CONVERGENCE

By
Jesse Clary

Cover art by Greg Carr
Michigan map sourced from Nations Online Project

For Kristyn

To my angel who holds my world together. My Anti-Anomaly.

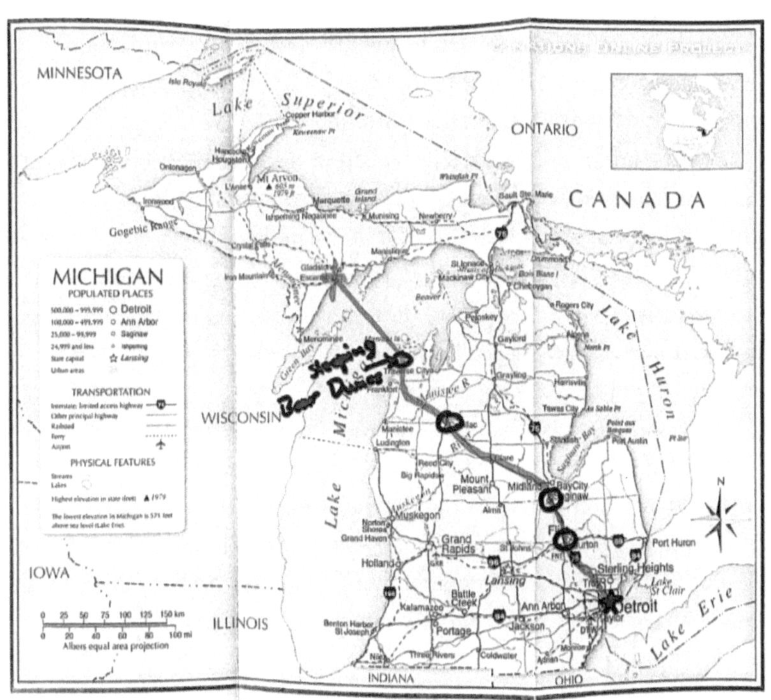

MINNESOTA
Lake Superior
ONTARIO
CANADA
Lake Huron
Sleeping Bear Dunes
WISCONSIN
Lake Michigan
IOWA
ILLINOIS
INDIANA
OHIO
Lake Erie
Lake St Clair

MICHIGAN
POPULATED PLACES
500,000 – 999,999   Detroit
100,000 – 499,999   Ann Arbor
25,000 – 99,999   Saginaw
24,999 and less
State capital   Lansing
Urban areas

TRANSPORTATION
Interstate limited access highway
Other principal highway
Railroad
Ferry
Airport

PHYSICAL FEATURES
Streams
Lakes
Highest elevation in state (feet)

The lowest elevation in Michigan is 571 feet
above sea level (Lake Erie).

0   25   50   75   100   125   150 km
0   20   40   60   80   100 mi
Albers equal area projection

Detroit
Ann Arbor
Jackson
Lansing
Grand Rapids
Holland
Kalamazoo
Portage
Battle Creek
Benton Harbor
St Joseph
Three Rivers
Coldwater
Adrian
Monroe
Sterling Heights
Port Huron
Flint
Saginaw
Bay City
Midland
Alma
Mount Pleasant
Muskegon
Grand Haven
Norton Shores
Big Rapids
Reed City
Ludington
Manistee
Frankfort
Traverse City
Cadillac
Grayling
Gaylord
Petoskey
Rogers City
Cheboygan
Mackinaw City
St Ignace
Sault Ste Marie
Newberry
Munising
Marquette
Ishpeming
Negaunee
Ironwood
Ontonagon
Hancock
Houghton
L'Anse
Copper Harbor
Keweenaw Pt
Mt Arvon
Gogebic Range
Iron Mountain
Escanaba
Gladstone
Menominee
Green Bay
Manistique
Isle Royale
Whitefish Pt
Grand Island
Beaver I
Bois Blanc I
Tawas City
Au Sable Pt
Saginaw Bay
Point aux Barques
Port Austin
Standish
St Johns
Tittabawassee R
Muskegon R
Manistee R
Au Sable R
N

{Chapter 1}

9:13:0:00

A loud ringing filled the dark. It paused for a moment, then rang again. Each sequence louder than the last, as if desperately trying to reach out for a response. It echoed throughout the small, dimly lit room, bouncing off each of the walls. After a fifth time, a hand came down on a little flat screen with pinpoint precision and struck the "snooze" option. The room lay silent for a few minutes, granting the few moments of precious sleep he needed. But then, the incessant buzzer began again. His hand came down but, this time, hovered over the alarm and gently tapped the "turn off" icon.

With a groan and stretch, Jay sat up in his bed. He peered around his small, dusty room through barely opened eyes and saw that sunlight had started to seep through the window. He closed his eyes, rubbed them slowly but harshly with his fingertips, and shook his head fitfully to wake himself up. Pulling the bedsheets off himself, he swiveled over to the edge of his bed and sat there.

He never liked waking up early.

It was always easy to sleep. The mind wandered freely through fantasy and solitude. During a truly peaceful sleep, no noise from the outside world could invade the sanctitude of thought. Jay used to enjoy this peace in the waking world, but not any longer. Only rarely would he ever get himself up after one snooze session but, on important days, he could find the motivation to resist the temptation of sweet ignorance.

Now was the time for work, and Jay had already slept in thirty minutes. He stood up and grabbed the pull cord of his bedroom blinds and, with a quick tug, brought light into the room, illuminating particles of dust and debris that floated wistfully in the air. Jay squinted hard and, for a moment, saw nothing. His vision cleared up and was met with that same familiar sight he had seen for the past three years: brick and glass.

At least, he assumed it was brick. He wasn't exactly sure what the Guardian Building was made of. Its distinct art deco structure consisted of multi-colored "bricks" and was a gorgeous thing to behold. Jay admired the building and was thankful this city hosted landmarks that weren't all dreadfully similar and mundane. Admittedly though, he had grown rather tired of seeing it. After three years, the big city novelty had worn off.

He glanced down at Griswold Street to see a typical Detroit morning. People were hastily moving up and down the road, presumably heading to work. From high above, Jay watched them move like lemmings. He could spot the conga lines moving steadily until someone tripped on their shoelace and scattered the papers he was carrying. A few bikers stopped to help him up while, from across the street, a man and his wife just watched. Behind them, an elderly man shivered harshly and breathed hot breath into his hands.

Some of the pedestrians had already donned jackets and winter hats while others still insisted that summer had not yet ended this late in September. Nevertheless, the weather was as unpredictable as ever, which was made doubly so when combined with Michigan's tendency towards chaos.

Jay had always preferred to wear winter clothes as much as he could. He didn't own a single pair of shorts and rarely showed his arms past his elbows. Of course, he was still human. He had enjoyed the warm summer days when he could cast away his winter outfit and head out for a drive in his Miata or work on a project in his garage. But those days had long passed and would not come again.

Jay decided he'd stood in his underwear long enough. It was time to get dressed. He walked across the room to his closet and picked out his typical attire—jeans; a random, graphic tee; and his favorite, loose-fitted, gray beanie. Grabbing his phone, keys, and wallet off the nightstand, Jay walked towards the door. He turned, scanned the room, and took a moment to gaze upon it a final time.

He slept in a small bed meant for one that was often unmade and messy but never unwashed. It was located about an arm's length from the window and on its left was that small, simple, wooden nightstand he'd made himself. Opposite the window was a bookshelf with various knick-knacks and collectibles. The few things he had collected over the years encompassed some of his favorite media and hobbies—model kits of robots; a handful of toy cars; small, wooden creations; and a smattering of novels and comic books.

Jay lingered particularly on the model kits. He had worked meticulously to perfect the techniques he had learned years prior—the techniques he had learned from Her. The models showed the progression of his skill from the first time he had splattered paint on a completed kit to perfectly airbrushed and weathered displays—at least, what *he* would define as "perfect." There was always room for improvement—always room for change. But now, these skills he had learned for a focused task were no longer useful. He found no motivation in the little things he loved ever since he lost Her. He let out a deep sigh, walked through the door, and shut it.

The small one-bedroom apartment faintly glowed from the sun fighting its way through the long, slender, vinyl blinds that adorned the large, sliding glass door. Jay walked over and quickly pushed the blinds along the rail. The incoming light revealed a sparsely furnished room. All that occupied the floor was a couch, a small coffee table, and a TV that rested atop an entertainment center along with its remote. Hung on the wall were a handful of movie posters from some of Jay's favorites: *Evil Dead*, *Robocop*, *The Matrix*, and *Tremors*. In the same living area was the kitchen.

Jay made his way to the kitchen and popped open the fridge. Not much occupied it; milk, eggs, butter, cheese, and some lunch meat were all that he typically kept. He didn't keep much because he didn't know how to make much. She was always the cook, and the few meals She had taught him how to prepare were unbelievably simple, even for a child. He snatched an egg, a tub of butter, and a slice of cheese. Then, he closed the door and faced the countertop and stove behind him.

Upon the stove, on the back burner, sat a small frying pan and to the left was a half loaf of bread and a microwave. He opened his nearly empty cabinet above, pulled out a plate, and set it aside. He pulled the pan forward onto a burner and placed the ingredients he was clumsily holding in his right hand onto the plate. He then turned the knob slowly to a setting slightly above medium, and the low hiss of the gas started to flow.

There were no matches or lighters in this dwelling. No mechanical means to start a fire aside from the flaky igniters located in the stove; however, Jay didn't need them. With his right hand, he pinched his thumb and index together and curled his other three fingers. A small smoldering began at the base of the mid-knuckles, blackened the skin, and traveled towards the fingertips. A pocket of heat formed around the met fingers and began to glow brightly. Tiny embers started to crackle forth from his skin as his ignition point popped into flame.

He gently held his newborn fire in the space underneath the pan as the flame *whooshed* around the burner and lit it. Jay moved his hand away, towards the knobs, as the fire at his fingertips fizzled out and the skin returned to its natural appearance. He turned down the burner precisely and brought it to low heat. One-by-one, each ingredient entered the pan: first, a small dollop of butter was placed and swirled around, then the egg was cracked open with the least bit of finesse. He let the egg cook thoroughly. Finally, a slice of cheese topped the dead-simple meal.

As his egg sandwich began to sizzle, Jay walked over to the TV and flicked it on with the remote. He set the remote down on the coffee table and returned to the kitchen to attend to his cooking. As the TV worked through its startup routine, a familiar voice came through the set.

"Well, it's gonna be a cold one later today, Michelle. As you can see here in the Detroit area, temperatures are going to be dropping to the 30s later today and we'll *actually* hit the minuses in the night."

Jay had always preferred listening to the weather rather than checking his phone. It brought sweet nostalgia of the days he had as a kid—waking up early for a school day, hearing the weatherman fire off the forecast from down the hall where his uncle watched. Jay had always checked the weather when preparing for a trip. His obsessiveness with being prepared allowed him to never get caught in the rain or snow. But the journey he was about to undergo could not wait any longer, and checking the weather was just a formality at this point.

He plopped the contents of the pan between two slices of bread, turned off the stove, and took a seat on the couch. As he ate, the weatherman continued his report. He had finished up the local area, and the graphic behind him now zoomed out to show the entirety of Michigan, attended by familiar soft jazz. The area had changed so much in the past couple of years. Many towns and cities were missing from the report. Temperatures appeared for a handful of cities— Lansing, Flint, Grand Rapids, and a few regions in between.

The fabric of reality had been torn and with it came unruly and unnatural weather. Across Michigan, temperatures ranged from sweltering to freezing; some were marked with a simple question mark. Communication ranges had continued to shrink and getting accurate reports across the state proved exceedingly difficult at times. It wasn't even assured that the screen Jay was currently staring at was entirely correct.

"And now your weekly forecast," said the optimistic, disembodied voice.

The next seven days were shown along with temperatures and conditions just as sporadic as the entire map. The image held for a minute and then moved on to the following week; however, only two extra days were displayed. Jay had just about finished eating but had interest in next week's forecast; his great trek would possibly spill into it. *I always try to plan a week in advance*, he could hear his uncle reply when Jay had asked why he was so obsessed with the weather. *You don't want something as predictable as the weather to ruin your plans!* A complete sarcastic contradiction Jay found humorous, especially in the face of what he was staring at now.

The screen faded to black and slowly returned with a large, red typeface timer. Above it read the words:

TOTAL CONVERGENCE

An automated female voice chimed in, "Total Convergence in… Nine days… twelve hours… twenty-eight minutes… and… fifty-eight seconds."

Total Convergence. At one point, that phrase meant something incredibly horrific and unimaginable, but now it was just an acceptable inevitability. Despite his anxiety, Jay glanced over at a large hiker's rucksack near his front door and let out a deep breath, whispering: "Plenty of time."

"And now, an all-new episode of *Tornado Tamers*—" Jay quickly cut off the foreboding voice and walked over to the kitchen with his dirty plate. He placed it in the sink and nearly began the habit of washing it. Sponge in hand, he remembered: Total Convergence. Setting the sponge back down, he left the dirtied plate at the bottom of the sink. He then opened the cabinet, retrieved a glass, poured himself some water, and downed it in one gulp. He was done wasting time.

He knelt by the rucksack. Its dark green canvas was thick and sturdy, with a strong, metal support on the back. Strapped to the top was an ultralight, nylon sleeping bag with a small backpacking tent secured at the base. A silver pot and ladle were looped and dangling on one side and, on the opposite, a lucky charm—a red-dyed rabbit's foot—was tightly tied. The frontmost pocket held a Leatherman, a compass, a packet of tissues, a battery bank, and a charging cable. In a large side pocket, a hefty water bottle. Jay undid the buckles to the main compartment and opened it up for one final check: five compact MREs (Meal Ready to Eat), a handful of energy bars, a bike pump, a tire patch kit, a collapsible stove top, a tri-folded map outlining his route, a spare set of clothes, and finally—near the bottom—a petite, delicate, pewter urn.

Jay reached in and pulled it out. He cupped it in his hands and ran his thumb across the relief of carnations. Each one precisely and lovingly cast. He was reminded of Her beauty and light. This was the object of his obsession, yet the subject of his ire. The urn was sealed shut with a little lid adorned with a sphere. A significant piece of him was housed within. Turning the tiny object in his hand, he reminisced about their time together.

①

"Eh, it's not really my kind of music," he said in response to Her attempted persuasion.

She assured him it would be fun. That the time they spent together would outweigh his boredom.

"You already bought the tickets, didn't you?" he asked.

She recoiled for a moment with a meek smile, Her face red with embarrassment, and nodded.

He snickered and shook his head, "Guess I don't really have a choice, do I?"

With both her hands, She grasped one of Jay's and tried to relieve his judgment by claiming She could ask a friend instead.

Jay looked up, smiled, and replied, "No, I'll take ya. I want to spend any sorta event together. I'll try to enjoy myself and at least it'll make for a good memory."

①

He clung to that memory and memories that came before and after. He could still hear the thumping of the Fox Theatre as the shrills of fangirls overpowered the pop music blasting through the speakers—the rumble of the floorboards beneath and the shaking of the seats. The energy was unreal, and yet Jay couldn't bring himself to move to the music. As he said, it wasn't his music. But he remembered Her joy and what that brought to him.

The little urn yanked him from his reverie, and he snapped back to the task at hand. He placed it back into its nestled spot and pulled out the map. The unfolded map revealed a dated Michigan. The spiderweb of roads and highways were no more, and only a scarce amount remained. A red "X" had crossed out the Mackinac Bridge, destroyed by a monstrous tornado that ripped the massive bridge to smithereens. A red line had been drawn from Detroit, spanning across the mid-section of the state horizontally, cutting through key cities, extending Northwest, and stopping at Sleeping Bear Dunes. From there, a straight line connected the dunes to Escanaba across Lake Michigan. Therein lay his goal: a small cemetery on the outskirts of the sleepy Upper Peninsula town.

He double-checked the route and traced his index finger along the major points. He pictured the trip in his mind and saw success— although, he remained realistic. It would not be easy, and many obstacles, sentient or otherwise, would impede his progress. But Jay had to do this; he made Her a promise. By bike, the pilgrimage should take only three days, but he packed extra things in case of trouble. The world had fallen into ruin, and journeys were no longer effortless.

He packed up the map and buckled the straps. Above him was a coat rack with a single black, hoodless, winter jacket. He snagged it down, slipped it on, and rolled up the sleeves past his elbows. Slinging the pack through his left arm and over his shoulder, he shot his right arm through the other side and pulled the straps taut. As he stood, he rolled his shoulders and bucked them forward; the backpack was heavy, yet balanced and comfortable. Jay found his shoes to the side where the backpack had been and knelt to put them on. The worn and grimy Chucks were not well suited for long-distance walks or bike rides, but they were all he had—and they were all he ever felt comfortable wearing.

He quickly patted his pocket and felt for the essentials he had always walked out with every morning: phone, keys, and wallet. He opened the front door to his apartment and nearly walked out when, suddenly, he felt a hesitation. He reached into his left pocket and pulled out his keys. The dull silver keys rested in the palm of his hand: the key to his car, the key to his bike lock, and the key to his apartment.

Guiding the apartment key through the key ring, Jay released it from its familiar home and tossed it into the living area. It skidded off the coffee table and landed somewhere out of sight. He paused then turned away and shut the door.

The long hallway stretched far into the distance. Jay's apartment was located at the very end, opposite the stairwell. Although they were closer, the elevators were always hit-or-miss in their operation, so Jay decided on the stairs. The pot and ladle clanged, and objects in his bag shifted and slid as he trotted down the hall. As he neared the stairwell, apartment 1302's door opened on Jay's left.

Out stepped a short, middle-aged man with scruffy, raven-black hair holding a stuffed trash bag. He was a scraggly fella of average weight and build. Days of unbathed grime smattered on his clothes and skin complimented his messily shaved face and bulging eyes. He wore a loose-fitted tank top along with a pair of blue sweats; he was barefoot. As he scratched the side of his hip with his free hand, he caught wind of Jay's presence and exclaimed with a small wave, "Mornin', Jay!"

As Jay approached, he replied, "Hey-ey, mornin', Jed."

"Lil' early to be headin' to work isn't it? Yer typically outta here by nine-ish."

Jay was now standing opposite of Jed, keeping his distance from the potent stench. He took a second to quickly blink hard and wriggle his nose, steeling himself from the smell and, hopefully, masking his disgust.

"You're not wrong," said Jay. "I'm heading out of town until Convergence."

Jed set the trash down by his feet, twiddled the tied end with his fingertips, and asked, "Work is givin' ya the days off?"

Jay rolled his eyes and smirked, "Jed. It's the end of the world buddy. I doubt my boss would care if I—or hell, *anyone*—showed up today or tomorrow or the day after until the end of time… which happens to be next week. Besides, I quit my job last week."

"You what? But you were guaranteed that job for life!"

"Next week. Convergence. Remember?"

"Oh, come on," Jed exaggerated. "You really believe that shit? Fifty bucks right now: you knock on my door next Friday and I'll still be here, livin' the dream." He shot out his hand for a shake.

Reluctantly, Jay grasped it. The eccentric Jed always amused him, and he was willing to humor him one last time. "Eh, what is it that you did again?" Jed asked, still shaking Jay's hand.

"You ask this every time we talk, I swear," Jay replied, exasperated.

"Yeah, yeah, I know but, c'mon: do I look like the kinda guy with an elephant's memory?"

Jay freed his hand. "I was the repair guy for the med equipment at the main campus of the Henry Ford Hospital."

"Ah! That's right! Well, you could probably fix this Convergence shit! Ha-ha!"

"Yeah, sure! I'll tell 'em to crank down their bolts to thirty-five newton meters," Jay said as he made a ratcheting motion, "on their magic fix-a-ma-tron and that should do it!"

Jed laughed heartily, and Jay chuckled.

"It's probably that easy, ain't it?" Jed said after calming down. "Well, I've bothered ya enough. Ya have a good one!"

"Yeah, you too!" Jay replied as he gave Jed a small wave and watched as the man set the hefty trash bag in the hall and shut the door.

Jay made his way to the stairwell entrance and stepped through the large metal door. It slammed with an industrial thud that echoed down the chamber. Jay worked his way down the twelve flights of stairs. As each floor passed, his heart weighed heavy with anticipation and fear. Thoughts raced through his head to the point that his movements became autonomous. He pulled out his phone and checked the time: nine days until the end. He could hear his pulse in his ears. Before he realized it, he was facing the front entrance.

Through its all-glass structure, Jay could see the busy and shifting world waiting to consume him. He put his hand on the brass handle and gripped it tightly. In the stillness of his breath, his heart sank. The hesitation was more potent than ever. His hands began to grow clammy, and his mouth turned dry. A miasma of regret seeped into his mind, begging him to return to his cozy, familiar home thirteen stories above.

He closed his eyes and began to let go until he felt something. At the small of his back sat the urn, pressed against him. Its warm presence permeated through the canvas and enveloped his body. He opened his eyes, gripped the handle once more, and was pushed into the waning world.

{Chapter 2}

9:11:51:08

It was hard to tell the state of the old city from the apartment above but, from street level, the disarray was evident. Great structures decayed under the heavy vegetation growth, despite workers' best efforts to repel nature's reclamation. The roads and sidewalks had fallen into severe states of disrepair—cracked and fissured, with large amounts of flora filling in the gaps. Street signs and lampposts were all warped and rusted in various ways. Trash littered the streets as trace amounts were tossed through the air by the morning breeze.

A cold chill brushed across Jay's face as he looked toward the Detroit River as it ran south along Griswold. A thick fog hovered over the border and shielded any view of Canada. Detroit's maple-leaf neighbor hadn't been seen for over two years. Many expeditions had been made across, but none had returned from that dense fog.

Jay peered upwards towards the morning sky. The sun was still rising in the early hours. Offset to its future path loomed a great black diamond—The Anomaly. Jay stared at it—the catalyst for the world's destruction—and recalled its arrival. How, five years ago, physics and the inner workings of the world began to succumb to The Anomaly's unrelenting will. The red light that engulfed the Earth that day was a moment Jay would never forget.

The Anomaly was disorder incarnate. It perched itself high in the sky and never moved from its throne. Somehow, ever watching the little blue marble. Despite all known laws of physics declaring it could not be always present, The Anomaly kept to its namesake. Astronomers couldn't detect a gravitational pull from it—and every probe sent towards it disintegrated into fine dust within 2,000 miles of its destructive gaze. It could be seen in the brightest day and the inkiest black of night, accompanied by a faint, red glow that had now receded from the initial bath it had submerged the world in years ago.

It occupied an orbit that was three-quarters of the moon's—and roughly shared its size. People yearned for any semblance of rules or meaning but, to their dismay, no explanation was given. Logic and understanding dissipated under its sinister gaze.

Jay quickly averted his eyes and turned away. He had heard tales of an infectious madness caused by staring at The Anomaly. People had rumored that one could witness the collapse of reality surrounding the diamond as it swirled and bent, collapsing tightly at its centroid. Jay would not risk it. He loathed the great mystery for its devastation yet felt a strange comfort in its existence. Like many others, he too felt anguish when The Anomaly began its rampage. But, as time passed, people began to grow accustomed to this new constant. This new familiarity was now in stark contrast to the old, mundane world it had now corrupted—and Jay found a reluctant safety in knowing the black diamond would find its place in the sky always, until the end.

I cannot let it take me, Jay thought. *I need my sanity for this trip. Concentrate on Her. On Her request.*

He felt livid in the moment. Perhaps it was a small influence from The Anomaly—or just a lapse in his emotional regulation. Jay took a deep breath, grabbed the straps of his pack, and pulled them up and forward—re-situating the backpack a bit higher on his shoulders. He began to make his way through the sparse crowd, towards the bike racks at the corner of Congress and Griswold.

The human population had become so thin. Even in this morning rush, the sidewalk was barely filled. The road fared a bit better, with more people preferring bikes as a quick means of transport since cars and motorcycles were no longer an option. Just a year ago, the streets would have echoed with the roar of combustion engines as they rushed the power of their fuel-injected pistons to the wheels, providing precious, perpetual motion. The pops and cracks of exhaust would bounce endlessly against the crowded city buildings. Even the whirl and hum of electric vehicles would cut through the primitive, fossil-fueled explosions.

The manic weather made air travel a high risk no one was willing to take—and trains ran few and far between, with unpredictable breakdowns and schedules. The last working freight train from Detroit was sent out nearly a year ago and never returned. But now, the roads sat silent. The mutation of reality had caused all other land vehicles to stall and crumble. Their batteries would not charge and engines would no longer turnover. Experts had torn the machines apart and could successfully start individual components and even small assemblies—engines, water pumps, and headlights—but, when all put together, they would all begin to rapidly fall apart. The engineers poked and prodded but, despite their efforts, the transports refused to serve their purpose. It was as if The Anomaly had grown tired of the noisy streets and flipped a switch to turn them off.

"Riggin' it with remote controls work," some frazzled GM engineer had said to his supervisor. "We can move a box! We can move a fridge, lawnmower, or even a cat! Hell, I'll tie a goddamn Mustang over the top of this Blazer and drive it up and down the River Rouge all day if ya like! But as soon as you want the fucker to move a *person*? It just flat-out refuses and falls apart!" He chucked a wrench in the direction of The Anomaly and heard a yelp from a coworker across the testing lot as the tool pinged off the pavement.

After a while, the population had whittled down to so little and the world had become so treacherous that the Poindexters had to focus more on survival rather than figuring out how to strap a Ford to a Chevy. They had done all they could but, no matter what, the black diamond refused to let anyone travel across its cursed earth by anything other than bike or carriage.

But The Anomaly had a sick sense of humor. During their testing, chemists and engineers found that their gasoline was no longer growing stale. Year-old fuel would still combust and fire off pistons as if it was refined hours before injection—no stabilizers required. No one knew when the last barrel of gas rolled off the production, but they considered the never-aging fuel a blessing—as it provided a reliable source to power the many generators the few pockets of humanity ran on. Others considered it a curse—a tainted liquid born of the black diamond.

As Jay made his way towards the bike rack at the street corner, he noted the ever-rotting state of the abandoned cars parked on the street side. Their paint had all but peeled away, replaced by dark orange and brown rust. Every nook and cranny had been invaded by some sort of plant or animal nest, with flurries of broken glass occupying the interiors. Most were plundered and gutted for some precious components, while some were left mostly intact.

"It's the human spirit made manifest," Jay said, replying to Her question as to why he loved cars so much. "They embody every aspect of human ingenuity. Man's desire and perseverance to go beyond his physical limitations."

She smiled at his unrelenting enthusiasm for something he was passionate about. They commonly had these long conversations after dinner.

He continued: "To take a group of complex mechanisms and fashion them into somethin' neat and orderly. I guess I appreciate how cars encapsulate so much about what makes us human." Jay looked away, red in the face, with a coy smile. He had always let himself get too philosophical about what others would consider boring. "Sorry for talkin' yer ear off. I'm sure you're tired of me talkin' about the dumb ol' things."

She shook her head quickly and urged him to go on; She reveled in his passions.

"Well," Jay went on, "do ya remember what car your parents took you to middle school in?"

She nodded, reciting the make and model.

"What was the color? What were the seats made out of? Any sorta quirks about it?"

She looked up, searching Her thoughts, as She recounted every minute detail of the vehicle. An old Ford Bronco, maybe from the 80s? Red with an off-white stripe down the sides. She remembered the rust that started to eat up the hood and the knock off the engine whenever it kicked into high gear. She recalled the leak her dad constantly had to fix every ten thousand miles and the butterscotch, leather front seats; cracking like the flaking crust of the leftover pie they'd bring home nearly every Thanksgiving from her aunt's. The sweet aroma wafting out of the partly rolled-down windows of the old Ford as they cruised down the open highway.

"Ya see, people claim cars aren't that important. That they're just a means to get from A to B. And yeah, that's true, but even to you, someone who doesn't have a huge interest in them, you can recall such small, precise details about them. Why? If they're *just cars?*"

She was starting to be persuaded.

"They're not *just cars*, are they? I remember how we danced outside on prom night to "Inspiration" blastin' outta the doors of my Accord because the DJ wouldn't play it." They both smiled. "Or how, in the first year I bought the Mazda, I parked on a mound of ice outside our first apartment. And, when I took off for work, the side sill didn't come with me!"

She chuckled and noted how Jay was nearly on the verge of tears when he walked back into the apartment, car part in hand. They continued late into the night, recounting the precious memories they had shared. This bonding was fueled by the simple mention of a motor vehicle.

Not just cars, he thought.

Jay snapped himself out of his trance and realized he had arrived at the street corner. He worked his way down the bike rack and found his own locked up at the far end.

It was an older mountain bike he had purchased when his car finally gave up the ghost. He bought it locally from a Detroit manufacturer, and it shared the same rugged, industrial look and feel the city was known for. It was a sturdy, well-made thing that served Jay well throughout the past few years. Its flaking, blue, metallic paint shimmered in the sunlight, and the old rubber grips were beginning to wear and discolor. Over the rear was a backpack rack and on the front handlebars sat a headlight.

If he had a boat, he would've been sailing his way through the rivers, canals, and lakes weeks ago. And *if* he had the skill, he would've made the journey. But The Anomaly's influence caused the world's waters to rage. Piles of shipwrecked wood, iron, and fiberglass littered the shores of the Great Lakes and along the riverbanks—all that was left of amateur sailors and ferrymen attempting to tame the roaring tides. Scant veteran captains were known to have made it back from perilous journeys, but most demanded a high price for the venture of a passenger. They went where the money was plentiful and where demand was high: the shores of the Great Lakes.

Jay needed a plan to cross the vast expanse of Lake Michigan. He had turned to Jed for help. Although his neighbor was a coot that smelled of stale tuna and spoiled milk, Jed knew people. He knew people all across Michigan. He had told stories of his young, drunk outings in the heart of Kalamazoo, illegally bungee jumping off the Mackinac Bridge, and all the way down in Monroe, where he stole an old Buick and crashed it into River Raisin. Tall stories. But told with such vivacity that some truth fringed the falsehoods. So, Jay had asked him—asked how he could get across Lake Michigan to Escanaba.

"Oh, sure! There's a way, no doubt!" Jed had told him. "Sleepin' Bear Dunes. Ya know the place, right? Well, I heard from a drifter the other day that a guy down in Lansing hitched a ride on a carriage from Muskegon; the *driver* said he came *alllll* the way down from Sleepin' Bear Dunes off a sailboat that crossed Lake Michigan. Even got the captain's name for ya: Quigby!"

Jay's hopeful expression had sunk into prying eyes and a lowered head, "Quigby? What kinda name is that, Jed? If you're gonna make up a name, at least pick a real one!"

"I swear! I swear!" Jed had raised his hands in defense and Jay could tell the ol' bastard was being serious. So, he made it his plan to trust that some seadog named Captain Quigby was waiting for him with a sailboat to take him to Escanaba.

Jay weaved his arm, key in hand, through to the bike frame and found the u-lock. Feeling around for the keyhole, he blindly inserted the key and gave it a quick twist with a grunt. The lock came free, and he shimmied the bike from its prison.

As he pocketed his keys, Jay kicked out the kickstand and propped up the bike. He took off his pack and secured it tightly onto the rear mount and tugged on the connection points, ensuring a proper attachment. He opened up the larger pocket and placed his u-lock inside.

The kickstand was tucked away, and Jay hopped on. He had one final stop before heading out of town. He set off down Griswold towards the city center of Campus Martius—a large city park. Traveling only a block and taking a sharp right, he entered the roundabout that circled the park. As he biked through, he looked south down Woodward Avenue—the great central road that all of Detroit and the surrounding suburbs had been built around.

Even in this time of despair, the grand avenue spanned proud and wide. It had suffered only minor damage and was well-kept by city officials. The street cut through the center of Detroit and stretched Northwest for over thirty miles into the city of Pontiac. Of that distance, only about six miles were maintained.

Detroit had been reduced to a minuscule portion of its former self. What was once a city whose footprint could easily fit San Francisco, Boston, and Manhattan combined inside it had shrunk to a mere six-by-five-mile block. Within this perimeter, only a scant amount of people remained, trying to live lives that mimicked the old world. Some feared it as a mad god and preached of its power at street corners. Most people had accepted The Anomaly's influence and decided to make the best of it by nonchalantly ignoring it.

They moved about their days working, relaxing, and shopping. Never once paying mind to the destruction around them. Jay could never tell if it was an oblivious choice or a spell cast by the black diamond. Either way, Jay had given up long ago on persuading people of the significance of The Anomaly and its convergence. While, at some point, he saw those who could band together and relent against the torrent tide of chaos—he now only saw blank, content faces and uncaring dispositions.

He continued around Campus Martius. Its magnificent marble fountain had been dry for years, and a mound of broken stone and bent bronze statues occupied the once-intricate Civil War monument. From the exposed earth towered an unnaturally large oak tree that reeked of fungal infestation. In its heyday, this significant city center was host to holiday celebrations and city festivities; however, the park Jay was passing through was a desolate, overgrown wasteland surrounded by towering skyscrapers and nary a person.

Jay coasted along the curved street on the South side of the great tree and pointed his bike straight for Monroe St. The city was quiet now with most finding themselves at work; only the wind and sounds of rustling trash occupied the space. With just a few pedals, Jay found himself in front of his destination: the old Campus Martius parking structure.

Was it the third floor or the fourth? he pondered.

He rode into the structure and began ascending. He pedaled through, taking time to stare at the exposed rebar and crumbling concrete scenery, and scanned the rows of cars. He moved onto the second floor and caught a glimpse of some people in tattered clothes, loitering between two cars. He paid them no mind. It wasn't uncommon for squatters to nest in any part of the city.

Jay made his way up the ramp to the third floor and circled it twice, searching thoroughly for his little sports car. *Nope, not here,* he thought. *Gotta be the fourth.*

As he turned the corner from the fourth deck onramp, he noticed a familiar sight on the ledge that overlooked the city. Small, black scorch marks littered the concrete wall. Each sunburst scar surrounded small, baseball-sized craters.

He now saw afterimages of tin cans he had placed on the ledge and how, from a distance, he had practiced the offensive capabilities of his powers. He traced the trail of craters, recounting each failed attempt to strike a can with a fireball. He looked down the rows of cars and remembered taking aim with his hand—stepping back with each successful attempt. Following the visions, Jay caught sight of the tail-end of his car parked on the left, against the guardrail, flanked by two dismantled SUVs.

An excited smile stretched across his cheeks as he rushed to the small convertible. He stopped behind it, skidding his tires. Sitting barely over waist high was a compact, sun-bleached red 2004 Mazda Miata.

It was a depressing sight to behold. The soft-top had completely rotted and crumpled into the interior. What could be seen of the beige leather seats was water damaged with excessive growths of mold and filth. Puddles of putrid water filled the footwells and housed birthing grounds for mosquitoes and other insects. The brilliant red paint had all but flaked away, and what remained of it was discolored to a chalky pastel pink. Broken glass littered the floor around the vehicle, and the poor creature rested on its brake rotors—all four wheels maimed.

But despite the disgusting state of his beloved steed, Jay still saw beauty. He hopped off his bike and rested it against the SUV to the right. Running his fingertips across the bodywork, he felt the personality and soul of the spirited coupe. Its spree and fervor coursed through Jay's body, and he recounted the days he'd spent with Her in it. He spurted out a dorky chuckle and retracted it quickly.

This was his first major responsibility. The hours upon hours he'd worked, day and night, had paid off in a glorious package of finesse and speed. The brilliant Miata mirrored Jay's desire for freedom— freedom to weave and fly through the world without the stress of the points in between.

He lingered on these emotions briefly but gathered himself. Now was the time to say goodbye to that dead world. He felt the new one yanking at his mind, ripping it violently from that preferred past. Jay was forced to refocus on the task at hand.

He reached into his pocket and pulled out his keys. He freed the car key from the keyring, placing the latter back into his pocket.

Facing the rear, he knelt on one knee and jammed the car key into the rusted lock. He began to jimmy and twist the stubborn lock when, suddenly, he heard the echoing clang of metal come from across the deck.

The sound grew louder as it approached. As Jay slowly rose, he turned to face two armed hooligans walking towards him. The cause of the ruckus came from a metal bat one of them was skipping along the ground. The other brandished a small pocketknife.

"Y'know, there's a parking fee!" shouted Metal Bat with a commanding voice. The gargantuan man had barely any teeth and black grime caked his face. He wore several layers of tattered clothes and a beanie riddled with holes.

"And it ain't fuckin' cheap," squeaked Pocket-Knife from behind. He had a strangely acute voice for a man of average height. He wore nearly the same outfit as Metal Bat and sported a bushy, squirrelly beard.

"Look," Jay said softly, showing his hands, "I'm just here to grab something and then I'm gone. We don't gotta do this."

"You dun't really have a say in thu madder," spat Metal Bat as he took a step forward. "Imma crack yer skull open like a fuckin' egg unless ya give us whateva you got in dat trunk and bag."

"And it better be fuckin' worth something," chimed Pocket-Knife.

Money, Jay thought. *You fuckin' kiddin' me? Nine-ish days to live and these dumbasses wanted something as worthless as money.*

The thugs were now standing a little over arm's length from Jay. They had circled around and had Jay's back to his car's trunk.

"C'mon, guys," Jay began. "This *really* isn't worth it."

"Heh," Metal Bat snickered. He looked back at Pocket-Knife— then swiftly lifted his bat over his left shoulder and took a wild swing downward at Jay. Instinctual reflexes kicked in as Jay dove to the ground. The weapon had glanced the trunk of the car with a heavy bang and struck Jay's right shoulder.

Metal Bat's head was in clear view. One fiery blast would be enough to kill. Jay had a perfect shot and took aim with his left arm outstretched—his hand spread open with fingers pointed forward. He lingered on the thought, but only for a moment, then decided against it.

He altered his focus and aimed at Metal Bat's right shin. In a split second, the searing heat coursed its way through Jay's veins, starting from his mid-forearm and ending at his fingertips. Again, his power began to manifest as his lower arm crackled and popped, turning a charred black with embers springing forth.

A baseball-sized fireball had now formed in Jay's palm as the flames engulfed his entire hand. The projectile shot out blindingly fast with a veracious *foom!* It struck Metal Bat on the side of his shin and exploded into a flurry of fire.

Metal Bat bellowed in pain. He dropped his weapon and grasped his freshly scorched leg. Jay's attack had burned a hole in Metal Bat's pants and penetrated deep into his leg. The meat had lost a significant chunk and was now severely torched and blistering. The smell was immediate: burnt, bubbling flesh.

Metal Bat had now fallen to one knee. Jay pushed himself off the ground and lunged towards the giant. He gripped Metal Bat's face tightly—a cheek in each palm—and ignited his hands. Jay stood over the brute and stared menacingly into his eyes with a soulless expression.

Metal Bat screeched as his face was melted. He released his leg and attempted to grab Jay's hands. Metal Bat's palms were met with sudden heat as the brute instantly forfeited the attempt to free himself from the torment.

Jay could see the thug was no more a threat than a sickly field mouse. He retracted his attack and tossed Metal Bat to the ground. He looked around for Pocket-Knife and realized he had run off long ago, possibly under the guise of Metal Bat's screaming.

Jay's bike and backpack had remained untouched. *They were planning to take you,* Jay thought as he stared at his bag. He looked back at the pathetic man still lazily wriggling on the ground.

"Please," Metal Bat squeaked.

Jay lowered his head and drooped his shoulders.

"Go. I ain't gonna hurt ya no more," Jay replied as he waved the wounded man off.

Metal Bat scurried to his feet in disbelief and limped off down the onramp as he whimpered. Jay placed his left hand on his right shoulder and rolled it. It was warm and slightly swelled. *That'll bruise. But nothing's broken,* he thought.

He turned his attention back to his prior task. The key was left in the lock during the ordeal. He continued to wrestle with the aged lock for a few minutes when, finally, he heard a small click. After pulling out the key and placing it in his pocket, Jay flung the trunk lid open. Inside sat two things: a compact toolbox and a small first aid kit in a clear-red, plastic case gifted by Her.

The small red case was covered in stickers of walruses—Jay's favorite animal. Bandages, antiseptic wipes, dressings, gauze, a pair of tweezers, painkillers, and burn cream were all included. She had forgotten a few things, notably some latex gloves, but he coveted the gift.

Even years after his car broke down, Jay was a creature of obsessive compulsion; everything needed to be in its rightful place. He had left the gift he held dearly where it had always been, nestled in its home within his car. Many times, he had thought about retrieving it, but he couldn't bring himself to accept that his car would never run.

Jay reached in and pulled it out. He popped the small plastic clips, opened the case, and checked the contents. While the case was slightly damaged and dirty, the supplies were surprisingly in good condition and still usable. Jay fingered through the bandages and packets and pulled out the burn cream. "Well, no need for this," Jay said under his breath. He returned the cream to the case and closed it.

He held the first-aid kit in his left hand and placed the other on the trunk lid and shut it. Placing the kit into his backpack, Jay backed the bike away from the parked cars. He had nearly jumped back on the bike when he felt that familiar hesitation he had when leaving his apartment. His mind was begging him not to reach into his pocket, but he needed to let go. Without lingering on the thoughts, he reached into his pocket and held the key to his Miata. He looked at it briefly, then tossed it into the interior. He heard it ricochet around a bit, then settle somewhere with a splash.

Jay mounted his bike and took off. He coasted down the three decks and noticed that the bums on the second floor were now tending to a large man with severe burns. He slowed to a stop, shot them a quick glance, and was largely ignored. He sighed, pulled out his first-aid kit, and tossed the burn ointment at their feet. Picking up the pace, Jay then made his way out of the parking structure, back down Monroe, and up Woodward Avenue.

Traveling down the road, Jay took note of the oddities he passed by. Some buildings were warped in winding ways that didn't make any structural sense. Small granules of rock were ascending slowly into the air. The same sort of decay the skyscrapers experienced was shared with some of the storefronts and restaurants he had regularly visited. The collapse of reality became more prevalent as Jay approached the city limits.

In the far distance, a great sprawling forest could be seen. What appeared to be tall evergreens surrounded the tiny city. Jay saw the trees grow more intimidating as he approached a security checkpoint.

His eyes were fixated on the tips of the trees. They dwarfed the smaller shops that lined Woodward Avenue and even seemed to challenge the skyscrapers downtown. Power lines and telephone poles seemingly disappeared in the dense forestry.

Jay moved his eyes down the length of the forest and came to see the checkpoint was now close. A great fifty-foot wall, made of metal and cinderblock, surrounded Detroit. Arborists were working tirelessly along the top of the wall to keep out the encroaching woods. Some were buried high up in the bundle of green needles, suspended by systems of ropes and pulleys. They hacked and chopped away at the rapidly growing branches.

Horse-drawn carts full of essential food and supplies were moving into the city—the morning deliveries. On the opposite side, a small line of empty carts was being checked before being allowed to proceed out.

Jay rode alongside the outgoing carts and reached the gate official. The guard motioned for another to take care of the outgoing patrons and held out his hand to halt Jay. Jay slowed his pace and came to a stop next to the guard.

"Gooood moooorning sir," said the jovial guard. He was a tall, built man with an evident Detroit accent. He had his hands placed firmly on his hips with one cupping the sheath of a machete. "May I see your I.D., please?"

Jay reached into his back pocket and pulled out his wallet. He slipped out the I.D. and handed it to the guard.

"Where ya headed?" asked the guard.

"Immediately? Royal Oak. I gotta grab something from my old house," Jay replied.

"And eventually?"

"Up north. Then to the UP."

The guard laughed. His makeshift armor of sheet metal and leather rustled as his chest shook from the laughter. Twiddling Jay's card, he said, "Brother, ain't nuthin' up there but death. You wanna get ch'self killed so bad, you be better off doin' it here! At least, that way, we able to bury ya before Convergence!"

Jay chuckled at the morbid, yet lighthearted, tone. "Well, I'd like my death to be somewhere pretty… at least… somewhere that *was* pretty," he said.

The guard handed back the I.D. and said, "You tellin' me Detroit ain't pretty? Ha-ha. Well, normally, I'd have ya go through the office behind me to fill out some paperwork and whatnot—but why waste both our time? Next week, right?"

"Yeah, next week."

They shared a moment of silence. A scream from deep in the woods whipped their attention down the road. It bounced off the trees and echoed into nothingness. The clops of the horses stopped as their riders also turned towards the scream. The guard across the gate, who was checking the I.D. of a carriage escort, dropped the card he was holding. Jay looked down the road that stretched out into dense shade. It had been nearly three years since he had left the safety of Detroit. Rumors and prior news reports when The Anomaly began its reign told him of the dangers of the outside world.

"You sure you wanna go out there?" asked the guard grimly.

"Yes," Jay murmured. "I *have* to."

The guard studied Jay's eyes. There was determination and fight in those eyes. The guard could see if he held Jay back, Jay would fight tooth and nail to get out. And, if he wasn't a fighter, he'd find a way to sneak onto a carriage or find a way through or under the wall. He'd seen people like this before. When people were first walled up in Detroit, the guards were given strict orders to keep people inside, barred from the outside world. But people grew restless and soon the occasional group of misbehaved teens or guys looking for thrills would find their way to the other side of the wall. Soon, the people protested, and city officials decided people could come and go as they pleased. Sometimes, they'd come back bruised, battered, and bloodied. Most of the time, the guard and his troop would find their bodies only a few miles out—mangled, eviscerated, and dead. The guard was staring at a corpse, but a corpse who deserved to die with some pride—just as anyone should. He clicked his tongue off the top of his mouth and said what he had said to a dozen corpses before, "Then, you best get goin' while there's still light… and good luck."

Jay looked back at the guard and said, "Thanks. You take care."

"You too."

The guard waved at Jay as he set off into the forest. Jay looked back over his shoulder and could still see the guard waving. He waved back and set his sights forward.

{Chapter 3}

9:10:24:18

The sun trickled through the canopies above, casting shafts of soft light down the tunnel of trees. It shimmered and danced as gentle breezes whistled through the empty woods. Jay was pedaling along, listening to the faint rustlings of leaves and unseen woodland creatures. His bike tires clicked along as the chain worked itself around the gears. The clopping of horses could be heard in the distance behind him.

As he rode, he passed more broken-down vehicles that were pushed aside to make way for the carriages. The road was flanked by the dense, great forest of towering evergreens. Jay lingered on them in awe. These trees were tremendously huge—not native to Michigan. They resembled giant sequoias in appearance and size, but their bark was pitch-black, and their branches hung low. Their large, invasive trunks had sprung forth through buildings and had entirely infested the outskirts, leaving mounds of debris and refuse.

Intermixed were a variety of deciduous trees that occupied Michigan. Ashes, aspens, and birches were all beginning to lose their brilliant fall colors. Bright orange, red, and yellow leaves littered the ground and drifted in the wind. They twirled and zoomed across the road, coming to rest for a moment to then be carried off by the current kicked up by Jay's passing.

The potent scent of Fall permeated through the tunnel. Jay could smell the familiar musk of damp, aging greenery and strong, uncut grasses. The temperature was cool—made dry and fresh by the sheer abundance of woods. Jay could feel the oxygen-rich air rush down his nose and fill his lungs. He could smell small traces of wildflowers.

Jay reveled in the peace for a while. He was now the furthest he'd been from Detroit in three years. He felt oddly comfortable on his ride.

Maybe this won't be so bad, Jay thought as he took in the scenery.

The serene landscape was at odds with the stories he'd heard of the outside world. What he was experiencing now was the same solitude he had enjoyed in his dreams and reminiscent visions.

As he steered along the path, he felt a growing pain in his right shoulder. Jay winced a bit from the sudden tightness. He pulled to the side, hopped off, and rested his bike against an evergreen. Rolling his jacket and shirt from the collar and past the cusp of his shoulder, he could see that the brute's attack had certainly bruised. The deep-purple, palm-sized mark was surrounded by a putrid mustard yellow.

Jay grimaced and sucked at his teeth. The endorphins that had fired off during the fight were now quickly wearing off. He turned to his backpack and took off his jacket and shirt, draping them over the handlebars. Scanning his torso, he found no other wounds and started to unbuckle his bag when he noticed something.

The dark, craggy bark of the evergreen was odd upon closer inspection. It seemed to pulsate and writhe. Jay reached out his hand cautiously and ran his fingers between the crevasses. They felt scabbed and fleshy and throbbed against his fingertips. He retracted his hand in disgust but caught a piece of bark with his fingernail and tore it from the tree.

Jay looked down to where the fragment fell; it was still twitching. He looked at the finger that had inflicted the wound. A small pinpoint stain of red lined his fingernail. Turning his attention back to the tree, he now saw a gaping wound where the bark had been torn. A thick, deep crimson syrup leaked from the trunk as the area around it pumped and spurted. The smell of dirty iron filled Jay's lungs; the cool air no longer tasted as sweet.

With trepidation on his face, Jay took some time to calm himself. *This is the world now,* he reminded himself.

Turning away, he closed his eyes and took a deep breath. When he came to, he looked up beyond the light shafts. Leaves rustled and fluttered like waves against a bright, blue sky. Branches swayed high above, causing golden rays to glide along the forest ground like little spotlights. He turned back around and took out his first-aid kit.

Digging through the contents, he found some pain relief balm and painkillers. He closed the case and propped it on the seat against the tree, trying his best not to look at the wound he'd inflicted. He set the bottle of painkillers on top of the kit and twisted off the cap from the tube of balm. A viscous, cream-colored paste emerged from the tube as Jay squeezed it onto the tips of his left three mid-fingers.

He rubbed the ointment deep into the skin of his shoulder. He cringed at the pain but, with each circular motion, the medicine took its effect. The surface began to warm and soothe and, soon, Jay could roll his shoulder with minimal pain.

Screwing the cap back on the tube, Jay placed the balm back inside the kit, making sure not to topple over the bottle of painkillers. He then retrieved his water bottle out of his pack and popped open the medicine. Only a quarter of pills remained—good for about five more uses.

He tilted his head back, carefully guided two pills into his mouth, took a swig from his water, and swallowed. He placed his water bottle on the ground and reorganized his kit as he put it away and got dressed.

As he drank a few more gulps of water, the low rustling Jay had heard before took on a sinister tone. The small woodland creatures he had heard before did not seem so small anymore. A great uneasiness began to stir in his stomach and shivered up his spine, causing him to jolt slightly. He packed up his water bottle and set off before his nerves could completely take over.

Passing by some familiar streets, Jay noticed he was nearing one that would lead to his old neighborhood. He had been traveling for over an hour and could feel himself approaching the town. Despite the overgrowth and destruction, he still recognized key landmarks along the roadside: restaurants, bars, shops, churches, and parks.

A large, decrepit water tower peeking through the trees to his left confirmed his location.

DETROIT ZOO

The words were mostly worn off, with an overabundance of vines obstructing the mural of safari animal silhouettes. But no one from the area could ever mistake it for anything else; Jay had arrived in Royal Oak.

He rode up a few blocks and listened for any dangers that might be lurking. His encounter with the tree still had him on edge, and his senses were now hypersensitive. He was now deep within the forest; not a soul could be seen. The sharp clicking of his gears rang out into the woods.

Jay imagined each click as a pinball pinging off each tree, bush, and building—eventually striking an ill-begotten beast. He pictured the beast barreling towards him, catching him off guard, and prematurely ending his journey. Anxious, he tried to shake off these thoughts by thinking of Her.

When they had lived in Royal Oak, they frequented many places on Woodward. The street was a bustling hub, full of life and pleasantries. Weekends were typically accompanied by bar-hopping or late-night shows. The twinkling business signs shone brightly against the starry sky, dancing in brilliant displays.

"Just give it try," Jay said, pushing the pint towards Her.

She picked up the heavy glass and sniffed it. She cringed and stuck out Her tongue in disgust.

"Stouts always smell strong," Jay chuckled. "Trust me: it tastes a lot better than it smells… especially after, like, four." He stuck his tongue out to tease Her.

She reluctantly scooted the glass back towards Herself. Raising it, She brought it to Her lips and closed Her eyes. She tilted Her head back slightly, took a sip, and began smacking Her lips.

"Well?" he asked.

She continued smacking Her lips softly, tasting the concoction. She finally finished and nodded in approval. She agreed with Jay and took another swig—this time, a gulp.

"Knew you'd like it," Jay winked. "Happy Birthday, honey."

⊙

Jay was passing the ruins of their favorite restaurant: Vinsetta Garage. True to its namesake, Vinsetta Garage had been an old mechanic shop converted into a restaurant. Now, the large overhang that covered the entrance had completely collapsed, and the large garage doors that faced the street were mangled and torn apart by invasive plant life. He briefly lamented the state of their favorite hangout spot and pressed on.

Up ahead on the right, he could see the street he needed to turn down. As he approached, he took note of a toppled, rusted street sign. Jay had never learned the name of this street. He always used the large church that stood at its corner for guidance.

Rounding the church, he looked up at the massive stone structure that was this church's unique steeple. It looked more like a castle tower than anything else. The crumbling structure was missing a significant chunk off the top, but the large carving of a crucified Jesus Christ remained whole, constricted by vines.

Jay bobbed and weaved down a series of short, residential streets. He navigated deep into the grid-like suburb as disheveled houses blurred past him. Even with the overabundance of nature, he could find his way home without sparing a thought. As he turned into his neighborhood, he slowed to a stop.

His bike chain had halted its operation, but the clicking that had accompanied him continued. He listened closely, trying to pinpoint its location.

The noise stopped. Jay spun around in his seat quickly, his arm outstretched to strike, and saw nothing behind him. He then looked over his other shoulder—nothing. To his left and right, he only saw the remains of houses taken over by nature. Whatever was stalking him was hiding expertly... intelligently.

"Whoever's out there, come out!" Jay yelled. "I know you're—"

The whistling "woosh" of a bolt barreled itself towards Jay and lodged itself into his right shoulder, knocking him off his bike. A small grunt left his mouth as he hit the ground. The sudden attack had cut off his call and forced him to swallow his words. He grabbed the wooden shaft and began to pull it out. Jay began to let out a cry when a cold, delicate hand pressed against his mouth and pinned him to the ground.

"Shh!" said a young, dark-skinned, female face. She had a long, slender nose and dark, sunken, hazel eyes. As she looked around, her wild, coarse, long black hair jostled over Jay. Her olive, drab cloak was thick and appeared to be handmade. She wore a loose-fitted blouse with several layers underneath, beige pants, and sneakers. A quiver of a few crossbow bolts—both wooden and aluminum—was strapped to her hip.

"I am truly sorry for shooting you," she whispered. She spoke briskly with a slight Hindi accent and perfect enunciation. "But you were being far too loud."

Jay nodded, assuring her that he would remain quiet.

"I have many friends nearby. When I let go of you, do *not* do anything stupid. Do you understand?" she asked.

Jay nodded once more—and with a bit more vigor as the pain began to set in. She slowly removed her hand from Jay's mouth and backed off. Jay stood up and went back to pulling out the bolt still in his shoulder.

"I can help with that—" she muttered, but Jay held up his right hand to stop her, breathing heavily. As he begrudgingly pulled out the wooden bolt, fresh blood flowed down his hand and dripped onto the ground. A crimson stain began to form around the entry point. He had pulled out about an inch and reached the head. With a muffled grunt, he yanked the bolt out. The wound heated up immediately and began cauterizing. As it finished, Jay set the bolt aflame and let it burn to ash in his hand.

He raised his head to find the mystery woman staring at him with a cautious expression. She began to reach for a knife that was strapped to her belt, opposite of the quiver.

"Don't," Jay whispered. "I'm human. This… ability…" Jay pointed up towards The Anomaly. "It did this to me."

The woman stilled her hand and hovered it over her knife.

"I have seen many things here," she said. "The people, and this place, have been corrupted by that damned thing. Every day, I witness something new—something different. I cannot trust any creature—even one that claims it is human."

"My name's Jay. That house down the road…," Jay motioned, "…that was my house. I'm just here to grab something—something precious to me. Let's just go our separate ways. Forget this happened. You can have your friends watch me the whole time, but I'm gonna defend myself if need be—understand?"

"You are not in the position to tell *me* to 'understand.' But," the woman murmured, relaxing her stance, "the longer I stand out here, the more I am risking my life."

She unslung her crossbow and held it at ease. Another quiver was attached underneath her weapon, holding four out of five bolts—the fifth now caked in Jay's blood on the ground.

"Do not linger here long," she continued. "*If* you are human, Jay, this place will kill you. Look around. Do you see the vines growing on the houses and along the ground?"

Jay's eyes darted around. House by house, he could see black vines creeping in every direction.

"Yeah, they're definitely not normal," he said.

"No, they are not. Nothing here is. My advice? Stay away from your home."

With this final warning, the woman backed off and disappeared behind a house. Jay could hear the crunching of leaves fade into the distance and then a soft clicking.

Jay picked up his bike and scanned the area for more threats. If these friends of hers were watching, they were masters of stealth. He could spot his home just a couple blocks down. Forgoing any risk of making too much noise, he decided to walk his bike the rest of the way.

Creeping up the empty street, he examined the black vines closely. They pulsed and crawled their way along the ground like worms seeking to burrow. Jay could trace some of them back to the soil that surrounded the accursed trees. The gray leaves bore tainted berries underneath that glistened a sunset orange.

Jay stood outside his old home. The vines had encapsulated it, reaching up high to the second story, invading the gutters and through broken windows. The hip-high grass masked the trail of vines, but Jay could see how they crawled up the vinyl siding and spread out to cover the entire house. The long concrete driveway was in complete ruin and the walkway leading to the porch didn't fare any better.

He escorted his bike up to the porch stairs, stepping and running over squelching vines. The rusty metal railing was failing at the stone tread mounts. Jay took hold and tested it. It creaked and bent with lots of play.

Jay frowned at his decrepit home. The years spent turning the late 60's two-story into the perfect, quaint abode felt wasted. Jay could see the past beauty of his house, how the thick plane windows shimmered in the sun. He looked across to the extruded bay window and saw Her sitting there, drinking Her morning tea as She admired Her little garden.

He leaned his bike against the faulty railing and removed his backpack; he didn't want to tempt any potential thieves. Bag in hand, he ascended the few steps and thought of the woman's warning.

Is there something inside? Jay's mind was racing. *Was it a bluff? An empty threat to ambush me as I ran? No, she coulda killed me there in the street if she really wanted to.*

Jay steeled himself and swallowed. It had been three years since he had set foot in this home and seven since *She* was here. He knew this would be a strain on his emotions. Just the thought of the interior began to overwhelm his heart and cause a quiver in his chest, but he allowed the sense of duty to take over.

The thick, stained glass had been shattered, which allowed Jay to weave his arm through and check the lock. He felt the horizontal position of the doorknob switch and then worked his way up to the deadbolt; it, too, was flicked into the unlocked position.

He retracted his arm and checked for any cuts. Bracing his will, Jay opened the door and stepped inside. The large living area was in complete shambles. The furniture was mangled and torn with slats of wood from the collapsed ceiling scattered about. Various broken knick-knacks and possessions were strewn about and caked with layers of dust and dirt.

Jay shut the door and placed his pack against the doorframe. To his left were the stairs leading to the second floor and across from him was a doorway leading to the basement. He stepped a few paces and nearly passed by the mantel to his left. Only a lone picture in a cracked frame sat upright. The picture was of a vacation they had taken together.

Picking it up, Jay focused on it and felt a welling of tears in his eyes. He looked behind him into the living area and could see that his movie collection hadn't been completely ransacked. A variety of cases were piled on the floor in front of an overturned bookcase.

"Groovy," Jay said in unison with Ash Williams as he twirled and holstered his sawn-off shotgun onto his back. They were watching his favorite film: *Evil Dead 2*. He had seen it countless times and could recite nearly every line. The ones he missed, She would fill in.

"Ya know Bruce and Sam Raimi are from Royal Oak?" asked Jay.

She shook her head.

"Yeah, they're high school buddies," Jay replied.

She tilted Her head with a small expression of curiosity. As their weekly movie night went on, they shared quotes, facts, and opinions as they held each other on the couch.

Jay was now leaning against the doorway to the kitchen that sat between the mantel and the basement. He held the little picture frame close to his chest and looked up at the ceiling, trying hard not to weep. He was struggling to breathe as his chest trembled. He closed his eyes and cold streams began to trickle down his cheeks.

The light had gone from his world. A deep, indescribable pain clenched at his heart ever since he lost Her. In the solemn nights, anguish infected his mind and ripped out his ambitions and desires. Only Her memory kept him going—the only way She could exist in his life.

His lips quivered as he let out a low sigh and took a rapid breath to collect himself. Holding the picture, he turned into the kitchen. The bright white walls were now stained with mold and waste. Rodents could be heard scurrying behind the open cabinets and worn-down appliances.

Jay placed the picture frame on the island and began searching the cabinets. Digging through the junk, he vigorously searched his memories. *C'mon, I know it's here,* he thought.

He backed off with his hands behind his head and exhaled. Turning around, he thought: *Where, oh where can you be?* He moved his hands to his hips and curled his lips to one side. Then, he spotted an un-searched drawer by the backyard door.

"Ah!" he said to himself. Jay hurried over to the cabinet and pulled it open. He fingered through mounds of old notecards and whatnots. He started to grow impatient as the little object refused to show itself. Ripping out the drawer, he poured the contents onto the ground. The waterfall of items splashed across the kitchen floor as a distinct metal *ping* bounced around.

A warped, silver ring skipped towards the back door.

"There ya are, ya little bastard," Jay whispered. He bent down and held the ring between his fingers as he stood up. It was a dirty, silver thing with a few blue diamonds still embedded in the thicker half. As he studied the ring, he looked out the back door window and could see a wooden, free-standing trellis entangled in vines.

"Look, I don't wanna build it right now!" Jay yelled back. The myriad of personal projects he had started were beginning to pile up. He rarely built things for Her and prioritized his work.

She stamped her foot and pointed, reminding him of the date he promised he would do it.

"Please! Not right now! I've got other things to do, and I don't wanna build some stupid garden thing!" Jay said without thinking.

She was taken aback. Without words, She walked away; Jay could hear Her sniffling as She slammed the back door. He stood all alone now with his hands on his hips, shaking his head. He pursed his lips and held back the combination of frustration and remorse. He let out a deep, long sigh, walked into his garage, and powered on his table saw.

Jay let out an exasperated snicker and thought, *silly little thing took me like thirty minutes.* He wiped a newly formed tear from his face and smiled. Even in the heat of anger, he relished his time with Her. She had taught him so much about himself. The arguments brought them closer only because they both held respect for each other. The more they listened to each other, the closer they grew. No amount of road bumps could steer them off their course.

The pain in his shoulder started to peak; it pressed him to keep moving. He placed the small ring in his pocket and pulled out his phone. Jay clicked the unlock button. The flat screen illuminated and showed the time: 12:44 PM. *Shit,* Jay thought. *I really gotta get goin'.*

He tucked the phone away and turned towards the kitchen entrance. He froze in place. A chilling terror shot up his spine and paralyzed him. His hands trembled as he struggled to keep quiet. The horror staring at him tempted him to scream.

{Chapter 4}

9:07:45:14

The cloudy white eyes peered at Jay. He could feel the dead stare pierce his own and infect his mind with fear. The black veins pulsed around the pupil-less eyes as they glared, motionless—unblinking. The face they belonged to was emaciated—long and human-like with two small holes where its nose should be.

The head hovered a couple of feet off the ground. As it breathed, strings of saliva met the floor from its gaping maw, overcrowded by sharp, claw-like teeth that jutted out from its cheeks. Jay traced its smile from ear to ear. The albino, leathery skin was pulled tightly against folds that formed rolling mounds on the side of its head where ears would normally be. Small ridges and needles lined the earholes like a Venus flytrap, patiently awaiting its prey.

The creature stood there, unmoving—poised on four appendages. The front two were large blades that swooped up high above the head, nearly reaching the top of the doorframe. The slender, featureless body curved back onto bony, inverted knees that sat low to the ground.

Jay's body was ice—cold dread had encapsulated his being. He glanced towards the back door before shooting his gaze back into the beast's empty glare.

Two feet.

Two feet was all the distance he needed to travel to rush out the back door. From there, the massive creature would have trouble fitting through the narrow exit. It would give Jay plenty of time to round the house and grab his bag from the front door. Afterwards, he could rush down the porch stairs and hop on his bike. He wasn't sure how quick this creature was, but he played out the scenario in his head over and over.

He had heard rumors about these beasts before and how they were blind.

The beast's head was motionless save for the small needles lining its ears which twitched and flicked. Jay hovered a palm in front of him and drifted it from left to right as he watched the creature's eyes closely. The monster's eyes did not move, and its head remained still. Jay raised his hand slowly above his head—still, no movement from the monster.

So, it's true, Jay concluded as he lowered his arm to his side.

Two feet. That's all he needed to move.

He readied himself mentally. Sweat poured down his face and soaked into his shirt and beanie. The beast continued to pant; with each breath, a small wheeze and click could be heard. Jay planted his feet and tensed his shoulders. The sharp pain of his earlier wounds caused him to wince, but he didn't make a sound.

He swallowed.

Twisted slightly towards the door.

Dug the balls of his feet in.

Now!

As he lifted his back foot, he made a severe oversight. The drawer he had carelessly ripped to the floor had found itself in his path. He kicked it with a wooden *clunk* and lost his balance. Catching himself on the doorknob, he heard a ferocious screech. He turned to see the creature leaping across the kitchen—its knives pointed forward to kill.

Jay dropped to the floor. The beast bashed into the wall behind Jay and flailed around, forcing Jay into the kitchen with kicks from its hind legs.

Jay worked himself onto his feet. The monster was far quicker than he had anticipated. Jay realized he would not be able to outrun this thing. He had to kill it if he hoped to escape.

The creature located its prey and roared. Its jowls stretched as the webbing between its jaws vibrated vigorously. It steadied itself. Scraps of broken wood and shattered tiles slid about as the horror glided one of its blades across the ceramic like nails on a chalkboard.

Jay fired off a shot. It impacted the creature's face and interrupted its battle cry. The explosion sent small flames across the kitchen. As the smoke cleared, the beast shook its head.

Aside from slightly singed skin, the beast hadn't suffered any damage.

Jay threw another and another, striking the beast in several sections. Still, with the same result.

The beast lunged forward. It lifted its right blade and stabbed downward, aiming for his head. Jay tucked and rolled to the side. He had to change tactics.

From the ground, he manifested a steady stream of fire from both of his arms. The intense, concentrated flame began to burn the tips of his jacket sleeves and engulfed the monster in a bath of flame.

A horrid scream came from the creature as it reeled back. Jay pushed forth. With each step, the fiend relented, squirming and whipping from side to side. Jay's vision was filled with the warbling of heat and flame. Exerting this much power began to take a toll on his stamina.

Just for a second, he calmed his attack. As his vision cleared, he was hammered in the chest by a swipe from the blunt edge of the creature's left blade. The blow sent him off his feet and through the doorway. The creature was again on the offensive.

Its skin blackened and blistered; the beast continued its attack. It lurched forward, taking consecutive stabs at Jay as he shuffled on his back into the living room. The monster howled with each strike.

Jay stumbled to his feet but was knocked backwards over a recliner from a fierce slash that missed his face by mere inches. He bounced off the seat and landed at the foot of the chair. His head tapped the floor, which caused him to wince.

As he recovered and looked up, two towering swords were soaring over the recliner. The beast was on its hind legs, standing tall—ready to come down with fatal stabs. As the blades began to plunge, Jay kicked the chair into the monster's rear legs and sent it back as it pierced the floorboards with a scream.

Jay made a beeline for the front door; he wasn't convinced he could kill it anymore and had to attempt another escape. As he reached for the doorknob, an acute, intense pain exploded into his right calf and through his shin. He pulled away and could hear a sharp object rip itself from his leg.

He yelped as he fell face-first to the ground and flipped around to see the beast looming over him—blood caked on its right blade. A growing fire could be seen between its hind legs. It drooled onto Jay's abdomen, soaking through his shirt.

With an outstretched neck, the creature inhaled deeply, its nostrils sniffed the air above its prey.

Jay took his fleeting chance. With his left hand, he exerted as much fire as he could into the horror's face. As the beast recoiled, Jay reached back to his backpack, tore the pot free, and cracked it across the monster's cheek.

Stunned, the monster stumbled back. Jay took his chance and limped upstairs as he cauterized his wound. His mind raced. The fiend would not be occupied for long. He queried his memories—searched through his catalog of thoughts for a weapon that might still be in the house. Then, he remembered it.

He rushed into his bedroom on the right and locked the door. Dragging his feet, he located the gun cabinet in his closet. He had supposed that the guns and ammo were already likely stolen, but he prayed the countermeasure he left was of no interest to thieves.

Jay could hear the beast working its way up the stairs, cracking the wooden treads with its weight and brutishness. Approaching the gun cabinet, he grew pale. His final hope lay within that cabinet; this was his last chance. As he rounded the cabinet, his face lit up. A woodcutter's axe leaned against the back.

As Jay peered at the weapon in disbelief, a loud bash cracked the bedroom door. The wood began to splinter as the beast broke through. Jay snatched the axe in both hands and crept towards the door.

Jay positioned himself within striking distance. A large blade pierced through the door and retracted. It struck over and over again until, finally, the door split in two, and the creature burst through. However, Jay didn't move an inch.

He stilled his breathing. Kept his shaking as quiet as possible. The beast sniffed around; its tiny nostrils inquisitively twitched as it tried to catch wind of Jay's scent. It teetered and tilted its head around, aiming its flattened ears in every direction. It took a few steps into the room and turned towards Jay, still unsure if he was there or not.

Another step, Jay thought.

Another step.

C'mon: a little closer.

The monster paused, then moved closer.

There!

Jay brought down the axe hard on the creature's skull. It caved in the charred skin and cracked through the bone. Jay braced one foot on the monster's face and yanked his axe out. Black ichor sprayed across his face and stained the wall. The mixture of bone fragments and brain matter began to pour from the gash.

The beast let out a harrowing cry as it backed off into the hallway. Jay pressed the attack. Limping after his tormentor, he stepped over the broken door, rounded the doorway into the hallway, and swung again. This time, the axe buried itself into the right cheek and dislocated the jaw. More ichor splattered around as the beast pawed at the axe head with its blade.

Jay ripped the weapon out with great force, causing the beast to lose its balance and back partially into another bedroom behind it. The shower of gore sprayed across the hallway floor with a heavy splat. The monster attempted to poke at its predator with a weak stab, but Jay sidestepped it without effort. He was now standing over the beast's neck.

With each blow, the sinews and muscles tore; black fluid flooded its every gaping wound. Jay continued swinging. His injured shoulder burned with pain. Each whack sent vibrations up his shaking arm, but the rush of survival quelled his anguish. He cut through the bone, staining his face, arms, and shirt with the inky mess. With one final bellow and thwack, he lopped off the terror's head.

Jay backed off and gasped for air. His arms tingled from the surge of adrenaline. He was still holding the axe, bloodied and worn, as he slid down the wall behind him. Removing his beanie, he leaned his head back and closed his eyes in relief.

His head was empty. It was flowing with chemicals, fueling his survival instinct. As the rush began to subside, Jay could smell a noxious fume. He opened his eyes to find them blinded by thick smoke. Again, the chemicals kicked in.

Shooting up to his feet, he threw on his beanie. He slipped the axe further into his hand and held it just beneath the head. He tucked his mouth into the crook of his left elbow and hobbled towards the stairs.

Stepping over the dead creature, he slid on the blood-soaked floor. He pulled his arm away from his face and caught himself on the handrail. Violent, raspy coughs echoed through the sweltering air as Jay descended the stairs.

He turned to see a roaring pillar of flame flourishing from the kitchen. It spread across the living room, burning the slats above and below a cinder. He covered his face once again and swung open the front door. He dropped the axe, grabbed his bag, and ran out.

As the flames kissed his back, Jay threw his weight onto the porch rail. Jay's stumbling weight was too much for the flimsy support to take and it snapped at the base, sending him tumbling onto the concrete.

Senses still heightened, he braced himself and protected his face. An elbow and knee took the brunt of the fall which tore his pant leg and left a small stain of blood on the rocky surface. Jay got up and snatched his bike by the handlebars.

Bruised, battered, wheezing, and exhausted, Jay dragged his feet towards the street. Each step heftier than the last. Soon he could hear the clack of his bike hitting the ground as he fell to his knees. The asphalt felt cool and soothing on his cheek, lulling him into a deep slumber.

{Chapter 5}

1132:03:06:47

Jay honked the meek, little horn of his Miata at the person sitting still at the green light in front of them.

"C'mon!" He shouted, throwing a hand up. Under his breath, he said, "Get off your fuckin' phone man."

The SUV in front of him jutted forward as the silhouette of a middle finger could be seen through the rear window. *Jackass,* Jay thought, shaking his head.

He had just gotten off work and was now fighting the relentless Woodward rush hour. The cars inched and jerked. Jay had nearly reached the magical shifting point in traffic; the mystical occurrence when everything suddenly flowed like a steady stream.

One more light, Jay thought, his head thumping from the honks of impatient commuters. He pulled up to the red traffic light and gently slowed to a stop. He rested his elbow on the window trim and nestled his cheek in his palm. He stretched his other arm into the air and let out a groan.

He looked up to the sky and located the newly found object that had been discovered two years ago. The strange black diamond had made itself whole earlier in the year. Two years ago, it was naught but a small, curious blip discovered by astronomers as they searched the night sky; they marked this discovery as the First Convergence. But now, it had fully taken shape and began changing the world ever so slightly—Second Convergence.

Jay brought his attention behind him and looked at his retracted soft top; he drove with the roof down as much as he could. The perfect spring weather mitigated the long, strenuous commute. Even with the blaring of horns and firing of dirty, imprecise pistons, Jay still enjoyed his drives to and from work. It had now been four years without Her, and he needed to find solace in the things he loved.

Jay could feel it now; the light would soon turn green. He readied himself. An empty road stretched into the distance before him. Both of his hands were at ten and two. With the clutch still engaged, he lifted off the brake and hovered over the throttle.

Gonna make this a good one; c'mon.

Steady… Steady… Go!

The green light hadn't finished fully illuminating by the time Jay was off. He let the revs climb high before shifting into second. The engine calmed for a second, but Jay pushed back, shifting into third. Again, his trusty steed slowed its churning, but its jockey demanded one final gallop into fourth.

Jay was flying. The cops rarely pulled people over at this time of day. The sea of cars didn't demand their attention and wasn't worth their time. Jay's face chilled a bit as the wind whipped across and jostled his shirt. His vision was solely fixated on the road as the gale buffeted his ears.

As he approached Northwood Boulevard, Jay shifted down through the gears with precision. He took the corner, rolling the body of the small Miata just a bit and skidding the tires with some oversteer. Correcting his course, he continued down the familiar streets. Jay drove around parked cars and oncoming traffic, pulling down the street towards his home.

A billowing funnel of black smoke was rising a few blocks down. As Jay drove closer, he could see that the commotion belonged to a harrowing fire that had engulfed his neighbor's house. The reflections of the flames twirled in his windshield as Jay stared at the fire while he parked at the curb in front of his house.

He threw on the emergency brake and shut off his car. He jumped out and ran across the street where a small crowd had formed outside the house fire. His neighbor, Sharon, and her husband, Charley, were staring in disbelief with their arms crossed.

"Sharon!" Jay beckoned as he ran up.

"Oh, hey! Jay!" Sharon waved.

"My god, what happened?"

"Not sure. Someone saw the flames from their window and called the fire department, but no one's shown up yet."

"Probably stuck in that damn traffic," Charley chimed in.

"Yeah. This is horrible. Did Derek and Kendra get out?" Jay asked, looking around. "I don't see 'em."

The couple glanced at each other.

"Well, someone yelled for Derek earlier with no answer," Sharon replied. "But Kendra left this morning for work. Was Derek with her?"

"Maybe he left for work even earlier," Charley pondered, "or maybe he was with her and she took him to work? Dunno; not sure."

"No, no, no," Jay said in a panic. "Do you guys ever even *talk* to the guy? They only own *one* car and Derek works from home!"

"Oh shit," Charley said, his face sinking as his arms dropped to his sides.

Without a further word, Jay sprinted to the door with Charley following suit. An intense red glow had begun filling the evening air, but Jay was only focused on the danger before him. Soon, the house fire would evolve into a towering inferno; Jay had to be quick.

They rushed up the porch and swung open the outer screen door. Jay grabbed the doorknob and attempted to barge in but was met with the metal rattle of a locked door.

"Shit," he muttered. He tucked his arm in and faced his shoulder to the door. Motioning to Charley, they both readied themselves. Bobbing to the count of three, the men charged the door with a solid thud—no dice.

"Again!" Jay shouted. "One… two… three!" This time, the door nudged and creaked, but still denied them entry.

"C'mon! C'mon!" yelled Charley. With desperate vigor, the men tackled the door once more. The heavy wooden entry finally caved and swung into the adjacent wall. Jay and Charley tumbled inside, catching their balance.

The immediacy of the smoke smacked Jay in the face and violated his lungs. The men covered their faces and ducked under the wild flames. Jay peered through the sweltering terror. The flames were engulfing every aspect of Derek and Kendra's home. They blanketed the walls, reaching high up to the ceilings as they whirled into violent blooms.

The rumble of the inferno's orchestra echoed through the home accompanied by a symphony of crackles and the ear-piercing beeping of the fire alarm. Charley added to the performance, "Derek! Where are ya?"

"Derek!" Jay added as the two started to venture deeper. They continued to shout, checking a few downstairs rooms, when a timid voice cut through the noise: "Ahhh, ahh."

"Here!" Charley beckoned to Jay. Jay ran through the small maze and found Charley in the kitchen. On the floor was Derek, Jay's middle-aged neighbor. He was on his stomach with his head resting on his right cheek—his arms splayed out.

Deep crimson stained Derek's dark skin and pooled around his wooly, black beard. The trail of blood led up and onto the corner of the dining table above him. His legs were pinned under a massive, overturned, walnut hutch. Broken china and utensils littered the floor; some pieces rested on Derek's back. Orange flames flickered in the reflection of a cracked phone just inches from Derek's hands.

"I can't… ahhh…" Derek grumbled.

"Don't worry, bud. We got cha," Jay reassured. He stepped over Derek, one foot on each side of him, and squatted to place his hands on the hutch. The hefty wood was smoldering, cracked, and burning with a steady fire. Jay didn't spare a thought. He grasped the blackened corner and turned to Charley.

"C'mon! Help me with this!" he yelled.

Charley nodded and took position next to Jay. He placed his hands just as Jay did, but swiftly took them back. The hutch was a furnace. Heat instantly scorched Charley's palms. They blistered as he examined them.

He looked over at Jay's grip and saw it holding fast. The piercing intensity hadn't affected Jay's determination.

"The *fuck* are you doing? C'mon!" Jay yelled, commanding Charley's attention.

Charley braced himself. Grabbing hold, the hot wood ate at his skin. He could feel his palms cooking to a broil as they began to explode into balls of pain. Charley bore the brunt of the anguish and howled.

With their combined strength, the men lifted the fiery obstacle a few inches off of Derek.

"Derek!" Jay commanded under the strain. "Go! Man! Go!"

Dizzied, Derek summoned a small ounce of adrenaline to his arms. He pulled himself with all his fleeting might from under his shackles. Flopping another arm over, he snarled like a bear ensnared by a trap.

"Jay, I can't hold this forever!" hollered Charley.

"He's almost out! He's almost out!" Jay hollered back. "You got this Derek! Go, man!"

With a final garbled cry, Derek lunged forward onto his face; he was saved.

Jay looked over the hutch and could see the source of the fire. A cyclone of flame was barreling out of the kitchen oven. Glancing to ensure Derek was out, Jay and Charley dropped the hutch with a tremendous thud as they rushed to Derek. The large man's stocky calves were exposed, and severe bruises had formed on his legs. Without wasting any more time, they each took an arm over their shoulder and lifted the hefty man to his feet. They nodded at each other and marched forward.

With raspy coughs, the two men trudged towards the entrance. Derek's limp body weighed heavy on the men's shoulders. His fledgling beer gut hung out of his shirt and his meaty arms stuck to the back of his saviors' necks. He tried to aid in their endeavors, but his dragging feet refused to obey.

The fire was now pouring out of the door. All around them, hellfire whipped and cracked as the swelling smoke clouded their vision and clogged their lungs. The exit was nearby.

As they approached, the group turned sideways to ready themselves to fit through the door. Shuffling through piles of ash and debris, they gave one final lug as they stumbled out.

The blaring of sirens filled the darkened sky as firefighters rushed past the men to douse the flames. Gallons of water drenched the home and showered the three men as they collapsed on the lawn. Another group of firefighters ran to their aid.

"Help him first," wheezed Charley, pointing at Derek. The firefighters called over a pair of paramedics as they prepared a stretcher to carry Derek.

Jay sat back on his heels, huffing as he wiped the soot off his face. He tilted his head back as he noted the intense red glow that had now completely covered the land.

"We need a couple more medics for these guys!" shouted one of the firefighters near Jay. He turned to Jay and asked, "Can you walk, sir?"

"Yeah, just winded is all," Jay replied weakly.

"All right, good. I'll help you over to the paramedics."

"Sounds good."

As Jay and the firefighter walked away, Jay turned to see Charley being checked by another worker. They were examining his wounds, and Jay could see that Charley's hands were decimated. He looked down at his own and wiped away some ash—nary a burn to be seen.

Jay sat on the back edge of the ambulance. He was waiting for the medic behind him to retrieve some medicine. He heard a drawer close followed by approaching steps. The paramedic stepped down and handed Jay a couple of painkillers and a cup of water. Jay swallowed the pills, gulped some water, and handed the cup back to the medic.

"Well," the paramedic started, "doesn't seem like you suffered anything serious. Your breathing has stabilized, and the oxygen tank helped a lot."

"Awesome, thank you," replied Jay who was now relaxed from the adrenaline rush.

"No signs of injury either, not even burns. The other guy, uh- "

"Charley."

"*Charley* said you both lifted a burning china hutch?"

"Yeah, that's right."

"He suffered third-degree burns in both hands. He's gonna need some skin grafts, but you... seem perfectly fine."

Jay unfurled his fingers and looked down at his hands resting in his lap.

"Why?" Jay turned his attention back to the medic. "Is there somethin' wrong with me? Or?"

"No, not from what I or your vitals can tell," the medic replied. "I'd still recommend following up with a doctor but, in the meantime, we'll just call it luck!" He patted Jay on the shoulder.

The flooding red glow had started to subside. What now filled the evening air was a faint crimson bath. Jay heard a small, distant hum from above. He peered up in the direction of the sound and found himself staring at The Anomaly.

"It's been doing that for the past few hours," said the medic. "It was a lot louder earlier, and the sudden red light from The Anomaly caused a lot of accidents, so we've been swamped. But it's dying down, looks like."

"That's good," Jay added. "Is Derek gonna be ok?"

"He's in pretty rough shape, but... he'll pull through. He's pretty damn lucky. If it weren't for you two, he'd definitely be dead in that house."

"And Kendra? His wife?"

"We were able to contact her shortly after. She's stuck behind some accidents on I-75 but she's ok... if not stressed out of her mind, I'm sure."

"Yeah! Same."

Static started to hiss from a small walkie-talkie on the paramedic's belt. He lifted a finger to excuse himself from the conversation and turned away, answering the call. He replied with acknowledgment and a few callsigns, strapped the walkie-talkie back onto his belt, and turned back to Jay.

"Duty calls," he said, motioning Jay to get up from the bumper. "Just clean yerself up and take it easy. You'll be fine! Get better!"

"Thanks again!" Jay replied, waving as he walked across the street towards his house.

Charley was sitting on the curb with Sharon comforting him. As Jay approached, Charley looked up and said, "Ah, my partner in crime!"

"Crime?" Jay joked in a bewildered tone.

"Ha-ha. You gonna be ok?"

"Yeah, doc said just to take it easy. You?"

Charley flipped his bandaged hands around towards Jay with a coy smile, "Gonna be a while 'til I can swing a golf club, I reckon."

"You both were incredibly brave," Sharon chimed in. "But, don't you ever, *ever, e-ver* do anything so stupid and reckless again!"

"We're men," Charley replied. "Stupid and reckless is kinda in our programming." He glanced over at Jay with a smirk. "Besides, it's what neighbors do, right? We help each other."

"Damn right."

They shared a moment of silence, absorbing the still spring air. The suburb street was quiet now. The crowd had left the spectacle, and the firefighters had all but contained the fire. The charred and ruined skeleton of Derek's house puffed and sizzled as water continued to douse the home.

"Well, I better get going," Jay said. "Probably gonna clean up and pass out."

"Good idea. You take care… and thanks!" Charley replied.

"Yeah, you too!"

Jay waved goodbye to the couple as he walked up to his porch. His legs were shaking, but the sturdy metal rail supported his weight entirely. He ascended the short stone stairs and unlocked his front door. As he stepped inside and shut the door, moonlight shone through the stained-glass windows behind him.

A brilliant array of spring colors rolled out across the hardwood floor, past the mantle, and ended just before the basement stairs. Jay had now entered a silent, malformed world. Where he once found comfort and companionship, he now only dwelled in solitude and indifference. The heightened feeling of heroism had been swiftly drained by the dark empty home as he stood there, casting his motionless silhouette on the stained-glass light.

He flipped the light switch. The living room had remained untouched since Her departure. The couch had a small indentation where they would spend their time together and the objects on the coffee table had not moved. A layer of dust masked the mantel top along with the memorabilia that sat on it.

Jay sighed and headed upstairs to clean up. He turned into the bathroom and began running a bath. As he undressed in the mirror, he examined himself. He didn't recognize the malnourished figure that stood before him. His eyes were now dark, shallow pits and his expression bore a severe apathy.

He looked over to the neighboring sink. Her cosmetics and toiletries were still there. A frayed, pink toothbrush sat in a cup by the faucet. Bundles of Her hair were still tangled in a large, wooden comb. Various bottles full of skincare, perfume, and make-up crowded the counter space like buildings rising from a small city.

Jay turned away, still without feeling, and finished undressing. He removed his wedding ring and placed it on the countertop. He stepped into the steamy bath and plopped himself in, dipping a few times to let his body get used to the heat.

He splashed some water onto his face and cleaned any remnants from earlier. Relaxing, he closed his eyes and replayed memories of Her. The emotion swelled in his chest as if it were ready to burst. He decided to save himself the grief and focus on the earlier events in Derek's home.

The ringing in his ear confirmed he was remembering the volume correctly. He recounted his fear as the fires surrounded him, but a curious observation came to his mind: he could not feel the heat. The air in the house choked him; he could feel the collapse in his chest at the time. But the temperature was as cool and comfortable as the outside.

Jay opened his eyes and emerged his hands from the water. He brought them into the light. Carefully, he examined them for any discoloration or blistering. They were a warm pink from the hot bath, but no signs of burning made themselves present.

"Huh," Jay murmured in astonishment.

After slipping into some pajamas and putting on his ring, Jay went down to the kitchen to prepare dinner. The white, ceramic tiles soothed his tired soles as he stirred a small pot of soup. His mind was still fixated on his lack of burns. He had trouble believing he had just gotten 'lucky' when Charley was now expecting several hospital bills; Jay was still human after all.

As his soup finished, Jay scooted over a bowl and set the pan aside on an empty burner. He went to turn off the flame when he paused. Staring at the little blue flame, he remembered the burning hutch and how it failed to sear his skin. He let go of the knob, his eyes still focused on the burner.

He inched his index finger towards the fire; he didn't want to risk a severe injury if it could be helped. As his fingertip neared the flame, he felt no heat. Closer and closer it approached, hovering like the bow of a boat entering port. Jay winced as he continued to push.

He pictured the cooked skin in his mind and the smell it would produce. He pressed on. Inching and inching. Running every scenario in his head, until he felt a smooth metal surface. Jay could hardly believe it. When he looked down, an impossible scenario had come to fruition: his finger was in full contact with the burner.

Jay felt no heat.

No fire.

No flame.

He splayed out his hand and rested it on the burner. Still, no pain. Only a scant feeling of cool embrace wrapped his hand. He lifted it away as the fire followed. He stared with his mouth agape as he fluttered his fingers, making the flames bow to his whim.

He raised his left hand and felt a power growing inside it. He chased the feeling and encouraged its ignition. The hand blackened and crackled, heating up to a significant temperature. Before it could burst into flame, Jay noticed his ring had begun to deform and melt.

"Oh shit!" he gasped. He retracted the power in his left hand, but his right was still aflame. He bounced on the balls of his feet, trying his best to retract the fire until he caught sight of his soup. Without hesitation, he dunked his hand in the boiling goop.

Scalding needles shot into Jay's hand and down his arm as the fire extinguished and sizzled.

"Ah, fuck!" Jay yelped as he yanked his hand out of the pot, splashing heaps of soup across the pristine white floor. He shook his hand vigorously and brought it over to his left to slip off his ring. His mind blank from the shock, Jay rushed to the back door as he worked his warped ring off his finger and tossed it into a junk drawer.

As he exited into the backyard, he felt the chilly evening air against his scalding hand which helped quell the pain, but Jay was searching for something more potent. Scanning the overgrown garden, he thought to himself: *C'mon honey. I know you tried to grow aloe vera around here somewhere.*

Jay peered through the darkness; his vision started to adjust to the moonlight. In the far corner of the garden was a small, spiny succulent, struggling to survive in the damp Michigan weather.

"Ah!" Jay gasped as he rushed to the puny plant. He dove into the soft dirt and snapped off a piece. He swiveled around and sat on the ground. Gripping the piece in his left hand, he rubbed the cooling juices on his scalding skin. He sighed in relief and looked up at the ominous, glowing black diamond.

{Chapter 6}

8:21:21:38

Flickering signs of muted orange and red lit the darkness. As they danced and glowed, pops and sputters could be heard alongside a muffled crunching sound. The sights and sounds lured Jay into the conscious world as his eyelids slid open and his hearing filled with the full volume of the room. Vision still blurred, he turned towards the source of the light as a small damp towel fell off of his forehead, plopping onto the floor.

"Finally awake? Good," said a calm, familiar voice.

The scratchy, dirty couch felt rough on Jay's bare back, but the ragged fleece blanket he was covered with was comforting and warm. He began to sway his head around as he scooted up—then he started to whip around in a frenzy. With small huffs and groans, he frantically searched the room, feeling the aftereffects of the fight with the monster.

"Hey-hey!" commanded the female voice.

Jay looked in her direction and recognized the crossbow-wielding woman, eating a cookie and sitting on the edge of a small cot.

"You are ok. We are safe here," She assured him.

He shot a glance at the fireplace. "Put that out," Jay whispered. "You want those things to find us?"

"Hmph, no worries. Female shabriri protect their nests at night and the males return from hunting during the day to rest. I have checked this house. There are no shabriri here."

"Shabriri?"

"The creature you fought. It is what they are called out here."

Jay looked down at his right shoulder. It was bandaged with perfect tautness and folds—the correct number of wraps to allow free range of motion yet still provide ample compression. He ran his hand along the blood-soaked gauze and noted its hospital-grade quality. He reached down and flipped over the end of the blanket, revealing his right leg. His pant leg was rolled up just below the knee and he saw that his leg wound was also bandaged with expertise.

"You know," the woman began as she took a bite of her cookie, "we do not cauterize wounds very often anymore. In particularly deep gashes, like your leg, it can cause serious infection."

Jay's eyes widened with concern as he held his injured leg in both hands.

"Do not worry." She rummaged through a red bag by her feet and pulled out a small bottle. Tossing it to Jay, she said, "Take a couple of those antibiotics for the next three or so days and you will be fine. Are you allergic to any sort of medication?"

Jay shook his head as he caught the bottle. He hesitated for a moment, wondering why his earlier assailant was now playing doctor. Investigating the bottle, he found it to be a normal course of antibiotics. At first, he suspected it could be poison but figured if this woman wanted him dead, she would've just shot him while he slept. He decided to put his trust in her, popped open the bottle, dropped two pills into his hand, and swallowed them dry.

Tossing the bottle back to the woman, he said, "Thank you."

"Of course. I would suggest staying off of it as much as possible, but seeing how you ran up those stairs—"

"Wait. You were watchin' me?" Jay asked curtly.

The woman pointed through a window behind Jay and nodded. Jay whipped around, pulling himself over the back of the couch to look over it. Through the window, Jay could see the smoldering remains of his house under a plume of smoke just down the block. He turned back around and stared daggers at the woman.

"You were here the whole time?" he asked.

"Well, not the whole time," the woman dismissed. "I set up camp here earlier today and set out to scavenge some supplies while the male shabriri were gone. Let me see… then I shot you… did a little bit of scouting… and… came back here."

Jay was beginning to grow annoyed with the woman's lackadaisical tone.

"As I was about to pack up and set off," she continued, "I saw the house fire through the window." She pulled out a small pair of binoculars from her bag. "So, I decided to watch."

"Why didn't you help me?" Jay asked through clenched teeth.

"Do not misunderstand me, please," she said, raising her hands in defense. "If I had not witnessed you spray that fire in the shabriri's face when you did, I would have gladly rushed over. But, after seeing what you could do, I would have just been in the way. I did not want to get burned myself, you know?"

"You coulda called your friends! We could've easily outnumbered it!"

The woman rolled her eyes as she laughed. She shook her head, taking another nibble of the cookie, and said: "If you are going to survive out here, you will have to learn to be far less gullible."

Jay let the petty insult glance off of him and asked curtly, "Why did ya shoot me? Ya coulda just came out and asked me to shush."

"And you would have *complied*? Stopped shouting?"

Jay looked away and grumbled: "Maybe... would've been less risky than me screamin' in pain from a fuckin' crossbow shot!"

"Well," the woman trailed off, scratching her cheek and turning red. "What if I told you that was meant to be a *warning* shot past you? I am... *not* the best shot."

A spark of anger started to build in Jay, but he was far too tired to let it burst. "Un-fuckin'-believable," he muttered.

"Hmph, I said I was sorry."

Jay peered at the cookie in her hand and then traced his vision down to an empty green packet on the floor. The MRE packaging looked all too familiar. He followed a trail of water to a pot with a wooden spoon resting inside. He looked by the foot of the couch and saw his bag—unbuckled.

"H-hey!" he called.

"Oh, come now. It is the least you could do to pay me for dragging you out of the street! Besides," she said as she stood up and walked over to the pot. Squatting down, she picked it up and brought it over to Jay. "I saved some for you. Eat. You will need it."

The pot hovered in front of Jay's face. He shot a few glances between it and the woman. He grabbed it by the handle, swiveled on his backside, and sat up. Peeking over the lip, he could see that, indeed, one of his beef stew MREs had been thoroughly cooked.

Jay couldn't deny the rumbling in his stomach. The energy from his measly breakfast had been expended long ago. He started with a small bite, tasting the lukewarm sauce. On any other day, the "Meal Ready to Expel" would have made him cringe and yearn for anything else—but, right now, it satiated his hunger like fine dining.

As he gobbled down his food, the woman walked over to the fireplace and lit a cigarette. She took a few puffs and sat back down, crossed her legs, then stared out the window. She held a stern expression as she stared off into nothingness.

Jay looked over and watched the smoke as it lifted from the tip of her cigarette. The soft glow of moonlight warped through the smoke as it illuminated the sparse living room. Small specks of stars through the canopies above twinkled through the cracked glass.

Stars.

Stars, Jay thought. He lingered on the word as realization set in.

"Shit!" he quipped, his cheeks full of stew. He threw the blanket off of himself in a panic and dropped the pot, splashing some food on the ground. Jay whipped out his phone and tapped on the screen repeatedly. The screen remained black—dead.

"What time is it?" Jay demanded.

"Ummm," the woman murmured as she broke out of her trance. She pulled up her sleeve to check her watch. "It is just about a quarter past midnight."

Midnight! Jay thought, running some calculations in his head.

"No, no, no," Jay murmured. "I've lost a whole… ten-ish hours!"

Jay shot up to his feet. The sudden flush of fatigue ran down his legs like a paralyzing wave. His knees buckled and jolted, sending him tumbling back onto the couch.

"I need to–" Jay grunted as he attempted to stand up again. Rising only a few inches off the seat, his legs refused to support his weight as he tumbled back once again with a defeated exhale.

"Rest, *dost*," the woman said, motioning with her hand for Jay to sit. "The day is lost. Accept it. You will need your strength when we set off tomorrow."

"*We?*" Jay asked as he lay back down.

She pointed at Jay's bag. "Your route... I too am traveling it. Not as far, though. I only plan to go as far as Cadillac."

Jay reached into his backpack and unfolded his map. He followed his red line across the state, searching for the little town to the northwest. He spotted the small print of 'Cadillac' and asked, "Cadillac? There ain't nothin' there."

The woman held a hint of contempt on her face as she replied, "A place with people cannot possibly have *nothing*—especially when two of those people are your mother and sister."

"Oh," Jay hung his head, "sorry."

"Hmph, no worries. I honestly cannot afford to get angry now if we are to travel together."

"I thought you couldn't trust a 'creature who claims he is human,'" Jay shot back, mocking her.

"I do not trust you. But... a creature does not carry an urn. A creature does not care for the dead."

The air stood still for a moment. Only the dying crackles of the fireplace could be heard in the solemn night. The woman took one last draw of her cigarette and snuffed it out on the heel of her shoe.

"Who is it?" she asked.

Jay turned away. Sinking into the couch, he replied, "Don't worry about it."

The woman grinned and nodded in acceptance, "Fair enough. Sorry I asked."

Jay's eyelids began to shut as the soft sounds of the fireplace lulled him to sleep. As he began to doze off, he had a realization. Turning over slightly, just enough so his voice would be heard, he stated, "Hey, I dunno your name."

"Oh! You can call me Benu!"

"Benu… is that a nickname?"

"Yes, ha-ha. Not common but," Benu tilted her head, "not uncommon."

Jay nodded, "Thank you again, Benu."

He pulled the blanket over himself and bundled it under his chin, between his hands. His eyes grew heavy as he nestled his head into the couch cushion. Soon, slumber took over his exhausted body.

Jay woke to the bright rays of sunshine gleaming through the windows onto his face. Weary-eyed, he sat up and yawned. He felt around for his nightstand. When he felt nothing but air, he snapped from the unfamiliar feeling of waking up somewhere new. The memories of yesterday came flooding back as he opened his eyes wide.

As he sat up, the pain in his shoulder was minimal and the one in his leg had subsided enough for him to stand. He stood up, half expecting his legs to give out, and looked around for Benu.

The fire had burned out, leaving nothing but ash and a small pillar of smoke. Benu's red bag was gone, and the cot was devoid of sheets. Distant bird chirps echoed through the broken windows as the potent smell of morning dew permeated the room.

Jay grabbed his shirt, jacket, and beanie that were draped over the head of the couch and got dressed. As his head popped through the collar, he noticed Benu on the front lawn with her thumbs pressed on the small of her back. She leaned back and bent her knees, keeping her feet flat. She let her wild hair dangle behind her as her head hung upside down. Her eyes were shut with a slight twitch in her cheek. She rose slowly and started to twist from side to side.

As Jay stepped onto the porch, his backpack in hand, Benu caught sight of him as she twisted and said, "Ah, good morning, Jay."

"Mornin' Benu," Jay replied. The low orange glow of the rising sun was peeping over the horizon. Jay looked in its direction and said, "Did ya sleep at all?"

Benu leaned forward on one leg, striking a warrior's pose.

"There are a couple hours when the male shabriri return and rest—and the females are still sleeping. I slept then," she said as she stretched. The speed of her words took Jay a moment to comprehend.

"How do ya know all this?"

"Hmm? Oh, I have been out here ever since Second Convergence. You know, when The Anomaly really started to mess things up. We were neighbors, actually. Well, sort of; I lived two blocks over. We never met, if you are trying to remember."

Second Convergence, Jay thought. *That would be when I got these powers. Three years, huh?* Aloud, Jay asked: "And you've been all alone?"

"No, not the entire time. When everyone was asked to evacuate, some of us stayed behind. People came and went, as they usually do. But, recently I suppose I have been *all alone,* save for the carriages I see pass by on Woodward. The growing shabriri do not exactly add to the curb appeal." Benu shot Jay a clever smile, gesturing to the patch of grass next to her. "You should join me. A cramp would be such a silly thing to waste time on."

"Uh, I'm good. Thanks."

"Suit yourself."

Benu continued through her routine as Jay stepped down from the porch. A modern, green mountain bike leaned against the wooden railing that lined the porch. Between it and the railing, a red bag and crossbow leaned against the support. The black vines that entangled everything were still writhing as they squeezed and crawled along the ground and up house walls. The warm, serene sun shower was at odds with what it shone on.

With a pat on her hips, Benu quipped: "Well? Ready to go?"

Jay patted his pockets and worked through his usual routine—phone, keys, wallet—and found them to all be there. An extra item had also joined his party: the wedding ring was nestled in his front-right pocket, neighboring his phone. He nearly nodded then stopped, remembering that his phone had died.

"Yeah, hold on one sec," he told Benu as he sat his bag down and retrieved his charging cable and battery bank. He plugged the phone in and waited for the screen to light up with an icon of a battery filling up. Putting the interlinked items away, he slung his arm through a strap and convinced his bag onto his back.

"Hmph, why do you carry that, anyways?" Benu asked. "It is not like the cell towers and satellites will suddenly start working again."

"I use it mainly for the time, honestly. But… I guess it just reminds me of my life in the old world. A sense of stability, I guess."

"To each their own," Benu replied, waving her watch in the air.

Jay scanned the yard and front of the house and asked: "Hey, where's my bike?"

Benu shot a quick point down the street towards Jay's wrecked home. There, in the street, lay Jay's bike, untouched from last night.

"Come," whispered Benu as she retrieved her bag, slung her crossbow around her body, and walked her bike over to Jay. "We will grab your bike and be off. And we should be quiet. The males may be nearby, and we do not want to wake any females as *you* did." Jay rolled his eyes and shrugged at the chide.

They walked down the empty street. Jay kept his eyes fixated on his smoldering home. His past, his memories, were now a pile of fizzling rubble. His gaze lingered on the house until he felt he was getting closer to his bike. Turning his attention forward, he nearly tripped over his overturned bike.

Jay bent down and stood his bike up. He propped it on its kickstand and examined it for any damage. Aside from a few new scuffs and paint chips, the bike was all good. Strapping his backpack on the rear rack, he continued to stare at the burnt remains.

"Hey," Benu commanded his attention in a low tone. "We should really get going."

"Right," Jay replied.

Benu jogged forward with a small start and leapt onto her bike. The clicking of her tires started to fade as Jay said one final goodbye to his home in his mind. With a heavy exhale through his nostrils and a frown, Jay followed Benu's lead and ran down the street. He leapt up and over his seat, balanced his weight on the handlebars, and came down onto the seat. He stood up and pedaled hard, catching up to Benu.

They rode down a path that led back to Woodward in silence. Coasting as much as they could to keep noise to a minimum, the two broke through the trees and arrived back on the main road. As they swerved onto the pavement, they were met with a conga line of carriages and trotting horses.

The morning deliveries were passing through; each cart flanked by guards armed with various weapons—axes, knives, crossbows.

No guns.

Guns did not share the same fate as vehicles. A fully assembled gun could be aimed, fired, and reloaded just as it normally would *if* it had ammo loaded. Guns were plentiful and easy to find, but ammo was rare. In three short years, The Anomaly had unleashed its chaos and people had fought the onslaught of otherworldly monsters using mountains of bullets. Wars between nations broke out. Eventually, the "sunk cost fallacy" took its effect and caused the large-scale wars to stop—but human-on-human violence continued between neighbors, bandits, and authorities. Survival of the fittest became the law of the land outside major city hubs. But as the ammo ran out, people had to resort to more primitive weaponry.

"Ah!" Benu broke out. "We can talk freely here. Shabriri rarely attack large groups."

"Why's that?" Jay shouted ahead.

"They are solitary hunters. They only attack stragglers. Like, uh, tigers going after deer!"

"Good to know!"

Woodward felt alive again. Although the sights and sounds were different, the clops of hooves and random chatter amongst the convoys filled Jay with a nostalgic feeling. A sense of routine as men and women went about their work. The tension was palpable as the guards eyed the woods for danger. Suspicious glares squeezed through makeshift, full-faced helmets—directed at Jay and Benu as they rode by.

Travelers were scarce and even scarcer in pairs. If people did travel, it was either in large groups or alone—to avoid the risk of shabriri attacks. Another person was seen as a burden. It was another mouth to feed. Another wound to bandage. Another risk of noise. Only true loyalty lay within those who traveled in pairs—or true stupidity.

"So why me?" Jay called.

"What do you mean?" Benu replied.

"Why choose *me* to travel with?"

"You can shoot fire out of your hands. That is pretty useful."

"I could roast ya in your sleep—take your things and leave!"

"You could… I guess we will see what kind of person you are, Jay!"

"So, you *do* trust me?"

"No, but I would like to. I believe I cannot make this journey on my own. And I believe *you* cannot either."

Jay rewound the past twenty-four hours in his mind. He recalled how he saw success in his trip—the naivety in his thoughts. The pain in his shoulder and leg struck a similar chord with Benu's words.

"So, ya don't feel like you're taking a risk here?" Jay shouted.

Benu laughed, "We have a week to live, Jay. If now is not the time to take risks, then remind me to take them in the afterlife!"

Jay and Benu were nearing the end of the convoy. As they passed the last carriage, Benu signaled back to Jay to stay quiet with her finger pressed against her lips. Jay nodded.

They continued up the road in silence. The familiar scene of yesterday surrounded Jay. If he hadn't driven up and down this road for years, he would surely be lost. But the bends and curves of the main street felt natural under his tires. As they neared the town of Bloomfield Hills, Benu spotted a commotion in the middle of the road.

She signaled to Jay to slow down. They rode up along the side of the road to a gruesome scene and stopped. A toppled cart was laying in the street—smashed fruits and vegetables strewn about. A gored and mangled horse was still hitched to the carriage. Its head had been caved in—barely recognizable amongst the mincemeat. A sanguine pool drenched the asphalt under the rent mid-section of the poor animal. Innards were piled and pulled from the gaping ribcage.

A massive shabriri, blanketed with bolts and arrows, was dead alongside the horse. The great beast measured the length of three men and would nearly reach as tall by the tip of its blade's elbows. The skin was a putrid green, the kind resembling dying moss. Jutting from its head were two massive antlers that spread and pointed in several odd directions—snow-white like bone. On its blades were small barbs and, down its spine, boney spikes pierced through the skin.

"That is a male," Benu whispered as she nodded over Jay's shoulder. "They were once human, you know."

"What happened to them?" Jay asked, still staring at the scene.

"Well, no one really knows. Some think it has to do with the trees and the black vines, but some claim they saw people change the moment they lost their way… their… meaning."

Jay nodded, speechless.

Benu sighed, "This convoy must have been running behind. Unlucky."

A few guards lay dead around the beast. Others were tending to the wounded, retrieving bolts and arrows, and standing watch.

"We should get on I-75," Benu continued. "The highway will keep us off ground level."

"Hey," a guard commanded in a low tone. "Can we help you?"

"Come, we should move," whispered Benu to Jay as she began to pedal off. Jay kept his eyes on the shabriri as he pushed off and followed Benu down a neighboring road.

The road was cramped, flanked by vehicles that hadn't been pushed by the wayside. Jay and Benu coasted as silently as their cycling gears allowed them. Soon, they came upon the onramp to the interstate. Benu motioned with a tilt of her head as she banked onto the ramp; Jay followed close behind.

They swayed and pushed hard up the ramp. Jay's leg was pulsating with pain, but he knew the top of the incline was soon to come. As he came over the apex of the ramp, he looked up at the evergreens. The tips were now visible, so he figured they were about two-thirds from the top of the ramp. The sky was more visible, with its milky blue filling the space between the trees.

Benu moved forward slightly, pulled over, and beckoned to Jay: "Hey! Pull out your map."

Startled by her willingness to immediately throw caution to the wind and yell, Jay reached behind him and retrieved his map. He tip-toed, straddling his bike, over to Benu and handed her the map.

She whipped it open and spread it over her handlebars. She looked forward and around, then back down at the map. Studying it, she puckered her lips and nodded with self-assurance.

"Mhmm, should take us… a little under four hours to reach Flint," she said. "That would mean," she continued as she checked her watch, "we should arrive by noon!"

"Y'know," Jay replied, "unless we're eaten."

"Hmph, come now. You have to stay positive," she patted Jay on the shoulder and handed back his map. "Once we are free of the forest, it should be smooth sailing."

"The forest ends?"

"Of course! Oh, do not tell me you thought Michigan was all trees?"

"It's just…"

"You have not been out in a long time, huh? It is ok. Come. You will see for yourself," Benu smiled and took off unexpectedly. Jay stuffed his map back in his bag and rode off after her.

They pedaled on in silence for what seemed like hours, cutting through the sea of cars at a steady speed. Jay could now see why the highway wasn't suitable for the carriages. The staggering number of vehicles wouldn't allow enough space for significantly sized carts to fit. They could have theoretically moved them off the highway via the ramps but, with the shabriri around, the task could result in several casualties.

The blinding streaks of green raced past Jay's vision. The flutter of the branches and streaks of wind brushed his ears. Everything around his focus was a blur. His eyes were fixed on Benu's crossbow slung across her back.

✦

The arrow flew fast and true, piercing the small red circle at the center of the target.

"Wow! Nice shot, honey!" Jay expressed from behind Her. She bobbed on the balls of Her feet as She spun on Her heel, smiled at Jay, and took Her place behind the safety line.

"All right! Next shooters!" called out the archery range supervisor.

Jay smiled and stepped up to the firing line marked with the number '4' on the ground. He stood perpendicular to the target. Looking down, he checked his footing. Shoulder-width apart. Flat on the ground. Knees slightly bent. He straightened up and looked down the range.

He peered at the little red dot that sat forty yards into the distance. She had hit two bullseyes and a yellow—the circle encompassing the red. Extending his left arm up and out, he gripped the bow tightly and focused hard on his goal. The vision around the small dot began to blur and drain of color; all he could see now was bright red in the center of his vision.

Only moving his right arm, he reached down and retrieved an arrow from the quiver that was mounted on a small stand. Unmoving as a statue, he guided the arrow between the string and rested it on the shelf. Jay notched the arrow and wrapped his fingers around it.

Slowly… gently… he drew his bow. He shut his right eye and lined up his shot. Sweat rolled down his temple and carried itself down to the corner of his lips. He paid it no mind and let it seep into his mouth. The salty taste worked its way around his mouth as he let out a deep breath…

Fire!

"Number 4: miss!" yelled out the supervisor.

Jay dropped his stance in defeat and turned around to see Her clapping as She laughed.

Ⓐ

Jay's tires screeched as he squeezed hard on his brakes. Benu had come to a stop to overlook the wondrous and terrifying view that stood before them. The open fields of the mitten popped into Jay's vision as he broke himself of his reminiscing. He looked left to right to see the highway flanked by younger evergreens, marking the end of the forest.

Farms of various livestock and crops were spread out across the rural land. Golden waves flowed as the chill wind brushed across their tips. In the distance, another highway could be seen with a scant number of carriages finishing up their morning rounds. Watchmen were posted around the farms to protect them from threats—both human and inhuman. Fields of scavenged solar panels blanketed the open land, providing precious power to what remained of Detroit.

But for all this beauty came a stark contrast. The Anomaly had proven to be a ruthless force. Enormous funnels of air and rock could be seen far and wide as they were slowly being sucked out of existence. Hairline cracks were scattered throughout the land, emanating traces of purple light that leaked across the surface. Jay looked up towards the black diamond to see the warping of clouds around it—the destruction of his world.

"Time to go, *dost*," Benu said. "Two more hours to Flint."

{Chapter 7}

8:08:12:59

The gates of Flint faded into view as they drew closer. The roughly two-hour journey was arduous but free of any significant turmoil. The surrounding area mimicked the dense vegetation of the Metro Detroit area, but the accursed evergreens were not present. All the same, the plant growth was immense from years of neglect. Infrastructure was mostly intact but buckled and strained under invasive elements.

Soon, Benu came upon a ruined truck whose tailgate was swung open. She signaled to Jay to pull over next to it. As she came to a stop, Benu dismounted her bike, propped it on its kickstand, and pulled her medical kit from her bag. Jay coasted to a stop next to her and asked: "What's up? Ya hurt?"

"Nope. We need to change your bandages I think," she replied. She patted the tailgate and said, "Up. Come on."

Jay stepped off his bike and obeyed. Benu motioned for Jay to place his right leg onto the tailgate as well. He swung his leg up with a grunt and leaned back on his hands. Benu rolled up his pant leg past his knee. The bandages were soaked with crusted blood and dusted with dirt. Benu bent Jay's knee slightly and began undoing his bandages.

As she worked, she asked: "How badly does it hurt?"

"I mean," Jay began, "it hurts about as much as a stab wound can. But honestly, the pain hasn't been bad at all."

"That is good to hear. It was a pretty serious wound… but it is almost completely healed. Strange."

Jay couldn't explain it. Perhaps it was his unrelenting determination to complete his task before the world died or a gift from The Anomaly, but rarely did he ever sustain an injury for very long. His altered body belonged to the machinations of the black diamond, but he was still human. He could still bleed. He could still die.

Benu finished removing the bandages and revealed Jay's gash. Small, interweaving wires lined the closed folds surrounded by tacky globs of dried blood. Benu gently lifted and turned Jay's leg and examined the exit wound as his face twitched on one side.

Benu's face held a robotic expression. Her eyes were unblinking as she scanned Jay's leg with the meticulous focus of a jeweler searching for defects in a gem.

"You… gave me stitches?" Jay asked, bewildered.

"Yes," replied Benu in a low, contemplative tone.

"While I was… asleep?"

"Yes." Her gaze returned to the wound on his shin as she set Jay's leg down.

Benu's demeanor had changed to that of a professional. In the moment, Jay was her patient and required succinct answers and explanations.

As she reached into her medical bag, she informed: "I used lidocaine to numb the areas. Your cauterization worked very well, in fact." She retrieved an alcohol packet, ripped it open, and began cleaning the dried blood. As she treated Jay, she continued, "The wounds were mostly closed, but it seems you did not have enough time to close the skin. So, I used a running suture to finish it up. It looks to have healed up well. You should only need bandages for another day or two."

Jay felt like he was back in his primary care doctor's office getting a routine check-up and had a hard time keeping up. Benu spoke with eloquence and speed.

As she bandaged his leg, Jay chimed, "So, *were* you a doctor?"

Benu chortled, "Hmph, what gave it away?" When she finished, she rolled down Jay's pant leg and patted it to indicate he could put it down. He obeyed as she motioned him to take off his jacket and shirt to check his shoulder.

As she worked, she continued, "Yes, I *was* a doctor…well, I *was* going to be. I was in the last year of my residency at the big hospital in Royal Oak. But, the big bad diamond had different plans for me… for all of us really. Your shoulder looks fine. I think you can do without bandages."

She started to put her supplies away as Jay said: "Y'know, I worked in a hospital too."

"Yeah? Where at?"

"Henry Ford. The one in Detroit."

"Ah, I had some colleagues there. Big hospital. No offense, but your medical kit is lacking from what I saw of it last night. Especially for a medical professional."

"Oh," Jay chuckled as his head popped through his shirt. "I wasn't a doctor or anything. I fixed the x-ray equipment."

"Ah, the handyman," Benu smiled as she packed her bag. "Good to know. Come, Flint is just ahead."

"Would be nice to eat somethin' decent," Jay said, slipping on his jacket and beanie.

Benu nodded as she mounted her bike and took off with Jay following in tow—his eyes still fixated on her crossbow. While his treated wounds made him more inclined to trust her, the uneasy pit in his stomach urged him to take caution. Although her demeanor came off as friendly, Jay remembered an adage his uncle once told him: *a sharpened, silver tongue cuts deepest at night.*

The massive steel gate that towered over Jay was different from the gates he knew back home. These large, dark-green structures were well-defined and manufactured with absolute precision. Huge bolts and rivets lined the steel panels, suggesting impenetrable construction.

The military had secured Flint in the early days of the Second Convergence. At that time, Flint required immediate attention due to reports of hordes of manhunting creatures. Riots and civil distress reigned over the streets amongst the chaos; the city needed order.

Guards were posted in watchtowers at the corners of the wall and had signaled Benu and Jay's arrival. Jay had his neck craned upwards. He looked across the top as they waited for someone to let them through the double doors they faced. The metal-on-metal squeak of the sliding peephole caught Jay and Benu off guard as they jumped and turned their attention to a pair of eyes peering through.

"Can I help you two?" asked a stern voice through the door.

"Hello," Benu replied, jovial. "My name is Benu, and this is Jay. We are just looking to get something to eat and head out to Saginaw."

The eyes shot a few glances at the two and their things.

"Where ya comin' from?"

"Detroit," Jay replied.

"Hold on," the man replied as he shut the peephole. Muffled words and shuffling papers could be heard through the door when finally, it slid open again. "Alright, yer clear to come in. As soon as you do, please submit yer bikes and bags for search and head to the office on the right for screening. Understood?"

Jay and Benu nodded. The peephole closed once again, and a voice shouted, "Opening the gate!" A whirling yellow light above the double doors flashed as the entrance dragged across the ground and opened inward with a hefty metal clunk.

As Jay and Benu walked in, a pair of guards greeted them. They were fully kitted in military garb. Although the material was worn in many places, their helmets, boots, and body armor appeared to be in adequate shape. Rifles were slung across their chests; however, each soldier was also equipped with a crossbow or bow, and melee weapons were secured on their hips. Jay couldn't be certain if their guns were loaded. If anyone still had ammo, it would be the military.

A female soldier approached them and said, "We'll need to search your bags, and you'll have to leave that crossbow and knife with us, ma'am."

"Am I getting them back?" Benu asked, annoyed.

"Private Carl tells us you guys are headed to Saginaw. We can move your things to the North Gate, but we can't allow weapons in the city."

"Ugh," grunted Benu as she rolled her eyes and handed over her weapons. A couple of soldiers unmounted their bags from their bikes and began their search on a table nearby. Jay's throat felt tight as he watched the guard remove Her from his bag. His eyes were permanently glued to the urn as the guard turned it in his hand, concluded it was harmless, and put it back in his bag. His attention was broken by the female soldier when she asked, "Any weapons on you, sir?"

"Uh nope," quipped Jay.

"Nothing?"

"Nothin'."

"You traveled all the way from Detroit unarmed?"

"What can I say? Benu's a good shot."

The guard looked over at Benu as she gave her a wink and smirk. The guard shook her head, handed their bags back, and said, "Alright, well, head over to the office to get cleared."

Jay and Benu thanked the guard and turned towards the office. A large sign reading "MAIN OFFICE" was mounted in front of what obviously used to be a coffee shop. A couple letters of the old neon sign jutted out on one side while the logo of a mermaid peeped out on the other. As Jay and Benu approached, a pair of guards patted them down, nodded at each other, and held the door open for them to enter.

A lone desk worker manned the empty lobby of the "main office." Foldable chairs lined the dining area and most of the tables served as shelves for military supplies. Jay and Benu looked around for a moment, then walked over to the counter and greeted the desk worker. Behind the uniformed man were the remnants of old barista equipment.

Blenders and coffee pots were pushed to the side to make way for stacks of documents and office machines. Planks of wood sat over the sinks to provide extra counter space and filing cabinets occupied a majority of the floor space behind the serving area. The desk worker asked for Jay and Benu's IDs and handed them each a clipboard with a form to fill out.

"Ya fuckin' kiddin' me?" Jay said under his breath as he and Benu took a seat.

"If anything can survive the end of the world, it is bureaucracy," added Benu.

They filled out their forms in silence, penning in general information and answering questions like: what is the purpose of your visit? Any symptoms of being sick? Have you ever been convicted of a felony? Are you an American citizen? Jay felt like he would spend the last of his days filling out this torturous, mundane, insignificant form. This part of the old world, he did not miss.

Eventually, Jay and Benu finished their orders and returned them to the clerk. He glanced through the papers and directed the two through the employee door and into the manager's office.

The office was a montage of clutter. Filing cabinets lined the back wall with hints of papers sticking out of various drawers. Papers and boxes were stacked high. The yellowed and crumbled nature of some of them suggested they hadn't been touched in years. A large metal desk separated two metal folding chairs from a seated woman wearing a commander's uniform. Thick binders crowded her desk along with miscellaneous office supplies. The one iota of organization was in the form of a small, metal cup that held a bundle of pens.

Jay and Benu took a seat at one side of the desk. The office worker handed the woman the forms and left. The decorated commander hunched over, resting on her elbows as she examined their IDs. On the desk sat a small plaque that read "Commander Silvers."

They sat for a bit until Commander Silvers broke the silence, "So, Jay, and—"

"Benu," Benu interrupted. "You can just call me Benu, ma'am."

"Jay and Benu. Ok. So…" she handed back their IDs as she scanned the forms, "…heading to Saginaw huh?"

"It's our next stop, yes, ma'am," replied Jay.

"*Next* stop? What's the final one?"

Jay and Benu explained their plans.

"Well, that's quite the journey," exclaimed Commander Silvers. The fair-skinned woman leaned back in her chair and brushed a loose strand of her chin-length, brunette hair behind her ear. "We haven't heard from Saginaw in months. I can only hope they're ok. We'd send out scouts, but why risk it with the rapture coming up, right?"

"What about the weather scouts?" Jay asked. "Not sure how accurate it is, but the weather for Saginaw was listed yesterday on the morning news."

Benu looked over at Jay with a raised eyebrow, but Command Silvers could see his earnest eyes didn't lie. She sighed and leaned forward. "You're from Detroit huh? I don't know how to tell you this, but all that shit you see on the news there… it's all fake. All those shows and broadcasts and weather reports, et cetera… it's all just make-believe to keep you guys happy and make the rapture a little easier. The Anomaly does whatever the hell it pleases with our world! Weather could suddenly take a left turn whenever; it'd be impossible to accurately predict it. Farmer's Almanac's no good anymore either."

"But the local weather was always right!"

"*Always?*"

"Well… usually."

"And what's *usually*? 80% accurate? 70%? 50%?"

Jay remained silent, recounting the several times the weather report was indeed incorrect.

"It looks like Detroit's little happy bubble worked. It's like a phony fortune teller or self-proclaimed seer predicting your dead grandpa's name. 'Does it start with a J? Maybe an S? Q? L? M? Ah! That's it, isn't it? Ok, I'm seeing… Marty. No? Mark? Mike?' et cetera, et cetera. Until he finally lands on 'Matthew', and you respond with 'Wow! How could he have known?' People are *so* focused on hearing what they want to hear that when they hear otherwise, they tend to ignore it. As if it never happened. *Or* they get upset and cast it off as the obvious 'wrong' answer. If the weather report predicts clear skies and warm weather for summer and it snows for a week… well, all is good if that same report is correct next week. 'Weatherman got it right for a whole week!'"

Jay stared at his hands cupped in his lap. He felt like he was back in high school, getting a lecturing from the principal about how he'd 'go nowhere in life if he kept playing hooky' or how 'breaking his bully's nose was immoral and barbaric' despite the oaf terrorizing him for weeks. Either way, Jay was proving Commander Silvers' point; he did not like what he was hearing and would rather it be a lie. An insignificant white lie that he could ignore, bundle up, tie to a brick, and toss into Lake Michigan. But he felt it deep in his gut: she wasn't lying.

"Sorry," Commander Silvers said, "I didn't mean to go off and ramble like that. It's just… I was in the same boat at some point in my life. To answer your question, we… haven't heard from a weather scout from the rest of the state for nearly a year. I think they all just gave up on reporting something that could change as soon as they were an hour out of whatever area they were observing. Hell, we've been living off local emergency generators and solar panels for a while now. Using them only for the essentials. Detroit's no different."

Jay's heart sank. It's not that he was surprised that the façade of Detroit had come to light, it's that he blamed himself for accepting it so blindly. He let himself become so comfortable in a world that refused to acknowledge the true deformity of the outside. Now, Jay had a cursory introduction to the real world, and the tailored illusion of "preparedness" he'd been so obsessive about had shattered completely.

"Sorry, *dost*," Benu said softly, placing a hand on his slumped shoulder. "I thought that is why you left when you did."

"Umm, it's ok. Thanks," Jay whispered, patting Benu's hand.

Commander Silvers sighed, "Well, any questions for me before I let you go?"

Jay scanned the room and spotted a rifle with a missing magazine behind Commander Silvers.

"Are you cut off from the rest of the U.S.?" Jay asked.

"No… no, not completely. Lost communications with interstate bases and commands two years ago. Then, the local regional bases a few months later. Then… nothing. Of course, we fell back on older methods until those all went kaput. Short-wave radio… telegraph… even went back to using pigeons at some point, but they became unreliable with all the sporadic weather. Eventually, we settled on good, ol' runners. Last message we got from the nearest base was about a month ago."

"So… do you get any supplies?"

"Yeah, sometimes. Mainly the essentials."

"Any ammo?"

Commander Silvers sucked her teeth, straightened her lips across her face, and shook her head. "That's on a need-to-know basis."

"That means 'no'," Benu grumbled.

Commander Silvers peered at her. They sat in silence as Commander Silvers awaited more questions until she looked between the two and asked, "Will that be it?"

Jay and Benu looked at each other and nodded.

"Alrighty then!" She picked up a small office stamp and smacked it down on both forms, looked up, and said, "Welcome to Flint!"

Jay and Benu roamed the thinly crowded streets of Flint. They were in a suburb just west of downtown, but locals had told them this was all that remained of the city. What was left was a small population of around five hundred people living the rest of their days under military jurisdiction. However, the people had no issue with their protectors.

Cut off from the outside world, the soldiers that guarded the gates and patrolled the streets were residents of this small community all the same. Many were marooned from their original homes across the country, but they had quickly adapted to their new Michigan home. The days were running short, so accepting this place as 'home' was necessary for peace of mind amidst impending obliteration.

Soldiers bore scars of battle across their cheeks. Men and women alike passed by with various wounds—a limp, a missing arm, a bandaged head. But, despite their previous torment, the people of Flint held optimistic expressions on their faces, enjoying the newfound freedom from the monsters that had taken the main city years ago.

A portion of downtown could be seen in the far distance from where Jay stood. A shimmer of silver webs could be seen strewn across the crumbled skyscrapers. He remembered the news footage well. How swarms of arachnid-like creatures emerged from the city sewers, indiscriminately feasting on the population. Their bodies were shaped like spiders but consisted of fleshy, grafted parts. Masses of animal and human bundled together to form horror that bit and fed through sharpened, talon-like fangs. In the end, the military had won at the cost of severe casualties and the loss of the main city to the structural damage and fear of the creatures returning. So here, they fled—to start anew.

Jay and Benu turned down what seemed to be the main street of the newfound Flint. The streets were lined with vendor stands selling various commodities as patrons walked all around. It was like being transported to a different country or different time. Fishmongers flaunted their daily catches from the river that ran through the city. Bakers set out their finest loaves in the hopes of drawing buyers with their tasty aroma. Second-hand shops were organizing their random goods in their varied categories.

Jay's nose caught the allure of something umami. The smell of cooked lamb was somewhere nearby. His belly let out an audible grumble as he grasped it. Benu nudged him with her elbow and asked, "Hungry? I could eat as well. Let us find something."

Jay nodded and searched around for the source of the smell. He looked through the passing waves of bodies and spotted what looked like an outdoor restaurant near a broken-down food truck. Motioning Benu to follow him, Jay weaved his way through the crowd toward the little bistro. A large sign hung across the top reading: "SHAWARMA CITY."

"This work for you?" Jay turned to Benu.

Benu nodded as they walked up to the counter. The greasy cook greeted them as Jay went on to scan the menu. His eyes darted between the various items on the list with indecisiveness. After letting out several expressions of long contemplation, Jay finally arrived at a decision.

"I'll just have a shawarma plate… with lamb and just some water, please!" Jay ordered.

"Just a chicken shawarma for me and water as well," Benu added.

"Ok, no problem," replied the cook. "That'll be fifteen bucks."

Jay pulled out his wallet. Even in the end times, money still held value. The Anomaly exhibited unfathomable power; however, nothing could ever sway mankind's love of cash. Jay could understand it. The monetary system was order in a disorderly world.

He opened his bifold wallet to reveal a singular ten-dollar bill. Pulling it out, he thought to himself: *Shit.*

Turning to Benu, he asked, "Ya got any cash on ya?"

Benu just smirked and shrugged. Jay rolled his eyes and turned to the cook. Before he could begin to bargain, a young man wearing thick-brimmed glasses spoke up next to him, "Let me help ya with that."

"Oh, no, no. I'm good," Jay replied.

"Ya got any way else to pay for yer food?" the man asked. Jay opened his mouth to answer, but the man had already pulled out his cash.

The man flashed a five-dollar bill at Jay, then handed it to the cook. "I just ask that you two join me and my wife for lunch. I'm Perry, by the way." The man pointed behind him with his thumb over to a table where a young, blonde woman sat with an infant in her lap.

"Uh, sure. Sure. I'm Jay."

"And I am Benu. Nice to meet you," Benu chimed in as she shook Perry's hand.

As they made some small talk, the cook called their orders. The group took their food and sat at the table, placing their bags on the ground by their feet. Perry took his place next to his wife; Jay and Benu sat across from them. The old picnic table sat amongst an eclectic collection of dining areas comprised of different tables, chairs, and tablecloths. Jay's plate was set on cracked, decaying wood that had rotted from exposure to the elements.

"This is my wife, Ellie," Perry said.

"Hello, nice to meet you," Ellie said, looking up from the infant that was feeding from a bottle.

"And this one is Isaiah," Perry said as he gently pinched the infant's arm.

Jay and Benu introduced themselves. As they ate, they discussed many things: the weather, life in Detroit, hobbies, and interests. However, Benu barely contributed; her eyes were glued to Isaiah.

"Benu?" Perry called. "Is something the matter?"

"Well," Benu swallowed, "it is just… well…"

"It's *just?*" Ellie pressed.

Perry placed a hand on Ellie's shoulder and pushed up his glasses with a smile. The small crack in its left lens glinted in the afternoon sun. "Yer wonderin' why we have a child?" he asked.

"Yeah," Benu trailed off with bewildered criticism in her tone. "Just how old is he anyways?"

"He would be one next month," replied Ellie, refusing to look at Benu.

"Hmph, *would be*," Benu pressed back.

"Let me ask ya somethin'," Perry spoke before Ellie could snap back. "Why do we choose to have children in the first place?"

Benu went to answer, but Jay—his eyes now fixated on Isaiah— interrupted, "Because we're mortal."

All eyes were on Jay. Perry's open mouth slowly morphed into a pleased smile, "Very good. Ya see… we are finite creatures. Even when

we know the date and time of the rapture, it changes nothin'. So…"
He wiped Isaiah's face with a napkin as the infant cooed and dribbled.

"We find a reason to keep going," Jay finished. It was the same for
him. The little urn in his bag reminded him of his mortality—his
purpose.

"That's right," Perry looked over with a grin.

"But," Benu spoke up, "is it not cruel—to bring a baby into *this*
world—at *this* time?"

"We've given a person a chance at life," replied Ellie. "How is that
cruel?"

"You have sentenced it to death! It has no chance to *live!*" Benu
raised her voice.

"And yet here *he* is—with a name, voice, and, in the short time
I've known him, a personality."

"But…" Benu slumped, sympathy in her voice.

"Now, we're not stupid," Perry interjected. "We fully knew
Isaiah's fate… our fates… when we decided on it. Even after Ellie got
pregnant, we… considered savin' him from being born into *this*
world—even considered… doin' it ourselves. But… we always wanted
a little boy… so we decided to take our chances with the rapture."

"What if the end is painful?" Jay asked with a stone-cold
expression.

"Then," Ellie began, "we'll face that together. All three of us." She
tickled Isaiah's belly as he giggled, grasping at her fingers.

"We can't predict how our lives will go," Perry said. "And, even
when we can predict the end, we can't predict *how* it will go… how it
will feel… or even what comes next. Some people obviously think
they know—whether it's heaven, hell, or nothing at all—but I guess
we decided to give Isaiah here a chance to find out with us. Maybe
we'll be punished for this in the end… maybe not… What do you
guys believe? Either of ya religious?"

Benu shook her head. "At one point, yes, but in light of the shit I
have seen—excuse my language—I am having trouble staying
faithful."

Perry looked over at Jay.

At one point, he could have answered that question with ease. He had dabbled in various religions and beliefs before, coming to identify with one in his early adult years. But, ever since She passed, he found himself in faithless limbo.

"I… don't really have an answer," Jay shrugged. "Sorry."

He looked back at Isaiah.

"Mmm, a daughter," Jay replied to Her question. "Yeah, I'd want a little girl."

He leaned back on the park bench—his arm wrapped around Her shoulders. She rested Her gentle head on his shoulder and placed Her hand on his leg and rubbed it. She smiled and went on to talk about Her plans with their daughter. How She would raise her to help in the garden. How She would teach her to paint and cook.

"I'd like to get her into cars… somehow," Jay said.

She giggled and slapped him lightly on the chest. She protested his statement, claiming She would never let him steal their daughter away. She wanted their daughter all to herself—a mommy's girl.

The sun raced across the sky as they passed the day, discussing plans that never came to be.

Jay's eyes grew warm from the moisture forming in them.

"Ellie," Benu said, pulling Jay from his daydream, "sorry for snapping at you earlier."

"No problem," Ellie replied. "The rapture is in a week; no point in arguing over anything, really."

"Hmph, you are correct. In a week, we will all be the same. I may not agree with you but… I do admit, I am happy to see a baby again. And he *is* very cute." Benu reached over and gently pinched Isaiah's cheek, eliciting a playful laugh from the child.

Jay and Benu thanked the couple, finished eating, and said their goodbyes. They decided it was time to head to Saginaw and started heading to the north gate. As they walked, Benu pulled out her pack of cigarettes and yanked one out with her lips. She reached into her pocket and retrieved her lighter. With a few flicks, she ignited her cigarette and took a few puffs.

Jay spoke up, "Ya think they actually moved our bikes to the gate?"

"We can only hope so," Benu replied through the side of her mouth. "We do not have any money to buy new ones. So, we will be walking otherwise."

They walked in silence for a bit before Jay asked, "Did you ever want kids?"

"Hmph, those days are long gone," Benu chuckled as she swung her arms and looked up at the sky. "Besides, we should focus on things that *will* be rather than things that could have been."

"Well put."

"That being said, yes… yes, I did."

"The feeling's mutual."

Benu looked over, smiled, and patted Jay on the back. "We have many things in common, *dost*."

"What is that by the way? *Dost*? You've called me that a few times now."

"Oh! It is Hindi for 'friend,' but it is more for the sake of being… *friendly* rather than admitting to someone being your friend."

Jay contemplated what Benu had just said. So, was he a friend, foe, acquaintance, or tool?

The sound of the noisy Flint city center died as they approached the north gate. They met with a couple of guards, exchanged information, and were given their bikes. Benu was also given her weapons back, as promised. She tucked the knife away in its sheath and slung the crossbow across her back. Jay and Benu mounted their backpacks and hopped on their bikes. Another whirling yellow light flashed as the large metal doors lurched open, leading out to the next stop: Saginaw.

{Chapter 8}

8:02:55:16

Clouds swirled and merged overhead into great masses that slunk across the sky and covered the land in shadow. They moved and morphed—layers upon layers. A great rumble shook the air and quaked the ground below their tires. The booming roar of thunder deafened Jay and Benu as lightning crashed from the growing storm.

The purple gleam of the earth illuminated the stormy nightfall, bouncing across the trees and road. Soft, fertile aromas rose from the earth as the pressures above forced the smell out—the signal of rain. Whispered trickles pinged along the craggy highway and clinked atop the rusty car roofs before transforming into a steady rainfall. Trees whooshed and whistled as the wind buffeted their thick branches and weak, Fall leaves.

The outskirts of Saginaw mirrored Flint's. Buildings existed in ruin along piles of concrete and steel rubble. The same deciduous overgrowth was now drowning in a plentiful shower.

Jay had a hard time keeping his eyes open. The rain splashed across his face, causing him to constantly wipe it away. The water gathered and seeped into his mouth despite his best efforts to spit it out.

"Benu!" cried Jay.

She looked back, wiping her face as she corrected her swerving bike. "Yes? What is it?" she replied.

"Let's walk for a bit!"

Benu spat out a glob of fresh rain. "Yes. I agree!"

They slowed to a stop and hopped off. The rain felt light compared to the assault they faced when riding at speed. It was a calming storm; the kind that could lull one to sleep on a late summer's evening. Jay and Benu let their eyes dance around as they wandered.

Shafts of the setting sunlight cast pillars across the city, while the soft red of The Anomaly intermingled with it.

Jay felt his cold, soaked shirt begin to stick to his clammy skin as the rain began to pick up. It would soon become a torrent. He felt a pit of anxiety grow in his stomach; the highway to Saginaw was in far worse condition than anything they had faced before. They needed to find shelter; it felt like they had wandered the streets for hours. The fading of the setting sun's orange glow was creeping proof of this. Benu checked her watch: 8:06 P.M.

They were in the suburbs—far from the downtown area. Only houses and the occasional shop filled the gaps between the overgrowth. Every structure they came across was either leveled, boarded up, or completely burnt down. Something terrible had stricken Saginaw.

Benu felt this too and started scouting out buildings with her keen eyes. Through the flickering slits of buildings to the west, Benu spotted the light of something man-made. The bright, white glow elicited a hum in her ears—fluorescent bulbs. She nudged Jay and pointed, "Someone has electricity over there. Could be the city center."

Jay peered through the cracks, "Yeah… no wall though."

"A checkpoint maybe?"

Jay shrugged and picked up the pace towards civilization. The light grew brighter as they worked their way through the gridded streets. The beacon beckoned to them as they shivered in the pouring rain.

The world began to warp around Jay. His vision was wavering as his legs grew weak and buckled under each step. He looked over at Benu to see her stretched figure struggling in tandem. As he lifted his concrete feet, he slopped onto his bike. Tingling jolts weaved across his face as it grew numb and heavy. He dropped his bike and glanced, once more, at Benu.

She was down on the ground, groaning out of a slack-jawed mouth. Her cracked, battered hands twitched as she attempted to lift them onto her neck. The attack had been silent—swift. Jay pressed on for a few paces and slid his hand on the back of his neck. As the numbness set in, he could feel the slim, cold needle between his fingers.

Jay fell to his knees. With the last ounce of his sobriety, he plucked the needle from his neck. The ping of the needle hitting the concrete echoed through the pitter-patter of rain. He lay, slack-jawed, on the wet asphalt. His vision was a jumbled mess. Desperate moans escaped his mouth but received no answer.

The creaks of heavy, soaked boots approached Jay. He could hear doom in their stomps. Turning his head with what little strength he had, he could see a large figure looming over them. He watched as the shadowy figure reached down and tied Jay's hands. He rolled his eyes over to Benu. She, too, was sharing the same treatment.

Jay's upper body lifted off the ground. His arms were suspended by two meaty hands at the bicep. Their toes dragged along the rough pavement. Jay's strength was returning. The sedative hit like a bullet, expelling all its energy before slowly dissipating. But lasting effects still lingered.

To his left was a gargantuan, flabby man with bloated lips and eyes. Mounds of festering pustules caked his bald head and traced themselves down his arms. Jay could see the growths on his hands. Pitcher-plant-like flaps covered the swelled pores—which oozed a slick puss. To his right, a similar creature carried his other arm, but long, mangy hair drooped over her shoulders onto a slim, feminine frame. Their faces were caked in grime.

He looked past his captor towards Benu. Two malformed women were carrying the limp, groggy Benu by her arms. One carried her bag. The other held a blowgun in her free hand. Jay swayed his head to his left to see the giant carrying his bag as well.

Jay felt full consciousness returning to him. He called out to Benu in a quivering voice, but she gave no response. Her eyes were glazed—her mouth dribbling a steady stream of drool. The dart was still lodged in her neck and continued administering a steady stream of sedatives.

Fuck, man, Jay thought. *What is this? How'd this happen?*

He was rife with turmoil. The sedative had drained him of his strength and will. In his mind, Jay teetered between life and death. His thoughts raced through the possibilities of his fate. Had he come this far just to die here? To live out his days as a plaything for these monsters? Or to be served as tonight's dinner? As the blinding lights grew closer, the structure they belonged to made itself clear.

"Voom – cha – cha – hoom! Voom – cha – cha – hoom!"

The crowd of disfigured men and women chanted. A ritualistic dance accompanied the repeated word. Their legs were spread, shoulder-width apart, and squatted. Arms outstretched forward with a clenched fist, swiveled, pulled back, and tucked close to the body in sync with each *cha.* Their splayed hands jutted out quickly as if expelling a demon at the final "*hoom.*"

The small tribe consisted of twenty, maybe thirty, people, not counting those unseen. But the occasion seemed special; attendance seemed required. As Jay and Benu were dragged into the parking lot amongst the crowd, the source of the light appeared.

Before them was a gas station, brimming with bright, fluorescent lights that illuminated the stormy night like a lighthouse. The canopy was lined with chimes and omens bearing collections of bones and metal objects. Atop the roof stood a handful of people dressed in scraps of plastic and metal. Each wore a headdress, cobbled together with various mechanical trinkets and tools. A wooden tower loomed above, built on top of the main convenience storefront standing roughly fifteen feet. Its flimsy construction looked weak in Jay's eyes—skirting and proper bracing were missing—but it held fine for the object they worshiped above.

A mighty V8 engine was sitting atop the tower like a king on his throne. A large fuel tank was mounted on one of the four posts of the tower, feeding the beast. Down below, wires from the starter dangled near a table where a tribalist waited with a battery, ready to fire it up.

A ladder stretched high above to the front of the display where the radiator waited for coolant. Torches were lit at the four corners of the tower.

"Voom – cha – cha – hoom. Voom – cha – cha – hoom," the people chanted.

Jay and Benu were thrown to the ground. One of Benu's captors bent down, plucked the needle from her neck, and tossed it aside. Jay scooted his knees forward and sat back on his heels. He looked over at Benu as she groaned and squirmed; the sedative still ran through her veins. Warm condensation puffed in Jay's face as he gasped for every breath.

As he peered around, through the torrent, he could see every person shared the same disgusting features as his captors. They chanted and stomped in the rain, splashing pools of water under their feet.

The thunderous boom of the sky grew as the chants racked Jay's ears. He closed his eyes and tried to drown out the sound, but the cacophony continued to ricochet in his head. He could feel his face twitching from the needles of rain striking his skin. Then, the chanting abruptly stopped.

Jay opened his eyes and looked above, at the roof. A gigantic, mountain of a man with folds upon folds of bare fat oozing around tight suspenders stood at the edge of the rooftop. His bare chest bore boils and sickly swollen growths that popped and spurted the same puss as the others. Fastened around his neck was a thick, wooly cloak. His head was lined with a circlet made of bent tools and parts.

"Hark! Hark!" bellowed the chieftain through bloated lips and bulging eyes. "The almighty V8 wishes to sing! It wishes to shake the very earth beneath our feet! It longs to bring us salvation for the cost of worldly flesh and blood!"

The crowd rejoiced.

The chieftain continued, "It knows! It knows! It has always known our fate...our salvation...our... sins! It wishes to tell us more. It wishes to impart... knowledge!"

A ritualist walked up, her head hung low, and presented a large oil pan to the chieftain. He took the pan, bowing to the ritualist as she backed away, her hands tucked in her sleeves. Raising it above his head, he continued. "This is the catalyst—the black blood it shares to allow communion! May it bless me, The Voice of the V8, and pass through me, ascending me to temporary… godhood."

Claps and roars echoed through the crowd. Thunder grumbled as the storm began to die down. The Voice lifted the pan high above his head and tilted it over his flabby body. The black oil showered his malformed figure, seeping and absorbing into the folds. His face became stained and blackened by the liquid as it soaked into his pants and pooled in his boots and around his feet.

A small remnant of motor oil remained in the pan. The Voice flicked it towards the crowd and sprayed the ground with the holy blood. The fanatics nearest the store rushed the pools before they could be swept away and smeared as much of the blessed liquid onto their faces and bodies.

The Voice handed the pan back to the ritualist and raised his hand to quell his mass.

"It is ready. Yes! It is ready, my people!"

The crowd roared with insanity and began chanting again.

The Voice flicked his finger around at the ritualists as the process began. One ascended the ladder to the radiator, carrying a massive jug on his shoulder. When he arrived at the top, he removed the radiator cap and filled it with a translucent, slick, green liquid as rain mixed in with it. From behind the engine came a short man who turned a valve on the mounted fuel tank. Precious, immortal gasoline flowed through the tubing and into the fuel pump. A signal was given to the one waiting by the battery. She howled an animal's cry, attached the wires of the ignition coil to the battery, and touched the alligator clip belonging to the starter to the positive terminal.

With a thunderous 'bang', the V8 roared to life. The pistons chugged and churned as the beast shook the wooden structure. Fumes of dirtied exhaust billowed from the header as the crowd's chanting transformed into deafening praise.

The Voice beckoned to the sky with a monstrous growl. He looked down at the crowd, smiling with jumbled, unsightly teeth that mimicked staggered, rotted wood.

"What is this *Mad Max* shit?" grumbled Jay.

"Shaddup!" shouted the captor to his left as he struck Jay across the cheek.

"Dick."

"Shaddup!" Again, another slap.

The Voice caught wind of this commotion through the calamity and raised his hand to silence the crowd. "More sacrifices?" beckoned The Voice.

"Yes, chief!" replied one of Benu's captors. "They were caught trying to sneak into the compound!"

"Oh," The Voice pondered as he dragged his greasy, oil-stained hand across the folds of his chins. "Oh! See this? The V8 *demands* sacrifices! If it did not want, why would it deliver? It brings us its sustenance for us faithful to prepare! Just… as… it… has… before."

Sacrifice.

The word echoed in Jay's fatigued skull. The word could not be minced. Jay was going to die here. Cut up and splayed across a V8 in the middle of Saginaw. His adrenaline struggled to kick in; there was enough fuel in his system to retaliate. But Jay still held logic in his mind. Surely, an untimely death at the hands of several outweighed one of torture over a car engine. Before he could enact his final attack, The Voice cried out, "Raise the sacrifice!"

From behind the tower raised a tall wooden stake that had previously rested out of view. Strapped to the top was a twig of a man—naked and drenched in rain and dirt. His soulless expression lifted to the pouring rain—mouth agape. Soft moans could hardly be heard through the wind.

The Voice faced the V8 and raised his arms high above his head, "Hear me! Hear me, oh, great machine! Accept this, the blood of our kind—blood of the ones that made you. Accept this: our sacrifice!" He signaled the short man at the top to begin.

The stake was leaned forward over the throbbing machine. It chugged and sputtered in the face of the broken man. Below, the little person brandished a large sickle. He stepped up on a platform and plunged the sharp end deep into the crevasse between the sacrifice's collar bones. The man jerked and grumbled but couldn't muster the voice to scream.

Pulling the sickle down the length of the man's torso, the ritualist winced and struggled against the meat and bone that stood in the sickle's way. The jagged gash splayed open at the yank of the tool from the corpse's lower stomach. A gush of crimson showered the V8 and caked its sanguine, stained chassis. The churning pistons flung blood all around as the corpse continued to fuel the ritual.

The little person walked over to the front and stuck his hand deep into the belly of the beast. As the engine revved higher and higher, red splashed from the rapid pistons and violently shaking frame. The fanatics went into a frenzy. Chanting began again as The Voice turned to the crowd with a sneer. He peered over in Jay's direction and wore a pleased smile.

Sacrifice.

{Chapter 9}

7:07:47:49

Benu sat against the headboard of her stained mattress. She rested her forearm on a bent right knee and kept the other leg stretched out. A chain clenched around her left ankle kept her anchored to a locked, metal loop embedded in the floor. She leaned her head back and stared apathetically at the solid, wooden door. Her eyes were tired. Worn from the restless night on the stiff, bare bed riddled with holes.

Surrounding her was an empty hotel room—save for a few, scant things: the bed she slept on, a plastic bucket serving as her toilet, and plywood that boarded up the bathroom. The patterned carpet of burgundy and black hexagons was stained and reeked of mold. Brown splotches of sitting water blotted parts of the popcorn ceiling. The wallpaper had all but been torn to shreds; traces of the striped pattern could be seen in the remnants. All she had to her name was this hovel and the rags she had been forced into.

She recalled the incidents of last night. How she found herself tossed to this room's floor after the sedative had worn off. How the tribe stripped her of her possessions and clothes and left her naked to writhe and recover from the muscle relaxants. She feared for her dignity, but no lust flowed in these creatures' veins. They cared not for temptations of the flesh, but for other things: the fuel—the engine.

Benu was a prisoner to these savages. The words they left her with were scarce but potent. "Tomorrow, you work." What would that work entail? She could only imagine the plethora of torturous tasks.

Benu felt her heart rate rising and attempted to calm it. She took a deep breath through her nose and out of her mouth slowly. The odor of the hotel was nauseating. Her nostrils were assaulted with the stench of black mold and sewage that lingered in the bucket across the room. Shafts of muted sunlight dimmed the room through the mucky, barred, southeast window behind her.

Doors could be heard opening in the hall just outside. One by one, each creaked open, followed by a commanding voice ordering the occupant out. The sounds grew closer. Next door, Benu could hear it clearly: a creak, a shout, a rattle, and a shuffle.

The steps now stopped outside her door. A lock outside rattled as it was unlatched from its hold. The door crept open.

"Get up! Work!" yelled a cyst-covered woman armed with a crossbow.

She hobbled over to Benu's anchor, slung her crossbow over her shoulder, and bent down to undo the lock. Benu glared at the back of Cyst's head. She was about Benu's size. Benu could take her.

The scene played out in her mind. She would mount Cyst on her back as soon she undid her chain. Reaching down, she would grab the chain in each hand and pull it taut against Cyst's throat. It would take ten seconds, maybe fifteen, and the woman would be dead.

Benu looked up towards the open door and saw another standing guard. No, she couldn't attempt escape now. Cyst stood up with the chain and lock in hand. She tugged at it, yanking Benu from her sitting position. "Up! Work now!"

Benu complied with searing heat in her eyes as she peered at the woman. She was led out into the hall. Her room was at the end, and a line of about ten prisoners—all female—had formed down the hall to her left. To her right was the corner of the L-shaped hallway that led deeper into the hotel. Cyst reached down and attached Benu's chain via the lock to the prisoner in front of them. She signaled to another down the hall who then nudged the prisoner at the front of the line.

One-by-one, the prisoners stepped forward. Benu felt her foot get pulled from under her as the prisoner in front began to march. Benu quickly stepped in tow and followed.

As they passed by the lobby, Benu saw disrepair and disorder in the crumbling hotel walls. She noted the lack of guards. The only ones seemed to be the two escorting their group. As they passed the front reception, Benu noticed something else—a small, metal cup with two pens inside. Her observations were cut short when Cyst bunted her on the back and pushed her forward.

The formation was led out of the front and into the gleaming morning sun. The weather had taken a sudden turn from the night before. Sweltering heat beat down on Benu's head and scorched her face. Through squinted eyes, she could see her entourage was walking towards a gas station that sat adjacent to the hotel. Two large craters, peppered with broken concrete, were located between the two rows of pumps. Pickaxes lined the left side.

Directly southeast, across the four-lane street divided by a median, was another gas station. A large, wooden tower sat atop the store with what appeared to be an engine sitting on its peak. Several people could be seen lounging on top of the store with others standing guard around it. Tribe members were going about their day. Money and goods were exchanging hands. Young and elderly alike were making small conversations. The population was scant, but it appeared to be a functioning community.

Through the hazy glass of the convenience store Benu headed towards, she could see a singular worker organizing clothes and various supplies on large plastic tables. Empty backpacks were piled to her left while newly ransacked ones were to her right. Only one other guard waited for them near the craters—three guards in total.

The chains rattled and bounced along the ground as the women shuffled into place. The third guard held out a hand to stop the frontmost prisoner. A wave of clattering traveled down the line until it reached Benu. They were lined up along the pickaxes, facing the store, with the other station over their left shoulders. The craters were only knee-deep.

"Dig!" belched a guttural, male voice at the end.

Benu watched as each prisoner picked up a pickaxe and began swinging. Benu hesitated. Stared at the pickaxe. Tested Cyst's patience.

Cyst stepped over and put her lips to Benu's ear. "Dig."

"Fuck off," Benu whispered back.

Benu felt a hardy thwack to the back of her head. It brought her down to one knee. Benu grasped the back of her head with one hand and, with the other, picked up her tool. *Bitch is strong,* Benu thought, *but impulsive. Stupid.*

"Dig!" Cyst commanded.

Benu stood back up and obeyed. She stepped into the crater and began working. The concrete was rough and craggy under her bare feet. Each swing chipped at the solid barrier of rock. Five feet below, the fuel was buried and housed in a tank. Precious sustenance for the almighty.

The sun boiled Benu's dark skin as the day wore on. Her mouth dried. Her head ached. The rocky surface ate at the bottoms of her feet. She could feel the blisters forming. She stood up straight for a moment and wiped the sweat from her brow. As she took a small break, she observed her tormentors.

The third guard stood watch by the street corner. Cyst was walking towards her, down the left side of the crater. To her right, the other guard walked away. The two crossed paths and nodded at each other. There it was: a blind spot. As Cyst approached Benu, she sneered at her and growled, "Keep. Digging."

Benu stared her in the eye, unfazed, and picked up her pickaxe. She shot Cyst a glare and went back to work. As Cyst walked away, Benu looked up once. Their paths crossed. They nodded at each other. *Yes, a blind spot indeed.*

"Do you know why they only make *women* dig?" the short-haired woman in front of Benu suddenly spoke, her voice squeaky and weak. She looked over her shoulder and continued, "Apparently, we have a higher pain tolerance." She showed her right palm to Benu. The skin was battered and torn; barely anything remained of the bloody mat. "I can hardly feel it no more."

Her wavering voice shook Benu's resolve, but she closed her eyes and thought of her mother. Her mother's thin-lipped, smiling face as Benu showed her acceptance letter. The warmth of her tight embrace as she exited the auditorium of her graduation. Her joyous, proud voice as it echoed in celebration of Benu's residency assignment. Benu opened her eyes and continued digging.

Darkness settled over the city streets of Saginaw as the sun slowly dipped below the horizon. The cooling wave of shade soothed Benu's neck as she reveled in the brief sanctuary. The soft haze of red engulfed the evening as the purple glow of the earth's spreading cracks floated along the surface.

"Stop!" cried Cyst.

The prisoners obeyed and set their pickaxes outside the crater where they had lain. Benu mimicked their actions.

"Out of pit! Now!" Cyst screeched. The endurance and strength of Cyst's vocal cords impressed Benu. She wondered if it was talent, training, a gift from The Anomaly, or a combination of the three. Whatever it was, Benu had already grown tired of it.

As the group stepped out of the pit, Cyst and the other guard signaled to each other. They led the group back towards the hotel. As they marched, Benu could see the glow of fire bouncing off the brick of the hotel. She whipped her head around to see torches had been lit at the four corners of the wooden tower. She turned her attention forward and kept moving.

As she entered the lobby, chanting could be heard from outside. The chanting sounded familiar. She thought back to last night and could recall the ritual through a cloudy, garbled lens. The muffled commotion grew as Benu led the line down the hall. The trudge of the chains banged against the wood floor as Benu stopped in front of her door.

Cyst went down the line, unlocked each woman's chain, and lead them into their rooms. Benu saw the latch and lock that kept her door locked from the outside. Cyst continued down the line. Unlock the door. Unlock the chain. Drag the prisoner in. Anchor them to the ground. Lock the door.

Soon Benu stood as the lone prisoner. Cyst worked through her routine and began anchoring Benu to the ground.

Benu stood over Cyst and stared daggers into the nape of the mutant's neck. She watched Cyst like a hawk. Studied her prey as it worked its routine. As it slinked around the chain like a lowly snake, slithering with threats of death.

Benu's target was weak. Bore fangs of empty venom. Benu let her predator instinct gestate inside her chest, but she bided her time. *Not now.*

Cyst finished her task and stood up to find Benu standing face-to-face with her. Benu's eyes were piercing her enemy's skull. Benu's glare tore into Cyst's brain, ripping it apart from the inside out. A primal terror shot up the captor's spine, but she resisted the urge to jump. But it was too late, Cyst had shown Benu fear.

Cyst shoved Benu out of the way and exited her room with a slam of her door. The clunk of the lock ensured Benu would not be leaving for the night. Benu regained her composure and walked to the window. She squeezed her hand between the bars and wiped away some of the grime.

The quiet, star-filled night was an odd beauty. The starlight shone and twinkled amidst the lack of light pollution from the dead world. Scant clouds drifted amongst the sea of celestial bodies like whirls of soft currents in the ocean. A sharp whistle leaked through cracks in the window frame as a gust shook the glass. Benu stared on into the blackness that was lifted by a blanket of violet that sat above the ground like fields of lavender.

A creak from behind broke her trance. She was so enthralled in the solitude that she had failed to hear her room's lock being undone as her door swung open. Cyst placed a paper plate of bread and water on the ground and slammed the door.

This isn't enough to eat... Benu thought...not *for what they expect. How stupid can they be?*

Benu's mouth watered. Her stomach grumbled under her hand as she grasped it. She began walking over to the plate until she felt an abrupt tug at her ankle. She looked back to see the limit of her chain had been reached. The plate lay just out of reach.

Benu lay down on her stomach and reached out for the plate. She stretched and groaned as her fingertips kissed the edge of the plate. With her teeth clenched, she pulled at the chain with the whole of her body as the cold metal dug deep into her ankle. Her index and middle finger could now grip the paper plate. She pinched them together and scooted the pathetic meal towards her.

She flipped on her back and bit into her bread. It was stale and tasted of dirt. She closed her eyes and imagined she was back home. Imagined an afternoon lunch with her little sister at the dining room table. Fresh-cooked food carried from the kitchen by her mother. Steam rising from the plate of chicken biryani served in the traditional style —no utensils, with slices of naan to pick up the food.

Tears welled up in Benu's eyes, but she didn't let them fall. She steeled her beating heart and took a deep breath. She swallowed the last bite hard, forcing the dry clump down her throat. She leaned back and grabbed the cup of water that sat closer. The water was murky, with hints of contamination floating about. Benu had no choice. She needed this.

She sat up and held her nose. Tilting her head back, she downed the putrid water. Her stomach fought hard to resist, but Benu clenched hard and balled up into a fetal position. She let out a small grunt and held a wince. Weak and nauseated, she crawled over to her bed and onto the mattress.

Her back smacked the headboard hard as she leaned her head back and began to slow her breathing. She was sweating bullets but allowed herself to relax. She had to focus. She could hear pacing outside her door. Benu leaned forward, touched her chest to her knees, and listened.

Cyst patrolled the hall. Benu recognized her lofty footsteps. The lazy hobble of the disgusting woman faded from Benu's door. She listened closely and heard it stop at the opposite end of the hall. Benu shut her eyes and counted in her mind. *Five minutes.* Then the pacing began again. It went on like this for approximately an hour. Then, another noise.

A door opened down the hall. A few words were exchanged. The pacing began again as the same door shut. This pacing was different. Heavier. It was another guard. A shift change had occurred. Then, the boom of machinery sounded out the window.

She rolled out of her bed and peered out the window. A familiar scene began to play out at the gas station down the road. Chants and praises could be heard from the small crowd as a nude man tied to a stake was raised high above the tower. Benu watched in silence as the man was bisected, showering the engine in blood. The distant revving of the engine rumbled through the mass.

Benu's eyes widened. She had witnessed horror. Violation of human dignity and body. Her lips quivered as she stared on. She wanted to puke but her stomach was empty, denying her the pleasantry. *Jay,* she thought. *Are you to be up there next?*

A knock came from the wall to her right. She peered in the darkness at the weathered drywall. Again, this time, two knocks came. She crept over and returned the gesture.

"Hey," whispered a small, high-pitched voice. Benu heard it come down from below her knee. She knelt to find a quarter-sized hole in the wall and stuck her finger in.

"Yeah! Hey!" the voice startled Benu as she retracted her hand. She got on all fours cautiously and peeked through the hole. A bright-blue eye stared back at her from an opposing hole; it appeared to gleam amongst the black innards of the wall.

"Did ya see it?" the voice asked in a slightly higher volume. Benu recognized it now. The short-blonde woman that worked in front of her. "The sacrifice? Did ya see it?"

"Yes…" Benu murmured. "Yes, I saw it."

"Crazy, huh? Fuckin' crazy. Every night, they sacrifice one from our group."

"Your group?"

"Yeah, we came as a big group from downtown. Every night, I look for Tim."

"Tim?"

"He's this homeless guy I like. I was homeless too, ya know! Well, still am, I guess… But yeah, he's got a great attitude and bright, red hair. Every night I look for him on that stake… I don't wanna… I know, eventually, it'll be him! I don't wanna look… but… I can't… I can't *not* look!"

A tear dripped from the eye as it pulled away. Benu could hear the woman walking away. She was done talking. Benu backed away from the wall and sat on the edge of her bed. She bent down and held her ankle chain in her hand. She studied the shoddy construction. A cobbled-together assembly of foreign forged metal. Thin and weak from rust. Benu unfurled, returned to her sitting position, and began plotting.

{Chapter 10}

6:10:16:35

The low drone of the fluorescent lights above buzzed in Jay's ears, vibrating his brain and straining his eyes. They were always left on—a beacon to lure sacrifices. The low gurgle of a generator could be heard somewhere deep in the store. Jay sat against the wall and stared at the stained ceiling tiles.

Last night, another ritual raged on above him. The incessant chanting and quaking of the tribe's dancing was encapsulating a tight grip of oppression around his cell. Jay's ears were still ringing. Screams and hollers deafened him as the V8 above burst into wails of power. He struggled to find the urge to cover his ears.

He and his fellow prisoners had eaten scraps of bread and rotten fruit yesterday. The three—now two—men he shared the space behind the counter with scrambled for the meal, but Jay ate very little. He hadn't learned their names; they were to die soon anyway. One huddled near the back door next to the bucket full of excrement and flies. He was an elderly man, beyond the years of self-reliance, and was nothing but skin and bones. He hadn't spoken a peep and remained there, motionless and staring wide-eyed at the floor through sunken pits.

The other man was more talkative and still held a fight in his soul. His short, red hair complemented his freckled, white face. The tattered sweater he wore reeked of iron and urine. The length of his cargo pants suggested a short stature, but Jay hadn't witnessed him standing yet. The hems of the pants ended just over his ankles and bare feet.

Jay's clothes were also worse for wear. They had stripped him of his possessions, save for his clothes. The guards were instructed to keep the sacrifices presentable, but the brutes couldn't help but have their fun beating him before tossing him into his prison. Dried blood caked his face, complemented by an aching bruise on his left cheek. Purple splotches that lined his abdomen made it hard to breathe; if he conjured a flame now, it would be naught but a spark.

"Yo, Beanie," Red called to Jay. Jay rolled his head along the wall and looked at the man sitting across from him through droopy eyelids. The shadow of the countertop where the register would have been masked Red's face partly in shadow. Jay motioned his chin towards the ceiling, acknowledging Red's call.

"I've gots a plan to get outta here," whispered Red.

Jay simply repeated his acknowledgment.

"When they come to take Bones ova der, we jump 'em and take their weapons."

Jay peered at him in disbelief. "That's it?"

"Whaddaya mean 'that's it?'"

"Did ya try that with him before I showed up?" Jay nodded towards Bones.

Red shuddered, looked away in embarrassment, and sat back. Jay rolled his head back to its original position and took a deep breath. The stench of the store was incomprehensible. Jay had never smelled such potent rot and death before. It ripped at his sinuses and burned his eyes. He could only imagine how many bodies the bloodstains along the yellowed tile beneath him belonged to.

"Hey Red," Jay said.

"Yo," Red replied.

"How long ya been here?"

"Hmmm," Red looked up to ponder, "two weeks, I think. I was part 'o a large group these fuckers caught. There used ta be, like, twelve dudes crammed in here."

"All sacrificed?" Jay rolled his head over once more.

Red shuddered. "Yeah. Every day since."

"I'm sorry."

"Nah, nah. They weren't important ta me anyways. I just tagged along so's I coulds be safe gettin' outta this shithole, but," he started to pick at the muck on the ground, "we didn't get too far."

"Coming from downtown?"

"Yeah, tryin' to get away from that damn flower."

"Flower?"

"Yeah, man. Ya not from around here?"

Jay shook his head.

"It popped outta the ground about a year ago," Red began. "It stayed all… uh… closed up. I dunno the word for it. But about, like, six months ago, it opened up. It shot out weird yellow powder all across downtown. A whole bunch a people just died. Some of us, like yours truly, were fine. But some… went fuckin' crazy, man." He nodded in the direction of the store's entrance. "They just… started killin'. We held out as long as we could but decided to run and, well…" Red shrugged and told his story.

The Great Blossom, as it was known, burst from beneath the downtown streets of Saginaw. It towered high above the lowly buildings, curled tightly in a spiral mass. It resembled a corpse flower and reeked of horrid, rotten meat just the same. The bloom of a corpse flower is exceedingly slow; it bides its time, exposing those near to the slow creep of death.

However, The Great Blossom's metamorphosis was sudden—swift—quick. The phallic center had rested upon the support of an unfurled pedal while the opposite opened up and crashed down upon the streets below. The pollen had spread and taken its casualties.

Jay's attention was broken when the chime of the entrance's bell dinged. The rustling of heavy, chafing clothes came through the door. Jay stood up and looked through the bulletproof glass that separated the cashier from the main store. The Voice had waltzed in, breathing heavily through his flabby, swollen mouth.

A tribe member was taking inventory of the now-improvised warehouse. Crates of salvaged food, weapons, and tools were stacked against the walls. The shelves had been emptied of their original goods and were now lined with various supplies. A wooden, bloody table was set up near the back with flies hovering over a mound of meat scraps; a cleaver was embedded in the surface.

The Voice greeted the tribe member and exchanged some orders. He turned towards the cell and saw Jay staring through the window.

"Ahhhhh…" he trailed off as he approached the window. His blubber swaying and folding as he walked. "Look at you. That soulless gaze!"

Jay met The Voice at the window. He looked up at the gargantuan man that towered over him. The Voice placed his hands on the counter and spread them as he brought his face down, his fat undulating as he lowered to Jay's level. Red shot up, standing as high as Jay's chin, and started shouting obscenities; but Jay and The Voice were locked in an unbreakable stare.

"I like you. Oh yes! I like you," The Voice grumbled as he licked his lips. His voice was a guttural gurgle of phlegm and rumbled deep like distant thunder. "The engine will like you. Mmmmm… it will drink your putrid blood… and bathe in your death."

Jay stood, unmoved and silent. He simply let the fat man's threat pass over him.

"But you'll have to wait your turn. Oh yes… those two come first," The Voice let out a long, drawn-out chuckle—his chins jostling beneath his mouth. His bulging, grotesque eyes glared at Jay, rich with scorn. He enjoyed the power he held over the helpless. If he had known the scorch of Jay's hands, would he feel different?

The Voice backed away, barked an order to the worker behind him, and left. Red spat a glob onto the glass and snarled, "Fat fuck," before sitting back under the counter.

Jay looked out of the broken windows of the store, past The Voice as he walked across the parking lot. At the corner of the street in the distance sat another gas station. He could see a line of what appeared to be women mining for something. Towards the rear, he saw a familiar figure. She looked up and their distant eyes met. Jay broke his gaze from Benu and took his place on the floor behind him.

"Hey," he called over to Red.

"Yeah, whassup?" replied Red.

"Why do they do this?"

"Do *what?*"

"Sacrifice people."

Red leaned forward onto one hand, "Yer askin' me why a buncha pimple-covered freaks and their whale of a leader, who wears a crown of wrenches and screwdrivas on his head, cuts people open over a fuckin' car engine and worships it?"

Jay tilted his eyes toward him and lifted his eyebrows, egging Red to go on.

"I don't fuckin' know!"

"The chief screams about 'salvation.'" Jay tilted his head away and back. "There ain't no salvation from the Convergence."

"Well, you dunno that."

"Oh, so you're one of 'em?"

"Nah! Nah, man! It's just..." Red lowered his voice as he slumped back. "Just cuz it's the end don't really mean it's the *end*, right? Like, there gotsta be sumthin' after—or maybe we'll get lucky or sumthin'."

"*Lucky?*" Jay peered over in disbelief, ridicule in his voice. "No one gets *lucky*, you dumb fuck. The universe is constantly moving towards chaos. The good things that happen to ya aren't based on luck, kudos, or karma. They're based on your own decisions and actions. So, unless the world's got some sort of planetary nuke to blow The Anomaly outta the sky, we're fucked."

Jay hadn't noticed his raised voice had caused Red to recoil. Jay settled his huffing and stayed silent for a moment.

"Just sayin'," Red squeaked, "you never know what's at the end until yer actually there. And when yer actually there, maybe what you'll find is luck."

"If there was luck," he said under his breath, "where was it for *Her?*"

Red's ears perked up; he had caught a snippet of what Jay muttered.

"Yo, Beanie," he piped up. "I'm sorry, man."

"No, no," Jay replied, "I shouldn't have yelled. It's just... the journey's been hard... even before all this."

Jay looked away.

Red's demeanor softened. He could now see Jay wore his emotional scars plainly on his sleeve, but his callous eyes had blinded him. Red opened his mouth to speak but closed it at the lack of anything empathetic to say. A smack at the glass had interrupted the thought, anyway.

"Food!" screamed the worker through the thick glass. He walked out of the front entrance with a handful of cans. His wide and hefty shoulders scraped against the doorframe, causing the glass windows to rattle slightly.

The cashier's area behind the register had two entrances. The first was a short, swinging door that allowed entry from the main store floor that had been thoroughly boarded up. And the other was a rear metal door that led outside, behind the store.

Jay could hear the clunky footsteps of the worker rounding the building through the wall behind him. He looked up towards the door and could hear the jiggle of a lock near the top. Two bolts were penetrated through the door, secured by a couple of nuts—a hastily installed latch. The door swung open outwardly, revealing the worker from earlier holding three tin cans. The sacrifices were fed better than the lowly slaves—only the best lambs for the engine.

He tossed them on the floor and slammed the door shut. Jay could hear the familiar creak and click of the latch being locked. Red scrambled to the ground and snatched a can. The emaciated Bones, who sat nearest to the cans, let out a pathetic moan as he reached for a can. By the time he reached it, Jay had walked over and picked it up.

"Let me get it open for ya, old-timer," he whispered. Bones looked up at Jay, his mouth agape, and huddled back into his nest. Jay pick up his can as well and looked over at Red, who was studying his can.

"Dumbass didn't give us a can opener," he muttered. "Hey!" he yelled through the glass. "Ya didn't give us a can opener, dumb fuck! Hey!"

The worker snickered and shook his head as he sat down and kicked his feet up. Red huffed and backed away. He looked down at the edge of the counter and immediately started beating his can into it. The side crumpled and bent as the rancid odor started to exude from small cracks Red had achieved. Potent fermentation and rot filled the air—expired beans.

Red had made enough progress to nearly split the can in two. Guck and mush dribbled into a pool below him. With what little strength he had, Red took each end into his hand and twisted the can open, splaying it down the middle. He panted like a dog and went to dig in—when Jay tapped him on the shoulder.

Red whipped around. "What?"

Jay pointed at one half and motioned Red to hand it over.

"Fuck no, ya gots two yerself. And shame on ya for taking the old guy's food."

Jay sucked his teeth, set one of his cans on the counter, and quickly snatched a half from Red's hand. "I want that can back after I'm done with this," he said.

"Hey! What the fuck are ya gonna do?"

"Just wait there. Don't eat your other half. You'll puke."

Red reluctantly complied. Jay turned his back towards Red. He held the little half in his hand tightly. Summoning enough stamina to heat his hand, he cooked the measly meal. The beans bubbled and boiled in the mangled bowl. As he finished, he turned around, placed the cooked beans on the counter in front of Red, and held out his hand for the other half.

The odor of freshly cooked beans floated into Red's nose. He turned to the steaming can and hesitantly touched it. The immediate sear of a burning metal shocked him. He reeled his hand back, turned around, and asked, "How the fuck..."

Jay simply raised his eyebrows and motioned again for his other half. Without a word, Red obeyed as Jay turned away and repeated the process. Red was still staring in disbelief as Jay placed another cooked meal upon the counter. The pains of hunger ripped him away from caring. He plunged his fingers into the boiling goop and scooped up a clump of beans into his mouth.

For the entirety of Red's imprisonment, he had eaten like a rodent. The decaying slop that had been served to him caused endless nights of nausea and indigestion. An overwhelming sense of joy started to well inside him as the miraculous, hearty beans filled his stomach. He held back tears as he wiped away snot with his sloppy hand.

"Hey, Red," Jay chimed, grabbing Red's attention. He held out the two unopened cans. "Open these for me, will ya?"

"Ah," Red said, blinking quickly to hide his tears, "Sure thing, man."

Red got to work and barbarically cracked the two other cans open. Jay took each half and repeated his cooking. By the end, he was exhausted. He slinked over to Bones and placed two halves next to him. "Careful, old-timer. It's hot," he whispered as he walked away.

Bones looked down at the beans with dead eyes. He floated his hand over the beans and hovered over them, feeling the heat. Carefully, he raised the hot stew to his mouth. A small blade of broken tin cut his lower lip as he tilted his head back. Globs of greasy beans poured into his gullet until the heat was too much to handle. He pulled the can away from his mouth. Hot steam expelled from his lips as he gummed the beans and swallowed.

"It's fucked up," Red said as he slid back into his spot under the counter, holding his two halves with sleeve-covered hands. "That's the first soft food old guy's had in days. Thanks, by the way."

Jay had also taken his place on the floor. He looked up from his meal and replied, "Yeah, no problem."

"Y'know, he has a daughter… probably a granddaughter, now that I think of it. Gots her working over there, diggin' for some shit."

"Fuel tank."

"What's that?"

"There's fuel tanks under the pumps. They probably ran out at this station or somethin'. Wonder why they don't use the pumps."

Red put a finger to his temple, "They ain't too smart."

Jay chuckled, "Oh yeah?"

"Oh yeah, especially the guards. I knows they gots, like, one guy who can work the generator here. Probably just needs gas. The other station probably has sumthin' *actually* wrong with it."

Jay shook his head and continued eating. The beans were awful—truly repulsive. But they gave him much-needed rejuvenation of the energy he had used earlier. He also needed excess if he was going to attempt an escape. He decided to relax a bit and imagine his meal was something far more pleasant. Something She had made.

The ear-piercing screech of the smoke detector buzzed through the household. She covered her ears as Jay yanked the fiery pan off the burner. She was teaching him how to cook fish, and it had gone horribly wrong. A puddle of spilt oil was evidence of the incident.

Jay panicked and headed for the sink. She rushed to stop him. Calmly and with grace, She reached down into a cabinet and pulled out a lid. She placed it over the barreling inferno without a flinch. Smoke gathered under the clear lid as the fire snuffed itself out.

She chided him for his mistake and urged him to turn off the smoke detector. With his fingers buried in his ears, Jay grabbed a step-stool they kept in the kitchen and placed it under the smoke detector. He stepped up and held down the reset button until the beeping stopped.

"Uh, sorry honey," he said as he returned the stool.

The burnt clump that used to be a fine cut of salmon was now glued firmly to one of her best pans. She sighed heavily and started to giggle. The cleanup would be a complete pain, but She should have known Jay had the unique skill of obliterating anything he cooked; salmon was a tall order.

"Pizza?" Jay asked as he pulled out his phone.

"Hey, Beanie," Red called through stuffed cheeks.

What now? Jay thought. He looked over and acknowledged Red as he chewed.

"Ya said you was from Detroit?" Red asked. "Why come here?"

Jay swallowed and replied, "This wasn't our—*my*—final destination."

"What was, then?"

Maybe it was the threat of inevitability staring Jay in the face. Or the same inevitability staring at Red. It could have been the incessant hum of the fluorescent lights. Or the aftereffects of eating expired beans. But despite the fact that Jay felt conflicted sharing his plight—his purpose—with Red, he felt this might be the last chance he would get to tell someone of his pain.

"I… lost my wife. Two years before the First Convergence. Her ashes are—*were*—in my backpack. She knew her time was comin', Red… I did too, but I was too stubborn to accept it. I always said things like 'don't worry, it'll get better' or 'the doctor's'll figure somethin' out!' But, really… I was just lying to myself. She *insisted* I accept reality. Her cryin' face is stained on my memory—the day that she ordered me to 'be strong and let her go.' Her face… the tears didn't roll down a solemn expression. It's like her body knew it was supposed to be cryin' but her mind didn't. She showed no fear… no sadness. It was an absolute face—one of bravery, I'd say. I was being told to 'be strong' by the strongest person I knew!

"Before she left me, she made a request. She… asked me to, when she was gone…" Moisture began to flood Jay's eyes as he looked away, "to take her ashes. Bury them in her childhood hometown of Escanaba… next to her mother." A swell of heavy anguish filled Jay's lungs. He took a moment to let out a trembling exhale. "I told her I couldn't let her go… I wanted to be with her no matter what. So, she told me I could hold onto her just a little longer… and bury her and my ring when I was good and ready. I promised… I promised I'd do that for her. So, here I am seven years later… finally ready to keep my promise."

Jay's hands were shaking. He couldn't look Red in the eye, but he could feel the man's solemn gaze at the back of his head. *The ring,* Jay thought. He patted his right pocket and felt a petite bulge. The guards had stripped him of everything, he thought. He reached in and pulled out his warped wedding ring and looked at it in utter disbelief. He shot a glance at Red who was gleaming a great, dimpled smile.

"I told ya," Red said with freshly cried, bloodshot eyes. "They put the real stupid ones on guard."

{Chapter 11}

5:12:18:57

Benu woke to a familiar smell—human waste. The bucket hadn't been emptied since the start of her imprisonment. Her nose twitched as her eyes burned from the early sun. Last night, another sacrifice was made. She had watched an elderly man bleed over the engine from her window. She half expected Jay's naked body to be displayed high above since meeting his eyes yesterday. Thankfully, he was still alive as far as she knew.

Rising from her bed, the heavy chain around her left ankle clattered onto the ground and tugged at her shackle. The metal was pathetic, just as she had observed before. Only fit for securing small fences or weak doors. Her feet were aching and tender from trudging on the hot pavement. They were rough and coarse like the scales of an alligator. Dirtied black from the outside grime. Benu bent over and massaged them. It helped ease the pain momentarily.

She needed her might today. All the energy she could muster would be put into action. She brushed a wisp of scraggy black hair out of her face and shut her eyes. Meditating, she took draws of long, steady breaths. The beating in her chest became a steady thump. Next to her, on the bed, sat a half-eaten piece of bread from last night.

Rationing would be necessary in order to carry enough stamina through the day to enact her plan. Benu opened her eyes and picked up her food. She took a few bites, leaving about a quarter left. She took the rest and hid it deep within one of the many holes that populated her mattress. The metallic tang of the bed springs and decayed stuffing began to stick to the stale bread as it nestled within.

As Benu sat up on the edge of her bed, she could hear the distinct stomps of Cyst down the hall. It was time for work. Benu looked down at her chain and lock, taking another analysis of its quality. The

loud routine grew closer as Cyst completed her actions in the room
next door.

Unlock.

Unchain.

Escort.

Shut the door.

The fumbling of the lock outside her door began. She stood up as
the door crept open with Cyst hobbling in with the same scornful
vigor she had for the past two days. She could see Benu was already up
and didn't waste her breath. She bent down and began undoing
Benu's chain.

Cyst's head looked especially soft today. Benu's tormentor would
soon become a stain under her feet. The mutant's skin was stretched
and waxy, slickened by the puss that oozed from her sores. Benu
counted the protruding vertebrae from the base of Cyst's skull.

One... two... three... four... five... six... seven...

Between any two of those seven would do.

Cyst finished and rose, sneering at Benu. She held the chain up to
Benu's chest, snarled, and jerked her forward. Benu followed and
watched her target just as she did before, watching as she was chained
up to the group. Cyst shut the door and secured the latch. The familiar
march began.

Her swings were lax. Benu conserved her energy for the fight
ahead. She studied the guards' movements carefully. Watched as they
traded glances when they crossed—the blind spot. Cyst approached
her. Benu kept quiet and swung a convincing strike, chipping away a
hefty chunk of concrete.

Cyst kept that ugly excuse for a face stone-cold as she walked away
and continued her routine. The metal handle of her knife, sheathed
around her left leg, glinted in the sunlight. Benu peered over at the
opposing gas station. She could see a hint of a familiar gray beanie

peeking over, behind the register. She allowed herself a small grin and prepared herself.

Placing her left foot over the chain, she held it down. She braced her legs and focused on the excess chain, just before the lock. Her pickaxe was brought over her shoulder. She gripped it tight, one hand brought flush with the head, and squeezed; she had to be careful not to strike her foot. A thick bead of sweat rolled down her cheek.

She rolled her eyes around, looking at the busy community going about their day. She held this position as she turned her attention to the two guards. They were about five paces from each other. Cyst on the left. The other on the right side, blinded by the prisoners that were between him and Benu.

Three paces now.

One.

The blind spot!

Benu whipped the pickaxe down on the chain with fierce tenacity—her arms swinging across her body. The unmistakable metal-on-metal twang was masked by the others' digging. Benu brought the pickaxe back up and saw that her strike had deformed the chain but hadn't cracked it as she had hoped. She'd need to strike again.

She waited. Her opportunity came again. Another weighty twang filled the air. However, the crack still hadn't transpired. *One more. Surely, one more.*

Benu was breathing hard now. As she pretended to work, her eyes danced between the guards. They hadn't suspected anything, but could she risk a third? She had hoped the flimsy chain would break by now. Perhaps, it wasn't so weak after all? *No,* she thought. *One more. Come on.*

Again, the blind spot occurred. She swung hard, harder than she had before. It sent a vibration into her ankles. Benu stayed in her bent position over the head of the buried pickaxe. As she huffed, the woman in front turned to her and whispered, "Stop that! You'll get us both killed!"

"Shut up!" Benu snarled through clenched teeth. "Or I will bury this pickaxe so deep into your skull, the devil will have to pull it out when you meet him."

Color drained from the woman's face as she slowly turned forward and continued to work. Benu slipped the pickaxe's head to the side, revealing a link that was now severed in one place. She whipped the broken link under her foot and straightened up. As she stood, Cyst was walking towards her from a couple of prisoners away; her eyes locked on Benu. *Fuck,* Benu thought. *Did she see me?*

Cyst brought her face down to Benu's, breathing through her mouth. Her hot, tainted breath enveloped Benu's face. The putrid breath lingered in her nostrils and caused her to cringe. Cyst pursed her lips high and tight. She lifted her chin, revealing her undulating throat. A skipping, guttural sound fluttered at the back of her tongue as she hocked a glob of phlegm in Benu's face.

"No breaks," Cyst muttered, deepening her tone. "Back to work."

Benu squeezed her eyes shut and gathered the gunk off her face in one swipe and flicked it to the ground. The gesture caused her to shudder out of disgust. She composed herself, resituated her dignity, and continued "working."

"Stop!" cried Cyst. The prisoners stepped out of the crater and placed their pickaxes on the ground. Benu kept her eyes glued to Cyst. She couldn't give any hint of the broken chain until the right moment. Cyst walked along the line, sneering her ugly sneer. When she reached Benu, she bumped her shoulder with the butt of her crossbow, forcing her to turn towards the hotel. She flicked her head towards the building and yelled, "Move! Let's go!"

The group trudged on in the setting sunlight. The musical clatter of the chains along the pavement encompassed Benu's mind. Her vision tunneled as the sea of clangs and rattles crashed against her skull. She could hear each synchronous clash match her stride. Match the strikes she would bring down upon Cyst's head.

The boils, pimples, growths, and pustules on the back of Cyst's head taunted Benu. They tempted her to crush them. *Soon,* Benu thought. *I will try. I must. I will see you two, one last time.* Her stare was not of blind violence or animalistic desperation, but one of intelligence. Laden with senses of retribution and purpose.

Cyst barged into the lobby. As she entered the hallway leading to their rooms, Benu found herself in arm's reach of the pens atop the reception counter to her right. Now was the time to set her plan in motion. She looked over her shoulder and saw the woman behind her lift her shackled ankle for a step. With a swift tug, Benu shot her left foot forward and pulled the chain tight. The sudden jerk yanked the fatigued woman behind her off balance, sending her to the ground.

The woman yelped as she caught herself on her elbow. Cyst whipped around and hollered, "Get up!" She rushed over to the prisoner and snatched her by the upper arm. "Get. Up!" Cyst commanded as she bent down to lift the woman, wrenching her around like an angry ape. The broken prisoner groaned as she struggled to her feet.

As she pulled her left foot away, Cyst caught wind of Benu's trap. The broken link remained connected, but the damage was obvious. Cyst's eyes bulged with confusion. She scratched her empty skull as she bent down to inspect the damage. Benu glanced over her shoulder. Noticed the line was still partly out the door. The rear guard couldn't possibly see her next move. With speed and precision, she plucked a pen out of the cup and tucked it in her palm and up her sleeve.

Cyst's feeble mind struggled with the chain. In the time it took her to finally figure out how to undo the lock and secure it to an earlier, unbroken link in the sequence, Benu could've stolen an armory of pens. As Cyst rose, Benu looked away and rolled her eyes, thinking: *about time.* She almost found it comical. If it weren't for the torture these savages had caused her, she would almost feel bad for having to outwit one so stupid.

Benu was led to her room and chained to her anchor just as before. As soon as the door shut, she rushed to her bread's hiding spot and dug it out. She gobbled down the rancid, dirtied food and sat on her bed. Soon, her daily meal would be served. More fuel for her fire.

Moments later, the door creaked open. Cyst placed Benu's meal on the floor where she always had. She slammed the door and left Benu to dine on her familiar, stale bread and water. Benu placed the pen on the bed and worked through the routine of laying down and stretching out for her sustenance. She ate in silence and steeled herself mentally for the next step.

But she needed to do the same physically. She had an hour before Cyst's shift was up. She had the time to stretch. She couldn't let something as silly as a cramp hinder her in her upcoming task. She brought her hands together in a prayer pose, closed her eyes, and spread her legs shoulder-width apart.

Spreading her arms to the side, she breathed slowly as she reached as high as she could. She brought her arms down and behind her back. Pressing her thumbs at the small of her back, she bent back and could feel her muscles loosen as they stretched. She brought herself up and held her arms up to her chest—her fists hovering in front with elbows bent. As she twisted from side to side, she could hear small pops and cracks from her back. She returned to her original position and felt totally calm in her mind—ready to kill.

Benu twirled the pen in her right hand as she sat on her bed, waiting for Cyst to be outside her door. Five minutes had passed since the hobbling had ceased. Cyst had taken her first break. Benu could hear the steps once more. Each heavy step clunked its way down the hall. As it grew louder, the stomps seemed to match Benu's heartbeat. The intensity of the approaching threat beat against her sternum.

This was to be life or death. A short time was ahead of her—she knew this—but a chance to see her family was worth the risk. However, sprinkles of doubt sparked in her mind like fireflies in the dead of night. The world would be ending in a few days. Soon, she would be united with her family in death, outside of her own volition.

She could spend the rest of the time here. It would be suffering… but it would all end in a few days.

But there was something potently human about Benu. A combination of the will to survive and a distinct realization of her passions pushed her to fight. Could she face her mother and sister in death if she hadn't fought to see them alive? No, Benu would not accept this. The fire in her heart raged like frenzied flames that could not be contained. She gripped her pen and peered at the door, huffing through her nostrils.

Her ears drowned out the whistling wind and creaks of the hotel walls. All she could hear were the disjointed stomps of Cyst as she approached. They were now outside her door. She could see a faint, but distinct, silhouette through the crack beneath the door. Benu nearly hesitated as the silhouette lifted away, but gathered herself and yelled, "Hey ugly bitch! Fuck you!"

The silhouette lowered back down. The fumbling of the lock outside began. *Impulsive,* Benu thought. *Stupid and rash.* The door swung open, slamming against the wall, and bounced back into a drift. "What you say?" screamed Cyst as she hobbled over to Benu, her crossbow clattering on her back.

"I said fuck your fucked up face!" Benu retorted as she spit in Cyst's direction.

Cyst was close now. Just at the foot of Benu's bed. She snarled and huffed as she approached Benu from the side. Benu tightened her grip.

Cyst took another clumsy step.

And then another.

She was now in striking distance.

She lurched over to Benu and grabbed her by the shoulders with both hands. She yanked Benu toward her and shouted, "I'm gonna–"

Cyst didn't have time to finish her threat.

The next sound that exited her mouth was a bloodcurdling scream that rang only in her right ear. Her left ear was now occupied by about three inches of ballpoint pen.

Benu pressed the pen deeper into Cyst's ear canal and wrenched it around, destroying the innards. Milky, yellow puss spurted from the wound as it coated Benu's hand. Cyst was making too much noise. She would alert the other guard.

Twisting Cyst around by the pen, Benu grasped Cyst's mouth and pressed her onto the bed—full-mounting the wretched woman over her stomach. The pen was yanked out and hammered down into Cyst's left eye. A fountain of the same milky ooze burst from the socket. A muffled cry warmed Benu's palm.

Cyst was kicking, flailing, and scrambling for something to grab to stop her killer. She placed her right hand on Benu's face and tried to gouge out her eyes, but Benu twisted and turned her away. Benu brought the pen out and slammed it down again, further obliterating Cyst's eye. The bangs and rattles of her chain felt like a bustling conversation in the night as they tumbled around against the wood floor and tattered mattress.

In a desperate attempt, Cyst began bringing her left leg towards her hand to retrieve the knife strapped to her thigh.

Benu glanced over her shoulder and noticed Cyst's hand pawing for the knife. In a flash of succinct, accurate movements, Benu pulled out the pen, tossed it out of Cyst's reach, reached back, and unsheathed Cyst's enormous hunting knife. She held it high— reversed grip, edge out—and planted it deep into Cyst's forehead.

The corrupted yellow blood seeped out from between the knife and waxy flesh. It trickled down the bridge of the dead woman's nose and into the mush that remained of her left eye. Slowly, it traveled across her forehead and poured into the ridges of her bleeding ear. Benu could no longer feel the hot breath of a living soul on her hand as Cyst's limp palm slipped off Benu's face and fell to the side.

Benu held her left hand in position and yanked out her knife as she stepped off the bed. The gunk that had bled from Cyst's wounds now bubbled from the gaping slit. It seemed to pour endlessly as it smothered Cyst's face and stained the bed underneath.

The smell was unlike anything Benu could have imagined. She retched hard and successfully held back vomit once but couldn't help it the second time. Puke belched from her stomach onto the floor. For a moment, she felt lightheaded as she wiped her mouth with her sleeve, but she quickly regained her composure and began looting the dead Cyst.

Benu stripped the corpse of its keys. She undid her shackles. The elation of freedom washed over Benu but was fleeting in her time of heightened adrenaline. She unslung the crossbow off Cyst's back, placed it to the side on the bed, and continued pilfering the body of its clothes. Cyst was a tad smaller than Benu, but everything fit decently: nylon fingerless gloves, work boots, cargo pants, dirtied undershirt, a hefty blue sweater, and a handmade leather cowl.

Cyst's naked body was odd. It was devoid of genitalia and her breasts had no nipples. The same unsightly growths and mutations covered the rest of her skin, but some had begun to sprout small, pointed protrusions. They were brown in color and craggy to the touch. A cursory glance would describe them as "roots." Some zits were also exhibiting a strange appearance in the form of flaking ridges that resembled the petals of a blooming flower.

She wiped the putrid muck off her knife with her discarded prison garments and tucked it in her sheath. Picking up the crossbow, she inspected it. *What a complete piece of shit!* Benu thought. The crossbow was neglected in nearly every aspect. The mechanisms all squeaked and groaned. It was covered in splotches of rust and discoloration with several chips and dings. Benu ran her fingertips along the string—unwaxed.

Of course, she thought. *Has this thing ever been fired?*

She'd need to find a way to lubricate the strings. Dry strings ran the risk of snapping at the force of an unleashed bolt. Benu thought quickly. She cringed as she gathered globs of puss from Cyst's bleeding forehead and lubed the crossbow strings. Hurling nearly came again but Benu fought the urge.

Cyst's belt had her quiver attached. Benu fingered through the measly group of bolts.

Five, she counted.

She felt a small brush of grace when she pulled out the bolts to find that they were all carbon fiber. Now, she could only hope that same grace found favor in her aim. Benu had taught herself to make wooden bolts during her three years living in the wilds of Royal Oak. She had kept carbon fiber or aluminum bolts she had pillaged for desperate situations.

Peeking left down the hall, Benu saw no one. She was able to finish the job within an hour, but she was unsure how much time she had left before the ritual finished. Distant voices began chanting. She had to move quickly.

She stepped into the hallway and locked the door behind her. It was evident now that the latch's installation was ham-fisted and amateur. Anyone searching for Cyst would have no issue breaking down the door.

Benu whipped around, turned left down the corridor, and hurried deeper into the hotel. The hallway stretched on for nearly forty rooms, ending in a T-intersection. She poked her head around the corner, looking left and then right. At the end of the left hallway was a door leading outside.

Again, she made haste for the exit. It was a standard metal door with a long push mechanism to open it. Benu placed the base of her palms on the panic bar. With steady pressure, she gently depressed the bar until she heard a soft click.

As the door creaked open, the sound of thunderous chanting rushed into the hallway. Benu opened it just enough to slip half her body out, leaving enough room for the crossbow on her back. She peeked around the doorway, towards the lit torches from the V8 tower.

The door faced the backside of the store that accompanied the gas station. She looked to her left, down the side of the hotel, and could see the back of the second shift guard as he stood and watched the ritual with devout rigidity. His giant stature dwarfed the door to his left—the same door Benu had trudged through for the past two days.

She slinked the rest of her body through the exit and shut it gently, keeping her eyes on the guard to be sure he hadn't heard. With her eyes still glued to his back, she snuck behind the store and crept low to the ground with arms spread wide to keep her balance. She reached the employee's back door.

Placing her hand on the door handle, she closed her eyes and said a silent prayer to herself. She hoped this door would be unlocked. It *needed* to be unlocked. She prayed for luck, and it had found favor in her as she pushed down on the handle without issue. A tiny click rang behind her as she stepped in and shut the door.

Benu was still low to the ground. She found herself in the bathroom hallway at the rear corner of the store. The sights and smells matched that of the hotel. Gripping her nose shut, she stood up— hunched with bent knees—and moved forward.

The little convenience store had no lights. Under the veil of darkness, Benu searched the store for any signs of the worker she had seen there before. The place was empty save for the bare metal shelves and piles of pillaged clothing and backpacks. She looked out of the window above the decaying magazine racks and rusted shelving.

Across the street, the fat chieftain stood high above the crowd atop the gas station, spouting his drivel. Down below, the small tribe danced and hollered. To her left was a guard at the hotel door, totally entranced by the ceremony. At the street corner was another, his back to the store.

Benu turned around and saw the table before her, piled with various items. Shirts, shoes, pants, toys, photos, watches, packaged snacks, and jewelry were just a small portion of what these savages had pillaged. She grabbed a digital watch, checked to see if the time reflected what seemed to be correct, and strapped it on her left wrist.

To the right, on the floor, were stuffed backpacks. To the left were flattened, emptied backpacks.

In the discarded pile, Benu saw a sight that sunk her heart. Jay's green, canvas bag lay on top, devoid of any of its contents. Glancing behind her, she could see the attention of the crowd was still solely fixated on the fat man and his ramblings. No body had been raised. Benu had some time.

She started at the left end of the table and rummaged through the pile, searching franticly for the little, pewter urn. The task was daunting. The flickering of the torches at her back didn't provide enough light to properly aid her search. As she moved down to the opposite end, she caught sight of something familiar.

It lifted her spirits to find her red bag, completely untouched amongst the unorganized pile. She snatched it up and opened the main compartment. Crouching, she fingered through the contents. Everything was there: food, medical supplies, tools, map, and clothes. She took time to open the front pocket and found the lone item she had kept there: a picture of her mother, sister, and herself at her graduation.

As she smirked with elation, a timid voice behind her whispered, "Hey."

Benu whipped around and rested a knee on the ground. A small, mutated boy with bulging lips and eyes—covered in blemishes—stood before her and chided, "Thas not yours."

He couldn't have been more than three, maybe four, years old. The orange flickers shimmered off the few strands of blonde hair that dangled from his head. Dressed in a tattered, striped sweater and dirtied cargo shorts, he stood there—clutching a small, silver, pewter urn with both hands.

Benu's eyes widened as she pointed to the urn and whispered: "That is not yours either."

"Yea it is. Mom gave it to me. It makes a cool noise. Listen!" He shook the urn violently up and down. The fine ashes tumbled and clashed against the inner walls like clumps of sand being tossed. Benu's fury boiled inside her.

She should kill this vile monstrosity. Everything in her instincts told her this was no longer human. The wicked substance that had burst from Cyst's body proved this. She could do it quickly… silently… Reaching for her knife, she looked down at her other hand, still holding her photo.

Could she face her mother, in life or death, with the blood of what was once a child on her hands? She bit her lip and blinked hard. No, she would find another way.

"Stop," she commanded in a murmur, "Please, stop."

The boy complied and tilted his head like a curious cat.

"That is not yours. It belongs to my… friend," she muttered.

"No," he protested, "Mom said I could have it. Mom says it's mine!" He stomped his bare foot.

"Shhhh!" Benu pleaded as she brought her index finger to her lips and splayed out the others towards the child while still holding the photo.

The boy pointed a finger at the photo. "Whas dat?" he asked.

Benu looked down at the photo and flipped it around to show the boy. The dance of the fire's light dimly lit the picture.

"This," Benu pointed at the older figure, "is *my* mother. And this is my sister." She moved her finger to her shorter sibling.

"Are they here?"

"No, they are not," Benu said in a soft tone, shaking her head.

"Are they dead? Mom says evrywun outside is dead."

Benu was taken aback by the assuredness in the boy's voice. She took a deep breath and shook her head. "No, they are alive." She nodded as she wore a hopeful smile.

The boy smiled back and replied: "Thas good." He rocked back and forth on the balls of his feet and looked at the ground. For a moment, only the commotion outside could be heard until the boy spoke, "You said this shaker is your friend's?"

"Yes, it means a lot to him. Please, may I have it?" She stuck out her hand to receive it.

"Mmmm," the boy pondered as he held it to his chest and swiveled left to right on the balls of his feet. "Only if u be my friend. I don't have any here. I'm the only kid. And the grown-ups are all mean. They never let me watch the big thingy outside. They always make me wait there." He was pointing at the register, past Benu.

They were hiding him from the killings, she thought. *These troglodytes still had enough semblance of dignity to protect a child's innocence? Please.*

"Sure. Of course," she replied, bobbing her hand for the urn.

"Mmmm, but u have to prove it," he said, pointing at the photo. "Les trade. Dat way I can member you and you can member me."

Curse this child! Benu screamed in her head. The logic of a child was proving to be a greater hindrance than any number of chains, stale bread, or wretched guards. Benu lingered on the photo. She held that moment dearest to her heart. The sense of pride, accomplishment, and pure love she felt in that moment was branded into her memory. How dare this monster take it away from her!

But she had heard this kid's voice. The boy's naivety was no different from any human child. A gentle innocence unravaged by the cursed impurities of the people around him. The mind of a child, so easily swayed and driven by the essence of simplicity. For the time being, he was not taken by the horrid infection that plagued the others' minds.

A flash of logic raced through Benu's thoughts. She held a physical representation of that sacred moment, but the moment was a metaphysical thing that existed within her. She could soon share that feeling again with her mother and sister. Her dearests were still alive; Jay's was not.

With small tears welling in the corner of her eyes, Benu presented the photo to the boy and muttered, "Sure. Here."

The boy took the photo from her quivering hand and placed the urn in its stead. Benu reeled it in and placed it in her bag. The boy peered at the photo and looked up, smiling through his malformed lips. "Thanks, lady."

"Hmph, no worries, kid."

Outside, the chanting started to erupt. Benu crept upwards and peeked over the racks once more. She could see a naked, red-haired man being lifted for the sacrifice. She was hit with a crash of conflicting emotions. She was running out of time to save Jay. Soon, the ritual would end, and the mutant community would no longer have any morbid festivities to keep them occupied. Benu battled between two choices: attempt the rescue or save her own skin and see her family again. Apprehension and solace played tug-of-war across her mind, and apprehension was clearly winning.

Shit, she thought. She glanced to the left and caught the guard entering the hotel. *Oh, shit.*

She ducked back down and held her hands out to the kid and pleaded, "Thank you for the urn, kid, but I need to go."

"Where u goin?" the boy asked solemnly.

"I have to go save my friend we talked about. I cannot stay here. Sorry."

"I wanna help!" the boy shouted as he jumped up and down.

"Shhh!" Benu pleaded. "Ok. Ok. You can help. Do me a big, *big* favor, ok?" She was nodding her head quickly in an attempt to get the child to understand. "Stay here. If any of the grown-ups ask about me, tell them you saw me. And tell them I ran *that* way!" She was pointing in the complete opposite direction of the ritual site.

"Why are they lookin for u?"

"Uh, we are playing a game. Yes! And if they find me, they win. If they cannot find me all night, I win! You want to help your friend win?"

The boy smiled hugely and nodded his head repeatedly.

"Excellent," Benu replied. "Don't tell them about the game, ok? Now, you are playing and if you tell them, you lose. Do you understand?"

"Mhmmm!" replied the boy.

"Great!" She placed her hands on the boy's shoulders. "Thank you!"

She slipped her backpack on and started to head towards the back. The boy ran to her and called, "Hey! Good luck!"

Benu turned her head around to face the child. She smiled, nodded, and left through the back door.

Benu watched the gas station from around the corner of an adjacent building as the two guards rushed out the front and headed in the opposite direction into the nearby suburb. *Thanks, kid,* she thought to herself. She found herself in an alleyway, sandwiched between two rundown restaurants.

Weeds and invasive grasses had wriggled through the cracks along the foundations. Old, piled trash had decomposed so much that it had nearly lost all its rancid smells. The hairline slivers that emanated purple light were not as prominent through the pavement. The ground underneath had not fractured enough to cause the pavement to collapse, shielding the violet hue. But the surrounding exposed earth allowed enough light to cover the surface.

Moonlight met the purple barrier and illuminated Benu's path down the alley. She snuck to the end which led out to a parking lot and onto the street. As she approached the end, she peeked around the corner to the left. To the northeast, at the street corner, the ritual raged on. The Voice was spilling his drivel to the masses. The occasion must have been a bit more momentous, since the sacrifice was still dangling above the engine.

Benu studied the crowd and could see the reason behind the heightened commotion. Two men were pressed against the ground by a couple of guards—new prisoners. He bellowed and preached as the tribe continued to cheer. Twenty or so people were in attendance.

She had to make her way behind the ceremony. Time her movements to the pop and bangs of the roaring engine. Across two lanes, the median with overgrown grass would provide ample cover.

Benu glanced around—peered into the dead of night for any outskirt guards. They could be well-hidden, just as they were when she and Jay were sedated. She couldn't spot anyone and, with a loud bang and sputter of the engine, she didn't have any more time to linger. The red-headed man would soon be cut open and the killing would be complete.

She dashed for the median. Her bag and crossbow jostled and rattled as she ran. Diving into the grass, she steadied her breathing and focused her hearing. The engine had calmed, and the fat man preached on. She listened for any approaching footsteps and heard nothing. She had two more lanes to cross.

Crawling forward, she parted the grass and looked across the street. Before her stood the remnants of an abandoned house. A line of houses stretched on into the neighborhood, down the street, to the south. She could move between the houses to reach the rear of the store. She looked around again and waited for the roar of the engine to mask her movements.

Instead, the loud call of The Voice signaled the sacrifice and caused the tribe to raise their chanting. Benu took her chance and sprinted across the street into the overgrown backyard. She kept low. She was now crouching in the mess of high foliage, facing a chain-link fence that separated the backyards of the neighboring houses. To her left, a high stone wall blocked her from the gas station.

She could see the top trim of the store. When she saw Jay earlier, she figured he was located behind the counter. She decided she would search the rear of the store for an entrance. The high sacrificial altar loomed overhead, casting flickering glows of fire all around. She still needed to work her way around the back of the store. Hopping the stone wall blindly could place her in plain view of the crowd or any potential guards stationed between the store and the wall.

Sneaking up to the fence, she found it had been cut through and broken at the bottom. She searched around for a hole large enough for her to crawl under. Near the center, she found one and unslung her crossbow.

First, the crossbow was fed through the hole, and then her bag. She lay flat on her stomach and pushed them far enough to give herself room to crawl through herself. Making herself as flat as possible, she began squeezing through.

Her arms came through.

Then her head and breasts.

Then she heard a rattle from the fence as her hips refused to follow.

"Shit," she said under her breath, and she turned around to see that her sweater had been snagged in a jagged part of the broken fence. She scooted back and turned on her back, jiggling the fence slightly. The jingle of the fence sounded like firecrackers in her mind. She heard an intense cheer from the crowd as she looked up to see the red-haired sacrifice being splayed open. She had to hurry. The body would bleed out and there would be a small celebration. Then they'd be dismissed, and her cover would be blown before she could reach Jay.

The thick fibers of her hefty sweater were impossibly entangled in the sharp metal. She couldn't risk ripping it as the recoil would cause the fence to wiggle violently; she didn't want to risk any unnecessary noise. She panicked for a moment but remembered her knife. She curled up tightly and brought her left thigh up to the fence. Reaching under, she was able to unsheathe her knife and cut herself free.

As she crawled through, she brought her attention forward to the rear of the house that this backyard belonged to. She had just reached for her crossbow when the rear door creaked open. Out stepped a scrawny, male guard armed with a machete. On his hip, a blowgun. The blurred memories of intoxication flashed in her mind. Benu lay still in the thick grass.

Through the thin green shafts, she could see him peering around in the dark. *He must have heard the fence,* she thought as she swallowed hard. The guard stepped down from the porch and entered the yard. He stood about twenty feet from Benu.

His outstretched neck hovered his bony chin ahead of him as he stalked the area. His large, bulbous nostrils sniffed the cool, Fall air. Slowly he moved with sinister intentions. His head swayed left to right as he scanned the fence and grass ahead of him.

Benu was sweating bullets. He needed to come closer, but if he spotted her beforehand, he would surely yell for help.

Steadily… carefully… the man moved towards Benu. Each step felt like a quake as they crunched and rustled the overgrown weeds and waves of grass. Benu could hear his breathing now. She gripped her knife.

The guard stopped about five paces in front of Benu. The indentation of the grass was obvious to him now. He went to open his mouth when the sudden rev of the great V8 tore his attention away. In this instant, Benu lunged from the grass and brought her knife into the underside of his chin, tackling him to the ground with nary a sound but a slice and a thud.

The blade found its home deep in the guard's brain. The disgusting substance dribbled out from the entry wound and sprayed out as Benu yanked out her knife. This time, Benu made sure to hold her breath to avoid the retching. She sheathed her knife, looked over her left shoulder, and studied the backyard.

It extended down the backside of the stone wall which sat flush with the fence. Near another dividing fence, perpendicular to the stone wall, was a broken section—large enough for Benu to step over. Retrieving her crossbow and backpack, she made her way to the wall and peeked over it.

She caught a glimpse of her final obstacle as she quickly ducked her head back down. Raising it up again, she took another look at the man standing guard outside of the back door to the register area. He was distracted. Looking high above him at the bloodbath. Benu raised her eyes to the tower as well and could see the corpse had almost finished bleeding dry, merely dripping blood at this point.

Under the boom and shake of the engine, she loaded a bolt. The guard stood about twenty feet from her. Benu brought the crossbow up to her eye. She pulled the hard, composite stock tight against her right shoulder and rested her cheek on it. Closing her left eye, she lined up her reticle with her target's head. This target was a lot closer than the time she shot Jay.

She could make this shot. She *had* to make this shot.

Shakes… Nerves… Doubt…

I should go… If I miss, I will never see you two again. I already regret trading that photo. But… do I dare carry this urn without him?

Sweat trickled down from her eyebrow and into her eye, stinging it. She took a deep breath through her nose. In that time, a seesaw of decisions teetered on her crossbow fulcrum: leave now or risk it all to save a friend.

She exhaled and made her choice.

{Chapter 12}

5:00:23:16

The howls of the tribe pierced the night sky as Jay and Red sat helpless in their cell. Last night, they watched as Bones was injected with the hallucinogenic sedative and stripped of his clothes. He was too old and frail to put up any sort of fight, but Red pounced on the guards as they took him. In the scuffle, the snap of his elbow echoed through the store as he fell to the ground, writhing from the shock. Jay's bruises were all but faint discolored marks, his cuts were already scarred over; he had wished he could share some of his miraculous healing with Red.

Now, the ritual would begin again. The sound of the gathering crowd invaded Jay's skull like ants working and endlessly clamoring in their nest. Each footstep, murmur, or thing being moved was like another pick and prod that ate away at Jay's sanity. His eyes were squeezed shut as the cacophony continued to grow in his brain, causing him to wince. Jay clamped his palms over his ears but, like prying hands, the sound from outside worked its fingers past his shield.

As Jay's head was ready to explode, the tornado of noise was ended by a soft tap on his knee. Jay shot his eyes open to see Red leaning over him, his left arm hanging limp at his side. Red took a seat to his left, underneath the counter. His sunken, blackened eyes contrasted with his skinny, pale face. Jay could see that his injured hand was a puffy, swollen red.

"Hey," Red spoke in a meek, raspy voice.

Jay scanned Red from head to toe, taking notice of his poor state.

"We'll need to do something about that arm, y'know?" Jay replied. "It looks pretty bad."

Red chortled and shook his head. "Ya hear what's goin' on out there? I'll be dead in a couple o' hours, man."

Jay opened his mouth to offer a rebuttal, some parable of hope, but only air escaped his lungs. He closed his mouth and whispered a curse under his breath.

"Look, man," Red continued. "I came over to ask a favor of ya."

Jay looked up over to Red but was met with the side of his face as Red stared off into nothing.

"Yeah, what's up?" Jay replied.

"Could ya pray for me?"

"Pray? You're a God-fearin' man?"

Red turned his gaze towards Jay and smirked. His eyes held no light. Hope of leaving this place alive had ejected itself from his soul hours ago. But his expression held a weight of complacency and acceptance.

"Nah, but," Red started, "my ma was. I'd like to tell her I at least tried to save my soul when I meet her in hell… or heaven, if this works, I guess."

Jay leaned forward, "Hey, man, stop with that shit. We're gonna find some way outta this—"

"And this is comin' from the guy sulkin' in the corner with his hands over his fuckin' head?" Jay backed off. "Look, I'm glad I'm finally fuckin' rubbin' off on ya, but it's over for me. I wish ya had that spunk earlier, but nah. Ya gave up. Ya sat in yer corner and waited and have been waitin' for yer end. What happened? Huh?"

Jay peered over and asked: "Whaddaya mean?"

"What happened to yer promise? Huh? Some fuckin' husband you are. Can't keep his wife's dyin' wish!"

Rage boiled in Jay's veins. He wanted to rip Red's tongue out just for mentioning Her. A sullied imbecile with no respect had no right to speak about Her. But he was right. Jay felt his ring through his pocket and was flushed with a wave of guilt. Where had his fight gone? Had She meant so little to him that he'd allow himself to fall into despair so easily? Perhaps this imbecile had some wisdom that Jay lacked.

The two shared a moment of silence between each other. Outside, the chanting began to grow. Stomps and hollers of the tribe echoed through the streets. Footsteps above shuffled on the roof as the ritualists prepared for the sacrifice. Just outside the metal door leading to the back of the store, the sounds of people climbing up and down an access ladder could be heard. The glug of gas cans as they were hoisted up the side of the building. Voices of chattering guards just on the other side of the wall as they prepared to take Red.

Jay spoke up. "You're right y'know? You're right. I dunno what came over me. I thought this would be easy—that I'd just ride my bike from Detroit to the U.P. like nobody's business. I guess the shock of facing some opposition really fucked with me."

"That black diamond really fucked things up, huh?" Red replied. "But to be honest… for folks like me… it's as if it was always there. It ain't ever been easy for me… Like, that black thing just eats away at everything you love or find happiness in. Like, any time ya think things are lookin' up… BAM! It hits ya like a fuckin' rocket… sends ya spiralin' down like a plane out the air.

"But ya can't let it keep doin' that. Ya gotta pull yer 'chute and land on the ground. Pick ya self up and get up there again. I'm starin' death in the fuckin' eye, man… but that don't mean I'm gonna run from it. Gotta walk with the mother fucka and see what comes next. I dunno… maybe I'll get lucky."

Jay broke himself from his trance. The words Red had spoken sunk deep into Jay's subconscious and nestled themselves comfortably there. Jay let out a sigh and presented Red with his hand.

"Well," Jay said, "I'm not religious, but let's see if I can at least do a favor for ya, while you're still livin'."

Red flashed a weak smile, took Jay's hand, and bowed his head. Jay followed suit and began a faithless prayer of empty platitudes. He said the typical things people usually do in prayers. Asking God for his forgiveness, grace, and blessings. Asking Him to guide Red where he went afterward. Jay wasn't sure if he believed anything he said, but he could feel Red's comfort through the trembles in his hand. Whether Red would meet his mother in heaven, hell, or the void, Jay was glad he could provide his friend with some sort of consolation and closure.

Jay scanned his cell one last time. The bulletproof glass and metal shutter still proved impenetrable. The boarded-up entrance that led to the main part of the store was surprisingly sturdy with no clear means of escape. Jay could set the wooden barricade ablaze, but the ensuing fire would cause too much commotion—with not enough time to formulate a getaway. The metal door was also devoid of any fault. The heavy exit was sealed shut by a hefty latch and lock from the outside. Only the faint red glow of The Anomaly seeped through the space between the door and frame.

Plans upon plans raced through Jay's mind. His renewed determination had given fuel to his goal of reaching the U.P.. The two guards that had come in to take the sacrifices were well-armed. He'd need the help of another if he hoped to take them out, but Red was in no condition to fight. Since their prayer, Red had fallen silent and absentminded. The agony from his broken arm had exhausted his mind.

Jay had rested well the night before and reserved his energy. Although he was nowhere near his peak, he'd be able to muster some sort of substantial resistance. He felt thin and his stomach rumbled, but the burning desire to keep his promise was now bursting inside. Tonight, he *needed* to run.

Just as Jay nearly became totally lost in his plotting, a loud clattering could be heard outside the metal door. The lock was being undone. They had come for Red. Jay stood up and locked his eyes on the door. He awaited the two guards with bated breath as the metal clank of the latch swung and smacked the outside face of the door. With a rusty creak, the door swung open, and two guards trudged into the small cashier's area.

The larger guard looked all-too-familiar. His fat, towering stature was the same as the guard that had dragged Jay into camp the night he was drugged. Over the guard's shoulder was slung a crossbow that Jay recognized: Benu's. The abomination must've found it a suitable war prize for his capture. On his hip, a large knife was sheathed and strapped.

A smaller guard followed in behind him. He was of average size but dwarfed by the giant that accompanied him. Armed with a hatchet on his hip, he posed a comparatively lower threat than his counterpart. Still, he seemed to be in good shape and could easily overpower Jay if met head-to-head. Both men were covered in the putrid growths that the rest of the tribe had. The flowering buds that peppered their skin leaked waxy residue down their sweating faces.

Without a word, the larger guard bent down and pulled Red up by his swollen arm. Red squeaked out a whimpering cry as his head hung to the side. Jay took a step forward, ready to fight, but the smaller guard shoved him back against the wall and shook his head with a tight grimace. Jay could only watch past the guard's shoulder as Red was stripped of his clothes like a lamb being sheared before slaughter.

Red's body was covered in scars. A life filled with hardship and struggle was worn plainly on his skin. The bright, puffy inflammation of his left arm had been made clear now. The circumference of his elbow was a deep, black-purple that blended into a bright tomato-red that traveled down to his fingertips. The fat guard grasped Red's face in his palm and jerked it towards him, looking deep into his eyes. Red could only murmur unintelligible obscenities as he made weak attempts to wriggle away.

"Mmm, no need for the drug on this one," said the larger guard. "He's already gone."

He then scooped up Red over his shoulder and motioned to the smaller guard to grab Red's clothes off the ground. The larger guard was holding the door open with his foot, facing out into the blackness of night. As the smaller guard turned away from Jay and bent over to pick up Red's clothes, Jay took his chance.

With a fierce lunge, Jay clamped his hand around the kneeling guard's head from behind. He then plunged his index fingers into each of the guard's ears as deep as he could. In an instant, Jay heated his fingertips inside the guard's skull to a frightening temperature. Like two concentrated blowtorches, Jay's index fingers scorched the inside of the guard's skull. Jay could feel the smattered mass of viscous flesh drain out of the guard's earholes as the liquified brain matter caked around Jay's fingers. Digging his middle fingers into the guard's eyes, he lit them ablaze with the same force and melted away the entirety of the eyeballs, leaving nothing but empty caves of burnt flesh.

The guard had opened his mouth to scream, but Jay's assassination was so swift and precise that all the dead man could mutter was a soft groan as he tumbled to the floor. The thud of the fallen body alerted the larger guard at the door; but, by the time he turned to face the commotion, Jay already had an open palm a few inches from his face. Jay flashed a brief pop of fire in the larger guard's face, blinding him just long enough for Jay to slip past.

Three steps were only as far as Jay got before he was lifted up by his shirt collar from behind. Just on the other side of the door to the right, out of view, The Voice waited for any sign of escape. He had snatched Jay with his inhuman strength and held him off the ground. Reeling him in, he placed his other hand around Jay's neck. Like a reed in the wind, Jay's neck was just a twist away from being snapped by The Voice's clammy paw. Jay clawed away at the waxy wrist that escorted him back into the cell. With a raspy grunt, The Voice tossed Jay across the floor, causing him to collide with the wall at the far end. He was now back where he started.

The larger guard still had Red over his shoulder as he rubbed away the dancing stars in his vision from the blinding flash Jay delivered. The Voice stood there in the doorway, filling the space with his bulging silhouette against the evening glow. He produced a dribbling, mangled smile and grumbled: "Oh yes, you are special indeed. Heh-heh. But I told you. Yes… I told you. You have to wait your turn… The engine… At first, I thought it would merely drink on your blood as it did the others, but oh no… no… no… it will *feast* on you. And, in your death, you will bring us salvation. Yes…"

The Voice stepped forward into the cell and bent over the dead guard. The seams in his baggy cargo pants rustled and groaned under the immense weight of his bloated body. His shirtless upper body squelched as the folds of fat slid against each other. He retrieved the axe and a hidden blade from the corpse, looked up at Jay, and said: "Can't have you *sacrificing* yourself now, can we? Heh-heh."

With a motion of his head, The Voice ordered the larger guard to step outside and carry Red to his fate. Jay called out to him, but Red was already unconscious, taken by the overflow of pain and stress. The Voice chortled once more as he backed out of the cell and slammed the door shut. Jay rushed at the door and attempted to force it open, but the flip of the latch and snap of the lock confirmed the door had been secured. Jay was trapped, once again, for the night.

"Shit!" Jay exclaimed. He placed his hands over his head and took a few deep breaths. He knelt by the dead guard and searched his body for anything useful—*nothing*. Even if the guard had keys on him, the lock was on the outside. Jay still had a fair amount of energy in him. He could possibly burn a hole through the metal door, but that would be all he could muster before he'd need to seriously rest. On top of that, he had no idea where the latch was located. He should've taken note when he rushed out!

Jay did his best to calm himself but, now, he was next on the chopping block. Thoughts of his impending doom invaded his mind as he took his usual seat at the back of the cell. He pulled out his ring and twiddled it between his fingers.

Their wedding was small. Only a handful of friends and relatives showed. They were never much for gatherings or ostentatious displays of celebration. Everything they did was quaint—cheap, some would say. The spotlight of attention never appealed to either of them but, on such a joyous occasion, they allowed for some level of theatrics.

The wedding was held in a small conservatory on Belle Isle, the small island on the Detroit River between the U.S. and Canada. The sweltering humidity drowned both of them in their wedding attire.

Jay's tight-necked collar started to discolor from the sweat as he nervously adjusted his tie, waiting for Her to walk down their makeshift aisle flanked by folding, plastic chairs.

The thick air choked Jay as the sound of crickets and fluttering insects filled the high, glass dome. The room was bright—filled with the gleaming, diffused sunlight that hung overhead. Smells of a variety of tropical plants, flowers, ferns, and trees engulfed the sparsely populated room. She always wanted to be surrounded by the vast greenery of nature and its attributes.

No music accompanied Her as She was escorted through the double doors that sat at the end of the aisle. She walked with grace in Her pure white wedding dress. The laces that hemmed across Her breasts held an intricate, flowery design traced down the sides, ending at Her hips. The dress was sleeveless and featured a great, puffy skirt that made it look as if She was floating on a cloud. The ends dragged across the dirtied, concrete ground, staining them an earthly brown. Atop Her head sat a handmade flower crown that She had fashioned herself over months of gathering and preserving Her favorite flowers: carnations, roses, and lilies. Her uncle had his elbow locked with Hers as She hid flushed cheeks.

Jay could feel his face form an expression he hadn't felt before. One of anticipation and disbelief at the beauty of seeing their years of commitment soon come to a permanent bond. She was delivered to Jay as he took hold of Her hands. He looked Her in the eyes and studied Her face. Her soft, simple features looked no different from the day he met Her. He tightened his grip and hoped that the unrelenting love he felt for Her would miraculously pass from him into Her.

Jay wanted to recount Her long and affectionate vows, but his train of thought was derailed by the sound of the booming engine above. He could hear The Voice preaching his smattering of nonsense while the crowd hooped and hollered. The faint creak of a rising wooden pillar could be heard near the back of the store; Red's time had come. As Jay heard the rip of flesh, he winced at the imaginary sight.

A few moments passed, accompanied by the familiar ruckus of the sputtering engine and tribe clamoring. Jay was waiting out the end once again. Waiting for Red to finally bleed out; then the crowd would celebrate, disperse, and the dead quiet of night would lull Jay into a torturous slumber. He could hear the splash of blood against the rooftop begin to transpire into a lowly trickle. Soon, Jay would be left to his vices—left to wallow in his suffering.

But Red's words still stung. Jay couldn't help but hold that guilt he felt earlier tight against his heart. As he started to plot, a sound pinged against the metal door which he hadn't heard before. It sounded like a small rock had been hurled with force against it. What followed next was a muffled thud sliding against the back wall and falling to the ground, like a sack of potatoes had just slumped over and unfurled onto the floor.

Jay stood up and braced himself for the unexpected. He could hear some rustling just outside the door, followed by the fumbling of the lock. The fumbling stopped. The latch met the door softly. As it crept open, Jay readied himself to sprint out, but the familiar face that poked through the lower half of the door buckled his knees and nearly sent him to the floor.

He almost let out an elated call to Benu, but she quickly shushed him and motioned him to stay low and hurry over. He obeyed and crawled over to the door, being sure to keep below the counter—out of view of any onlookers that may be peering in from the front of the store. As he met Benu's face, he whispered, "Benu! Are ya ok?"

"Yes, yes," she replied curtly. "I am fine. Come now. We are leaving."

Jay nodded and squeezed himself out the back door. Benu carefully shut the door as Jay stood up and looked down to his left. The lumbering guard lay dead on the ground—a crossbow bolt penetrating completely through the front of his forehead and out the back. His open mouth was inviting a steady stream of infected puss that flowed steadily out the front wound. Jay snatched his nose shut as the piercing smell nearly caused him to gag. Next to the dead guard was a simple, rusty crossbow with a broken string; Benu had reclaimed her far-superior weapon and a handful of bolts to boot.

Jay looked over to Benu and thumbed over his shoulder to the dead guard. "Another warning shot?"

Benu smirked as she slung her crossbow over her shoulder and brought her backpack forward. She opened it and pulled out an energy bar from her stash. Handing it to Jay, she muttered, "Keep that sense of humor up, Jay. I bet it is what has kept you alive so far."

Jay gobbled down the food and tossed the wrapper aside. No point in worrying about litter when the world was about to end. The sweet chocolate that surrounded the wafer bar was like heaven in his mouth. The sharp rush of nutrition was nearly so foreign to him that he wanted to giggle with joy, but he kept his composure and finished it off. As he gulped the last bite, Benu pulled out something that helped ignite Jay's vigor more than any prepackaged energy bar.

The little, pewter urn glinted in the moonlight and reflected a soft bath of red from the black diamond. Jay met the sight with a quivering sigh and frown which then morphed into a timid smile. He peered at Benu with moistened eyes and whispered, "Thank you."

"Here," she replied, motioning the urn towards him.

"No, I have nowhere to put it. Go ahead. Hold it for me please."

Benu was stunned for a moment but quickly agreed, placed the urn back in her bag, and re-situated it on her back as she unslung her crossbow and held it at the ready.

"We should go *now!*" she quipped as she started to walk towards the broken wall. Just then, the noise of the crowd began to simmer down. Jay turned around and shot his attention up towards the tower on which the engine sat. He could see the ritualists begin to work their way around the tower to lower Red's corpse and shut off the engine. Jay traced his view up to a joint at one of the top corners of the tower. The bolts appeared rusted. The construction was poor, missing the simplest of bracings and skirtings. The tower creaked and groaned with unsteadiness. Jay aimed his hand at the weakened joint and turned to Benu.

"Get ready to run," he said.

Benu, wide-eyed, shook her head furiously.

"We need a distraction!" Jay rebutted.

Benu sucked her teeth, rolled her eyes, and braced herself. Jay shot out his open palm and peppered the tower with a volley of tennis ball-sized projectiles. It only took three hits from the small shots to blow away a main support. The howls of ritualists filled the night air as their god began to topple over the side of the tower.

The tower buckled and swayed as the fire from Jay's attack began to engulf the oil-soaked wood. The Voice could be heard bellowing out pious curses and orders in an attempt to quell the panicked crowd. Wooden beams began to splinter as embers fluttered in the breeze. The clear tubing of the fuel lines flung free and whipped fiery fuel across the rooftop. The blaze traveled up the tube and popped the gas reservoir with a deafening bang, sending shards of plastic all around. The crackle of the torches whistled through the air as they snapped from their pedestals and spiraled down. With a low groan, the tower finally collapsed inward, sending the great, fiery V8 crashing down through the roof of the store.

The fluorescent lights flickered for a moment as debris of dust, flames, wood, and concrete shot up into the air. Then, like the screeching howl of a dying bear, the engine within the storefront exploded, producing a monstrous boom through the funneled hole above it. A whirlwind of fire shot up for a moment as Jay turned to Benu.

"Let's go!"

{Chapter 13}

4:21:57:57

The uproar of the tribe faded as Jay and Benu sprinted through the suburbs. In the cold, dead darkness, they ran through overgrown lawns and hopped broken fences. They could faintly hear the rustle of disturbed grasses behind them as pursuers were hot on their trail. Jay could see that the gas station's lights had now become a small pinpoint between the houses and storefronts, but the fanatics wouldn't dare let the god-killers escape.

Benu was leading. She motioned back to Jay to turn down a narrow road, flanked by duplexes with barely any space between the structures. Her heavy breathing was like a hurricane in her ears accompanied by the thundering stomps of her boots. Her vision began to tunnel and blur; she needed to take a breather. She pointed over to an open door and headed towards it with Jay in tow.

As Benu crashed through the door, it slammed and buckled under the blow. It hung for a moment from its top hinge before succumbing to its weight and collapsing to the floor just in front of Jay. The falling door caused him to recoil and nearly lose his balance, but he regained his composure and stepped in behind Benu. She had moved into the kitchen at the back and was leaning against the back wall to catch her breath; her crossbow was placed on the countertop.

Jay jogged in and placed his hands behind his head. They both said nothing as they caught their breath. Benu stood up straight, still gasping, and pulled out a half-empty water bottle from her bag. She gulped down half of what was left and tossed it to Jay. He took no time to say anything and just as swiftly downed the rest and tossed the empty bottle back to Benu.

They could hear the growing cries of pursuing guards from outside the front door, including one that rumbled with a fierce tenacity that had plagued them for three nights: The Voice. Orders and directions were being shouted every which way as the tribe shifted into a methodical search. Jay looked over his shoulder, down the hallway that led out to the front door, and scooted out of view.

Finally, he whispered: "We're in no shape to outrun them."

"I know," Benu replied as she finished taking in one final, deep breath before wiping the dried snot off of her nose. She looked out through a window above the kitchen sink. In the red-bathed darkness, she scanned for any means of losing their hunters. The back of the duplex was facing a large city highway that separated residential from commercial. On the other side, Benu could make out a row of big box department stores that could prove to be suitable mazes in which to buy them time.

One, in particular, looked as if the powered, sliding doors were left wide open. This entrance belonged to a large tan hardware store, lined by trims of orange. Over the entrance was a large, muted-orange, metal awning that encompassed a small glass foyer. Inside, rows of bright-orange shopping carts were scattered about. At the top of the building, built at the center, was the silhouette of the idealistic rooftop—peaked perfectly and spanning across a majority of the front of the building.

Benu pointed towards the hardware store and looked over to Jay, "We can lose them in there. I doubt they have the manpower to search all those buildings in any reasonable time. When they are preoccupied with another store, we can slip out the back."

Jay nodded. "Sounds like a–"

"Hey, over here!" shouted a voice down the hall. Jay whipped his head around the corner to see a mutated woman armed with a bat signaling to others through the front door. "They in here!" she cried.

"Shit!" Benu exclaimed. She snatched her crossbow, loaded a bolt, and fired down the hallway. The bolt whistled through the air and struck the woman just above the left breast. She yelped a succinct cry of pain as the blow sent her stumbling out the front door and onto the lawn. Benu was already bursting through the back door as Jay listened for the encroaching threat. He could hear approaching war cries as he turned tail, swung open the back door, and booked it for the hardware store.

As they weaved through the sea of abandoned cars on the highway, Jay looked back to see pillars of dancing lights flickering between the duplexes. The tribesmen were now far from home, no longer caring for subtle pursuit. Their flashlights were like the glowing eyes of a beast in the night, stalking its fleeing prey. Jay turned his attention forward and focused on Benu. They had just finished crossing the crumbling highway and were making their way across the pothole-riddled parking lot.

The shower of light that washed over Jay felt like a blast of ice-cold water against his back. Someone had their flashlight fixated solely on him, and it sent a jolt of shivers up his spine. The stain of yellow light jostled past him and lit up Benu as well. He could tell that the illumination caused her to pick up the pace. The 'whoosh' of a crossbow bolt whistled somewhere to his left and skipped across the pitted asphalt. Another, to his right, shot past Benu and plinked off the glass of the foyer. They rounded the entrance and hurried into the store.

The old hardware store was in a state of severe disrepair. A large shaft of sparkling moonlight shone through a twenty-foot-wide hole in the roof onto the tool aisle where a large slab of concrete and rebar lay—a remnant of The Anomaly's pull. Underneath the slab was a multitude of crushed products: hammers, jigsaws, lights, toolboxes, levels, and screwdrivers. The large steel shelving of the aisle next to it had taken the brunt of the blow and sat, mangled and partly unscathed at the end, towards the front of the store.

From the hole, streams and drips of rainwater flowed onto the floor below, echoing 'plips' and 'plops' throughout the empty store. Jay and Benu worked their way down Aisle 5: Cleaning. Along the shelves sat a variety of overturned and broken cleaners, detergents, mops, paper products, and degreasers. A majority of the store had been pillaged and pilfered from the early days of the apocalypse. Old stains of blood mixed with the spilled chemicals from the struggles and scuffles of times long past littered the ground.

The store was devoid of sound, save for the echoing creaks and groans of strained supports and crumbling shelving. The soft blue moonlight that permeated the area barely lit the way for Jay and Benu. They crept down the aisle and took a seat at the end cap. Above them sat waterlogged boxes of clearance items: power tools, gloves, power cords, and tape.

Jay felt as if his short breaths were pinging off every wall in the desolate store, somehow reverberating back to the entrance and leading The Voice and his cohorts back to him and Benu. Jay scanned the area. They were sitting in the large section that bisected the store, separating the front aisles from the back. Part of the slab that had pierced the roof was laying in the large, central aisle. Scattered tools peppered the floor. Directly to Jay's left, across the section, was the appliance showcase. Every appliance was caked with a thick layer of dust and grime. None were taken—too heavy and useless to be bothered with. Down the long section were overhanging signs.

At the very end, one sign reading "LUMBER" dangled vertically from a singular chain; the other was broken and swaying around, kissing the concrete floor. Jay had visited hardware stores like this often. Whenever he needed parts or tools for his job, the big orange store would be there for him to provide the bolt, nut, washer, drill bit, or driver he needed. He knew the loading dock, where workers would take in product from delivery trucks, was located at the back. That would be their exit.

As Jay cooked up a plan, the yellow gleam of flashlights cast shadow puppets against the mosaic of shelves and items before him. The tribesmen had entered the store and were drifting their lights across the aisles. Rays of amber passed through the pinholes that lined the metal shelving and flickered across the walls of the store. The reflected lights bounced off the sheen of the concrete floor and dimly lit Benu's face.

She waited as the light passed and peeked around the aisle. Two guards with flashlights flanked a blubbering giant. His rusty, cobbled crown of fasteners and hand tools caught small glints of twilight. He was panting—no doubt from carrying three-men-worth of weight in blubber. Benu could hear no other footsteps besides those three. She retracted her head and nudged Jay. Holding up three fingers, she mouthed '*three.*'

Jay nodded and gathered his thoughts. He systematically worked through every scenario he could that would guarantee them escape without confrontation—but found none. Even offering up a howling distraction would simply delay the inevitable. Their dwindling strength wouldn't allow them to lose these beasts in a chase. Jay figured that cutting the snake off at the head would be their best option.

Jay looked over to Benu and gestured his thumb across his throat, cutting it. He motioned over in the direction of the men with his head. Benu sucked in her lips and bit them. She exhaled with reluctant acceptance and prepared herself.

"Come out!" bellowed The Voice. "Come out, you heathens—you who have destroyed everything we worked so hard to build!" As The Voice continued, Benu loaded a bolt under the veil of his roaring dribble. "Oh, I am *not* pleased! *Not* pleased at all! You have sullied the names and lives of those who were given to the great engine… Have you no shame—no sense of self-hate?"

Jay and Benu rose to a crouching position, their backs against the endcap. Jay positioned himself to ambush the left side; Benu took the right. Peeking between the pillars of the shelving, Benu could see one of the men making his way down the cleaning aisle. He was but a dark, human-shaped blob with a spotlight in his hand that he swayed left and right, near his waist. As he slinked down the aisle, The Voice spoke again:

"Do you believe this to be righteous? Oh no… no… no. *I* have heard from Him up above! Oh yes… the V8 was but a physical representation. But *His* voice—*His* soul—lives on in me! And *He* demands sacrifice. Yes… I will appease Him without fail… just as I always have…"

The shouting from The Voice was moving across the store. Jay could follow it as it moved away from him to his left, towards the lumber. He turned to face the front of the store, now. Searching for the other light, he could see it moving somewhere near the center aisles, to his right now: Tools. It was working its way down, just over two aisles from Jay. He waited for the spotlight to move away from his direction. As it drifted away, he snuck over to the next endcap.

Benu shot a glance at Jay, hoping his movement hadn't compromised her position. She turned her attention back towards the approaching threat and could see that Jay's scuffle had caught his attention. He dipped and ducked his head around, trying to peer through the shelving. The rapid movement of his flashlight stung Benu's eyes. She took a small step back, turned on the balls of her feet, and shouldered her crossbow.

The man slinked forward, now standing fifteen or so paces from Benu.

Now was her chance!

With a robotic pop and lock, she leaned over into Aisle 5 and fired her bolt. The projectile whizzed through the air and planted itself deep into the man's jugular. He dropped his flashlight, causing it to flicker, and grasped his neck. Benu wasted no time and rushed him. As she ran up to him, she pulled out her knife and plunged it upwards through his chin. The waxy puss oozed out and splattered as she ripped out her blade.

As the man slumped to the floor, his head smacked a shelf and knocked down a few scarce bottles of Simple Green. The spray bottles bounced by his bleeding head with a buoyant thud that echoed down the aisle and through the store. Benu was suddenly illuminated by a light from the center of the store. The other pursuer had fixed his light on her through the slits of product and shelving.

Jay sprang into action. He rounded the endcap and bolted for the man before him. The man whipped his light in Jay's face, blinding him for a moment, but Jay continued to press on and tackled him to the ground, full-mounting him. The flashlight ejected from the tribe member's hand and skipped away towards the front of the store. In his other hand, he wielded a hatchet. As he brought his arm back for a swing, Jay took hold of his wrist and placed his other hand on the man's face. Simultaneously, Jay heated up his hands.

As the tribesman's waxy skin boiled, the smell of bursting pustules shot up Jay's nose. The assault on his nostrils caused Jay to recoil and retch. Gagging, Jay released his hands and stood up to instinctively remove himself from that wretched odor. The weakened man clamored to his feet. Jay had burned away a majority of the man's face. Bubbling, black flesh encompassed the left half of his mutated mug. The ball of melted eyebrow had fused over his left eye. Snow white cheekbones and jawbone could be seen peeking through the strings of meaty sinews.

His left wrist shared the same properties. Jay had cooked away enough meat to reduce the man's wrist to a smoldering twig, held together by strands of dead muscle. However, miraculously, the man held a tight grip on his hatchet. Panting from the attack, he looked up at Jay with his one good eye and let out a howling scream as he stepped forward, raising his hatchet high above his head.

The lumbering strike was slow and clumsy. Jay quickstepped to the left and aimed a kick at the inside of the man's left knee. The snap hadn't guaranteed a break, but it was enough to cause the man to buckle onto Jay. As he fell inward, Jay took hold of the hatchet with his right hand and gripped the man's wounded wrist with the other. Again, he heated up his hand. This time, the immense heat caused Jay's hand to burst into flame.

The mutant man yelped as he collapsed to his knees. Jay ripped the hatchet from him and let him go. The man curled up and gripped his bloodied and charred wrist, crying obscenities as he rolled over. Jay loomed over him, breathing heavily.

The thought of letting this pathetic creature go was but a blip in Jay's mind. As Jay hacked away at the man's skull, he had nearly forgotten where he was. The bloodlust was coursing through his veins. The bloodied mess he had made of the once-human skull was completely unrecognizable.

"Jay!" screamed Benu from behind him. Jay whipped around to see The Voice facing him, standing tall at the end of the aisle. To his left, where Jay had initially been, Benu was reloading. Benu's bolt was lodged in The Voice's meaty left shoulder while Jay was lost in the slaughter. The Voice smiled that same drooling smile Jay had grown so accustomed to and pointed a fat finger at Jay.

"Gotcha," he grumbled.

Jay gathered himself. He realized he was in the center aisle of the store where small tanks of propane needed for blowtorches were stocked. He looked near The Voice's feet, at the bottom of the shelves, and caught a glimpse of dark green bottles amongst the shadow.

The Voice took a waddling step forward. As he squeezed into the aisle, his massive arms bumped the shelving and caused the metal tanks to clang off each other like chimes. Without hesitation, Jay fired a flurry of flames towards the sounds. An orchestra of hisses sounded off just before erupting into a deafening bang that exploded into the left side of The Voice.

Fire whooshed up his blubbery mass as shrapnel from the tanks dug itself deep into his leg. Jay shielded his eyes from the blast and looked on as the explosion died down. The resulting blast had scorched the aisle and set it ablaze. Bits of metal shards whizzed through the air behind The Voice, barely missing Benu. Jay could see The Voice was still stunned when he decided to turn back down the aisle, circle it, and regroup with Benu. As they met, The Voice worked himself out of the aisle. Benu took aim.

The Voice stared down at them through slitted eyelids. He still held his sinister, nearly toothless smile. His blackened skin creaked a bit as his folds of fat slid about. The flickering light of the inferno to his right danced across his face. His breaths gurgled as he panted.

Benu wriggled her nose. Even after four kills, the burning, mutated puss still stung her nose. What was one more? She fired her crossbow, aiming for The Voice's head. However, the bolt launched with a metallic snapping noise that reverberated with a twang from her bow. The mechanism jammed halfway and sent her shot wide, missing the giant completely.

"Fuck! Fuck!" shouted Benu.

The Voice let out a rumbling, mocking laugh as he lunged across the large dividing aisle and picked up a dryer over his head. With a belching grunt, he hurled the dryer at the shelving to Jay and Benu's right. The white Kenmore lodged itself neatly in their path and tempted the high, orange shelving to topple. It creaked and groaned for a short while until it finally succumbed to The Voice's monstrous blow.

The domino effect of the toppling shelves caused Jay and Benu to brace themselves as the clangs of steel shelving boomed throughout the store. As the dust settled, Jay peered over the overturned shelving to search for a means of escape. He was looking for the loading dock, but it was nowhere to be found. *Shit,* he thought. *It's one of those stores. Gotta be back by Lumber. Fuck!*

As The Voice straightened up from his gargantuan feat, Jay looked through the moonlight shaft towards the corner of the store and could see his suspicion was confirmed. The loading dock, their escape route, was located just down the Lumber aisle… past this beast.

Benu slung her broken crossbow over her back and tightened the strap so it wouldn't jostle when she ran. In the distance, towards the front of the store, shouting could be heard.

"Hear that?" said The Voice. "It's over. Oh yes, no more. See how devout they are? How loyal they are to the engine? To its voice? They figured we was gone too long." He pointed another fat finger at Jay. "I don't know what you are… but… killing you… oh yes, I think this is the sign I've been waiting for. The last sacrifice for salvation!"

"Benu," Jay said, ignoring the fat man. "Follow my lead, ok?"

Benu nodded and bent her knees to make a break for it at Jay's signal.

Jay swiveled the hatchet in his hand. He took the same stance as Benu and focused his attention on The Voice's bulging eyes. He watched as they danced between him and Benu. Soon, he could tell, The Voice would make his move. Jay only hoped his retaliation would be as precise as he had envisioned it. A jolt of numbness shot through Jay's body as he felt The Voice's reinforcements draw near. He dug his feet in.

All that could be heard was the crackle of the growing fire that Jay had created. In the stillness of the blue hue of moonlight, Jay could feel his heart skip a beat—an instinctual signal that fired like a starter pistol.

The Voice bolted forward, his arms wide open. The quake of his thick legs slammed the ground with each stomp. Jay shot out his free hand and fired a fireball right at the charging bull's face. It collided with a thunderous explosion, causing The Voice's vision to be filled with blinding flame. In that moment, Jay ducked to the right, under The Voice's sweeping arm, and buried his hatchet into the crevice of The Voice's knee, leaving it there.

The Voice cried out in agony as he fell to one knee.

Jay and Benu rushed past. As they hopped over the slab that sat partially in the center aisle, spilled tools and items were kicked out of the way. They bolted under the hanging "LUMBER" sign and found themselves at the T-intersection that led into the lumber aisle. Turning around like a couple of deer in headlights, they saw that Jay's strike had little effect on The Voice. He had already recovered and was charging in hot pursuit, spurting heaps of infected blood out of his left leg.

In a frenzy, Benu scanned the endcaps they stood between. Immediately to her left were a few bottles of lighter fluid. A sign hung above them: "CLEARANCE: 2 bottles of Zippo lighter fluid for only $5.99!" Benu took the deal and snapped the caps off the bottles. She chucked them at the charging giant. As they flew through the air, splashes of fluid sprayed the floor. One smacked The Voice squarely in the chest, and the other skimmed off his shoulder, coating his face.

"Jay!" Benu ordered.

Jay outstretched his right arm and splayed out his hand. This would be his final attack for the night. The short stint of energy he had reserved was wearing off, and he could feel his arm waver and his knees tremble. He fired off two quick shots. Both mirrored Benu's lighter fluid toss; one struck The Voice in the chest and the other glanced his cheek. With a fiery boom, The Voice's upper body was engulfed in flames. The raging fanatic continued charging, screaming bloody murder at the top of his lungs.

Jay and Benu dove out of the way and into the aisle towards the back as The Voice barreled past them into a stack of 2x4s. He braced himself with his ignited arms and held himself there for a moment. The flames spilled off of him and transferred onto the wood, setting them ablaze. The towering inferno turned towards Benu and Jay.

The lumbering mass of melting blubber plodded towards them. The sea of growths, pimples, boils, and cysts popped and burst under the rolling flame that encompassed The Voice. Each swollen pustule bloomed and unfurled as they spewed hot, boiling ooze across the crackled and crispy flesh. His metal crown had become heated to a point of searing through his face's skin and cartilage. As it sunk into his flesh, it began to slip down his skull, scraping away the goopy meat and exposing bits of pure white bone. His arms were slumped to his side, swaying and sticking to the boiling fat of his upper body. A murmuring could be faintly heard through the roar of the fire, but whatever words The Voice was trying to speak were being strangled by his collapsing throat.

Taking a few steps back, Jay and Benu winced at the repugnant display of human mutilation. As The Voice trudged near, he fell to his knees, reached out a hand, and slammed onto the ground face-first. The hardy splat of his enormous body felt as if it had shaken the entire store. Traces of fizzing, yellow blood sprayed out from around his eviscerated body. All around, the store fire raged on, spreading rapidly down the aisles. Jay and Benu hurried towards the back of the store and out the rear exit, through the loading dock. As the metal door slammed shut, The Voice let out a final, gurgled breath.

{Chapter 14}

4:18:26:38

Once they were sure they were clear of the tribe, Benu tossed Jay a half-eaten energy bar. He gobbled it down to the wrapper and threw the trash to the ground. That was her last one.

They had stumbled to the northern border of the city. In the far distance behind them, a billow of smoke rose into the starlight. Ahead of him, Benu dragged her feet, her crossbow slung on her back. Her arms had tired of carrying it, and she was far too tired to aim it, even if she had to.

It was raining again. It was just a drizzle, but the chilling September air made each drop sting like a needle against Jay's face. Through the cold, the two headed towards a supermarket to resupply. They had spotted the supermarket from down the road and decided to try their luck at finding supplies and shelter for the night.

Benu looked back to check on Jay. His face was sagging, and his shoulders were slumped. She could tell he was ready to pass out at the drop of a hat. She did her best to fight off her own fatigue, but she was fooling no one; she was ready to drop to the floor as well. "Come on," she called with wearied breath. "Not much further."

Her Hindi accent and rapid speech were accentuated by her fatigue. Jay had to contemplate what he'd just heard for a moment before nodding silently in reassurance that he was ok.

As they approached the store, Benu noted the glass on the powered door was completely shattered. The horizontal, metal bars that reinforced the doors created a barricade that Jay and Benu would have to crawl under. Benu ducked and wormed her way inside, being mindful of the blades of glass that remained intact. As she stepped inside, she turned to see Jay slinking his way in and rising to meet her. They scanned the dark, open space at the entrance. Benu slipped off her backpack—careful to make only faint noise—and reached in, retrieving a right-angle flashlight. She flicked it on and moved it towards the registers.

"Shabriri?" Jay whispered.

"Unlikely," Benu replied, peering where her light shone. "They prefer houses—more enclosed spaces—but… all the shit we did back there would have definitely attracted one." She swayed her light towards the produce section. "One could be hiding, so we should–"

Her light stopped. Jay had seen it too. Two bright, reflective, yellow eyes were lit up just behind a stand of rotten apples. Two erect ears twitched in response as it gnawed one final chew before leaping over the stand. Benu held her light on the doe as it pranced past Jay and out the front entrance, clearing over the metal bar with grace. Two more emerged shortly after from the dark and galloped out the store. Jay and Benu let out a breath they'd been holding since spotting the first deer.

"We should be safe," Benu continued, "Deer do not typically hang around where shabriri hunt."

Jay shot Benu a relieved smirk; she replied with one of her own. She clipped her flashlight to her cowl and clapped her hands, rubbing them.

"All right," she said, "looks like we have the store to ourselves!"

She turned to grab a shopping cart when Jay clasped her shoulder.

"We should scope out the store first," he said. "Shabriri aren't the only monsters out here." He motioned his head towards the entrance.

"Hmph, you are right," Benu replied, embarrassed by her fatigued-tainted logic. She unslung her crossbow and turned off her light. Blackness washed over their eyes briefly as they adjusted back to the dark. "I will take the left half of the store and check the back— where the storage is. You take the right and meet me there. Sound good?"

"Yeah," Jay replied with a nod. Benu had taken a step to her right before Jay stopped her, "Thanks, by the way."

Benu turned around, walking backward, "Hmph, that is *twice* I have saved your life, *dost*. Do not forget it!"

Jay chortled and shook his head. He began creeping through the registers. The layout was a typical, cookie-cutter supermarket. They had come in through the "produce" entrance that led into a large, open area, lined down the middle with empty stands. Jay moved through the self-checkout area. The machines were all broken and busted, looted of their cash. Along the small shelves that surrounded the area were stacks of old magazines and celebrity newspapers. The scowling faces of celebrities facing rumored divorces, scandals, and affairs were masked by layers of dust and grime.

As he exited the area and moved into the right half of the store, he looked down the front aisles that held seasonal items. Above the row of shelves hung a banner that read "Back 2 School!". Jay moved up and down the aisles. Mice and cockroaches scurried away from his feet as he walked. Coming across a row of backpacks, he pulled a blue schoolbag off the hook. He dusted it off and inspected it for any gnawing from rodents… or deer. It was untouched—just dirty from sitting around. He slipped it on and continued moving through the store.

Passing by the toys, he took note of the few bikes that sat on the upper racks. Office, home supplies, automotive, and paint were all clear. The shelves remained mostly stocked. People were mainly after food, clothes, and maybe a few tools. As he passed through electronics, he could see Benu by the storage area where they planned to meet. He passed by the shattered TVs that hung crookedly on their displays. Glass cases were all broken into and emptied of their expensive contents. It seemed that, even at the end of days, people still longed for their high-end gadgets—either for entertainment or for profit. As Jay neared Benu, he looked down the aisle that housed the portable speakers and other audio equipment. The slumped remains of someone were being gnawed on by a group of rats. The body was mostly decomposed; only small strings of meat were being pulled off exposed bones. Its skull was bashed in—probably over a wireless speaker or pair of headphones. Jay paid it little mind and met up with Benu.

"Well? Your side clear?" he whispered.

"Yeah," she replied, "and yours?"

"Yup," Jay said, speaking audibly now. "We're good."

"Good," she flicked the light on her cowl and walked into the back area, returning with a shopping cart. "There is still some good food and medical supplies. I will go grab what I can."

"Cool. I spotted some bikes by the toys. I'll see what I can do."

Benu nodded as Jay turned around. She noticed his new backpack.

"Hold on," she called as she slipped off her backpack and retrieved the urn. She handed it to Jay who took it delicately in his hands. The cold pewter was ice to his skin but warmth to his heart. The relief he felt washed over him like a tingling wave, and he was partially upset with himself that his fatigue had caused him to forget that he had the means to carry Her again. He sighed and slipped the urn into his backpack.

"I… don't know how to thank you, Benu," Jay said.

"Hmph, find something that will make *me* thank *you*," she replied, sticking her tongue out the corner of her lips. "Scream if anything crazy happens."

Jay smiled and slipped his backpack back on. The lousy rattle of the clunky shopping cart wheels began to fade behind Jay as he headed towards the toy section. He pondered Benu's resolve. She had just fought through hell and back, yet still maintained her quick-wittedness. The tone of her voice was neither somber nor hopeless. There was a fiery drive inside her that burned hotter than any flame Jay could produce.

Jay stopped by the tools section. Various hand tools, parts, and packages were scattered on the shelves. The disheveled mess proved difficult for Jay to make out anything useful in the dark. Bringing his left thumb, index, and middle fingers together, he manifested a torch for himself. He hovered it over the myriad of items until he found a hard, blow-molded case near the bottom. Pulling it out, he could see the thin, cardboard slip that wrapped the case was still intact. He wiped away the dust to reveal a picture of various useful tools and a label that read: "Homeowner's Kit: everything you need." Jay ripped off the cardboard sleeve and popped open the plastic latches. Inside, the tools were loose, but all accounted for. He popped each item back into their respective places and tucked the closed case into his bag.

Continuing down the right wall of the store with a flame in hand, Jay could see he was coming up on the sports and camping supplies. *Would be nice to have some sleeping bags*, he thought. He searched through the products: dumbbells, tennis balls, yoga mats, cooking stoves, fishing rods. Finally, he came upon a pile of the store's cheapest sleeping bags. Since anything could be taken for free, why not go for the highest quality items? Unfortunately, Jay had come long past that opportunity and had to settle on two thin sleeping bags. He tied the pull strings of each of their cases around the straps of his backpack. As he walked past the airsoft guns, the plushy cases bounced against each of his legs.

Jay thought of Benu's words.

Find something to make me thank you.

He held a flame to the empty shelves of airsoft guns. Only a few spring power pistols and accessories lay scattered across them. Squatting, he could see a few sights and scopes had been left behind. Near the back, he could spot a box with a picture of a sniper scope on it. He reached back and pulled it forward. Tipping it towards the light, he whispered the contents to himself, "Six times magnification… adjustable… comfortable… yadda yadda… fits standard tactical rails…" Jay rolled his eyes towards the ceiling, searching his memory. He closed his eyes, lifted one corner of his lips, and thought hard. Forming the image of Benu's crossbow across her back, he recalled that it *might* have a tactical rail. He relaxed his face and opened his eyes, "Yeah, yeah… it's got one…" As he stood, he placed the box in his backpack and continued towards the bikes.

With his light in his hand, Jay had now noticed how empty the shelves of the toy section were. Jay sighed with grief as he thought of the daughter he could've had with Her. The early mornings of walking his daughter to school or afternoons playing make-believe with the toys he would have surely showered her with. But the world moved away from that timeline. The Anomaly had different plans.

He let the moment pass over him and held his light up to the bike rack above him. In the far distance, he could hear Benu's cart skating along, stopping at various times to supposedly gather supplies. Jay could spot two bikes that looked to be in decent shape, right above him. At the end of the aisle where he stood, a service ladder was parked against the bike rack. Putting out his flame, he grabbed the ladder and moved it into place. He ascended the ladder and retrieved the first bike, being careful not to lose his balance. Backing down near the bottom, he lifted the mountain bike over the railing and leaned it against the ladder.

He went to retrieve the other one. Pulling it from its rack, he could see its aquamarine paint was nearly pristine. A small basket was mounted at the front. It was a utility bike. The low, swooping frame made it easy to mount. The handlebar was simple, with no gear selector. No hand brakes were present either; the bike relied on backpedaling to stop. The bike was nearly identical to the one She rode over seven years ago.

She had asked Jay about the people he'd want to invite to his birthday. They were pedaling their usual route around their neighborhood. She rode hands-free; she had done so since she first learned to ride a bike. Every weekend, they would spend a couple of hours riding together. The fresh summer air provided no excuse to get out and enjoy it. Jay cruised on alongside her as he replied over his shoulder: "I dunno. I don't think Keif or Danny would be able to make it. They're still movin' into their new places across the state."

She suggested a few more names. Names that Jay hadn't heard since high school.

"Nah, they're way too far away."

Most of Jay's friends had moved out of state. Many found jobs elsewhere in the nation. Others who came from transferred in from out of state went home. Some simply grew tired of Michigan. But Jay found his life here. The hardy people of Michigan resonated with Jay's blue-collar attitude. His buddies from college longed for Silicon Valley, but Jay preferred the knuckle-busting turn of a wrench against a plate of steel. Still, he loved his friends and felt lonely from time to time. But anytime he had the light of his life next to him, he could never feel completely alone.

She started to fall behind a bit.

"My ma will be here anyways, and your aunt and uncle are always welcome!" Jay called, looking over his shoulder.

They banked a neighborhood street and coasted fast down a hill. As they slowed, She came up next to him and began to ask what he wanted for his birthday. The skid and crash of Her bike interrupted Her question. Jay squeezed his brakes, bringing his back wheel slightly off the ground, and hopped off his bike. He rushed to Her side. She was gripping Her chest as She lay on the asphalt, Her bike resting between Her legs. A small streak of blood was brushed across the road, leading to her elbow. Her eyes danced from side to side as she gasped for air.

"Hey!" Jay cried as he pulled the bike off of her, knelt, and held her in his arms. "What's wrong, honey? Is it actin' up that bad? Oh, God." His words were thin between his hyperventilating gasps. She looked at him with dull eyes, breathing through her mouth, and asked for an ambulance.

"Ok! Ok! Oh, God, honey… keep breathin', ok?"

The harrowing memory of sirens rang in Jay's skull as he tore himself from that painful memory. He took a deep breath and stared dead-eyed at the bike he held in his hands. Looking over his shoulder, he peered through the darkness and down the rack for any other option. All the bikes he could spot were child-sized or had their tires stolen. He took another accepting, deep breath and walked the bike down the ladder. He bounced the bikes a bit to test their tires. *Could use a little air,* he thought.

He scrounged around the area and found a bike pump and a small repair kit. All the good pumps had been stolen, so he had to settle on a cheap hand pump. He slipped the kit into his bag and pumped up the tires. His arms burned with fatigue as he pushed the air into the tires; he was craving something with more nutrition than a bar of chocolate, nuts, and whatever chemicals gave you "energy". Jay held his ear to parts of the tires to listen for the high-pitched whistle of a leak and found them to be good. The rattle of Benu's shopping cart could be heard near the back as it disappeared somewhere near electronics. *Must be all done*, Jay thought.

Jay could see Benu's light through the metal shelving of the stockroom as he walked towards it, leading the bikes by their handlebars. As he turned into the open area between the shelves, he could see that Benu had changed into a new set of clothes. She had replaced her stained sweater with a couple of layers of loose blouses with floral designs. Her cargo pants had been swapped out for nearly identical pants of a different brand; the hems tucked into the same boots. She had removed her nylon gloves and cowl, placing them on the ground to her left. Her right-angled light sat upright on a cardboard box, shining in Jay's direction. Benu was sitting on a milk crate, hunched over, with her crossbow in her lap and a cigarette in her mouth. Clicks of her failing lighter echoed through the storeroom as she whispered soft curses at it.

Jay parked the bikes via their kickstands and presented the tip of his finger to Benu. As she turned, he ignited it with a small flame. She drew in Jay's fire and exhaled smoke through her nose. Gripping the cigarette between her index and middle fingers, she pulled it out of her mouth with a dry 'mwah' and raised her cigarette towards Jay in gratitude.

"No problem," he replied.

Benu motioned over to her shopping cart, parked by the cardboard box. It was filled with a collection of packaged foods and a few bottles of water.

"There was more food than I expected," she said. "Take your pick. I got the good stuff." She reached down by her side and held up an empty jar of Skippy. Jay didn't hesitate. He snatched a bottle of water and took his pick from the cart. Peanut butter, a plastic spoon, a bag of potato chips, and a vacuum-sealed pack of beef jerky. Jay took a seat on a milk crate opposite from Benu and placed his bag beside himself. He cracked open the jar of Skippy and peeled back the plastic seal. The nutty aroma rushed down his nose and swirled in his stomach. Anticipation caused a small tinge of pain in his stomach as it yearned for Jay to eat. He buried his spoon into the creamy paste and shoveled out a mound of the stuff. Sticking his spoon in his mouth, he teared up at the glorious taste of something other than the slop he had at the gas station or puny energy bars. He continued to devour his peanut butter.

"Hmph, slow down, *dost*," Benu joked. "It is still expired."

"Don't taste expired right now," Jay replied, his mouth stuffed with stale chips. "Tastes like heaven."

Benu chuckled as she took another drag from her cigarette. Jay finished his meal with a swig of water to wash it down. The sealed bottle kept the water relatively fresh. He had to wipe away some mold on the lip but the liquid inside tasted like spring. As he took off his beanie and placed it on the ground, he noticed Benu was fighting with her crossbow. She whispered obscenities to herself as she struggled to unjam it. Jay reached into his bag and pulled out the scope. He stepped over to Benu and held out his free hand.

"Lemme take a look at it," Jay said as he bobbed the scope in his hand, "and I got you a little gift. Thought it could help that wonderful aim of yours."

Benu simply replied with a shrug and handed Jay her crossbow. He sat back down with it, placed the scope box on the ground, and pulled out his toolkit. Pliers and a multibit screwdriver were all that he figured he needed. As he inspected the weapon, he could see the issue. It was a modern crossbow with cables that were strung around pulleys on the end of each limb. The string that held the bolt went across the top, looped around the pulleys, and was fed underneath, through, and across the barrel. At one end of the cable, where it was strung around the left pulley, something had lodged itself in there, causing the pulley to jam. Jay stood up, placed his foot in the stirrup, and attempted to cock the crossbow. He brought the left pulley up to the light and could see a piece of sharp metal had jammed itself between the limb and pulley, hindering its operation. He recognized the green paint on the metal—a piece of propane tank.

Lucky it didn't find itself in your side, Benu.

He shook his head and yanked out the metal shard with his pliers. The bowstring snapped forward, dry firing; he smiled to himself over a successful repair. As he inspected the crossbow, he asked Benu, "Do your shots usually pull to the left?"

"Lately yes," she replied. "I have been compensating but sometimes I forget, why?"

"Well, you might not be as bad of a shot as you think. Your left pulley is loose. I'll fix it for ya."

"I thought your specialty was hospital equipment, *dost.*"

"It's just mechanics," he sighed as he sat down and began tinkering. "It's all the same shit. Fixin' a crossbow, car, dishwasher, etcetera… it all just comes down to figurin' out how the nuts and bolts work. No difference with hospital stuff… except I'm sure your crossbow doesn't make any radiation or cost billions in taxpayer dollars."

"Hmph, not that I know of. Did you like your job?"

"I loved it, to be honest. I always preferred workin' with machines over people. Just me and the mechanics… only time anyone ever bothered me was when a doc or tech came in to ask: 'is it *done* yet?'"

Jay finished up his repair on the pulley and checked his handiwork. He unboxed the scope and held it in his lap for a moment. He looked off to the side at his bag and said, "Hey Benu."

"Yes? What is it?" she replied.

Jay went on to fulfill the promise he had made to himself when he was with Red. He repaid what he had owed to Benu—the full story of why he carried his urn. He felt a great weight lifted off him again—a lesser one than the time he told Red. It seemed that, with each iteration, it became easier to talk about Her… about himself. He felt weak in his chest and out of breath, but he held back his tears and kept his composure. He hung his head for a moment, then looked up at Benu.

Benu could see his distress and calmed it, "Thank you, Jay. I can see this is hard for you."

He forced a small smile and began working on mounting the scope. As he worked, he asked, "Do you have anyone?"

Benu curled her lips into a tepid smile. She took one last draw of her cigarette and dropped it on the concrete floor, stamping it out. "Yes… I *did* have someone."

"Oh yeah? Tell me more."

Benu crossed her legs and set her left arm across her lap. She then rested her right elbow on her thigh and nestled her chin in her palm, sighing: "She was beautiful— blonde, slim… I admit: I came on to her based off of those two things. But, if you had seen her, you would understand… she was the barista at the coffee shop on the first floor of the hospital. I swear, she never got a day off. Every weekday, she would be there… eventually she memorized my order… masala chai—made just how my mother would."

Jay glanced up with a warm smile as Benu continued.

"It took me a long time to work up the nerves to ask her out on a date. You will *never* understand how many times that is multiplied when you are gay." They both shared a small chuckle. "But… I could feel it. The way she shot small signals my way… how our hands would sometimes meet when she handed me my coffee. It happened *just* enough times to be more than a coincidence. Oh, *dost*. You have no idea the butterflies I had when she agreed to meet me after work."

Benu looked off into the dark corner of the storeroom in silence, a solemn smile across her face as she swayed her head. She daydreamed of happier days, lost in the chasm of lost opportunities. She took a heavy breath through her long, slender nose and tucked a tuft of her messy hair behind her ear. Jay had finished mounting the scope when he asked: "What happened to her?"

She sighed, "I do not know, to be honest. We went steady for a long time—almost for the time of my entire residency—but I had a few years on her… and she dreamed of bigger things. That is what she was always doing. She was a dreamer—an artist. She finally had her break with some agency in New York… She broke the news to me over dinner. She was crying her eyes out, but so was I. I was so happy for her. She asked me to join but… I was too dedicated to my job. She moved sometime during the First Convergence. We kept in contact as long as we could but… even before the world started to go to shit, we fell out of touch."

Jay frowned and nodded to himself, looking away from Benu. He had a hard time finding the words to respond. He found some reassuring words and opened his mouth to speak, but when he looked over at Benu, he could see she was wiping her face. Jay held silence as he stepped over to Benu and rubbed her shoulder.

"Here," he whispered presenting her crossbow. "The scope should be good for six times magnification… if the box is to be believed. I zeroed it as best as I could without actually firin' it, so you'll have to do some adjustments, I bet."

Benu sniffled and took her weapon.

"Thank you, *dost*," she nodded. "Thank you."

Jay smiled and patted her lightly on the shoulder. Benu inspected her crossbow's new scope, puffing out her lower lip and nodding in approval. "Looks good. I always wanted one of these!" Her mood had already shifted.

"Glad ya like it. It's just some airsoft scope so I dunno how good it'll *actually* be," Jay replied. "I've got some sleeping bags here." He untied the two pouches and tucked them under his arms.

"Nice!" Benu exclaimed. "I could use the luxury after that shitty slab of a bed they had me on at that camp." Benu picked up her light, and the two walked over with their backpacks to a manager's office at the end of the shelves. They locked the door behind them as Jay rolled out the sleeping bags. As Jay removed his jacket and nestled himself within his bed, Benu asked, "Hey, why did they let you keep your clothes?"

"Whaddaya mean?"

"Well," Benu blushed, "they took my clothes and gave me rags. That is why I had some freak's clothes."

Jay chortled. "They were a group of lunatics that worshipped a fuckin' V8 engine… Ya think I got an answer for ya?"

Benu rolled her eyes and flicked off her light.

{Chapter 15}

4:10:29:58

The Anomaly balanced itself on one of its elongated points. Its vertex barely touched the reflective pool that spanned out to the horizon in every direction. The black diamond sent out periodic, whispered hums. Small ripples glided across the surface with each rhythmic pulse, dissipating into nothingness as they traveled across the water. The pool was like a mirror, perfectly flat and reflecting an exact image of the world above it.

The cloudless, aqua sky was slightly muted in the mirror's reflection. Along the horizon was a forest line of amber trees, so far off in the distance that they looked like strokes of oil paint. Jay stood about thirty paces from The Anomaly. The soles of his shoes dipped just underneath the pool's surface. He was motionless, locked in place by the oppressive hum of the black diamond before him. It was smaller here, no bigger than a two-story house. Yet, the malice it exuberated was overpowering.

Peeking out, just above the surface of the pool, were large stone faces. They peppered the barren water, wetted by the moisture. Jay recognized the faces: his relatives—both close and distant—and the few friends he had fallen away from. He could count the total number easily; there were so few. The ones he held dearest—his mother, uncle, college and high school friends—were nearest to him. Even Benu's face was amongst the sculptures. Their expressions were flat, with no sign of emotion in their open, dull eyes.

His wife wasn't there. Scanning his lucid eyes across the still surface, he could not find Her. She had already been lost to him. This was the black diamond's way of telling him so. He fixed his attention on The Anomaly. Outside his periphery, he could see objects rising out of the water. Toys and trinkets from his childhood. Model cars and DVDs from his apartment back in Detroit. Precious pictures and decorations from his house in Royal Oak. Now, the black diamond taunted him with his material things. Still, he was held in place by some invisible force.

A burning sensation began under his feet. Jay could feel the tinge of fire on his ankles. He looked down to see flames wrapping themselves around his legs. Next, came his hands and torso. Soon, he was completely ignited. He could feel it. The intense heat was torture and alien to him. He could feel his clothes fusing with his leathery skin. His mouth opened to scream, but only a raspy croak escaped.

The Anomaly began to rise; its humming was now becoming a steady sound. Ripples continue to be sent out from where it had touched, now with more frequency. Jay watched as the black diamond rose high above him, spreading its crimson filter across the land. He could hear the sirens in his head from the night of his neighbor's house fire. As he burned, Jay danced his gaze around the pool.

Inky tendrils emerged around the stone faces, wrapping themselves around each one completely until there were only rolling mounds of black. One by one, they were pulled under as black liquid tainted the water. Jay turned back to The Anomaly. It had stopped its ascent at two times its height and appeared to look down at Jay. Just as the fire crawled up his legs, the black tendrils did the same. Soon, Jay was bound by darkness and pulled down.

"Hey! Hey!"

Jay awoke with a jolt and a violent shake from Benu's hand; a beeping came from her wrist. He peered at her with startled eyes.

"My God, man," she said, crouching over him. "You sleep like a rock. Come; time to go." She silenced her watch's alarm. "I hit the snooze a few times to let you sleep, but we should really move now… Are you ok? Bad dream?"

Jay groaned as he wriggled out of his sleeping bag, "Yeah, you could say that."

"Well, come on."

Benu left Jay to his devices; she had already rolled up her sleeping bag and packed her things. Jay stood up with a great, big yawn and rolled up his sleeping bag as well. His back was aching slightly from the cheap bed and his limbs were fatigued from the insanity of yesterday, but any amount of soreness was worth escaping that hellhole. He tied the packed sleeping back on his backpack strap; threw on his beanie and jacket; and slipped his bag onto his back. His nightmare was still fresh in his mind but he reminded himself: *it was just a bad dream.* All things considered, he felt all right.

Leaving the manager's office, he caught Benu leaving through the backdoor to his right. The flash of sunlight blinded him for a moment before the door shut and he was once again in the palely lit storeroom. He walked over to the shopping cart and packed some food and water Benu had left behind. The bikes were gone. *Benu probably walked them out,* he thought. He did one last pass of the area and walked outside.

Jay held an open palm over his eyes to shield them from the bright mid-morning sun. The sky was a brilliant blue through the mild cloud cover. The warm rays felt nice against the chilly air. Near the sun, The Anomaly loomed, ever-present. Benu was straddling her bike, hunched over the handlebars with a map splayed out across them. Next to her, Jay's new mountain bike was parked and ready to go.

Jay walked up, placed his hand on his bike's handlebars, and quipped: "Did your morning stretches?"

Benu drew out her words, keeping her eyes glued to the map: "Sure did." Her eyes darted across the tangled roads and highways of the mitten. She placed an index finger on a town somewhere northwest and checked her watch. "Midland is just about two and a half hours away… Cadillac is roughly one hundred and ten miles. Should take us… six to eight hours or so in a straight shot. But with our luck… I am sure it will take longer."

"Don't think it's really luck anymore," Jay replied as he looked out across the empty backlot. His eyes traced the cracks and potholes across the pavement. Weeds and grasses filled the crevasses as overgrowth lurched over the stone wall that a couple of dumpsters sat against. Lumps of small rocks were drifting away towards space; the black diamond continued to pull the earth apart.

Benu let out a long, drawn-out sigh. "Yeah… I do not think so either. We will have to be more careful." She clicked a few buttons on her digital watch. The high-pitched beeps sounded off as she found the date. When she had found the watch, the time had been correct as far as she could figure; she had to trust the date as well. It seemed correct. She rolled her eyes to the sky and did a few calculations:

Four days.

"Hey," Benu said, pointing at Lake Michigan on her map. "How do you plan to get across the lake? Considering the fact that the bridge is gone, it looks like you are going to have to go by boat."

"Got a tip from a buddy that there's an old captain that can cross the lake," Jay replied.

"Hmph, sounds like a tall tale. Did they feed you something funny back at that gas station—something that made you as *crazy* as they were?"

Jay shrugged with a chuckle. He decided to leave out the details of his neighbor's crock of a story—Captain Quigby included—for fear she would put a bolt through his head for convincing her she was right.

"We should get going," Benu said as she folded up her map and tucked it into her backpack. "Midland should only be about a two-hour bike."

"Sounds good," Jay replied.

He hopped on his bike and motioned for Benu to take the lead. They rode off onto the main road and pedaled out of Saginaw. As they left the edge of town, the overgrowth of trees began to thin. They had reached an open clearing. The highway was filled with abandoned vehicles, flanked by fields of dense, dying grass and thick bushes. Peppered throughout were small yellow and white flowers belonging to tall, swaying weeds. Large craters emitted a deep violet light—fresh chunks of land that had been torn by The Anomaly.

As they crested over a hill and cleared a small forest, what should have been Midland came into view. Instead, a massive, barren crater stretched out before them. The giant basin glowed with the same purple that seeped through the earth's alien hairline cracks. A sharp fifty-foot drop split the highway the entire length of the absent city. Remnants of old foundations, sewer lines, and water pipes were scattered amongst the rubble in the crater. The ruins spread out over the horizon; the pair could not see the other end of the mighty crater. Midland had been lifted away, spooned out of the earth's crust like a scoop ripping through a tub of Stroh's ice cream.

"Holy shit," Jay said under his breath as he scanned the devastation. Benu shook her head in silence with shut, twisted lips. They didn't dwell on it long. The Anomaly's destruction had been a part of their lives for five years now. Ever since the benign power outages of the First Convergence–to the rampaging natural disasters of the Second Convergence–the world knew of the black diamond's ever-escalating fury. "We'll have to go around," Jay said.

"Yeah," Benu said, exasperated.

They set off into the open field. The grasses and weeds brushed Jay's hands as he led Benu. Various bugs leapt away and across his face as he and Benu raced to make up time. Jay was constantly swatting away swarms of gnats, but Benu paid them no mind; she was in her element outdoors. They bumped over and around severed roads and cut through the scant parking lots of the few businesses that survived the catastrophe. The detour took them a little under an hour and a half to complete. As Jay ascended the onramp to the highway, he looked back at the glowing crater just to confirm he hadn't gone mad. Yes, Midland had truly been plucked from the earth, and what was left looked like nuclear aftermath.

Jay completed his ascent and waited for Benu. He took a moment to rest and pulled out a bottle of water from his bag. As he drank, Benu pulled up beside him.

"Hey," she called for Jay's attention. "Sticking to the main road might not be the best idea. If we are in an open field, sure. But–"

"If we can avoid it, we should," Jay finished.

"Exactly."

"I dunno. What about shabriri—or whatever the fuck those people were? They weren't human. I think I'd rather deal with *human* thieves or whatnot on the main road than risk fighting whatever monsters that *thing* has planned for us." Jay pointed at The Anomaly.

"It is a fair point but staying on an open road deep in a forest—or city or what have you… We are completely exposed. If we move between trees or buildings, we at least stand a chance of avoiding confrontation altogether."

Jay felt a shiver of numbness crawl up his spine. That shot of anxiety when time felt short. "Do we have enough time for that?" he asked.

"Hmph, that is a hard question to answer, *dost*. The short answer is 'yes, if we are lucky' but as you said earlier, it is not about luck now. Towns will be far more spread out from now on." She pulled out her map and held it up to illustrate her thoughts. "I doubt we will see any friendly faces before Clare or Cadillac."

Jay let out a sharp sigh. "All right, we'll play it by ear."

They set off down Highway 10, towards Clare. The journey through the rolling countryside reminded Jay of the trips he used to take in his Miata. The open air tasted just as sweet and fresh as it did many years ago. The abundant greenery kept it that way and the few years without human smog had allowed the earth to breathe again. However, the world continued to feel alien to Jay. This was not the same road he had traveled long ago.

They passed over Sanford Lake—a place Jay and his wife had visited frequently. The lake was nearly emptied from the local dam collapsing. Rotting pontoons, speedboats, and sailboats lined the shores of the shallow water. Abandoned lake houses, with their peeling, pastel colors, were decaying under the mid-afternoon sun. A slimy film of algae covered the surface of the lake. Scraggly fins of something otherworldly cut through the algae, creating temporary slits in the thick green blanket.

Jay held on for dear life as the inner tube hopped and skipped off the crashing waves. The nylon rope towing the inflated raft was being pulled tight, stretching it to its limits. The speedboat banked left and right violently as the inner tube mimicked its force. The waves continued to build and build, curving viciously with the speedboat, but Jay held on tight. His face was buffeted by splashes of water that made it hard to breathe. The speedboat's sputtering engine revved harder.

It banked hard to the left and continued circling; the driver was determined to shake Jay off. Round and round it drove, building a whirlpool as it went. Jay could feel his grip weakening, but he was determined to hold on. The inner tube began to lift. Once, it took to the air and came slamming down on a wave, but Jay held on. Then again, but higher. Jay held on. Then, the driver came off the throttle and whipped the vessel to the right, stopping it abruptly. The inner tube caught the ensuing, monstrous wave and sailed through the air. Finally, Jay's slick hands lost their grip, and he went tumbling into the lake.

He plunged beneath the surface. The world went silent. Muffled rumbling of the speedboat's engine traveled through the water as he traced its keel from beneath. Wavering rays of sunlight pierced the clear, blue lake. Fresh water rushed past Jay's nostrils as he swiftly squeezed them shut. He could feel his life vest pull him to the surface as he paddled his feet and rose towards the sunlight. Jay broke through the water with a heavy gasp as he spit out gobs of lake water. As he breathed, he wiped his eyes clear and could see the speedboat drifting towards him. The side of it pulled up to him.

"Had enough for today?" the female driver asked. Her name was Stacy; she was Her best friend. Stacy's soaked, red hair stuck to her bare back, over her bikini's back strap; a few strands stuck to her forehead and traveled down her cheeks. Her fair, sunburned skin glistened in the high sun. Jay nodded as he gasped and climbed onboard. As they docked, Jay could see his wife sitting against a tree, reading a book. Lost in Her own world.

He thanked Stacy, jogged up to the tree and called Her name. She looked up, smiled, and asked if he had fun.

"Stacy went a little crazy today," he replied, "but she had to be to shake *me* off." He chuckled and stuck out his tongue. He sighed, "I wish you could join us, honey—like you used to."

She tilted Her head and smiled, hiding Her lamentation with veiled indifference across Her face. She reminded him of Her heart—how any amount of built-up pressure could cause it to burst.

Jay caressed Her back. "I know, sweetheart." He forced a smile of his own.

He stood up and said, "Stacy's makin' hotdogs inside; I'll bring you one." She thanked him as he walked up the sandy shore and into the lake house.

Jay and his wife visited Stacy often. They'd find themselves at her pastel blue lake house nearly every summer weekend.

Jay sat on a barstool at the counter of the kitchen. Stacy was cooking hotdogs over an iron skillet. As oil popped and sizzled off a flipped sausage, Stacy looked over her shoulder at Jay. "I heard she had an episode earlier last week. How's she doing?"

"Better," he lied.

After two hours, Jay and Benu were coming up on the tiny town of Clare. Taking advantage of their respite from last night, they had picked up the pace and were making good time. They passed through dead fields and abandoned rural neighborhoods, stopping to scavenge for supplies here and there. They were coming around a large bend, their view of the upcoming clearing blocked by forest trees. Benu had reluctantly agreed with Jay to stay on the main road. He argued that, in broad daylight, ambush would be unlikely and, if it did happen, they'd see it coming. Total Convergence *was* drawing near, and Benu wanted as much time with her family as she could get.

As they broke through the woods, they came upon a section of the highway that had been ripped out by The Anomaly. Jay and Benu stopped at the edge of it. The crater was shallow and spanned a couple of miles ahead and a mile wide; they weighed their options.

"Maybe we should go around," Benu suggested. "Avoid any possible flat tires."

"Yeah, I think you're–" Jay was looking out across the field. A dust cloud was being kicked up over the horizon. Jay stared, speechless, as the rolling wall of dirt barreled towards them. Benu caught Jay's silence and turned to face what he gawked at. She reached into her bag and pulled out her binoculars. A stampede of gazelle-like creatures was galloping across the open plain.

The quadrupeds were creatures of The Anomaly—monsters from another dimension… or twisted forms of earthly animals. Benu focused on a singular member of the herd. An array of large, cat-like eyes lined a mouth that spanned the entirety of its long, slender neck. Ridged horns swooped back from atop a head that had no distinguishable transition into its neck. Stripes of black covered its green, furry body which ended in a stubby white tail. Small, translucent domes flanked its spine down the entire length. Jay shook Benu's shoulder. She dropped her arms and could see that the stampede had become too close to avoid.

"Benu!" Jay cried. "Into the hole, now!"

"Yeah!" Benu yelled back as her binoculars slipped from her hands and fell to the ground. They jumped their bikes into the crater and coasted down its rocky surface. The handlebars vibrated violently in their hands as the stomps of hooves grew closer. Jay could see now that pebbles were beginning to bounce and wiggle across the crater. The stampede was like thunder that would soon be crashing above them.

"Drop!" Jay called out as he stumbled off his bike and dove onto the ground. Benu followed suit and covered her head. The remnants of concrete road jabbed into Jay's ribs as he fell. The sharp pain distracted him from the sea of leaping creatures above. He turned over onto his side and watched as the strange animals sailed through the air. Their long, worm-like necks and heads were extended out, pointing forward, and completely stiff. Their bodies matched the size and girth of a full-size pickup truck. Short, white fur covered the entirety of their neck-jaws down to their stomachs and their brilliant, jade coats shimmered in sun. Jay looked to the edge of the crater where the creatures leapt from. They ran up to the edge, tucked their front legs, and launched themselves high into the air with their muscular hind legs, clearing the entire mile in one magnificent bound.

Jay and Benu lay there for what felt like hours but, in reality, it was only a few minutes. The stampede's rumble began to fade as the rear of the herd finished their jump. When the sound became distant, Jay slowly rose to his feet. His ears were ringing as he extended a hand towards Benu. She took it and stood.

"You ever see those things before?" Jay asked as he picked up his bike.

Benu shook her head, "Nope, first time. They were somewhat… beautiful."

Jay chuckled dismissively. "Beauty is in the eye of the beholder, I guess. Those things coulda scrambled us!"

"But they did not," Benu replied as she picked up her bike. She looked back to where they entered the crater, saw the remnants of her binoculars spilled over the edge, and sighed.

"Either way, let's keep movin'."

The two backed their bikes out of the hole and rode around it as they had originally planned. They returned to the highway and continued their travels. As they came over the horizon, the tips of great sequoias started to come into view. Jay slowed, falling behind Benu. The black, fleshy bark was visible now. He looked down by the roadside. The accursed black vines were crawling along the pavement. Benu came to a stop as Jay caught up to her and parked at her side.

She held an index finger over her lips.

{Chapter 16}

4:1:12:24

Benu checked her watch—7:17 P.M. They had entered the dense forest a little over two hours ago. Deciding not to risk the open road, they walked their bikes through the thick brush and smaller streets. They had already passed through Clare. The small town was nothing but dust and rubble, nearly indistinguishable from the forestry Jay and Benu walked through now. Small splotches of the setting sun's light were spread across the ground like stars.

The pair moved slowly, trying their best to keep the noise of their tires and footsteps low. They had already spotted three male shabriri and avoided them by stopping in their tracks and waiting in silence. The woods were heavy with sounds of rustling leaves and swaying branches from the gusts that passed between the enormous trees; Jay and Benu moved under their guise. They both had their wits about them. Their eyes and ears stayed alert. Benu's hearing was sharp, trained from the years of surviving the outskirts of Detroit. She listened intently to the distant noises of the woods.

The scratching of bark.

A squirrel, maybe.

A crack of a twig.

The snap hadn't been very loud. Nothing to be worried about.

Crumbling sounds of falling rock.

Some building is falling apart.

The trickling of water.

A stream? Just ahead.

The sound grew as they carried on. After a while, Jay could hear it too. Now the sound was near, just beyond a wall of bramble. He carefully parted the thorny bush to reveal a pond that had formed in a small crater, fed by a steadily flowing stream to their right. Jay held the bush open as Benu ducked under his arm. He pulled himself through, his beanie and jacket caught by the thicket. Freeing himself, he joined Benu by the edge of the pond.

"I think we can take a break here," Benu said as she laid her bike on the ground and pulled out her map. "The sound of the stream should mask our voices… if we keep them low."

Jay set his bike down and took a seat on the ground. He unzipped his backpack just enough to squeeze his hand in and pulled out an unopened water bottle. Tucking the bottle under his shirt, he grasped the cap with the fabric from the outside and cracked it open. His heavy jacket and soft shirt muffled the sound. He took a few drinks of water, crouched down by the pond, and looked out across the surface.

"Hmph, something interesting about the water?" Benu asked as she squatted next to Jay.

"Nope, just takin' it all in," he replied as he moved his hand through the water. It was freezing, but the cold pool eased his tired hand. "We'll have to go around." Jay motioned with his head towards the stream that trickled down a steep slope. "We could try to find the end of the pond to the left, through the woods and shit, but if we climb that hill… I think the stream'll be small enough that we can step over it. Don't wanna risk any splashin'."

"Yeah, good thinking," Benu replied. She held her map in front of Jay and pointed to their current location. "It will be dark soon and we have only traveled this far." She traced her finger back to the outskirts of Clare. "We will have to find shelter—preferably one with doors and windows we can lock."

"Agreed, maybe here?" Jay pointed to the small town of Farwell, just west of where they were.

Benu sucked her teeth, "No. Too many buildings—perfect breeding ground for shabriri. We should find… Do you hear that?" Benu whipped her head to the right. Just beyond the stream, the fluttering of fleeing birds could be heard. Woody creaks echoed through the forest as heavy stomps grew closer.

Jay raised himself just enough to look over Benu's head. Through the tree line, he could see the sheen of emerald approaching fast, disturbing the smaller trees around it. Jay took Benu's shoulder and pulled her towards the thicket behind them. They slinked backwards and readied themselves to dive into the thicket when the massive creature halted its gallop with a skid through the tree line.

It was one of the gazelle-like creatures that had nearly squashed Jay and Benu in the clearing, but this one towered high above them. As it shook its head like a dog drying off, its tiny ears brushed against the lowest branch of the great sequoia it stood near. Three more galloped from behind. Smaller, like the ones they had encountered earlier. Jay and Benu were frozen, awestruck by the creatures' magnitude.

The adult looked in their direction. The many eyes that lined its upper jaw and neck were fixated solely on the pair. Two of the children looked on as well. Now closer, Jay could see that the creatures had puny, hippo-like ears that twitched and swiveled in curiosity. Jay readied his hand. He began to build a great amount of heat; the blast would have to be intense to take down such a beast.

Benu snatched his wrist; Jay immediately dissipated his energy.

"Wait," she whispered and nodded towards the third youngling. It hopped down from the tiny drop-off and into the pond with a soft splash. It glanced the tip of its mouth across the surface. Then, it lifted it slightly and opened its great maw. The mouth appeared to unzip itself, starting from the tip, and continued down the length of its long neck. Slender teeth, spaced out a few inches between each other, lined the top and bottom jaw. It submerged its lower jaw into the pond and scooped up gallons of water. As it closed its mouth and gulped, water dribbled out of the creases of its lips—waves of muscle pushing down the liquid in its throat.

The other two younglings jumped down and joined it. Benu released Jay's wrist, took a step forward, and sat down. Jay relaxed his shoulders and stood next to Benu. The adult held its gaze for a moment then swayed its lumbering head away to watch its offspring. Streaks of orange passed between the trees and bathed the area in the setting sunlight. Jay and Benu watched in silence as the creatures drank—their soaked emerald fur shining brilliantly now.

As darkness covered the land, the small domes on the creatures' backs began to glow with blue bioluminescence. Insects began to gather around the lights as the blue hue lit the pond. The adult's domes were shining the brightest, casting azure stains across the black bark of the sequoias.

Beautiful, Jay thought.

"Hmph, you know," Benu said. "As much anguish, ugliness, and shit The Anomaly drops on us, there are still things to enjoy in our world. Our time is short, but we cannot let it be filled with misery, can we?"

Jay looked down at Benu and smirked. She was right.

She would've loved this, he thought.

The two watched the creatures drink for a few minutes when the closest child perked up its head, slammed its mouth shut, and looked over Jay and Benu's shoulders. Its ears were dancing around furiously, whipping thin tufts of hair around. Benu heard it too; something was crashing through the woods towards them. A youngling ran off down the pond as the other two followed. The adult let out a deep, rumbling coo and followed its children, throwing large splashes of water as it stomped through the pond. Benu pulled Jay to the ground as she dropped to her belly. She looked over at Jay and held her finger over her pursed lips.

Overhead, a male shabriri leapt over and into the pond, scampered as it swiveled on the tips of its blades, and barreled down the pond towards its prey. Jay and Benu remained motionless as the sounds of pursuit faded. Benu clicked on her flashlight. "We need to move," she whispered. Jay nodded as they rose to their feet.

The forest ground was rich with the purple tinge of the dying earth. The light hovered amongst the thick underbrush and grasses. Jay and Benu waded through the waist-high overgrowth, guiding their bikes carefully over hills, rocks, and fallen branches. They had scouted many buildings for shelter, but the shabriri presence was heavy.

Why are there so many males still out? Benu thought. *They should not be hunting this late.*

As they spotted a large, dark log cabin through the trees, Benu brought her watch up to her face. She stopped and leaned her bike against her body for a moment as she pushed a small button on the side. The dim, green fluorescence washed over her face from the watch's light. She read the time—10:59 P.M. She must have caught the time seconds before the top of the hour because, as she scanned her eyes across the digital display, it changed to 11:00 P.M.

A shrieking alarm screamed into the night air. Benu scrambled to shut off the alarm as quickly as it had sounded. The pair stood silent. Benu looked up to see Jay staring at her with a cold expression—one that spoke of imminent death. The crashing of hooves and blades didn't take long. From deep in the woods behind them, they could hear the trampling rush of a shabriri.

"Go!" Benu yelled as she dropped her bike and sprinted towards the cabin.

Jay had already taken off by the time the word left Benu's mouth. They hopped over large roots and pushed through the overgrowth. The purple light danced and flickered off the black trunks as Jay and Benu disturbed the flora. Jay could feel the beast drawing near. Soon, the hot breath of the shabriri's tooth-flooded maw would be on his neck. The cabin just a couple of trees away. Forty feet if he had to guess.

They passed by a great trunk.

The shabriri was two trunks behind them.

Half a tree away now.

The shabriri had just passed the start of the trunk behind them.

They broke through the tree line.

Jay could hear the breathing of the monstrosity at his heels.

As Jay ran into the open area where the cabin stood, he could hear the stomps behind him stop. He skidded on the sides of his feet as he swiveled around. The massive beast had stopped at the tree line. Its bone-white antlers glistened in the starlight as the red glow of The Anomaly stained them pink through the break in the canopy above. It panted there, dripping hot saliva onto the ground. Cocking its head in curiosity, it pawed at an invisible force with one of its great blades. Clicks and growls vibrated its leathery, gray neck.

Benu stopped, whipped around, and chided in a hushed voice, "Jay! What the fuck are you doing?"

Jay stayed silent. He furrowed his brow at the confused shabriri. He took a few cautious steps forward—his eyes glued to the shabriri's.

"Jay! Jay! Have you gone mad?" Benu pressed further.

He hovered an open palm behind him towards Benu to let her know it was all right. He stopped a few feet from the monster, just far enough that its blades couldn't reach. The creature continued to pick at whatever stood between it and Jay. Jay rolled back his shoulders and stuck out his chest. Standing tall, he yelled, "Hey!"

The shabriri jerked its head at him. With a mighty roar, the shabriri spat globs of spittle and mists of hot breath at Jay; but, it did not move.

"What's going on out here?" shouted a deep voice from the cabin.

Jay and Benu looked behind them. A burly man was trotting across the barren, dirt field towards Jay. As Jay watched the man approach, he could see that the cabin was shining bright lights out of its many windows. Sounds of comradery and a live band screamed out of the door as it bounced off the door frame and shut, muffling the sound.

There wasn't music before, Jay thought.

The man passed Benu without paying her any mind and stood next to Jay, staring daggers at the shabriri. Jay had a clear view of the face that stood parallel to his. His chiseled, crossed arms fed into a white t-shirt that was practically bursting at the seams from his defined chest. Bulging veins fed up his neck and behind his ears onto his bald head that sheened in the moonlight. Deep wrinkles lined his eyes and cheeks and traced down into his bushy, white, full beard and mustache. His deep-set eyes were flooded in blackness under his thick brow.

The man took a step forward. The white, folded apron tied around his waist swayed as he shooed off the beast like a harmless mouse with his hands. In a heightened, commanding, Italian accent, the man yelled, "Get outta here, c'mon!" The shabriri recoiled slightly and grumbled at the voice. "*Porco cane!* Go! Now!" The beast began to slowly back off before lifting its blades, turning completely around, and galloping off into the woods.

The man placed his hands on his hips and turned to Jay. "You ok, *amico?*"

Jay, awestruck, replied, "Uhh, ye-yeah. How… how did you do that?" He thumbed in the direction of the fleeing beast.

The man pulled up his sagging jeans and replied, "Ah, they've never hurt me. I've always been able to tell them to fuck off. Ha-ha!" He clapped a beefy hand across Jay's shoulder. The force moved Jay a bit. "Come! You and your woman look like shit! I've got the good stuff in my bar, and my wife isn't such a bad cook. You can just ask my customers! Ha!"

Was there music playing? Jay thought.

Jay was skeptical. He traced his ring through his pocket and remembered the cage he had escaped just a couple of nights ago. But he could feel still feel the hot breath of the shabriri. He looked over at the cabin. Through the windows, he could see silhouettes of people dancing merrily. The sounds of laughter and conversation crescendoed amongst the clinks of glasses as the band continued to play.

Yeah, there was *music playing!*

Benu walked up to the two men, her hand resting on the hilt of her knife strapped to her thigh.

"*Ciao*," the man greeted. He stuck out his hand for a shake. "I'm Lorenzo. Lorenzo Bandini."

As Benu grasped Lorenzo's hand, he shook it hard, reeled her close, placed his other hand on her shoulder, and pecked a kiss over each check in a traditional fashion. He straightened up and released her hand. Jay could see the shock on Benu's face that slowly returned to normal when Lorenzo let her go. If it weren't for the fact Benu had mistakenly presented her knife-wielding hand, Lorenzo may have been gutted right then and there.

Lorenzo turned to Jay and introduced himself in the same way. Jay was taken aback by having another man come so close to smooching him on the cheek. He was used to the typical quick shake, wave, or succinct nod—not having woolly hairs brush his cheeks as Hercules blew kisses past his ear. Lorenzo went back to placing his arms on his hips and stood like a statue with a great smile.

Jay could only muster an embarrassed chuckle before he said, "Well, I'm Jay and this is Benu."

"Well met, Jay and Benu," Lorenzo said. "You are a lovely couple."

"Oh," Benu chimed in, "we are not together—just traveling buddies."

"Oh, *mi scuso*, sorry. You two don't look familiar—not like one of my regulars at least. Are you from around here?"

"Um, no we are not."

"Where are you staying?"

"Nowhere," Jay chimed. "Not for tonight, at least."

"Oh," Lorenzo said, his eyes widening, "that's no good. I've got a couple of rooms upstairs. You two can stay here for the night! Well, come on! Even though I close late, I *do* close."

Lorenzo began walking towards the cabin. Jay and Benu paused and looked at each other with concerned expressions. Benu was the first to whisper: "We should not stay here."

"I don't think we really have a choice," Jay replied. "It's way too late now, the shabriri here are… different… and you saw what he did. This is our safest option… I mean all that noise and no shabriri. We'll be safe for the night."

"And if he decides to kill us in our sleep?"

"I dunno," Jay looked over Benu's shoulder and motioned with his chin. "Look at the guy. He's harmless."

Benu turned her head. Lorenzo was humming along with the music seeping out of the bar when he turned around and called, "C'mon! The beds I have are far more comfortable than the cold, hard ground! Ha!"

Benu looked back at Jay. She raised a questioning eyebrow. Jay shrugged and jogged to Lorenzo. Benu sighed to herself and caught up with the men. Lorenzo's stride kicked up small clouds of dust under his sneakers as he walked. Jay trotted up to Lorenzo's side and asked, "Hey Lorenzo, can I ask ya somethin'?"

"Sure, what's up?" he replied.

"Do you know a lot about the shabriri?"

"Is that what you call them? I like that. Better than what they call them around here: 'Demons.' So boring… but yes. I'd say I've learned a lot since they started showing up a few years ago."

"Then you know that males typically don't hunt at night."

"Typically, *sì*. But in the past year, they've… changed." He stopped in his tracks and crossed his arms. "Not sure what happened. Some people at the time rumored it was another curse from The Anomaly. Some argue their food supply was running low, so they've been getting desperate. The slackjaws are too fast for them to catch."

"Slackjaws?"

"You didn't see any? The big, green, deer that sometimes run around in the fields and forest."

"Yes, we have seen them," Benu replied, coming up on Lorenzo's side—opposite from Jay.

"They're so kind—*bellissima*—especially the really big ones. Whatever the case, the woods are no longer safe—day or night." His bushy mustache contorted into what Jay assumed was a frown. "Ah, but come on. Enough! Enough!" He placed both hands on Jay and Benu's backs. "The beer will get warm."

{Chapter 17}

3:21:7:13

Benu kept her hand steady over her knife as the trio ascended the steps leading to the tavern's entrance. The worn, wooden steps groaned as Jay and Lorenzo stepped off them and onto the porch in front of Benu. She wanted to keep her distance in case of an ambush. Adrenaline was still coursing through her body. She looked down the long porch for any signs of a hidden party.

A few sun-bleached benches with peeling paint sat against the massive log wall of the tavern. Plastered across the entire length were banners and signs for various Michigan breweries and beers. Lamps hung down the length of the porch from the wooden awning, lighting the entire length in gold. Benu could spot no danger and turned her attention to the entrance. Above hung another lamp; moths and other various bugs swarmed the amber glow.

As Lorenzo opened the front door, the full volume of the band blasted Benu's ears. It was a song she recognized. Immediately, the lyrics began flowing through her head. She swatted a moth out of her face as she stepped inside. As she stood in the doorway behind Jay, her toe began to instinctually tap to the beat. Yes, it was a song she recognized well: "It's the End of the World as We Know It (And I Feel Fine)" by R.E.M.

Without thinking, she began to hum along softly to herself. The band played the song perfectly. The pitch and timbre of the singer's voice were an exact match to Michael Stipe's distinctive Georgia twang. The tone of the guitars, beat of the drums, and punch of the keys all mimicked R.E.M.'s classic without fault. If Benu closed her eyes, she might as well have been listening to the recording straight off the album. She chuckled at the campy and felicitous mood the tune had mustered.

Jay turned over his shoulder and said in a heightened voice: "Kinda on the nose huh?"

"It is my favorite song, actually," she replied, trying her best to talk over the blaring music and loud conversations. The door closed behind her as Lorenzo walked towards the bar at the other side of the tavern—opposite the stage—and ascended the stairs behind it.

"Really?" Jay replied. "Why's that?"

"Hmph, I do not know," Benu replied. "I just always loved the tune of it ever since I heard it as a child."

Benu wore a solemn smile. The lyrics had become all-too-real now, but hearing her favorite song performed live with such precision flooded her with happy memories. The feeling wrapped her like a warm blanket, soothing her tense body. Her hand soon left the safety of her knife.

Jay could see Lorenzo exiting a room from a landing up above that overlooked the main dining area and stage. He followed the Italian as he walked towards the bar, disappeared behind a wall, and reappeared at the foot of the stairs.

Lorenzo walked from around the bar and began to approach Jay and Benu. He passed between long wooden benches and tables that were crowded with people sharing beers and meals—chatting about all sorts of things. The bar was packed with patrons, laughing the night away. He squeezed into the crowd that was gathered at the foot of the stage and vanished for a moment. Jay followed the tip of his shiny head through the crowd as he popped out in front of Jay and Benu.

"I've got your rooms ready," Lorenzo shouted. He held out his hands. "I can take your bags and your crossbow, *signora.*"

Benu hesitated. She looked at Jay and sighed. She unslung her crossbow and bag and handed them to Jay.

"Go with him," she said to Jay. Jay curled his lips, took her things, and nodded. Benu looked to Lorenzo and said, "Sorry, it has been rough out there."

"Ah, no worries. I understand," Lorenzo replied. "Come, come!"

Jay followed Lorenzo through the crowd. Some shot him visible signs of annoyance as the crossbow brushed against them and others were just too drunk to care. As they cleared the crowd, Jay and Lorenzo worked their way down the aisle of tables. All manner of persons were there: various ethnicities, genders, and ages—the full spectrum of Michiganders. The volumes of their hearty conversations were matched by the wails of the band as they moved into the final movement of the song.

He followed Lorenzo up the stairs that ran behind a wall parallel to the bar. Underneath the steps, he could hear the sizzle and pop of a grill and the clinks of silverware and plates. As they turned the corner and walked across the landing, Jay peered down into the crowd to see Benu had joined with a raised, cheering hand and a beer in the other.

When'd she get that? Jay thought as he smirked and shook his head.

Lorenzo opened two rooms, flicked the lights on, and turned to Jay, "Here you are! They're not the fanciest, but a bed's a bed right?"

"We're not picky," Jay replied. "Thank you, Lorenzo."

"*Di niente*, don't worry about it," he patted Jay on the shoulder. "Come have a beer when you're settled in. It's on the house!"

Jay nodded as Lorenzo walked back down the landing. Jay was beat, but the siren call of alcohol was too tempting to ignore. He quickly dumped their things in the rooms, shut the doors, and hurried back down.

Tiny bubbles of Jay's Dirty Blonde traveled up from the bottom of the glass and floated to the top. He traced a random bubble and watched as it followed the trail, crawling up the side before treading across the surface of the beer for a bit before merging with the small island of bubbles that floated along the inner wall of his glass. He grabbed the half-empty glass and took a huge gulp. The amber ale dribbled out the corner of his mouth as he set his drink down. He looked over his shoulder at the lines of dining tables, still occupied with guests.

The stage was empty; the band was outside taking a smoke break. At the far end, he could see Benu chatting away with random patrons as she enjoyed a hot plate of fried cod and French fries. A waitress retrieved the four empty glasses by her plate as she handed her a full one off her platter. Jay smirked and turned his attention back to a TV that hung in the corner.

A football game was on—Lions vs Browns. The score was six to seven by the end of the second quarter. Four fumbles had already been made by the Lions—six for the Browns. And both teams had issues dealing with constant interceptions. Jay never cared for football very much; he was always a hockey guy. Taking Her to see the Red Wings in the Joe Louis Stadium was one of their first dates.

The puck sailed across the rink and skipped into the goal as the buzzer sounded for the end of the second period. The Detroit Red Wings were now up two goals over the Toronto Maple Leafs. Jay sat down in his seat; his voice hoarse from the cheering he had just done. He looked over at Her and shouted, "Man, what a shot!"

She simply nodded with a smile. Jay could tell from Her forced enthusiasm that She wasn't completely enjoying herself. She wasn't miserable, but She wasn't ecstatic either. Jay had convinced his mom to lend him money for the both of them, and he even saved up his allowance to buy his date a commemorative jersey that She now wore. *Why'd She even agree to come?* He thought.

Jay picked at a pimple on his teenage cheek and said, "Y'know if you're bored, we can go."

There was a slight bit of sass in his voice. He didn't want to leave. No way. But he felt a slight bit of betrayal from Her disinterest, as if She had only said "yes" out of pity. That feeling stirred a small storm of anger in him. Jay liked this girl. He liked Her a lot. He liked Her so much that he wanted that feeling to be genuine. He wanted it to be beyond skin deep. But, he needed to be sure that the arrow that had struck his heart had also struck Hers.

"Why'd you come?" he asked plainly.

She tilted Her head in confusion.

"Why'd you say 'yes' if you really didn't want to come?" Jay elaborated.

She asked if he really wanted Her there.

"Yes! Of course! I want to do anything and everything with you— no matter what it is."

She simply retorted that the feeling was mutual and grasped his hand.

◉

The game between the Lions and Browns had ended. As the next one began, Lorenzo walked over to the TV and ejected a disc out of a DVD player that was mounted underneath. The game immediately stopped and a bright white screen, searching for a video signal, was displayed across the flat LED TV. A wave of sighs traveled down the bar.

"Yo, Lorenzo! I wanted to watch that one!" hollered a man from somewhere down the line.

"C'mon! You've seen that game a million times. The Packers win... just in case you were too drunk to remember yesterday! Ha!" Lorenzo replied as he squeezed the latches closed on the DVD case of NFL recordings. He pulled out a stack of DVDs from beneath the counter and started thumbing through them. "Let's have a bit of variety for once, eh? Baseball? No. Tennis? No. Boxing? No, no... Ah! How about this? Now, *this* is something different!"

He held up the DVD case to show the cover to his onlookers. Centered was a black-and-white photo of a trio of Ford GT40s crossing a finish line from the viewpoint of the grandstands. A man stood by the side, waving a checkered flag. Old trailers and foreign cars comprised the background behind the racetrack barrier. The picture was bordered with white in a sea of orange—with a baby-blue, horizontal stripe above it. Within the stripe was the title: *7,000 RPM: A 1966 Le Mans Documentary.*

Lorenzo looked at Jay, "It's a video I saved off the internet before everything went to shit. Made the cover myself!" He popped open the case and inserted the disc. The screen skipped a bit and then immediately cut to a title card. The low-grade audio of old revving started crackling through the TV speakers.

The crowd booed.

"Ehhhh, *taci!* Shut your holes!" Lorenzo shouted as he waved a dismissive hand. He started to refill their glasses. "Would be good for you lot to learn a little history, eh?"

As he tended to a drunkard at the end of the bar, the kitchen door behind the bar swung open and a woman backed through it, her hands full with a platter of fresh food. She approached Jay and placed a hot plate of chicken tenders and fries in front of him. "Here ya go, hon," she said with a thin-lipped smile. Jay was starstruck for a moment. The woman's face was young—in her mid-thirties perhaps. Bright red freckles dotted her soft white cheeks. Her scarlet hair was tied up in a ponytail with tufts of it covering the right half of her face, meeting at her collarbone. Jay couldn't be completely certain, but he could tell behind her white, greasy apron that she had a slim, fit figure.

"Um… thank you," Jay stuttered, trying his hardest not to blush.

She shot him one more tight-lipped smile and walked down the line, passing Lorenzo as he came back towards Jay. Jay took a cautious bite of chicken. He half-expected the taste of stale packaged food or worse: the aftertaste of expired beans straight out of the can, but he was pleasantly met with the hot and crispy crunch of moist, fried chicken. He had to catch a glob of drool that had escaped the corner of his mouth as he chewed away the delicious meat.

Lorenzo looked back at the redheaded waitress and then came up to Jay, placing his hefty forearm on the counter. He leaned in. "Hey, don't ogle my Mel too much, *amico.*"

His deep grumble kept Jay from swallowing for a moment. The air was silent between them as Jay gulped audibly. He knew one well-placed fireball could blow Lorenzo's head clean-off, if it came to that, but the old, muscular man that leaned over his plate of chicken tenders made that seem like an impossible feat; Lorenzo was fireproof.

He clapped Jay across the shoulder, causing Jay to drop the chicken tender he was holding back onto the plate.

"I'm kidding! I'm kidding! Ha-ha! Look at your face! Beet-red. Like a little tomato," Lorenzo bellowed as he laughed. "My Mel is way too out of *your* league. Though she was out of *my* league as well until she said yes to marrying me! Ha!"

Marrying you! Jay screamed in his mind. You *must have at least twenty… No: thirty … years on her!*

Lorenzo looked back to see Mel backing into the kitchen with a platter full of empty plates and glasses. He closed his eyes and blew a few kisses. She shook her head and rolled her eyes before replying with a wink and disappearing through the swinging doors.

"Ah… isn't she the best?" Lorenzo sighed.

The band started to set back up behind Jay. He could hear the shuffling of equipment as amps and mic stands moved about. The drummer had dropped a stick, and it clattered with that thin wooden verbose that should've been caught earlier. Vocals began coming through the house speakers as the singer ran a sound check. The guitarists began playing the ritualistic song of "tuning," plucking each string one by one.

Finally, they were ready. Jay swiveled in his stool as the house went quiet. A small squeal of feedback sounded as the singer spoke: "We've gots a couple more for ya'll. It's gettin' kinda late and we best get on gettin'. I think we gonna play a few slow ones, but let's start with one of my favorites."

The lead guitarist started to pluck away. Jay immediately recognized the string of notes and surreal tone of the guitar. As the intro faded into a sustain, the vocalist began to sing, and Jay mouthed along to a tune he held dear to his heart: "Black Hole Sun" by Soundgarden.

The verse opened up and spoke of emotions and true feelings masked by disguises so convincing, that others couldn't hope to decipher the meaning behind them.

Jay chortled as he stared on. The melancholy tune wrapped his body like a warm campfire on a chilly evening. The song was played without fault—more than without fault; it was downright perfect. The vocalist's southern accent was entirely gone, completely possessed by the inflection of Chris Cornell's rich voice. *These guys are fuckin' good*, he thought.

He returned to his meal. The rumbles and roars of the cars coming out of the TV were fighting against the growing crescendo of the band. Jay moved his attention back to the race and watched as the cars zoomed along the racetrack. To his left, the people at the bar were either watching the performance or talking amongst themselves. Lorenzo, however, was solely focused on the aged footage of old Fords and Ferraris.

"You know," he shouted to Jay. "I was named after Lorenzo Bandini… that guy! There!" He pointed to a sleek, rounded Ferrari 330 P3 as it zoomed past the camera—a black "21" in a white circle plastered on its door. "My father *loved* racing. '*Ferrari è la migliore!*'— 'Ferrari is the best!'—he would always say. He wanted me to always know that—named me in a way that I could never forget! Ha! And you know what? It worked. I love those damn, smog-spewing things! I can tell you do too, *amico*… just by the way you stare at the screen!"

Jay raised his glass in confirmation.

"Tell me, Jay. What were you and *signora* doing out here? I don't think I've seen any outsiders here in oh… a couple of years or so— shortly after that stupid diamond drowned us in red that one night."

"Well," Jay began raising his voice as the second verse was coming to a close, "Benu wants to see her folks in Cadillac. As for myself…"

He went on to explain the journey he had begun nearly a week ago. The trials and tribulations he had struggled through to get to this bar, and the ultimate goal of his ambitions. He left out some details— ones that drew out heavy emotions—but the primary facts were all there. A weight felt lifted again—smaller than the one that had dissipated with Benu. Jay still felt a quiver in his chest, but his body language hardly showed it. Still, a solemn force floated across the bar and into Lorenzo. Jay could see something had touched him deeply.

As the band moved into the chorus, Jay could feel the lingering presence of The Anomaly permeate through the walls of the inn. The black hole sun would soon wash away this moment and all that came before.

"Ah," Lorenzo murmured, barely audible in the fading chorus, "I see. Well, I wish you all the luck you could possibly need, *amico.*"

"Cheers, Lorenzo," Jay raised a glass. Lorenzo snatched a bottle of Founder's Porter from the fridge behind him, popped off the cap, and clinked it against Jay's glass.

"*Salute!*" he cheered. As he tipped his head back and began knocking back the beer, he turned to the TV and exclaimed, "Ah! Here is when Miles passes Lorenzo in the straight!" He wiped a few dribbles of dark, roasted beer off his snowy beard and mustache—now stained slightly by the porter.

Jay watched on with Lorenzo, trading their vast knowledge of everything four-wheeled. The band had moved onto a slower, quieter tune—one that Jay didn't recognize. He looked over to check on Benu; she had passed out onto her crossed arms, drooling a steady stream of saliva out of her gaping mouth onto her sleeve. Jay could see the drool had formed a dark spot as it soaked into her shirt. He chuckled to himself at the sight of his savior ugly-sleeping. *If only I had my phone,* he thought as he imagined showing her the photo he would've taken of her ridiculous face.

"Don't worry," Lorenzo assured Jay. "I'll make sure Mel gets her into her room."

"Thanks again, Lorenzo," Jay said. "This trip has been hard on us... hard on *her.*"

"Yes, I can tell."

Behind Lorenzo, the kitchen doors swung open, but no one came out. Jay thought maybe he had just missed the person who exited, but no waiter or waitress was out on the floor right now. As the door swung back and forth, Jay thought he had witnessed a paranormal event just as a chunky cat hopped onto the counter between Jay and Lorenzo. The hefty tabby meowed in Jay's face. Its dark green eyes let out a tiny, curious puff of blue mist as it blinked. The blue wisp faded so quickly Jay attributed it to an illusion caused by the four Dirty Blondes he had had.

"Nerf!" Lorenzo exclaimed as he scooped up the bowling ball of fluff. "Where have you been, silly boy?" He gave the cat a smooch on the head as it meowed in return. "Jay this is Nerf. Nerf, Jay."

He set the cat back down on the counter as it took a seat and stared daggers at Jay. Jay pulled off his beanie and presented it to Nerf. The cat flared its little brown nose and took a few whiffs of the hat before licking its nostrils. Jay put his hat back on and presented an index finger next. Nerf stretched out his neck and gave Jay's finger the same sniff and lick reaction. Jay held his finger in position. Soon, Nerf came forward and rubbed his left cheek across Jay's finger. Jay then cupped the cat's head in his hand and began scratching behind its ears. Nerf's eyes slowly shrunk into a squint as he began to purr.

"Wow, you sure do know how to introduce yourself to a cat!" Lorenzo said, astonished. "Typically, Nerf swats at nearly everyone he meets!"

Jay chortled and replied, "Ah, I'm just used to it. I grew up with cats. Had a couple myself for a while."

Nerf reeled back from the petting. He decided he was done and jumped off the counter. Jay watched as the kitchen doors performed another act of paranormal activity.

The documentary was in its last quarter now. Footage showed patrons from all over the globe making their way to the track in the early French morning. A man brushed his teeth at a spigot by his trailer. Children played with little wooden cars on the foldable, plastic tables. A woman yelled in French for her missing husband.

"Let me ask you something, *amico*," Lorenzo said. "Why do we hold onto the past so much?"

Jay opened his mouth to answer but retracted. He wanted to say something along the lines of learning from one's mistakes and how the preservations of mishaps can ensure people never make them again. But, he felt this was oddly morbid. So, he replied: "To give us a sense of immortality."

"Oh? Explain."

"Well, it's simple. If we continue to archive information and evidence of the past, then those people will continue to exist in some fashion in our world. Thus, makin' them immortal… in a sense." His thoughts always drifted back to Her.

"Ah! That whole 'you actually die twice' idea: once, when you are buried and again when someone speaks your name for the last time? *Sì?*"

"Yes, but some people, like Lorenzo Bandini, have gotten an even longer lease on life wouldn't you say?"

"Ha-ha! *Bellissimo!* Wonderful! I like that!"

They toasted again.

Jay had trouble drinking his toast in earnest. A thought came over him: *But soon that lease will end along with everything else.*

The documentary was finishing up. The three Ford GT40s were crossing the finish line as the man on the cover of the DVD case waved his checkered flag in a dramatic photo finish. The cars paraded through the crowd as the drivers sat on the roofs with the doors propped open. Lorenzo leaned over to Jay and asked, "Hey, can I ask you one more thing?"

"Sure, shoot," Jay replied.

"Why do you like cars, *amico?*"

"Well," Jay began. He considered giving the same answer he had given to Her long ago but instead, he tapped into a different avenue of thought. "Ya haveta be drivin' the right car—one free of rules, regulations, and restrictions. There's a point you reach when the speeding scenery flies by, you hear nothin' but the roar of the engine and smell nothing but fresh air. That's when the world outside your car feels frozen in time. You're *finally* free of the noise. There are plenty of ways to escape—movies… video games, and stuff like that. But I dunno… I guess when I'm drivin' and enjoying the winding roads and open air, I'm livin' my escape through something truly tangible in a way that doesn't deny me reality."

Lorenzo smiled, "Good answer." He tapped on the counter, "Come. Let me show you something. Mel! Take care of the bar for me for a bit!"

Jay downed his beer and made his way around the bar. He followed Lorenzo out the back door and through the kitchen. Nerf was sitting on the wooden railing. It swiveled his head around and gave Jay a 'meow'. Jay began scratching the back of his ear as Nerf began to purr. Crickets chirped in the chilly Michigan night. Small insects surrounded the dim incandescent lamps that hung over the rear exit. In the dark backdrop of the black forest, fireflies danced like flickering stars. The smell of the earth permeated the area as rain clouds formed overhead. Off to the side, a line of generators hooked up to a small yard of solar panels were humming away.

The two men strolled towards a small barn. On one side of the barn was a vegetable garden filled with all the ingredients Lorenzo needed. A chicken coop and pig pen occupied the other side. A line of burbot was hanging by the barn's entrance—Lorenzo's latest catch.

"Whatcha wanna show me?" asked Jay.

Lorenzo looked back and smiled. "Something I think only someone like you can appreciate."

Lorenzo led Jay to the large double doors of the small barn. He reached into his pocket and pulled out a large iron key ring that held a singular black key. The double doors had a matching black lock which Lorenzo took in the palm of his hand and clacked open with a definitive twist of his key. He motioned to Jay to open the right door as he opened the left. Jay nodded as he grabbed hold of the worn, wooden pocket-door and slid it open in unison with Lorenzo. As he turned to look inside, moonlight poured into the barn and illuminated a gorgeous object.

Jay could hardly believe it.

What sat before him was an immaculate 1966 Alfa Romeo Spider.

"Well? Thoughts?" Lorenzo egged Jay on with a big, goofy smile.

"Ummm… ahhh… Well, I *think* I like it!" Jay replied, outdoing Lorenzo's smile.

"I bought it back in Italy when I was young," Lorenzo began as Jay walked around, inspecting the vehicle. "It's a relic of my country's past! Ha-ha! I always wanted a little red convertible, but it had to be *Italiano*! Ha!"

"But, how? I don't get it. There hasn't been pristine car like this since The Anomaly!"

"Ahhh, don't ask how. Just be glad you are alive to ask 'how'!"

"Does it—?"

"Run? Yes! But it doesn't drive. Eh, something wrong with the differential or something. But… it runs. See for yourself."

"You're serious?" Jay asked, his heart skipping a beat. "Do you have the keys?"

"Heh-heh. Already in the ignition. Go on." He motioned with an outstretched, open palm.

Jay squinted into the cream interior. The leather seats were completely and utterly pristine. The glossy, wooden steering wheel hadn't lost a speck of its sheen, and the dash looked as if it had rolled off the assembly line earlier that evening.

Jay spotted the keys in the ignition, just as Lorenzo had claimed. He pulled at the door handle which gave a chunky 'clunk' only classic steel could make. It took him a moment to fully absorb the feelings he was exuding but, soon, he found himself sitting in the driver's seat. He ran his hands along the steering wheel—the same ritual he had done with his Miata. The spindly steering wheel felt smooth and flawless. He ran his hand across the spotless dash and examined his fingers.

This can't be real, he thought.

Nerf had joined him in the passenger seat while he was entranced by the vehicle. The thick tabby gave a faint 'meow', sat on its haunches, and began grooming an outstretched rear leg. Jay grinned and gave Nerf a few more scratches on the head. The cat halted its grooming and whipped its head at Jay without moving any other part of its body—its rear leg still suspended in the air. Nerf licked his whiskers and went back to grooming. Jay shook his head and placed both hands on the wheel.

He worked through the routine: engage the clutch, shift into neutral, wiggle the stick side-to-side, and start the ignition.

Jay closed his eyes, his hands trembling at the possibility of feeling the rumble of an internal combustion engine for one last time.

He turned the key.

The feeling numbed him for a moment; he couldn't believe it. The seat underneath quaked as the burst of gasoline-fueled explosions rattled the little sports car. The vibrations traveled up Jay's arms as he held his mouth open in astonishment.

"Give it some gas, *amico*! Rev it! Ha-ha!" yelled Lorenzo over the hood of the car.

Jay didn't hesitate, kept his foot down on the clutch, and pumped the gas. First, he commanded the coupe to grumble. Then, he commanded it to snarl. Finally, he commanded it to howl.

"Yes! Ha-ha!" Lorenzo shouted. "How is it?"

"It's perfect, Lorenzo!" Jay replied, matching Lorenzo's volume. He leaned his head back, closed his eyes, still revving the engine, and whispered to himself, "it's perfect."

{Chapter 18}

3:9:10:22

Cobwebs hung from the ceiling like safety nets for their eight-legged trapeze artists. In the far corner, the morning light glistened off the silvery strands of intricate webbing, wrapped and bundled in small white balls. The net fluttered in the breeze that flowed through the cracks in the weathered windowsill. Jay traced one of the performers as its spiny legs took it along one of the thin tightropes.

The room was different from the one he wearily stumbled into last night. The worn blanket he woke up under was a dirtied mimic of what he had pulled over himself last night. A dusting of dirt and rubbish was spread out across the floor, as if the room hadn't been swept in years. Dust lingered in the air, eliciting a small sneeze from Jay as he sat up on the edge of the bed. His jacket and beanie were draped over a rickety, wooden chair that was scooted under a dust-caked desk. Jay grabbed his clothes off the chair and wiped them off; puffs of filth dimmed the sunlight coming through the window.

He threw on his clothes and thought to himself: *What happened here? The room was immaculate last night.*

He looked above at the lightbulb that had supposedly lit his room to find it shattered, made opaque by grime. Jay reached into his pocket and felt his ring. His bag rested against the leg of the bed at the foot end. He checked its contents; everything was accounted for. Slinging it over his back, he tried to recount last night's events.

The Italian.

The band.

The fat cat.

The food.

The drinks.

Drinks! How many did I have? Five or six, maybe? Definitely felt like that many when I was pissin' for fifteen minutes straight!

Jay's mind was clear. Unaffected by the lingering effects of the heavy night of drinking he partook in last night. The feeling was a conundrum in that sense. Although the environment was unknown to him, Jay felt no panic. His slumber was pleasant, rejuvenating him. He went to open the door. The doorknob jiggled loosely in his hand as he turned it. A hefty creak sounded throughout the entirety of the door's travel, filling the empty tavern with an echo.

He stood over the wooden railing. Parts of it were splintered or entirely collapsed. Down below, chairs and benches were turned over with a smattering of trash strewn about. Banners and decorations that were on the walls were all broken, crooked, and fallen to the floor. The stage was completely barren—stripped of any audio equipment. Jay could spot tracks leading from the entrance to the areas he, Benu, and Lorenzo had been to; he could even see the bright red cushion of the barstool he sat at, now free of dust from him sliding off it. He patted his ass and brought his hand to his face to find that it had been dirtied. At first, he suspected foul play, but the undisturbed layers of dust on the turned-over chairs and tables confirmed no confrontation had taken place. Everything that Jay had seen and touched was there, but now looked like it had been abandoned for years.

The neighboring door creaked open. Benu stepped out, rubbing one eye—a befuddled look on her face that matched Jay's.

"Hey," Jay said as she joined him.

"Hey," she replied as she processed the scene. "What happened here?"

"Dunno. But whatever happened… didn't happen overnight." He pointed to the far end of the long table Benu sat at last night. "See the chair at the end there? See how your ass wiped off the dust but everything else is still dirty? We haven't been here as long as the dust."

Benu sneezed and said, "I do not understand… Are you missing anything?"

"Nope. You?"

"No. Nothing was stolen. All I remember was having a drink, then passing out. Hmph, I was totally exhausted... so how did I get to my room?"

"Lorenzo carried you. You were out cold when we came back in from checkin' out his car in the barn... then we came back and saw you were still asleep. Everyone had pretty much left at that point, so I decided to turn in for the night. Lorenzo scooped you over his shoulder and yeah... guess he put you to bed—probably tucked you in, too."

"This is strange. This is very strange." Benu placed a hand on her hip and another around her chin as she rubbed it. "Wait... why did you go to see his car? Was there something special about it?"

"Oh, you wouldn't believe it!" Jay's enthusiasm had thrusted out of the peculiarities of the current situation. "He's got a Spider, a little convertible, and it runs! It fuckin' *runs!*"

"Bullshit."

"I swear! C'mon, I'll show ya."

Jay rushed towards the stairs. He nearly tripped on the long, moldy rug that ran down the length of the landing. Benu hurried to catch up. As they descended the groaning steps, a tread cracked and split under Benu's feet. She caught herself on the railing, which sagged under her weight. She regained her footing to see Jay at the bottom, waving her over.

Where is Lorenzo? She thought as she followed Jay into the kitchen.

The kitchen was an absolute mess. Benu's steps lifted with resistance as she ripped her boots from the sticky floor with a definite squelch. Pots and pans were stacked like towers on the greasy stovetops. Shards of broken plates and utensils littered the floor. However, in the far corner, Benu noticed a deep fryer and stove were oddly cleaner than the rest—the smell of recently cooked food in the air.

Jay was completely oblivious, his mind focused on the car. He rushed out the back, forgetting to hold the door for Benu. She caught it before it could smack her in the face and called out, "Slow down, *dost*!"

Jay turned back as he trotted towards the barn. "It's right over here!"

He turned his attention back to the barn and caught a glint of the chrome bumper, with the rest of the Fiat covered in shadow. As Jay passed the vegetable garden, he could hear the clucks and oinks of the farm animals to the right. He turned into the barn and froze in his tracks. The sight before him was all-too-familiar.

A decaying, sun-bleached, and rusty-red convertible lay dead on the barn's dirty floor.

"What?" Jay murmured to himself.

Benu came up beside him, "*This* runs?"

"No… no, no. I swear, Benu. Last night, this car was *pristine*. I felt the engine shake the seats under me! It was… It was—"

"An illusion, *amico*," Lorenzo's voice approached them to their right. The two looked over to see Lorenzo walking their bikes towards them; Nerf walked alongside him. "I'm sorry," he said with a somber smile.

Benu started to unsling her crossbow.

Lorenzo stopped and stood up straight, "Ah, no need for that. You are unharmed and I don't have any plans to hurt you. I found these out in the direction you came from. They are yours, *sì*?"

Jay nodded to Benu to calm herself; she obliged. He walked over to Lorenzo and asked, "An illusion? I don't understand."

"It was just that: an illusion—not real," he replied. The same blue mist Jay witnessed last night puffed from his eyes as he spoke. "The people, the music, the *car*… All my doing—well, somewhat my doing."

"What do you mean *somewhat*?" Benu asked.

Lorenzo sighed, "Three years ago, Second Convergence, the big guy up there did its huge hum. *Terribile!* Awful! It made my headache worse! I was here at my tavern, trying to sleep off a cold. I struggled to get back to sleep… but, eventually, I did. When I woke up, this little *bambino*, was sleeping on my chest." Nerf responded with a 'meow'.

"I had never seen this cat in my life—figured he just wandered in through a door my manager forgot to lock… That guy was always forgetful… Anyways, I noticed this little guy was different. His warm, fluffy body brought me so much comfort. You saw it, yes? The blue smoke? The Anomaly shared something with us… something that could ease the pain in my heart. You see, Jay… you and I share that pain. I saw the look in your eyes… Mel was indeed my wife… *mio angelo*… If only I had seen her grow old with me."

Jay understood now. He kept a tight-lipped frown and continued to listen.

"So, the cat allowed you to bring her back?" Benu asked, tenderness in her voice.

"Not exactly… The Anomaly granted me with a blessing and a curse. As my friends and loved ones died all around me, I found I could bring them back as spirits… birthed from my memories. They moved and acted on their own, as if they were never gone. Just last year, my ghosts had grown so real, they could move the things around them. I could even bring those that I haven't seen in over thirty years! Soon… I could even recreate environments, feelings, and senses as I remembered them. I could feel the extent of my power, too. I can cover, ehhh, a fifty-meter-or-so radius—give or take. *Mica male!* Not bad! Eventually… creating this grand illusion became autonomous… something that just happened every night without my thinking. Imagine my surprise when two *real* people showed up on my lawn! I had to alter some things on the spot! Ha-ha!

"In my world, no one will ever perish again… even you will become part of this illusion when you leave. But," he let out a heavy sigh, "I know none of this is real. That realization can make the daytime painful. Living the illusion itself can be painful… every night… in my little, false kingdom, safe in this bubble. Which, believe it not, is Nerf's doing. Isn't he amazing? *Fantastico!* He's kept this place safe ever since I met him. Whatever force he puts up, those demons do not dare enter!”

“But the food… and the *beer*!” Jay chimed in. “The beer couldn’t have been fake.”

“Ha! I’d be a lousy bartender if I forgot the taste of the beer I stocked!” Lorenzo teased. “As for the food, don’t worry. My little farm provides.”

“So, what *did* we drink?”

“Water, *amico*. Fresh from my well.”

“So why end the illusion at all?” Benu asked.

Lorenzo opened his mouth to answer, but Jay beat him to it, “He’s too tired. Using our powers drains us.” He held out his palm and ignited a fire in his hand.

“*Figo!*” Lorenzo exclaimed. “We really are the same! Ha! It’s true, I’m saving my energy to do it all again tonight.” He presented the bikes.

Jay snuffed out his flame and took his bike. Benu stepped forward and retrieved hers.

“Thank you,” Benu said, appreciation rich in her voice. Jay looked over at the rusty Fiat.

“And the car?” he asked.

Lorenzo placed a hand on Jay’s shoulder, “I assure you, *amico*. It sounded and felt *exactly* as you heard and touched last night.” He tapped a finger on his temple. “I wouldn’t dare forget.”

“Hey Jay,” Benu interrupted. “We should really get moving.”

“Ah! Wait!” Lorenzo said as he picked up Nerf. “Here, borrow Nerf. He’ll keep you safe until you reach the edge of the black forest.”

“How far is that?” Jay asked.

“If you take the main road… an hour or so. Please take him! He’ll be happy to help, right Nerf?”

Nerf squeaked as he stretched his jowls wide and let out a big yawn.

“Are you sure? Won’t ya be vulnerable without him?”

"Bah! I'll keep quiet until he gets back… maybe take a nap or something. It wouldn't be the first time the little *bambino* has gone out on some adventure during the day. And he always finds his way home!"

Lorenzo stepped over to Benu's bike and plopped Nerf in her front basket. The cat's round body fit tightly into it. Rolls of fat drooped over the sides and tufts of fluff bulged out between the basket's wires. Nerf balled up and settled in, his paws disappearing in the sea of fur. He was nothing but a fuzzy loaf with a cat's head propped on top.

The trio walked around the tavern to the front. In the daylight, Jay could see a dirt road at the edge of the clearing that led out of the grassy parking lot and back into the black forest. Jay and Benu mounted their bikes. As Benu rocked hers to get on, Nerf let out an annoyed '*mrow!*'.

"Oh hush," grumbled Lorenzo. "You take care of them, ok?"

Nerf replied with a meek 'meow.'

"Stay safe Lorenzo," said Jay. "And thank you for everything."

"Yes, thank you again," Benu added.

Lorenzo walked up between them, his bulky body filling the space. He placed a hand on each of their shoulders and said, "*Prego,* and don't worry: we'll meet again." He patted their backs and stepped away.

Jay and Benu nodded to each other and set off down the dirt road. Jay looked over his shoulder to see Lorenzo waving goodbye. He set his eyes forward for a bit but was overcome by a strange feeling—an urge to look back again. When he did, Lorenzo was gone. Had he already gone inside? He looked over at Nerf; the cat's green eyes exuded blue mist.

An illusion within an illusion? No.

The tavern disappeared behind the tree trunks as Jay and Benu turned onto the main road.

The air was silent between the two as they strolled down the road. Even under the protective guise of the cat, Benu's years of surviving in the Royal Oak urban jungle had made her habits steadfast. Jay rode alongside her. He wanted to strike up conversation—something to pass the time. Benu had been a trustworthy ally and good friend; Jay wanted to get to know his companion. As he studied her facial features, he realized she wore a great deal of her personality outright. The glare of her deep-set eyes, surrounded by dark circles of insomnia, pierced the path before her. The silhouette of her long, slender nose was like an arrow aimed true. She held a cold expression—not one of discontent or animosity, but of determination and confidence. As her unkempt hair was swept back by the wind, Jay could see the dark skin of her sunken cheek had been made darker in patches from smears from dirt she hadn't had the chance to wash off.

Nerf mirrored Benu in his forward stare. The plump cat was as still as stone, with fumes of blue occasionally puffing out from its eyes before they were whisked away by the wind. The two looked like the perfect match. As Jay smiled at the cute imagery, Nerf let out a 'meow' as if calling to something. Benu quickly grasped Nerf's back and shook him, gently mouthing out a soft *'shh'*. As Benu looked up, she hit her brakes with a mild skid. Jay, still fixated on the two, reacted immediately.

"What's up?" Jay whispered.

Benu raised her chin towards a black tree about a hundred and fifty feet ahead of them. Jay squinted to see the distant face of a shabriri leering from behind the massive trunk, its antlers bouncing a glare as it exhaled misty clouds. Benu unslung her crossbow, careful not to make a peep. As she shouldered it, only the delicate clacks of its mechanics could be heard. She held the creature's head in her scope's reticle, ready for the charge. However, Nerf decided to handle this one.

Benu dropped her aim when her bike was suddenly rocked by Nerf's fat body leaping out of the basket and into the road.

"Shit," Benu murmured as she snatched a handle with her leading hand.

Jay and Benu watched as Nerf trotted a couple paces in front of them. As he did, they could see that the shabriri had been pushed out from its stalking place and forced into the road. Nerf stopped and plopped down on his haunches, his tail whipping with agitation. The shabriri clicked and growled as it stood tall on its hind legs and began clawing at the air. Nerf growled back and let out a drawn-out warning *'mrow'*... The monster didn't heed it.

The cat let his growl swell before letting out a vicious cry. The shabriri reeled back and dropped its blades to the ground; it stared daggers into the furball. Nerf scrunched up his round body and arched his back. His ears flattened behind his head as he let out a small hiss. Then, in a flash, he sprang forward a tiny distance with a series of screeching cries and swipes at the air. The forcefield was bashed into the shabriri with a tremendous blow that sent the massive beast toppling onto its back.

Jay and Benu jumped at the impact of Nerf's attack on the shabriri and found themselves looking on in amazement. Jay had only noticed his jaw had fallen to the floor when he looked over at Benu and saw hers had done the same. A single expression rang through their heads.

Whoa.

As the shabriri scrambled to its feet, it shook its entire body like a wet dog before sprinting off into the woods. Nerf followed the sound of the fleeing monster for a short while, growling before calming down. His ears made a flapping sound as he shook his head and scratched an itch under his chin with a rear paw.

"I suddenly like this cat a lot," joked Benu, speaking at a normal volume as she put her crossbow away.

"Sounds like ya suddenly have more faith in him too," Jay replied.

Nerf finished his pamper session and waddled back to Jay and Benu. He sat down between the two, tilted his head up at Benu, and made a requesting 'meow' with wide, black-filled eyes. She bent down and pet him, "Good job, Nerf. You are a very good cat."

'*Mrow!*'

"Is something the matter?"

'*Mroooow! Mrow…*'

Jay chuckled under his breath, "He wants you to put him in the basket."

"Oh," replied Benu with wide eyes of realization.

'*Mrow…*'

"Right, right. My mistake."

Benu leaned over and scooped up the chunky cat and nestled him into her front basket. He settled in, swiveled his head, and gave Benu two slow blinks of appreciation with a soft purr.

"He's thankin' you," Jay said. "Give him two slow blinks back."

"Are you serious?" Benu asked.

Jay nodded towards Nerf. "He's waitin'."

Benu turned back to Nerf to see he was indeed waiting for a response. Benu extended her neck towards Nerf. She looked deep into the total blackness of the feline's eyes. Slowly, she squeezed her eyes shut and smoothly opened them—then, again. Nerf gave her one fast blink and looked forward. '*Moaw!*'

"Hmph," Benu exclaimed proudly as she turned to Jay, "you know a lot about cats."

"Not much to know," he replied as he began to pedal off.

Benu caught up. "You must really like them, *dost*."

"Well, I grew up with a couple of cats so, yeah. I do like cats. What about you?"

"No… I am not much of a pet person in general. I like animals, do not get me wrong, but owning a pet just seemed like… too much responsibility, ha-ha. And trust me, I had *enough* of that already."

"I bet. Being a doctor ain't easy."

"Indeed! I know this is very… morbid, but I have seen a lot of people die, not just out here, but during my time at the hospital, we lost a lot of people. I could not imagine growing so attached to a pet knowing it will be gone even sooner than some of my patients!"

"Yeah…" Jay replied, trailing off in a somber tone.

"Oh," Benu said as a twinge of guilt brushed her heart, "my mistake, *dost*. Sorry."

"No, no it's ok."

Benu tried to change the subject, "Did you and your wife own any cats?"

"Oh, no. Unfortunately, she was allergic. Ha-ha. But she *loved* cats. Sometimes we'd go to the pet store while we were out just so she could play with the cats… and then she'd immediately turn to me with puffy eyes and a runny nose."

Benu laughed as she pet Nerf on the head, smushing his ears.

"Hey, *dost*. What was her name? You have not told me."

"Oh…" Jay replied. "Her name…"

A tight lump had shot up his throat and choked him of his words. He wanted to say it. How desperately he wanted to say Her name! But only bumbling sounds came out his mouth, as if he was trying to speak for the first time. He slowed to a halt. Benu did as well and looked back at him, asking: "Jay? Are you ok?"

No, he thought. He closed his eyes, shut his mouth, and bit his lips. Sucking in a swell of air through his nostrils, he held back tears. In the darkness, he could see Her name, written across Her hospital chart. He exhaled slowly through his mouth and opened his eyes, red with moisture. He felt the weight of his backpack, the little urn pressed against his back, and remembered the relief of the emotional baggage he had tossed off three times before.

"Sorry," he finally whispered. "It's… hard for me."

"It is ok, *dost*. I understand."

"With all due respect, Benu, I don't think you do."

"I have lost people too."

"But not your wife," Jay looked up with a pale face. "Some people marry because they have to… or they're expected to. Some people do it on a whim. Some for money. But… most people do it out of love. I initially did it out of love, of course. I loved her, Benu. When we first started goin' out, it was all because I just wanted a girlfriend, y'know? And she *just* wanted a boyfriend, I assume. But soon, it became more

than that. We shared our thoughts, ambitions, passions, our bodies…
but eventually sharin' turned into a singular act of givin' and takin'.
Somethin' more than just a kind gesture… it was simply our way of
life. We didn't just grow closer… we became a part of each other.

"The day I married her, I realized I gave her a portion of myself. I
married her not only out of love, but because I'd given somethin' to
her, and I couldn't live without it… without her. I was no longer
whole on my own… I'm still not. The little urn that's sittin' in my bag
holds a piece of my being that I can never get back. Do you
understand? If I speak her name… I'm invoking that lost portion of
what makes me, *me.* I can feel it… I can feel that swell of pain being
ripped from my core, up my throat, and off my tongue if I say her
name. I feel that if I even whisper her name, I'll lose myself… binding
it to a world that is doomed to expire."

"Jay…" Benu wasn't sure what to say; this was not a wound she
could mend.

"That's why," he pedaled next to Benu, "I haveta do this, Benu. I
have to get to Escanaba. I made her a promise—a promise I've sat on
for seven years. And I guess the only push I needed was the fuckin' end
of the world." He grimaced but calmed himself. "I dunno why… but
deep in my heart, I feel returning her physical remains to the earth…
makin' her final words ring true… It will release me from this
torture—make me whole again in this reality… the one where we
shared everything together… if only for a moment."

Benu placed a hand on Jay's shoulder and smiled. "Then, let us
not waste any more time."

Jay left behind a heavy weight as he and Benu continued down
the road.

{Chapter 19}

3:7:26:41

The great sequoias began to shrink as Jay and Benu neared the end of the accursed forest. As the canopy opened up, Jay could see muted light struggling to penetrate chilling overcast. Even the red glow of The Anomaly was but a pale, crimson spot amongst the clouds. The darkened land allowed the purple gleam of the earth to shine brighter than it usually would at midday. Jay and Benu stopped at the edge of the forest. They could see a large herd of slackjaws galloping across the field, heading towards M-115 to leap across it. As the herd hopped and skipped over the concrete barriers, Nerf slinked out of the basket and began walking back towards the forest. Jay and Benu looked back at the chubby ball of fluff.

"Guess he's headin' back home," Jay said.

"Guess so," Benu added. She called out, "Thank you, Nerf!"

Nerf turned his head, yawned with a squeaky 'meow', lapped his nose with his tongue, and jetted off into the forest—leaving a small wisp of blue mist from his eyes. Jay and Benu shared a smile. Benu swung her backpack onto her lap, pulled out her map, and checked her surroundings. She swiveled her wrist a few times—adjusting her watch—and said, more rapidly than usual: "We should be able to make it to Cadillac in about an hour and a half… If we hurry, we can save fifteen minutes, maybe!" Her voice was filled with enthusiasm, her Hindi accent strong.

Jay smirked, "Let's not rush things. I can see you're excited, but we gotta make sure we make it *alive.*"

"Hmph," Benu replied as she put her map away and retrieved her lighter and diminishing pack of cigarettes. She wrapped her cracked lips around the butt of a protruding cigarette and pulled it out. She flicked her lighter open and began striking it. Jay started raising his hand to offer a flame, but just as he began building the heat in his fingertips, Benu's lighter sprung to life. She brought the fire to her cigarette and cupped it with her other hand. As she took a drag, she puffed out a handful of gray clouds out of the side of her mouth. She continued to smoke freehanded as she put her things away and swung her bag onto her back, arching it as she wrestled it under her crossbow.

The slackjaws continued their crossing. Jay crossed his arms over his handlebars as Benu rested the elbow of her cigarette hand in her other palm across her stomach. She smoked as she slouched. "Did your patients know you smoked?" Jay teased.

"Hmph," Benu chuckled, "I started *after* I lost my job to The Anomaly, so I am going to say 'no.'"

"Ah, I see."

Benu took another drag. Her eyes traced each slackjaw as they leapt. She asked: "Do you remember First Convergence?"

"When The Anomaly was first discovered? Yeah. They didn't even call it 'First Convergence' until the second. Also didn't figure out the exact end of the world until Second Convergence… how on earth did they figure out that one?"

"I am not exactly sure myself. I remember watching some round table on the news with the top physicists of the world as they explained it. Some complicated explanations surrounding gravitational fields and the rate at which The Anomaly was breaking down the fabric of reality around it. They compared it to the third law of thermodynamics, how a closed systems tends towards entropy. But… they said it was not exactly like that. Honestly, I did not understand most of it."

"Yeah," Jay sighed, "me neither. I honestly didn't care too much for the reasoning, only that they had solid proof that it was happening."

"How long do you think they kept it from us?"

"Whaddaya mean?"

"Well, I am sure they discovered it long before announcing it to the public. A strange new, mysterious object appears in our orbit that defies all physics? I am sure the government wanted to keep that under wraps until they figured out whether or not a foreign attack or something."

"Yeah, I dunno. Maybe it's been around forever—hiding in the moon's shadow… waitin' for its chance to fuck us up. The Russians claimed to have found it first."

"And the Chinese."

"And the Germans," they both said in unison. They shared a small laugh.

"I guess it doesn't really matter anymore, huh?" Jay said.

"What were you doing at the time?" Benu asked as she flicked off some ash.

"God… I can't remember. I remember readin' that NASA had discovered some strange thing orbiting the planet… think I read it as a passing article on my phone off a post a friend shared. But as for what I was doing? Coulda been anything… work, sitting around the house, waitin' in line for groceries. Just my daily life… What about you?"

"I was visiting my mother and sister actually. My mother had the news playing on the TV, and me and my sister had overheard it as we were making dinner."

"How was growin' up in Cadillac, by the way?"

The slackjaws had finished their crossing. Their fading gallops could be heard as Benu threw her cigarette to the ground and stamped it out; she began to pedal. Jay rode next to her as she replied: "Well, it was… different—especially as one of two Indian kids in town. And for a few years of my life, I was the *only* Indian kid in town. I was twelve when we moved from India. Three years later, my sister was born."

"Oh, did your parents move there for a job or somethin'?"

"Yup. My father accepted a position as a pediatrician at the local hospital. And my mother was a nurse. Why he could not find a position in a larger, more Indian-populated city I have no idea."

"Feel free not to answer if this is insensitive but… was it hard?"

"Was what hard?"

"Being the only Indian kid in town. In school and stuff."

Benu let out a hardy laugh, "Hard? No, no. Sure, I was teased—more so in middle school than high school, but I had plenty of friends. And the people were very kind to my mother and father. They *did* constantly hound them to convert from Hinduism, but they never alienated them over it. I think it mainly had to do with my father and mother being very good at their jobs. Even after my parents divorced, people were kind to us, as far I could tell."

"Sorry to hear they divorced."

"Ah, it was no big deal, to be honest—at least to me. My father was not very involved in my life… or my mother's, for that matter. He was far too focused on his career—going as far as to hammer the idea of becoming a doctor into my head. Guess it worked… but that was all he ever gave me. It was not very hard for my mother either. I think she cried for maybe… an hour when he moved out, but nothing after that. He was never abusive… They just grew apart. But, as I said, the townsfolk were always sensitive towards us. Have to keep your kid's doctor on your good side, right? Have to treat his daughters, right?"

"I suppose so," Jay replied. As they entered a normal, overgrown forest, Jay felt a chilling twinge on his hand. He looked down to the remnants of a melted snowflake on the back of his hand. Craning his neck, he spotted a blanket of chilled white specks drifting from above. "Snow?" he said. "This early in the year?"

Benu looked over, her raven hair speckled with flecks of snow, "Looks like The Anomaly has decided to make our trip interesting." She flipped the hood of her cowl over her head.

"Great," Jay sighed. He had to contend with his beanie. "So, you were sayin'?"

"Well, I did not have much more to say. I suppose the hardest part of my life growing up was in high school. It was sophomore year that I discovered I liked girls. I kept it secret for a very, *very* long time. It was not until I achieved my bachelor's that I told my mother. But… people gossip. They talked about how it was strange that I had not shown any interests in their sons and how I never gushed over 'hot' male actors with their daughters. I was true to my feelings. I did not see them as wrong, but… I kept them to myself… for my family's reputation. For a short time, I could feel suspicious eyes on me constantly. I spent quite a few nights crying in my bedroom, I have to admit."

She speaks about this so easily… about her problems, Jay thought. *Why is it so difficult for me to do the same?*

"That… sounds like a *whole* lot more to say," Jay teased.

Benu chuckled, "Yes, I suppose so. It is just… that is all in the past. I am who I am now. And what I went through is part of my identity. I cannot really feel any sort of vitriol over it. I feel more for my mother, honestly. A lot of her devout friends pushed her to confront me over *their* suspicions about my sexuality."

"Fuckin' assholes."

"I mean… I agree, but I cannot be mad at someone for believing what they believe. Otherwise, we would all be hypocrites, in a way. Do I think they were wrong for wanting to change me because *they* thought something was wrong with me? Sure. Do I think they should change their closed-minded ways? Of course. But, in their minds… in their *beliefs*, they thought they were saving me. And I have *my* beliefs that may be negatively affecting someone unbeknownst to me. I just know approaching animosity with anger is the least effective form of persuasion."

Jay slightly shuddered in light of his previous statement. The steady snowfall continued to dust the road and stick to the overgrowth. Jay could feel the tip of his nose numb as the air became cold. The two weaved through a small series of snow-blanketed cars before returning to an empty stretch of highway.

Benu continued, "To be honest, I faced most of those kind of issues at the hospital. You get a whole variety of patients. And people's true personalities tend to 'shine' when they are sick—racists, sexists, homophobes, or all three rolled into one! 'There is no way a gay, female, pajeet is treating me!' You hear it all."

"I'm sorry, Benu. You didn't deserve any of that."

"No, and I knew it. For a while, I would get really angry—I mean, *really* angry. I yelled at patients, I admit it… Got into such heated arguments that I had to be asked to leave by other doctors one time… got reprimanded a few times too, ha-ha. But, one day, my mentor and I had a heart-to-heart. He told me that people are only the way they are from their experiences. They believe the things they do because of someone in their life, or some experience they had. So, I looked back at my own upbringing and decided if I were to respond with compassion, then maybe I can be that new person or experience that changes someone for the better."

Jay could hardly see Benu's face behind her cowl. He could only make out her prominent nose and faint outline of her mouth and chin. But as a gust passed by, her cowl fluttered back slightly revealing a gleaming smile. Eddies of sparkling snow twirled past her.

"You're a good person, Benu," Jay said.

"Hmph, I appreciate it, *dost*," she replied. "What about you? It is not fair I share my entire life and not hear about yours!"

"Well, there's not much to say—and *I* mean that. I was raised in Royal Oak. Felt like I spent most of the time out of school rather than in it, but I'm glad I at least showed up a few times because that's where I met my wife—sophomore year. I was such a bad influence—ha-ha—always convincin' her to skip class with me. Eventually, my dad lit a fire under my ass, and I got my shit together. Pretty sure he threatened me with takin' over his auto shop if I didn't graduate and get my ass to college. Funny how I ended up more like him than I had hoped."

"Yes… I *definitely* know what that feels like! Where did you go?"

"U of M, baby."

"No shit? Me too! Go Blue!"

Jay laughed, "Go Blue! God, small world after all. You'd think we woulda had a class together."

"We probably did, but you know how large those classes could get."

"Very true. But yeah, unfortunately, my dad died shortly after I got in. My ma was so distraught that her brother had to move in with us to keep her sane. After I graduated, she actually moved back to her home state of Texas to live closer to her parents. I don't blame her, though. I was pretty well set—hopped between a few biomed positions before ending up in Detroit."

"Is she still…?"

"No, sadly. She passed peacefully one night around the time of First Convergence. I didn't really keep in touch with her side of the family, and my dad's side had disowned him years before he met ma. If I'm to be honest, I got most of my support from my wife's family."

"Well, I am sorry to hear that about your parents, but I am glad you were not alone." Benu looked over with a compassionate smile. "You are still not."

Jay returned the smile. "Thank you, Benu."

Trails of snow swirled behind their speeding tires like fairy dust as they passed a rusty green sign with white borders, reading:

**CADILLAC
CITY LIMIT**

{Chapter 20}

3:6:7:15

Jay and Benu approached Cadillac from the South. They crossed over from M-55, following the long, sloping offramp onto US-131. As they rode, the gentle snowfall quickly transformed into a flurry. The afternoon sunlight was diffused over the small town in a soft blue hue that smeared into the gleam of purple from the cracks of the earth. It gave the town a fantastical tone—an alien environment amongst the heavy vegetation. Jay felt he had been transported to another world, but Benu remained laser-focused on their destination.

She was home. In a few moments, she would be introducing Jay to her mother and boasting about her adventures to her little sister. Her sister would stare in awe over her daring escape from Saginaw and question her in disbelief over the headshot she had landed on the guard outside Jay's prison. Benu's sister would fantasize about one day witnessing a slackjaw in all its emerald glory and shiver in fear at the tales of the shabriri. She would meet the heels of her palms together and clap rapidly at the tale of Nerf, the brave and almighty. Benu couldn't help but stretch a smile from ear to ear as she wiped specks of snow off her face.

Jay was having trouble keeping up. The snow had built up quickly and became a slippery slush across the road. He focused on following Benu down the streets of the Eastern suburb. They had already passed Lake Cadillac, the central lake the city was built around, and headed off deep into the residential jungle just North of the hospital. Benu had mentioned her house was on the Northeast side of town, and she didn't waste any time racing down the main road of Mitchell St. when they exited US-131. As Benu turned a corner, Jay could see a splatter of dirtied snow kick up into the air as Benu slid sideways and caught herself with her right hand against the asphalt, landing on her knee as well.

As she hurried to remount, Jay sped to her and called: "Whoa, whoa. Hold on, Benu. You're ridin' like you're gonna shit yerself, and your ma's got the only workin' toilet!" Jay dismounted and helped her up.

"I know! I know! My mistake, but we are only a few blocks away," Benu protested.

"You took a pretty nasty spill there. Lemme see your hand."

Benu reluctantly complied. Jay held her palm in his. He wiped away the bloody snow that had caked itself on the heel of her palm and along her wrist. Black stains bordered a deep scrape that was a scarlet red, brightened by the contrasting white snow that gathered in the hand. He looked down at her right knee to where the pant leg had torn, a small stain of blood soaked into the pant leg.

"I am fine, really. Let us move!" Benu rebutted like an impatient child.

Jay raised an eyebrow and asked: "Does this hurt?" He proceeded to poke the open wound in Benu's palm.

As she yanked her hand back, she cried: "Ahhh! Yes! Of course!"

Jay crossed his arms and, in an authoritative voice, said: "At least take a break here to patch yerself up."

"Fine, fine," she replied as she swung her backpack from under her crossbow. As she grasped a strap with her right hand, she grimaced and sucked her teeth. She retrieved her first aid kit and began treating her wounds. As she cleaned her scrapes with some Neosporin, Jay scanned the lines of houses.

Only a few were in wretched conditions. Aside from uncut lawns and heavy vine growth, the neighborhoods they passed by were all in fine condition. Jay could even spot a few faces peeking from behind curtains or through windows as they rode by; the city of Cadillac was not dead. The streets remained empty though, and this bothered Jay. He saw no signs of makeshift shops, food stands, or other services. Mitchell St., which was wide and ran past several storefronts, was barren of any human activity.

"Hey, Benu," Jay said, barely above a whisper.

"Yeah, Jay?" Benu replied as she wrapped her hand.

"Where is everyone?"

"You saw them. Inside I guess."

"Yeah, I know that. But… there is absolutely no one in the streets."

"I mean… it *is* coming down hard right now."

"Right, even so… there weren't any bikes parked in the streets—or food stands—or shutters on the storefronts if they decided to close. There isn't even any smoke comin' from the chimneys! Everything seems so well-maintained and yet… it's so quiet."

Jay and Benu paused for a moment and listened. Only the gentle rustle of leaves could be heard. The blanket of snow danced in swirls throughout the street as small white wisps were blown off the tips of growing snow dunes. The eerie silence pierced Jay's eardrums and drilled into his brain, striking a neuron that fired off a singular signal to his frontal lobe: 'leave.'

Jay opened his mouth to speak, but all he could mutter was a stutter as he turned to Benu and saw her mounting her bike. In Jay's contemplation, Benu had already bandaged her wounds and packed up her things.

"Alright, enough wasting time. We should move," she spoke before Jay could express his concern.

Jay held his tongue. There *were* people here. He saw their faces in the windows. But the gentle smiles they wore unsettled him. Jay convinced himself everything was alright, for Benu's sake. He owed her his life two times over. He'd keep her safe and deliver her to her goal, even if that meant accepting this suspected façade.

Benu had slowed down against her will. The heavy snow had become a slog. It had already come up to their pedals as the soles of their shoes shot out puffs of white powder. They trudged through the thick blanket, their tires crunching the slick, icy slush. They were approaching a T-intersection. Benu had indicated earlier that her house was just a left at this intersection, then a right at the next T-intersection (just a block away) and all the way down at the end of that road.

They rounded the corner, leaving thin canyons behind them. Down the street, they could spot something. At the top of the T-intersection, a body was hunched over, handling something on the ground. Jay and Benu looked at each other and nodded. They had seen enough danger and could communicate without a word at this point. The nod was simple conversation—one mutually understood: "Move slowly. Be ready."

They dismounted, careful to keep the sound of crunching snow to a minimum. They gently set the bikes into the snow, which left a neat outline. Jay's feet sunk into the chalky sea, its surface level reaching halfway up his shins. The snow soaked into the canvas of his shoes; he could feel the fabric begin to wet. As he walked, scabs of snow stuck to his jeans. Each crunch felt like a deafening echo in the cold silence. He peered over to the windows and saw grinning faces reel quickly into the darkness of their homes.

Somethin' ain't right, he thought. *Surely, Benu must feel it too!*

The sound of chewing pulled his attention forward. The body was clearer now, only the length of two houses away. It was squatted over the curb; Jay could see the hint of a human corpse laying partly into the street—its legs blanketed by snow. The upper half was underneath a creature now in full view. Its skin was a burlap-brown, ridged and calloused like warts. The back of the creature was large, with no distinction between its torso and hips. The bulbous end of its teardrop-shaped body was located at the top where a head would normally be. Instead, a small slit crested over the bulb and came down its back about a foot, coming to a point. Flanking its protruding spine were six small, circular vents measuring about ten inches wide, occupied by what looked like closed rose buds. From behind, Jay could see its twig-like arms—sitting about a third of the way down its body—were ripping strings of red meat from the chest cavity of the corpse that was splayed over the sidewalk.

Jay began heating his hands as he drew closer—the emanating heat melting the snow by his sides. Benu had unslung her crossbow and held it at a ready position. She motioned to Jay to stop; he obeyed. She slowly plunged the crossbow into the snow until it met the street with its stirrup. Benu snaked her foot inside and pulled back the drawstring. A definite 'click' indicated the crossbow was now at full draw. As she brought the crossbow back up, she loaded a bolt. She took aim at the creature and shuffled forward. Jay began to move as well.

The beast was a house-length away when it suddenly straightened up its back like a startled hare. Benu held a fist up to signal Jay to halt. Jay froze in his tracks and watched as the creature dropped the torso onto the sidewalk with a meaty 'thud'. The creature stood up straight on two spindly legs that ended in large, three-toed, webbed feet. A dusting of snow covered the tops of its feet that were tipped in stubby, black claws. Jay could see the palms of its hands now. The same stubby black claws protruded from five lanky fingers, including the thumb; the palms were a light beige and thick with calloused skin.

As it turned on its heels to face the two, it hunched its shoulders, causing its bulbous top to sag forward. A creeping chill traveled up Jay's spine as he gazed upon the creature's front. The eight-foot-tall monster was an abomination. Its torso was bisected down the middle from the slit that crested over the top and came to a V just above where its hips should be. Its splayed-open torso was lined with rows of sharp, yellowed teeth like that of a shark's. The teeth disappeared into deep, purple flesh. On the outer ridge, near the top, two reptilian eyes that blinked vertically darted between Jay and Benu. But the horrifying centerpiece was nestled within this splayed maw between its shoulders.

The soft, gentle face of a brunette girl, no older than five, had its lips caked in blood. The expression made Jay shutter fiercely; it was the same dead smile that the faces he had seen in the windows shared. Her hair was neatly combed, as if she were a doll. A small, pink hairclip decorated her glistening hair as snow collected on her head.

Her brown eyes were unblinking, staring forward, and emotionless—looking past the two of them. Her skin appeared supple and perfect, save for the crimson stain across her lips. Jay looked over at Benu.

She had a palm pressed tightly against her mouth as if holding back tears. She lowered her hand and opened her mouth to speak. Just then, the creature's child face did the same but out came a strange series of chirps and whistles, like a dove calling out. Then, it hummed out small laughter.

"Benu!" Jay shouted in a heightened whisper.

Benu steeled her emotions. Jay had snapped her back to reality, and she could now see the face she had recognized from her childhood couldn't possibly be real. She shouldered her crossbow and placed the space between the little girl's eyes in the center of her scope's red crosshairs. The snap of her crossbow fire was like a crash of thunder in the dead air. The bolt flashed before Jay's eyes and buried itself deep into the face's forehead. The creature made a series of high-pitched squawks as it clawed at its false face. It reeled back and stumbled over the corpse and lay motionless, its arms splayed out by its side.

Jay whipped around in all directions—his hands still ready to strike. He looked over to Benu, who was breathing heavily.

"You ok?" he called over.

"Yeah... yeah," Benu replied. "I just need a minute."

"I think that thing was callin' others, but I'm not seeing anything."

"Could have been a warning as well."

She started to make her way towards the creature to retrieve her bolt. Jay began to follow, still searching around. The two trudged through the snow as Jay made four trails behind him; two for his feet and two under the heat of his hands that formed little rivers of melted snow. They stood over the creature. The child's eyes were still open—its expression unchanged. Jay looked up its body and examined its reptilian eyes. They were dull and glossed over. The creature was truly dead.

"I knew this girl," Benu said in a flat tone. "I played with her at the park when I was around seven or eight." She looked over at the male corpse piled with snow. It lay on its back, its legs straddling a bike that Jay couldn't see beneath the smothering of white dunes. The corpse was a man. His chest cavity had been ripped open, exposing a mess of unrecognizable, brutalized organs encased in a shattered ribcage. Around him, snowflakes settled into pools of blood and drifted across them like little boats sailing a crimson lake. His neck was enflamed—swollen to nearly the size of a watermelon. A blackened puncture wound was on the left side of his neck with purple veins spiderwebbing out. He wore a bandana across his forehead. His skin was nearly as white as the snow that covered it.

"Did ya know him?" Jay asked.

"Yes. This was Mr. Bradford—her father."

"So, she turned into that… thing… and killed him?"

"No, that is impossible."

"Why's that?"

Benu stepped forward and placed her boot on the creature's false face. She grabbed her bolt and yanked it out, saying: "Because she died in a car accident when she was five."

Benu wiped the fresh blood off her bolt with her pant leg as Jay stayed silent, stricken with confusion over what evil The Anomaly had wrought upon Cadillac. When he finally decided to speak, Benu spoke instead: "Could you grab our bikes? I would like to cover up Mr. Bradford and get him off the road. He was my high school physics teacher. He was very kind to me and my mother after father left."

"Oh, sure," Jay replied. He took a moment to examine Benu's face as she stared coldly at Mr. Bradford's body. She lowered her hood and placed her bag on the ground. Light was starting to leave her eyes as she struggled to cling to hope of seeing her family. Jay left her to her devices as he trudged back to the bikes. He kept his eyes on the houses to his right where he had seen the faces. He knew now what they were and feared them. The faces had vanished from the windows. Jay could only hope Benu's suggestion that the cry was just a warning was true and that the creatures were now hiding deep within their stolen homes.

As Jay knelt to pick up his bike, he noticed the snow melting away around his hands, creating a little pocket. He was so on edge; he had nearly grabbed his bike with heat that could revert the rubber handlebars back to liquid petroleum. He took a deep breath and cooled his hands. He began walking the bikes back to Benu.

Benu had finished fitting Mr. Bradford's shirt on backward to cover up his mutilated torso. She looked over her shoulder to see Jay about three houses away, dragging the bikes through the heavy snow that reached his knees. She focused her attention back on Mr. Bradford and shimmied over to his legs. Pulling the bike away from him, she freed his legs. As she tucked a leg into each armpit and stood, she heard a gentle cooing from behind the house that Mr. Bradford lay in front of.

She looked over to see a creature that resembled the one she had just killed moments before standing in the shadows of the house. However, the splayed open maw—like the one that had contained the face of Mr. Bradford's daughter—was sealed shut. Only a thin, black seam separated the two halves. The reptilian eyes fixated on Benu.

She began unslinging her crossbow and nearly had it held at ease when the creature made another cooing sound that hypnotized Benu. The reptilian eyes began to pulsate in its sockets as they glowed a fluorescent green.

'Coooooo.'

The creature began walking towards Benu.

'Coooo.'

It was now halfway across the yard.

'Coo.'

Jay had his head down to avoid getting flurries of snow in his eyes but, as he looked up, he could see the maw of another creature unfurling just an arm's length in front of Benu. He dropped their bikes back into the snow.

"Shit!" he cried through the snowfall. "Benu!" He began plowing through the snow. He tried melting away the snow with a steady stream of flame; but the coverage was thick, and he couldn't risk immolating his clothes in this freezing weather. He continued wading through the snow. "Benu! What are ya doin'? Run!"

But Benu could not hear Jay. She was entranced by the siren call of the creature. As its maw split open, it revealed a sight that soothed Benu's heart. A young, female face was nestled between razor-sharp teeth. Its blank, smiling expression stretched across dark skin. The face had bushy eyebrows that sat above two brown eyes. Its nose was slender like Benu's. Even its hair bore the same raven waves that sat upon Benu's head.

"Benu…" the young face whispered. "Where have you been, Benu?"

As the maw fully blossomed, Benu whispered, *"Behan…"*
Sister.

"Benu!" Jay cried as he passed the point where Benu had taken her shot. "Move!"

Jay heated up his right hand and aimed it at Benu's back, then faltered. *Shit! I can't get a clear shot!* he thought.

All she had to do was move two steps to the right. Just two steps and Jay could incinerate this monstrosity, but Benu was lost in a trance. She dropped her crossbow into the crunchy snow and leaned in to touch her sister's face. As she reached out, a slithering stem tipped with a rosebud emerged from the creature's back and over its shoulder. A thin black needle extended two inches from the center of the bud. Benu walked forward and caressed her sister's doppelganger.

"Get the fuck away from her!" Jay shouted. He was now just across the street from Benu.

As Benu whispered something to her sister in Hindi, the creature grasped her shoulders and, with the speed of a scorpion's sting, the rosebud plunged its black needle into the side of her neck and pumped something down its stem. Benu froze as if hit with a taser and gasped out of her gaping mouth.

Fuck! Jay screamed in his head. He planted his feet and aimed his hand at the stem. He unleashed a series of fireballs. As the projectiles shot through the air, they left valleys of melted snow in their wake. The first one struck true, severing the stem at the midpoint and scattering flames to the sides. The others zoomed past the beast and collided with the face of the house behind it, sending splinters off vinyl siding into the yard. The creature released Benu as she fell into a bed of snow, gasping for air. The creature recoiled as Jay pressed the attack.

One after another, Jay fired his shots into the gaping maw, blasting away chunks of mutated flesh. Streams of fire twirled through the air from the impacts and peppered holes into the snow like a miniature meteor shower. The monster caught aflame as it desperately tried to shield itself with its arms. As Jay stepped onto the sidewalk, he tripped over Mr. Bradford and caught himself on soaked grass beneath the melted snow. He scrambled to his feet to see the burning monster had retreated beyond the house.

Jay gathered himself and rushed to Benu. He ripped the bud and needle out of Benu's neck, tossed it aside, and could see the purple veins begin to form as her neck swelled. The veins crept along her skin like lingering lightning bolts across the night sky. Her eyes were wide open, dancing around wildly. She was grasping her neck tightly with both hands, one on top of the other, as she gasped for air.

"Oh shit, oh fuck…" Jay said to himself in a frenzy. "Benu! Benu! What do I do? I'm no doctor! Just tell me what to do!"

But she was unresponsive, fighting a losing battle for her life. He scooped her up into his arms and stood up, looking around frantically. He didn't know what he was looking for. His mind was just filled with explosions of panic. His instincts just told him to look around for anything that might help. But he was in a frozen wasteland now. Creatures of false faces filled this town; Jay and Benu had walked into their deaths. As despair began to flush Jay of all hope, he looked down the street where Benu said her house sat at the end. He had heard a woman's voice beckoning to him. Across the street, about three houses away, a woman was calling to Jay from her porch. She waved her right hand at him. In her left, she held a lit lightbulb by her fingertips.

"Lay her down on the couch there," the woman instructed, pointing at the maroon loveseat to her right. As Jay came through the door carrying Benu, clouds of snow eddied into the living room as the outer screen door clattered shut. The woman, still carrying the lightbulb in her hand, flicked on a light as she disappeared around a corner.

Jay hadn't known what persuaded him to trust this mystery woman. She was the first being to appear completely human since Lorenzo. He guessed the familiar sight of a friendly face and accommodating voice had earned his desperate trust. Then again, those were the same qualities that incapacitated Benu. Jay set Benu down on the couch. He rested her head on a throw pillow at one end and pulled off another one at the opposite end to make room for her feet.

Benu was in rough shape. She clutched at her swollen neck with white knuckles, fighting for gasps of air. Her neck had now swollen to nearly the width of her head as prominent purple veins traveled along the length of her chin. Darting around the room, her eyes were unblinking and bloodshot. As she kicked the arm of the couch, the thin, wooden legs skipped and skidded along the cherry, hardwood floor.

"Shut the door," the woman said as she emerged from the room she had entered. Without looking at her, Jay turned on his heels and complied. As he turned back, he raised his head to see the woman standing over Benu at the end of the couch—a hypodermic needle attached to a syringe filled with clear liquid in her right hand. Jay held out his open hands low to try and calm the situation, but the woman remained still—unfazed by the dying woman beneath her.

"Hold her still," the woman commanded.

Jay began to approach slowly, his hand bobbing up and down. "Whoa, whoa. What do you think you're doin'?"

"I said hold her!" the woman shouted.

"What the *fuck* is in that needle?" Jay matched her volume as he ignited a hand into flame; he was now at the other end of the couch.

With an annoyed groan, the woman lazily bent her left elbow and pointed at Jay. Lilac bolts jumped across the tiny chasms between her balled-up fingers and finally zipped down her index fingertip. The thin bolt of bright blue leapt across the room and into Jay's collarbone, casting a flash of white light across the room. Jay felt the bolt shock his entire body as he collapsed, stiff as a board, onto his back—his teeth clamped shut by the attack. His fire was extinguished in an instant.

The attack only took a split second. In that time, hurdling to the floor, Jay saw nothing but white. He had been utterly shellshocked by the woman's attack. He lay there, staring at the eggshell ceiling, as feeling slowly returned throughout his body. He could feel the tip of his nose, the twitching of his fingers, and the bitter coldness in his toes. He scrambled to his feet, took a fighting stance, and ignited another flame in his hand.

Benu had relaxed. Her chest moved up and down in a steady rhythm. She had stopped convulsing with her arms slowly drooping to her sides. The purple veins had all but receded as her neck began to return to normal. Jay could see her eyes had shut and that the woman's left hand was lifting her chin gently as she removed an emptied syringe from her neck.

"Put that fire out," she said curtly, "or I'll make sure the next one keeps you down."

Jay complied and stood up straight. He studied Benu intently, reassuring himself that she was still breathing.

"She'll be fine. Just needs to rest 'till tomorrow," the woman said. "This stuff always knocks you out for a solid twelve hours."

"Why didn't ya tell me what was in it?" Jay demanded.

"If I had wasted time answering you, she'd be dead."

Jay let out a heavy sigh through his nostrils. He looked over at Benu one last time and saw her fast asleep—peaceful. Relaxing his shoulders, he turned his attention to the woman. She was an older, fair-skinned woman, perhaps in her fifties. Valleys of early wrinkles lined her cheeks and crow's feet spread out from the ends of her eyes. Gray streams of hair split fields of wavy, brunette hair that hung just above her clavicle. She was thin and small in stature—a stark contrast to the effortless power she unleashed to send Jay to the floor.

She held the needle with an open palm under it, catching drips of unspent medicine. Her wiry hands protruded from the sleeves of a striped, turtleneck sweater of blue and gray. A stiff bracelet was clasped around her right wrist—a leather-strapped watch on her left. Laying around the high collar was a necklace of various charms: keys, angels, crosses. She turned and began to return to the room behind. Her sweater was hemmed over her belt, just above the rear pockets of her jeans.

Jay looked behind him to see a cluttered shoe rack and realized he had tracked dirtied snow onto the woman's floors. He quickly removed his shoes and went to Benu's side. He knelt by her face and placed the back of his palm against her forehead and another against his. *She's fine,* he thought to himself as he let out a relieving sigh.

"You can take her upstairs," the woman said, causing Jay to jump. She had seemingly materialized at the end of the couch again. "There's a guest bedroom—first door on the left. She'll be more comfortable there."

Jay stood, readjusting his bag on his back. The woman extended a hand for an introduction, "I'm Carla."

He shot a glance at Carla's hand, then looked back at her face.

She smiled, rolled her eyes, and shook her head, "I'm not gonna zap ya."

Jay cautiously gripped Carla's hand as she shook his gently. "I'm Jay," he said. "And this is Benu." He motioned over to the sleeping beauty.

"Ahhhh, Deepti's girl."

"You know her?"

Carla released Jay's hand and patted him on the shoulder once. With a smile, she said, "Take her upstairs. I'll make you something to eat. We'll talk more then."

{Chapter 21}

3:3:35:33

Jay pulled the plushy comforter over Benu as she lay peacefully on the large, queen-sized bed. Her head was sunk into a soft, white pillow. Diffused amber from a lamp sitting on the nightstand next to the bed bathed Benu's face in golden light. The guest room was huge and could easily be mistaken for a master bedroom. Paintings of sailing boats and lighthouses hung on the forest-green walls. There was a recliner—where Jay had set his bag—and an ottoman in the corner next to an entertainment center with a large flat-screen TV sitting on top of it. An extravagant dresser with precise carvings of pedals and flowers was located behind Jay in the large, walk-in closet.

Jay went to the foot of the bed and lifted the blanket, revealing Benu's feet. He undid the laces of her boots, careful not to disturb her, and slipped them off her petite feet. Placing them on the floor, he could see patches of her dark skin peeking through several holes in her black socks. Just as he went to grab the comforter to pull it back over, the smell hit him like a truck—her feet stunk to high heaven. He pinched his nostrils and threw the comforter over the stench.

Standing up, he still smelled a lingering fume and sniffed around. He searched around like a hyena that caught the scent of something dead. He followed the trail down to his own feet and threw one into the palms of his hands, balancing on one leg. Hunched over, he took a big whiff and gagged silently. Jay dropped his feet and composed himself. He looked over to Benu and saw that she had turned away, onto her side—still asleep.

Jay reached under the lampshade and turned the knurled knob one click. He walked over to the window to shut the blinds. Outside, the snowfall had calmed to a sprinkle. Across the alley, he could see the face of someone he didn't know smiling at him from the upstairs window of the opposing house. He leered at the face, making out the razors that flanked its cheeks in the darkness. He shut the blinds and pulled the curtains closed. Opening the door to the bedroom, he took one last look at Benu before heading downstairs.

Jay shut Benu's door slowly until he heard a tinny *click*. Then, he turned to his right and descended the stairs, grasping the thick, glossy handrail. The stairs made nary-a creak as he admired the craftsmanship of the wood his hand glided down. He could hear the distinct drag and clack of a wooden spoon stirring in a metal pot. The handrail ended in a right-angled turn to the left and placed Jay in the living room, about eight feet from the lefthand side of the front entrance. He could smell the strong aroma of a fresh meal snaking its way across the living room. In the insanity, Jay hadn't noticed the extravagance of the massive space.

A crystal chandelier hung over the intricate, cherry coffee table. It cast small rainbows against the off-white ceiling. The table itself was also a thing of beauty. A glass inlay floated above a carved jungle scene. Thick leaves were recreated so meticulously that Jay could imagine reaching in and feeling their waxy exteriors. Various wild animals were hidden amongst the leaves: tigers, elephants, flamingos, and monkeys. Along the edge of the table, a Roman ogee cut lined the molding. The legs were hefty and curved, ending in feet that were carved in the shape of lion paws.

Against the staircase, across from the couch, was a hutch filled with expensive china and small porcelain angels—its construction just as intricate as the table's. As Jay walked along the plush rug that the table sat on, he could see a small staircase of four steps leading into a large den. Jay looked over the iron railing to the left of the small staircase and saw a massive brick fireplace at the opposite end. On either side of the fireplace were built-in shelves lined with thick, hardcover books.

Jay wanted to explore some more, but Carla called from his right.

"Hey," she said, standing in the kitchen doorway. "Food's ready. C'mon."

"Alrighty, sounds good," he replied as he walked towards the kitchen. As he entered, he realized this was where Carla had turned into when retrieving the medicine that saved Benu. He investigated an open trashcan that sat against a marble island and saw an emptied syringe sitting atop piles of rubbish.

"Take a seat at the table," Carla said from across the island, her attention focused on the pot in front of her. "I'll bring this over. There's already a couple of plates set."

Jay obeyed without saying a word. He walked across the stark, white kitchen. The place felt eerily clean compared to the vile environments of the outside world. He passed by the large pantry and sat himself at the head of the oblong table. It stretched far, extended by a leaf insert at the center; eight chairs surrounded it. The dining area was attached to the kitchen, separated only by a change from white tile to hardwood. At the other end of the table was a bay window with an adjacent door leading to an expansive deck. Along the wall to Jay's right was a line of large double-paned windows, each flanked by opulent curtains. Behind him, a carpeted reading nook. His filth made him acutely aware of his presence amongst the pristine.

Carla walked over to the table set down a cloth, then walked back to the stove and retrieved the pot with a ladle in it, placing it on the cloth just in front of Jay's empty plate. She picked up Jay's plate and poured a serving of thick curry from the pot. As she set his plate down in front of him, she began serving herself, saying: "It's masala curry. Deepti, Benu's mother, taught me how to make it a while ago. I was thinking she'll want something to eat if she wakes up hungry. Hope you like it." Then, she took a seat to Jay's left.

Jay nodded, "I'm sure I will." He scooped up a spoonful of the milky, orange curry. A small piece of chicken draped over the side of his spoon. He blew the steam off the top, causing small ripples to travel throughout the red-speckled liquid. Taking a bite, he was hit with the sweet taste of Indian spices and creamy curry followed by a buildup of heat at the back of his tongue. He chewed for a bit before the spicy flavor was too much to handle. Swallowing quickly, Jay attempted inhaling and exhaling wafts of cold air to cool the burning sensation.

"Oh! I forgot to get us water," Carla exclaimed as she stood up and walked to the kitchen.

"Yes, please," Jay wheezed.

Carla opened her brushed steel fridge and retrieved a large pitcher of water. She pulled two glasses out of a cupboard above the countertop and filled them. She returned to the table after putting her jug away and placed a glass in front of each of their plates. Jay quickly snatched up the glass and gulped down nearly half the water at once. As he finished swallowing, he gasped for air as if he was drowning.

"It's really good! Thank you, Carla," Jay said between breaths.

Carla smirked, "Glad you like it, but what's wrong? Human Torch can't handle spicy food?"

"Well, it's only the heat from a fire or object heated by fire I can't feel. Spicy food doesn't seem to meet that criteria, I guess." He took another sip of water and reached out to the searing pot with an open palm, placing it against the super-heated metal.

Hot!

He recoiled, startled by the sudden burning sensation he hadn't expected. Dropping his spoon onto the table, he gripped the wrist of his pulsing, bright-red hand. His bewildered eyes met Carla's laughing face as she covered it with the side of her spoon-gripping hand. She hooked the thumb of her free hand over her shoulder and said: "electric stove."

Jay exhaled an embarrassed breath and picked up his spoon. They ate as they continued their conversation.

"So how did you meet Benu?"

Jay explained his entire journey thus far. He went into every detail he could remember and answered every one of Carla's questions with precision. Royal Oak, Flint, Saginaw, Clare. All retold over their meal. And when he went on to discuss Her, he felt no stutter in his voice. No tears had welled up in his eyes, and not a tremble could be seen

darting across his lips. Another weight had fallen off his shoulders—
this one microscopic, but still present.

As Carla set her spoon on her empty plate, she said, "Well, Jay,
that's quite the journey you guys made. Sounds like you guys have
taken care of each other."

"Yes, well… I feel like she's done more for me than I have for
her," Jay replied, taking a final bite.

Carla placed her elbows on the table and clasped her hands
together. Leaning forward, she said, "Well, Benu's real lucky that you
got her to me when you did. I'm guessing you ripped out the
nopperubo's stinger fairly early. Typically, when they grab hold of
you… they don't let you go until you're dead. You… wouldn't happen
to be the reason she got in *that* situation, would you?" A thread of
lightning jumped from one of her pupils to the other across the bridge
of her nose.

"Oh no, no! We spotted one of those things had killed someone
Benu knew. What was his name? Um… Mr. Bradford! That was it."

"Billy, you dumb bastard… did he have his blindfold on?"

Jay remembered the bandana around the man's head and replied,
"It was around his forehead. He must've lifted it at some point."

"How about earplugs?"

"Nope, didn't see any that I recall."

Carla leaned back and craned her neck to the ceiling. "Ugh, why
do I even warn people anymore? He was on his way here for an
appointment. I was wondering why he was running late, then I heard
some explosions outside and stepped outside to see what was going
on."

"Well, I'm glad you did. What appointment did he have with ya?"

"Eh, don't worry about it. Just something he wanted to talk to me
about when I saw him a couple weeks ago."

"So, there're people still alive here? A community?"

"Oh, I'd hardly call it a community. There are maybe ten left? We
rarely, if ever, visit each other's houses unless it's a real emergency—
too risky with all the monsters. Everyone's become a damn recluse

here… I'm the only one that goes out to stop by everyone's house and discuss things, like: if we need to do a supply run, if everyone still has running water, if anyone needs their generators charged by yours truly, et cetera. I've got the route memorized at this point—only gotta peek under my blindfold every so often."

"Did you visit Benu's ma and sister?"

"They didn't answer the door, but they did two weeks ago, yeah. Even her father was there. I charged their generator and brought them some food."

"You think that means…"

"Can't say. Billy didn't answer his door last week either, but he was obviously alive as of yesterday."

Jay took a moment to contemplate this. He stared down at his barren plate and asked himself if he should tell Benu. As he looked up, Carla had taken the pot and was setting it on the kitchen stove to keep it warm. "So how did you meet Benu's folks?" he asked across the kitchen.

"I live down the fucking street, how else?" Carla replied, sass in her voice. "Ya know, I hardly recognized Benu when you brought her in. I hadn't seen her in nearly ten years, and she looks like she's been through some serious shit. Obviously has, if what you told me was true." She returned to the table, took the dirty plates, and began walking them to the sink, saying: "But to answer your question, I met the Udathas through my husband. He worked with Ajith, Benu's dad."

Udatha, Jay thought. *That's half of the equation solved.*

"And your husband?"

"Dead. Died only a year ago."

"I'm… sorry to hear that."

"It's ok. I'm used to death, unfortunately. I've mourned him plenty." Carla took her seat at the table.

"So, your husband was a doctor?"

"Ah, so Benu told you about her dad. Yes, he was a pediatric surgeon in the same department. Many times, Ajith would have to hand over a patient to Rich, my husband, and he'd do the dirty work.

They were both *real* good at their jobs. They worked with other doctors in the hospital to develop that antivenom for the shit the nopperubos pump into ya."

"The nopperubos…"

"Yeah, funny name huh? It was actually a Japanese fella that worked at the auto shop on Mitchell St. that coined the name. He lost his wife to the first one and caught a glimpse of the face changing into her grandmother, calling it a demon. He said it resembled a spirit from Japanese folklore called a—and his pronunciation was *obviously* better than mine but I'll try my best—'no-peru-bo.'" Carla held out the last syllable slightly longer than the others.

Jay found her enthusiasm in the entomology of the creature's name a little unnerving. Her tone held an air of morbid fascination as opposed to repulsiveness that he found uncomfortable. But he was just as curious about the fake people he had witnessed throughout the town. He said, "I saw many of them in several houses. There's even one next door, across from Benu's room!"

"Yes, they like to occupy houses, mainly. That's usually where they hunt their victims. Don't worry, though, they're not smart enough to open doors. But they do knock… even figured out doorbells. They just trick ya into letting them in. People here are too afraid to answer the door anymore… They lure you in with that damned cooing noise they make. Sounds just like a pigeon—a *loud* pigeon. It's just curious enough for you to look in their direction. I don't know what it is, but we humans have a weird affinity for birds."

"Maybe we're jealous of their ability to fly?"

"Who knows? But we always seem to turn our attention to them as soon as we hear them. Either way, once they have your attention, and get their eyes on yours, they cast a spell on you—some sort of hypnosis that keeps you in place just long enough for them to approach. But it's not just hypnosis, they read your mind somehow… searching deep for someone you can trust with your life—or someone you hold close to your heart: your mother… your best friend… your lawyer…"

"Your sister…"

Carla paused and met Jay's eyes, understanding his implication. "Yes," she said solemnly. "Once they've got someone, they form that false face within their mouth. It's always recreated perfectly, down to the fucking voice. And once you hear that voice… the nopperubo is close enough—close enough to grab hold you and—" She mimed a fist holding a syringe and lanced the imaginary needle into her neck.

"They don't seem very aggressive… or tough, for that matter."

"They're not. You've seen their limbs. Even I could break one of their arms over my knee! They're both ambush predators and scavengers. They can only form a face once. Once they've transformed, they have to rely on another, unchanged nopperubo to kill their prey. Then, they can swoop in and eat up the scraps. If I had to guess… Billy boy out there is gonna be nothing but bones by tomorrow morning."

Jay placed an elbow on the table and nestled his chin in the webbing between his thumb and index finger. He rubbed his lower lip, moving it slightly—his mouth partly agape. "So, these things killed Cadillac?"

Carla blinked slowly, pursed her lips, and nodded.

They had been sitting in silence for a moment when a muffled groan came from upstairs. Jay shot up out of his seat until Carla stopped him halfway with an open hand in his direction. She called out over her shoulder. "Benu, sweetie, stay in bed! I'll bring you something to eat!"

Jay stayed in his bent position until he heard a weakened "Ok…" echoing from Benu's direction. He sat back down and relaxed. As he did, the lights in the kitchen flickered for a moment.

"Ah," Carla said, looking up at the white, recessed LEDs, "gotta recharge the generator. And it's getting a little chilly. I'm gonna bring Benu some food, head down to the basement, and add some more logs to the furnace… Also gotta charge the generator." She held up her hand and twiddled her fingers; bolts of static jumped between them. She smiled coyly.

"All right, sounds good. And… thank you for everything, Carla."

"Of course, anything for Benu. But as for you… I'll need a favor… Can I be perfectly honest?"

"Sure, of course. Whaddaya need?"

Carla leaned over the table and chided, barely over a murmur, "You smell like… hot garbage. There's a bathroom in the guest bedroom with a shower down in the den. Clean yourself up and I'll leave you a change of clothes on the bed. My husband was about your size."

Jay went beet-red and lowered his head, replying: "Will do."

Carla nodded, made a fresh plate for Benu, and exited the kitchen. Jay slipped his beanie off his head and sniffed it. He instantly jolted back in his seat and wrinkled his nose, clamping his eyes shut.

Hot garbage…

Dirty, gray water drained into the circular grate between Jay's feet. The stream swirled around like a whirlpool as Jay scrubbed his head. He could hardly believe the amount of mud and grime that was coming off his body. Had he really been out here that long? The days felt as if they had rushed by, speeding towards total obliteration. Ever since he left the ramshackle walls of Detroit, he felt as if he had experienced a lifetime of events. The rivers of filth that washed from his body felt like he was shedding a second skin—armor that had been tempered by The Anomaly's world. The warm water soothed his aching muscles as he traced his finger down new scars he had unknowingly earned during his travels.

The comfort of the luxurious bathroom was foreign to him. The shower was large enough for two or three people, with stone-gray tiles on the floor that matched the stone bench at the opposite end of the shower head. Black tiles covered the walls with white grout in between. The sweet scent of the expensive body wash he was lathered with was nearly too pungent for his nose which had become accustomed to the smells of fresh blood and forest dew. Beyond the foggy glass door was a dark, ceramic sink with a bronze faucet that sat atop a natural stone counter.

Even before the apocalypse, Jay hadn't known such luxury. He knew plenty of doctors from his job, but only by name. Although he worked on machines whose cost was well over Carla's house ten times over, his job was a thankless one. As he told Benu before, fixing an x-ray machine was no different from fixing a bike, car, or crossbow. In the end, he was a handyman. The only real difference between him and the average plumber or carpenter was the small dose of radiation he reported off his dosimeter every six months.

He had finished rinsing off the last grouping of suds on his back and turned around completely under the shower, just to be sure he was free of any more soap. The water dissipated as Jay turned the temperature handle to the right, passed the blue streak that rounded the control, and into the "off" position. Jay placed a hand on the side of his neck and stretched it around, hearing a small crack amongst the dripping of the shower head above. The gurgling beneath his feet had begun to grow distant as the flow of water reached somewhere deep in the pipes underneath the house.

①

Stacy had shut off the water she was using to clean some dishes. The dishwasher to her right began to drain as water rippled through the pipes within the cabinets beneath the sink. It was the next morning after her birthday, and she was busy cleaning up the dirtied dishes, utensils, and beer bottles that were strewn across her lakeshore home. She turned around and placed her hands—one gripping a towel—on the countertop in front of Jay.

"Ya know… you could *help*," she chided.

Jay rocked in his barstool and swiveled its chair as he took a sip of coffee. "I gathered all the dirty plates *and* swept the back patio. Picked up all the trash too. I'm on break," he quipped as he took another sip.

Stacy rolled her eyes and brushed a lock of her red hair behind her right ear. She looked across her open-concept home into the living area. On one of the couches slept Jay's wife.

"She sleeps a lot nowadays, huh?" Stacy asked, still looking over at Her.

"Yeah…" Jay replied as he stared at the ripples in his coffee. "She hasn't had much energy lately."

"Did she drink at all last night?"

"Nah, she still can't have any alcohol with what she's on. The meds just make her sleepy."

"She still on the same meds?"

"They're tryin' something new again… They said it's helpin', keepin' her pressures down, but… they said that about the last medicine before she couldn't get on with it anymore." Jay set down his coffee and leaned his temple on the heel of his palm, his elbow resting on the countertop.

"Hey," Stacy called to Jay, turning her attention to him and raising her chin in his direction. Jay looked up. Stacy asked, "How ya holdin' up?"

He let out a deep sigh. Rarely did people ask about him. The mask he wore was as dense as stone and just as rigid. In just a short time, he had to juggle his job and Her needs. She had to quit Her last job due to Her condition and, even though She found a job in which She could work from home, there were many days when She was sick. If it were not for Her expertise, She would surely be let go for the overabundant workdays missed.

Her garden had begun to wither. Jay did his best to take care of it, but he had no green thumb. He struggled to keep Her lush flowers from drooping. Every day, they would hang a little lower. There would be many days during Her bouts of sickness that he would have to wash dishes, do the laundry, mop the floors, and cook, preparing food for a few days in advance so She would have something to eat while he was at work. Normally, these chores would be split between the two. The past few years took a toll on his mental well-being. Motivation was hard to come by, and they would resort to ordering takeout several days in a row. He felt sick and drained.

But.

None of this could ever amount to Her suffering. She was the one stricken with disease—one passed down to Her unwillingly through genetics. Every day, She fought against the torrent of invasive emotions and physical ailments that plagued Her mind and body. There were days when She faltered, and Jay would need to be Her rock. He would stay up late with Her as She cried in his arms. He would rub Her arm and peck Her head with kisses, assuring Her he would always be there for Her. That She was never alone. He would always carry Her burdens because She was a part of his life. A part of his life that he could not bear to see hurt or distraught because it did the same to him. So, the days of aching bones and chore-filled days were all worth it in his eyes as long as he could be with Her.

One night, She had told him She felt She hadn't done the same for him. That She felt Her shoulders had been barren of any duty to keep him stable.

Jay had replied: "Honey, you've already done everything you need to by simply existing."

Jay finally answered Stacy, "I'm keepin' it together."

Jay finished putting on the clothes that were left for him on the guest bed. Carla had left him a fresh pair of black socks and weathered, slim-fit jeans. Underneath, he wore a pair of boxers that made him feel a little weird; it was slightly awkward to wear another man's underwear—especially a dead man's. Jay had used his own belt to tighten the pants against his waist and left the button-down plaid shirt of orange and blue untucked. He rolled up the sleeves just above his elbows. Carla had even left him one of Rich's beanies—a tight-knit, black thing devoid of any branding. He pulled the beanie over his ears and walked back into the bathroom where he had dumped his clothes on the ground. Rummaging through the pile, he found his pants, retrieved his ring, and stuffed it in his new pocket.

He strolled out of the guest bedroom and into the den where he saw Carla—a pair of glasses perched on her nose—sitting in a leather recliner by the lit fireplace, reading a book. The flickering light from the fire and a soft orange reading lamp next to Carla dimly illuminated the den. Past the top of the small staircase, Jay could only see the faint silhouette of furniture in the living room, bathed in winter's weak light. An ornate clock sat on the granite mantel above the fireplace to his right—quarter past six.

"How's Benu?" Jay asked.

"She's fine," Carla replied without taking her eyes from her book. "Gobbled down her food quick. I took her dirty clothes and gave her a fresh set from my wardrobe before she passed out."

"Good to hear."

"Did you leave your clothes in the bathroom like I asked?"

"Yes, I did."

"Good. I'll take care of them tonight and have them clean by tomorrow morning."

"Appreciate it," Jay said as he strolled around the den, glancing at the various furnishing and decorations. Carla had a vast collection of paintings on the walls. Only slivers of blue could be seen between the flooded walls of canvases, only broken up by the occasional bookcase. Some appeared to be originals from unknown artists, while others were prints of well-known pieces. Picasso, Monet, Jackson Pollack, Diego Rivera, and many more were all present. One painting caught Jay's eye near the staircase. He peered at the scene of swirling blues and yellows as he walked over, his arms crossed.

Vincent Van Gogh's *The Starry Night*, was perfectly recreated within this black-stained frame. The inner edge of the frame was trimmed with gold. Jay had seen the original in New York City years ago when he and his wife made a pilgrimage to The Museum of Modern Art. It was Her favorite painting, and she idolized Van Gogh.

The thick buildup of oil pigments flowed across the canvas like waves, crashing together and swirling into golden stars. The recreation of the village below the night sky was immaculate, even down to the periwinkle rooftops of the church. Every tiny house was painted with absolute precision. Jay followed the village across the rolling fields and up the great cypress tree that twisted up the left side of the canvas.

Is this place another illusion? Jay thought to himself as he continued to study the painting. As he leaned in, he heard the soft thud of Carla's book closing. The leather recliner squeaked as Carla stood up and walked up next to Jay. She crossed her arms and closed her book around her left index finger, bookmarking her spot. In her other hand, she held her reading glasses.

"It's incredible, isn't it?" she asked, motioning with her glasses at the painting.

"Ye-yeah… almost *too* incredible. It's practically the original in every way," he replied.

"That's because this *is* the original."

Jay stood up straight and looked down at Carla with astonishment. His mouth could only mutter an exasperated '*huh*'?

"Yup," Carla began as she let out a brief chuckle. "I bought it from some guy who was passing through town, who bought it from some guy in Toledo, who probably stole it from some gal in Pennsylvania, who probably killed some family in Jersey for it, who originally tore it off the wall of the MoMA."

Jay scanned the room once more with this new information. How much of this opulence was bought? How much of it was stolen? How much of it was earned in blood? Jay brought his attention back to the section of paintings that surrounded *The Starry Night*. He pondered: if he hadn't known the exact time and date of earth's obliteration, would he pillage any of this? Believing that material wealth brought longevity. A sense of worth.

"I wish I could've gotten one of his self-portraits," Carla said as she danced her eyes between other framed Van Gogh prints. "I think the one at the art museum in Detroit had an original. Wish you could've snatched that for me!"

Jay curled his mouth to one side in a tight-lipped smile and shook his head. "Even *if* I knew you wanted it, the DIA's still heavily guarded. People still visit it as if The Anomaly doesn't exist."

"Ah, that's good to hear. That's *really* good to hear. Rich and I would visit it every time we went to see his cousin for Christmas. It's good to know I'll be able to go again someday."

Jay raised an eyebrow at Carla's statement.

There won't be a 'someday', he thought.

Jay opened his mouth to speak, but Carla interrupted his train of thought and asked: "Do you know why Van Gogh painted?"

"Wasn't he poor? Artists were makin' a lot of money during his time, and he wanted in on that."

"Yes! Exactly!" Carla exclaimed, strong sarcasm in her voice.

"All right, no need to be a jerk about it. Enlighten me."

"No, no. That's the common misconception. Van Gogh had financial support throughout his entire life, even from the moment he was born. He was an art dealer at first, making good money off of other people's works. After jumping from job to job, his cousin took him in as an apprentice and that's when he seriously began painting. Now, you know he was rather depressed throughout his entire life?"

"That's… putting it lightly. Man was a wreck."

"Indeed, but not from being 'poor' or without success. Even though he supposedly only ever sold one of his paintings himself, he was never without support. His brother, Theo, was behind him until the day Van Gogh shot himself in that field. No… I think it goes deeper. The man was surrounded by yes-men—people willing to carry him to the top. And yet… he strived to paint. Why?"

"Maybe it was to prove he could carry himself?"

"No, I don't think so."

"Then, maybe it was to give himself a sense of purpose— something to ease his depression."

"Ah, you're close, but no. Not that."

"Then, it was all that he knew. He painted because it gave him a sense of humanity. It was as natural to him as breathin' was."

"That's pretty good… but I'm thinking it was something else."

Jay shrugged, "I could go on with guesses, but I can see you've got the answer."

Carla looked over with a wry smile, then back at the painting, "He had *all* this sadness inside him and *all* these people lifting him up, calling up to him, and yet… he didn't call back. Or I should say, he didn't know *how* to call back. He wanted them to understand the extent of his pain but didn't know how to explain it in *his* way. They couldn't understand *his* words. He didn't paint for fame, or to make an impact in modern art. He had hoped to, I'm sure, but… I think he had hoped the ones closest to him would feel the impact first."

Jay placed his hand over his mouth and rubbed his cheek with his fingertips. He continued to listen silently.

"Some people can just express their woes through words. Maybe some keep a journal. They go and talk to a shrink or something about what they've written. But for others… the pain cuts so deep, it penetrates the soul to a point that traditional remedies can no longer quell self-destruction. I think, at some point, Van Gogh reached that event horizon and was immune to such remedies. He was so desperate to find a way to cry for a cure that he spent most of his money on supplies and ate very little. Finding a way to express himself became so important that it was literally life or death. And so… he painted. He painted, hoping those who mattered the most to him would translate his oil-lexicon."

{Chapter 22}

3:0:22:10

"So, did ya know Carla your whole life?" Jay asked.

"Mrs. Marlow? Yes, for the most part," Benu replied as she readjusted her back against the headboard. "She was one of those 'devout followers' I talked about earlier."

Jay sat in the recliner he had set his bag on. He pulled it up to Benu's bedside when he came to check on her after his chat with Carla, moving his bag onto the ottoman. When he came in, Benu was already awake, staring at the ceiling.

She sat up in her bed with a grimace and moan, her muscles feeling like heavy sandbags. Her pillow supported her lumbar as she leaned back against the headboard. They talked for what felt like an hour. When Jay had come in, he asked for the time, and Benu had picked up her watch off the nightstand—seven o'clock sharp.

They talked about the little things. Their hobbies, favorite TV shows from the old world, the adventures they had been through, their thoughts on which flavor of Doritos was better, and even their favorite colors. Jay's was green; Benu's, purple. Benu told stories of Cadillac, its history she learned in school, shenanigans she got into by the lake, and how nervous she had felt to have the newly crowned title of "older sister" when her sister was born.

"My mother named her Alexis," Benu had said. Her voice was low, fatigued from the gasping and swelling from earlier. "She wanted an *American* name for her *American*-born child. Ah, I suppose that was the beginning of the end for my parents' marriage."

"Your dad wanted a more traditional name, huh?" Jay had asked.

"Yes… 'Ishanvi' I think is what he argued for—named after the goddess of knowledge. Mama thought it was too… pretentious. Papa thought it guaranteed her future."

"What do you think?"

"Hmph, I think Alexis is a fine name. I could not care less, if I am honest. She could be named anything for all I care. She will always be my *behan*—my sister."

Benu sighed as she looked towards the window, still covered by curtains. Her hands lay on her lap. Scraggly shadows from her hair were cast upon her thighs by the lamp on the nightstand. She turned her head back towards Jay, but her eyes remained on the comforter that covered her legs.

"Mrs. Marlow apologized to me when she brought me food," she said, voice still raspy.

"Oh?" Jay replied. "For what?"

Benu balled a roll of blanket in her hands, suppressing a tinge of anger.

"I think she knew I was *different* for a while... possibly when I first found out myself... back in high school."

"I see..."

"I hated her for a long time, *dost*. I overheard her once, talking to mama. I do not think she knew I was home sick from school. I do not know *how* she knew... gossip... people always gossip. I can hear her words clearly." Benu's eyebrows hid her eyes from Jay's gaze above, but Jay could see streams of tears had trickled down her cheeks, cutting paths through dirty smudges. "She said, 'Deepti, if you do not do something about her, she *will* go to Hell! There is still time... for both of you.' Mama argued back. But she did not argue for who I was, but for what she hoped I was not—denying my sexuality. 'What that is... is inhuman!' Mrs. Marlow finally said."

"Benu..." Jay murmured. He began stretching out a hand to place on her shoulder, but she began speaking again. Jay retracted the motion.

"But she apologized... and it was earnest. I could see it in her face." Benu met Jay's eyes. "You know someone is genuinely sorry when tears run down a stern face." Benu balled up the blanket tighter within her fists and grimaced. "I guess it takes the literal end of the world to change a bigot!"

Someday.

The word rang in Jay's head.

"No," Jay whispered, "I don't think that's it."

"Well," Benu said, wiping tears with the hem of her sleeves, "does not matter, I suppose. I cannot deny I owe her my life. I owe you as well. Thank you, *dost.*"

"That's two." Jay held up his middle and index finger in a 'V' shape.

"Two what?"

"Two times you've thanked me. We're even now."

"When was the first?"

"When I gave you that scope."

"Oh, come now, *dost*!" Benu rolled her eyes along with her head and relaxed her hands, slouching back against the headboard. "That does *not* count!"

The two shared a laugh, Benu's noticeably quieter.

"Well, we should move," Benu said as she began to get out of bed. She leaned over the side of the bed and winced hard at the pain that shot down her spine. Jay shot to his feet and gently pushed Benu back against the pillow.

"Nuh-uh, no, *no*. Not tonight. You're in no condition to do anything but lay there and sleep."

"But they are just at the end of the road, Jay!" Benu protested through a slight grimace. "Four, maybe five blocks!"

"And we will bike down those 'four, maybe five blocks' *tomorrow*. Besides, there's still at least a foot of snow out there… Carla says she saw them, by the way."

Benu's eyes widened, the pain seemingly gone from her face entirely.

"Really! Are they safe?" Benu asked, fighting against her rasp.

"Well, she met them at their house two weeks ago. I'll ask her if she knows any more."

Benu slipped under the comforter and sank her head into her pillow.

"Please do, and thank you, *dost.*"

Jay stood and placed a hand on Benu's shoulder through the comforter. Smiling, he said, "What was it that you said to me last week? 'Rest, *dost*. The day is lost.'"

Benu shook her head and turned away.

"Fuck you," she said playfully.

Jay spotted Carla at the end of the deck through the bay window, leaning over the rail with a wisp of gray smoke trailing off in the breeze by her face. The black shoes she wore were dusted with snow. Jay had searched for her throughout the house. He had found her book on the coffee table. The featureless, deep-blue hardcover was missing its dustjacket and no words were printed on the spine save for a shimmering, red symbol of a spoked wheel, intersected by an ouroboros—twisted in an infinity—at the top corners. A "6" was printed near the bottom. A blue braid draped onto the glass surface from the midpoint of the hefty hardback. Jay peeked inside to find the title.

Lord of Chaos
Robert Jordan

Jay exited the back door. The outer screen clattered behind him as he walked across the snow-ladened deck. The weather had calmed, and the snow had already begun to melt. Rhythmic drips could be heard under the boards as they formed little puddles beneath. The night air was stale and dry, chilled by a soft breeze. Jay stuffed his hands into his pockets as he crossed the deck, crunching the layer of ice beneath the powder.

Carla looked over her shoulder, a cigarette gripped between her lips. She took a drag, pulled the cigarette from her mouth, and exhaled a puff of smoke as Jay joined her. He pulled his hand from his pockets and crossed him arms, leaning on them over the rail. He looked out into her vast backyard. The twilight of night illuminated the small field of corn, wheat, and vegetables; clucks of chickens came from a small coop to the left. Down by the deck supports, a few garden supplies were leaned up against a hose reel: a bucket of seed packets, potting soil, fertilizer. All caked with snow. On the opposite end of the deck was an electric lawnmower with jerry-rigged wires soldered onto the leads and ending a pair of alligator clips. Carla powered the thing herself, no doubt.

The clouds had dissipated into wispy trails, and as they drifted across the sky, moonlight shone against the sparkling blanket of white. The purple hue of the earth was diffused evenly across the land, smothered by the snow. Jay looked up and found it— The Anomaly. Its red aura was shining bright tonight, and the size…

Was it always that big? Jay thought, a visible cloud of hot breath leaving his mouth.

"Why are you cold?" Carla asked.

Jay jumped a little. He was so lost in thought; he had forgotten she was there.

"Ah, it wears me out whenever I use my power," Jay replied. "I could keep myself heated, but I try to save my strength for when I really need it."

"I see… so it works the same way…"

"How'd it happen? If ya don't mind me askin'."

"I was a lineman… Linewoman? Lineperson? Bah, whatever the case, I was on a job one day with an apprentice. A distribution line had gone down somewhere off US-131. We were in the cherry-picker, finishing up the job, when the big, bad diamond in the sky let out a horrendous hum. The sound startled us."

Second Convergence, Jay thought.

"There was a miscommunication. I'm guessing someone at the company misunderstood my call when I said we were 'done.' They must've thought we were on the ground so there was still voltage on the lines. My apprentice lost his footing so he went to grab the line for support… His other hand was on the cherry-picker's rail. We were far too lax that day… far *too* lax! Why the fuck did we take our gloves off? Just a series of fuckups that day," She took a heavy drag from her cigarette. "You have any idea what 37,000 volts feels like going through your body? I couldn't tell ya… As soon as I lunged to grab my apprentice's hand, the earth shook the base of the cherry-picker, and the next thing I remember… everything was bathed in red light. One of my hands had his wrist in it, and the other one had the line. At first, I thought 'good thing we have protocol!' but as I looked down at my apprentice… Christ, Jay… you ever seen a man's eyes melt from their sockets?"

Carla's face was pale, drained from reliving her vision. Jay looked out to the field for a moment, unsure about what to say. He felt a strange pit in his stomach as he contemplated her rhetorical question. He looked back at Carla and said softly, "Go on."

"I let him go. I tried to save him, but he just dropped in the carriage… smoldering. As I lifted my hand from the line… I realized someone didn't follow protocol. Little bolts danced from my bare skin across the metal as I hovered over it."

"And now you can shoot lightning from your fingertips."

"And now I can shoot lightning from my fingertips," Carla repeated flatly. "So, what about you?"

"Saved my neighbor from a house fire."

"That's it?"

"That's it."

"Did he survive?"

Jay shuffled his feet, kicking a few clumps of dirty snow off the porch. He watched as it broke apart into tiny pieces and pitted the pristine surface of the blanket below. He stared off into the field, "At the time? Yeah. Presently? No idea."

A chasm of silence formed between the two. Carla continued to smoke. They reminisced of the people they knew in the old world and where they might be. Jay thought of his uncle down in Texas. Maybe he was reclining in his favorite, black, leather chair watching an episode of '*The X Files*' off one of his many DVDs. Or he could be like

Bill Mulder, lying dead on his living room couch. Jay stood up straight and wrapped his palms around the soggy, wooden railing. Traces of slush were pressed beneath his palms.

He hooked a thumb over his shoulder and broke the silence, "I didn't take you for a high fantasy kind of reader."

Carla raised her chin away from Jay and huffed, "Found my book, huh? Yeah, I'm halfway through it. I've got the rest of the series. Gonna take me another six months or so to get through the rest."

She wasn't being sarcastic. Her voice was straight and genuine. Jay could feel the confrontation he wanted to pursue burning a hole through the back of his skull.

"Carla," he said, a tone just above a whisper with a tinge of patronization, "you *do* know the world is ending in a couple days?"

"No, I don't," she replied curtly, pitching the butt of her cigarette off the deck. It sizzled in the frigid snow. She met Jay's eyes, "Do you?"

"Yes! Yes, I do! You and I are proof!" Jay scooped up a fist of snow and shook it towards Carla. "*This* is proof!"

"That's just snow—strange weather caused by The Anomaly— something that has *naturally* occurred as time *naturally* moves on and the earth *naturally* changes."

"How can you say that?" Jay asked, confusion rich in his voice.

"How?" Carla replied with her chin held high.

"I don't understand… you're so…"

"*So* what? Naïve? Stupid? Blind? I've been called it all."

"Educated! Kind! Thoughtful!" Jay retorted.

"And I have been called all those things, too. People are so sure of what I am, but struggle to understand my reasoning."

"Then, help me. Enlighten me." He taunted her with a lavish bow.

Carla turned to him completely and leaned on her side against the railing. She asked: "*If* you are so sure the world will end soon, then what will happen?"

"The Anomaly is pullin' reality towards it. Gradually tuggin' and tuggin', harder and harder. Earth will be torn to pieces, and that'll be it."

"And you are sure of this? Why? Because the scientists have told you? News? Friends and families? How can you really know without experiencing it yourself?"

"So what? Believe nothin' until I've seen it myself?"

"No. Live as if you are seeking the unknown. You don't know where or *what* you will be tomorrow or even forty-five minutes from now. If you have already seen what you will become, then why are you not that person now?"

"Because I haven't been there yet," Jay murmured.

"If you are *so* focused on what you will become, rather than figuring out how you will achieve that… then you are already lost— without growth—without meaning."

Jay shifted his frustration, recalling his conversation with Benu. "And this is coming from the woman who believes Benu will go to Hell for being gay?"

Carla pushed herself from the rail and turned towards the field. Her eyes glossed with moisture, her face as rigid as wood. Her gray-brown hair fluttered against her face. She brushed it to the side and gripped the railing tightly. *"Believed,* Jay. *Believed."* She focused on Jay's eyes. Tears streamed through the deep crevasses in her cheeks like rivers against an unchanging earth. "I am still changing—still figuring out how to become *that* person. A person I'm proud of. I am still true to my faith—despite my sailor's mouth—but… I love that girl, Jay. I recognize who she is. And she recognizes my disapproval. However… never would there be a moment I wouldn't lay down my life for her. Part of my metamorphosis was realizing that that love transcends all else."

Jay leaned against the rail with his hands and let out his anger in a heavy breath. The frozen cloud that wafted in front of him reminded him of the cold air. His body was so rife with a mixture of frustration and critical contemplation that his blood boiled. As he calmed himself, he could feel the breeze like pricking pins and needles against his cheek. Carla wiped her tears, crossed her arms, and came up to the rail. Her hips pressed against it as if expecting the next question.

The question came: "And what about Benu's parents and sister? Do you know anything more about them?"

"I told you what I knew," Carla replied. "I last saw them two weeks ago. They asked about an appointment."

"Carla… what is this 'appointment?'"

Carla looked down at her feet and mimicked Jay's kick of snow. "I can make it quick y'know?"

"Excuse me?" Jay said, trying hard to convince himself otherwise of what he had just heard.

"It's easy—quick, clean, painless… I place my hands on your chest." She held her hands out and splayed her fingers. "37,000 volts across your heart—instant death." A string of lilac bolts sparked from one hand to the other. She placed them on the railing.

"So then… Mr. Bradford…"

"Whenever I meet with someone, we discussed the things I previously mentioned, but… the last topic is 'appointments.' We discuss where they'd like it to be done… most prefer here, at my place. I think for them it feels… spiritual. Guessing they take time to reflect as they head over." She twiddled her thumbs over the railing. "The other methods are too painful. And no one wants to be killed by a nopperubo masquerading and sullying the face of someone they love. I offer a mercy."

"A mercy? Carla, you've killed people!"

"Of their own request!" she protested as she whipped a grimace towards Jay. "Would you believe the first one? My husband… my fucking husband as he choked on his own tongue! See? I made my partner a promise too… that if it came down to it… I'd make it easy for him. Others eventually found out. And so, as people drove themselves mad… when they couldn't take it anymore… they came to me. Yes, Jay… I've killed people."

"And you never denied them? Never encouraged them to keep on living?" The anger in Jay's voice was vicious and passionate.

"You think this is the first time I've had this conversation?" Carla shouted. Her voice reverberated through the wooden deck, causing Jay to shudder.

Jay sucked in his lips and bit them; he turned his back to Carla. He wasn't sure what to think or if he should even think at all. Perhaps, he should have just stewed in the silence for a while and let this moment pass over him like a bad dream. He imagined walking down the street to Benu's house the next morning—this conversation with Carla but dust in his memory.

"I could make it quick," Carla repeated from behind Jay. He squeezed his eyes shut as if he hadn't heard her. "The shock will move at the speed of light. Your pain will end. You hide it well, but I see right through you like glass. Benu is no different."

Jay opened his eyes and spoke over his shoulder, "No, that is not my decision to make for her. Neither is it yours, Carla."

"And you?"

Jay looked to The Anomaly. It *was* larger. Its growing pull perpetuated the madness in Jay's mind. Was he really considering Carla's offer—to rid himself of the struggles that were sure to come ahead? The potential of perpetual failure and the grief that would come along with it. He could take this mercy. He could be with Her sooner.

'I could make it quick.'

Her words rang in his head like a siren's song, lulling him onto the living room couch. Shirtless, he would lay there, his eyes closed as he waited for the inevitable. Carla's soft hands would place themselves against his weathered pecs. Her fingers would spread out and envelop him in an aura of comfort. Slowly, his chest would expand and contract as his hands twitched by his sides. He would feel an instant jolt and then nothing, waking to the immediacy of the unknown. There, he would find Her, or he would find oblivion.

"Shit," Carla said to herself, breaking Jay of his trance.

He turned around to see Carla staring off into the cornfield as she pulled a blindfold out of her back pocket. Jay turned his attention to the stalks of corn. Flecks of snow flung through the air as the tips of maize danced, parting and crashing back together. A whispered 'coo'-ing came from the approaching wave. Carla descended the three steps that led into the field and positioned herself a few feet from the wall of corn. She could see slivered streaks of brown, warty skin between the stalks. Tying her blindfold around her eyes, she spread her legs shoulder-width apart and outstretched her hand.

"Jay! Tell me when it exits the corn! Look at the ground, not at its eyes!" Carla commanded.

Jay watched intently. The 'coo'-ing continued to grow closer accompanied by the whips of green stalks through the air. The ears of corn thumped together with each approaching step. Jay followed each clash, one by one.

Two more thumps until it reached Carla. Jay shot his eyes to the ground as instructed. For just an instant, a thought fired across his brain. Should he let this murderer receive retribution? No. Then he would be no different. The thought had expelled itself from his mind as soon as the last *'thoomf'* echoed and the nopperubo emerged from the field.

"Carla! Now!" Jay shouted over the railing.

Small traces of blue static traveled across Carla's sweater towards her outstretched palm. Her hair began to rise, lifted by the growing static. The blue streaks quickly gathered around her fingers, arcing across the gaps between them. Then, all signs of electricity disappeared as each fingertip produced a lilac bolt that met together about three inches in front of her hand. From the conjoined bolts came an enormous streak of hot, blinding-white light that shot through the air and clashed with the closed slit of the nopperubo, cleaving the creature in two.

Jay jolted from the sound, raising his hands as if to defend himself. It started as a succinct, electrical buzz before exploding into a boom not dissimilar to two semis crashing head-on at full speed. The crash of thunder, compacted into the span of about fifteen feet, had

obliterated the monster that stood before Carla. All of this, in the time
she had described—the speed of light.

As Jay stepped down from the deck, a small chunk of charred and
bloodied meat landed at his feet. He stopped and looked up to see
strands and debris from the nopperubo were still descending from
Carla's attack. He looked over at the two halves of a corpse. Jay could
hear the familiar sound of sizzling flesh as dying embers flickered
amongst the blackened, rough skin of the nopperubo. A small fire was
flickering amongst the grass. The innards where Carla had struck it
were strewn about, mangled and turned to mush—and smelling like
burnt shit. Carla lifted her blindfold over one eye, "I might've
overdone it."

Jay trudged through the slush and stood over the corpse. Blood
stained the icy surface of the snow like cherry syrup. He examined the
mess and quipped, "Yeah, that's an understatement."

'Coo.'

Jay looked up.

'Coooo.'

It stood before him: another nopperubo. Its reptilian eyes pulsing
its green hypnotics.

'Coooo. Coooo.'

Jay stood motionless. Carla's cries were muffled. At some point,
he thought he heard her say to cover his eyes. She had already covered
hers.

'Cooo.'

It took a step forward. The gaping maw began to open.

Jay could see it forming, the face he'd known the creature would
form—perfectly recreated. It was Her. There was no mistaking that
delicate, soft expression. The hair upon Her head matched identically
to his memory. So beautiful were her eyes, feminine cheeks, and
dainty chin. Her smile was just as he remembered. This was the face of
his beloved! It truly was!

Jay stepped forward between the two halves of the dead
nopperubo. He stood before Her, only two arm-lengths away.

Carla didn't have a clear shot. Even if she stepped to the side, the air resistance between the two figures was too small for the power of her attack; her bolt would jump from the nopperubo to Jay. Besides, she couldn't risk removing her blindfold; if there were two here, there might be more nearby. She stood powerless in the blistering cold.

Jay could almost touch the face his beloved now.

The nopperubo stopped; its instincts told it to move on to the next phase. The creature's arms spread wide, ready to grab hold of its prey.

Jay held out a hand, ready to caress his wife's face. Her mouth opened, but nothing came out except small, struggling moans. Jay's trust faltered. He began to regain control of his legs, shuffling back from the monster. More groans and whimpers before the false face spoke in a voice Jay did not know:

"Jay… Jay! I'm here! Come to me!"

Jay regained control of his entire body, his mind now returned. He grimaced, staring deep into the eyes of the insult to his wife. Crackles and pops formed around his hand as the entirety of it blackened. Jay gathered his rage into the palm of his outstretched hand and delivered a steady stream of flames into the nopperubo. The creature squawked and screamed with the same unknown voice. Jay cried out as tears flowed heavily down his face. He pushed forth and added his other hand, forming a tunnel of fire that fully engulfed the abomination.

The nopperubo howled as Carla removed her blindfold to see a section of her field lit ablaze. She ran through the snow, turned the valve on the spigot attached to her house, and hurried to her garden hose.

Jay continued his assault, the flames now coming from his entire forearm. The nopperubo flailed and swatted at the rush of flames. Chunks of melted flesh dripped from its body like blobs of swampy sludge. Carla entered the burning corn, set her hose attachment to "shower," squeezed the trigger, and began dousing it with water.

As Jay calmed his flame, the burning nopperubo bashed its heel
into a rock and fell onto its back, creating a crater in the snow. Steam
rose from all around it as it kicked and swung its arms. Jay could hear
a squelching sound from underneath it as he stood over it; the flaps for
its stingers were scarred over by his flames. He leered down at the
immolated monster, a backdrop of flames behind him. With a splayed
hand, he fired a tiny fireball into the emaciated, porcelain face of what
paraded as Her.

The creature lay dead. Carla came up beside Jay and sprayed down
the burning corpse and the fires around him. The steam and smoke
rose into the air, reaching high towards the stars. Jay looked behind
him at his path of destruction. Blackened stalks were toppled over in
his path as they sizzled with glowing embers.

"Hey!" Carla called as she let go of the trigger and threw her hose
to the ground. Jay gave her his attention. "Don't you think you
overdid it a bit? Just kill the damn thing next time!"

Jay exasperated, "Sorry."

Carla looked down at the dead monster. "I heard it call to you… It
formed a face, right?"

"Yes."

"Was it your wife?"

"Yeah… Yeah, it was."

"How did you…"

"My wife was a deaf-mute," Jay sighed. "She didn't have a voice—
not one she could speak with, that is."

Jay quickly shot off a salute towards Carla. Then with his elbow
by his side, held out his left palm, upturned and completely stiff like a
chop—all five fingers pointed forwards. He formed the same shape
with his other hand, met his palms perpendicularly, and smoothed
across the surface of his upturned hand, rolling an imaginary marble
from the heel of his palm off the end of his fingertips. Next, he
pointed his two index fingers towards the sky and held down the other
fingers with his thumbs. A small thump came from his knuckles as he

bumped them off each other. Finally, he lowered his left hand and pointed his right index finger at Carla.

Hello! Nice to meet you!

Carla raised her chin at him with a smirk.

They walked back to the deck, carrying a conversation.

"So, she could read lips?" Carla had asked.

"Yup, she was damn good at it too," Jay had replied. "Could even tell what I was sayin' when my back was to Her. Don't know how. But… I learned to sign, just in case."

He had helped her drag the corpses off her property and offered to do a small patrol of the field. Jay had found no sign of any more nopperubo and decided to return to the house. Carla was waiting by the stairs, her arms crossed. Jay emerged from the corn and came up to her. He shot his hands into his pockets and stood up straight.

"All clear?" Carla asked.

"All clear," Jay replied.

Carla clapped her hands and began ascending the stairs before Jay stopped her.

"Carla," he said. She stopped, turned around, and simply listened. "My answer is 'no.' You're not the first encounter I've had with the easy way out. Those dark options have been brewin' in my head ever since I lost Her. In two days, I'll be dead anyways, huh? And… you're right. I don't know what's at the end. But… I think I wanna see for myself—see if the person I want to become is waitin' for me at that cemetery in Escanaba."

Carla formed a tight-lipped, quivering smile. For the first time since she was gifted her lightning, she felt powerless.

{Chapter 23}

2:12:15:27

Jay found their bikes in the same place he had left them yesterday afternoon. He had his backpack on and carried Benu's bag and crossbow in each hand. The snow had almost entirely melted, and all that was left were scant bumps of slush and ice. Jay had picked up Benu's things by Mr. Bradford's body… what was left of it, at least. Carla was right; Mr. Bradford's bones were picked clean. His skull was carried off somewhere along with his left leg. Only strings of red sinew and rotting ligaments held the skeletal remains together. His clothes were in tatters across the bones; a small portion of his pelvis flesh remained. Flies were already circling around it, pecking at the meat with their suckers. Soon, Mr. Bradford's corpse would be bursting with maggots.

Last night, Jay dreamt of the old world. He dreamt of something mundane and boring—ordering something off the Internet. That was it. That was all his mind really cared to think about. He was at home— on a Saturday evening—sitting on his living room couch with his phone in his hand, scrolling down pages of DVDs. It was an uneventful dream that felt like a lifetime amongst dreaming's twisted time. Many would wish to wake from such a dull tedium—but, considering The Anomaly's mutated reality, it was something he longed for.

When he woke, he found his old clothes by his bedside, washed and folded. He took his gray beanie, black jacket, drawers, and Chucks. Carla had made him an offer to take a pair of Rich's fitted jeans and a black and gray, plaid button-down. Jay had taken the offer and replaced his stained graphic tee and torn, scuffed pants.

Picking up their bikes, Jay placed Benu's backpack on the ground and slung the crossbow over his shoulder. It clattered against his lower back, causing him to wince slightly. Raising his bike, he noticed his front tire had gotten a flat. He propped it on its kickstand and picked up Benu's teal cruiser, looping her bag onto the handlebars. He looked around the sunlit neighborhood. The receded snow had revealed a town just as dead as the previous ones, occupied now by mannequins wearing the faces of its residents.

He began walking the bikes back to Carla's. His encounter with the nopperubo last night had given him confidence to stroll with some ease. If one of the creatures were to catch him in its hypnosis, he'd be able to break it. But the leering faces of the dead, smiling expressions that he could spot out of his periphery, kept him on edge.

He parked the bikes in Carla's perfectly-preened lawn and placed Benu's crossbow on the ground. Next, he went to his bike and turned it over, propping it on its seat and handlebars. Pulling out his toolkit, a repair patch, and handpump, he went to work. He placed his adjustable wrench around the nut that held the tire in place and unscrewed it; he went to the other side and did the same. Then, he removed the brake line and lifted the tire off. As he deflated the inner tube, he heard the front screen door clatter shut above him. Carla had stepped out—an unlit cigarette in one hand, a lighter in the other.

"Flat tire?" she called down from the porch.

"Yeah," Jay replied as he worked. He finished deflating the tube and began prying off the tire with a screwdriver. "Benu ok?"

Carla lit her cigarette and tucked her lighter away in her back pocket, saying: "She's taking a shower. Should be out soon."

"Good to hear. Thanks for takin' care of my clothes, by the way." He sniffed the shoulder of his jacket. "Best they've smelled in weeks."

Carla chuckled, "Don't mention it. You can take some more of my husband's clothes, if you'd like."

"Nah, don't feel right to take more than I need."

"Suit yourself."

Jay finished patching his tire as Carla leaned her back against the house and smoked. After he reassembled his tire, he put his toolkit and turned the bike back over. As he began pumping the tire full of air, Benu came out the front door and greeted Carla, who offered

Benu a cigarette and lighter. She took them and lit up. They shared some words, giggling a bit like high-schoolers gossiping by a line of lockers. Benu came down the steps as Jay finished up and flicked out his kickstand with his toe.

"Morning, *dost*," said Benu, flicking ash into the grass. She had taken Carla's offer of new clothes as well. A beige, hooded poncho, embroidered with roses and green thorns draped over her body, ending at her waist in a 'V' shape. Long sleeves of black were hemmed around her wrists. Her faded, green corduroys had their hems tucked deep into the same black boots Jay had taken off her the day before. Her knife was strapped around her left thigh.

"Mornin'," Jay replied. "Ready to go?"

"Sure am."

"Those pants don't really match," Jay teased.

"Hmph, I did not have much choice. They are an old pair. They were the only ones that fit. Probably fit Carla back when she had more meat on her bones."

"I heard that," said Carla leaning over the rail. She took a final draw from her cigarette and flicked the butt at Benu. It landed just before her feet as she gave Carla the finger and smirked.

Benu turned to Jay and said: "She told me about last night."

"Oh yeah?" Jay replied. *How much did she tell?* he thought.

"Your wife was deaf?"

Ah, so… everything.

"Yes," Jay replied as Benu finished her smoke, walked to her bike, and gathered her things.

"Any reason you did not tell me? I am not mad, just curious."

"Well, when you've known someone for so long, their quirks just sort of… fade into the background and you forget they were ever there. Understanding her signing and talkin' to her in that special way just became second nature after a while. She was as normal in my eyes as anyone else."

But not always.

She held up Her right hand and pinched Her index and middle finger together against Her thumb, the other fingers balled up.

"*No.*"

She did it again:

"*No.*"

"Ugh," Jay grumbled as he slouched his shoulders and sank back in his chair in their newly furnished house. They had just moved in a week ago, closed on the two-story bungalow nearly a month ago. The newly wedded couple had mostly finished unpacking. All that was left were a few cardboard boxes of knickknacks and miscellaneous things. They had been moving boxes all day and decided to take a break and practice Jay's signing.

She told him to try again.

Jay looked to the ceiling and allowed his growing frustration to abate. He sat up straight as his wife leaned forward to study his hands.

He pointed his index finger into his sternum—*I.*

He presented his open hands and pulled them towards his chest as if opening a dresser drawer—*want.*

He pointed two index fingers to the ceiling, then in the direction of the front door—*go.*

Finally, he upturned his left palm in his lap and froze, searching his memory for the next motion to finish his sentence. His wife leaned forward and motioned Her hand to encourage him to go on. Jay sucked his teeth and shook his head. He could see the word clearly in his mind written in English, floating there in the darkness in neon-white letters—"SHOPPING." He could speak it, write it, and translate it into German due to his required second language course in college. But, for the life of him, he couldn't perform the simple motion that he knew he had learned the other day from Her.

Defeated, Jay raised up his palms and shrugged cartoonishly.

His wife fell back into her chair and threw Her hands up—the universal sign for 'fuck this'.

"Hey, this really isn't that easy," Jay pleaded. "Sorry, honey, but this is gonna take some time."

A tear rolled down Her cheek. She had known this way of speech her whole life and had plenty of others to talk to. But she had married the love of Her life and wanted nothing more but to be able to talk to him the same way She had the others. Before this, She had written notes and taught him short, basic sentences, but wished to talk to Jay about so much more in Her voice. She wished She could impart Her knowledge upon him, instantly turning his hands into professional performers. She wished She could open Her mouth and tell him this. She closed her eyes and silently wept as Jay stepped over and embraced Her.

Carla came down from the porch and handed a blindfold to Benu. "Just in case Human Torch over there isn't around to blast one of those things to pieces."

Benu tucked the blindfold into her back pocket, thanked Carla, and pedaled into the street to a stop. Jay mounted his bike as Carla walked over to him, her arms crossed. He nodded to her—a silent show of gratitude.

"I hope you find what you're looking for at that cemetery, Jay," Carla said.

Jay gave Carla a solemn smile that was more meant for himself rather than her. He rode up to Benu and patted her on the shoulder. She nodded and began heading for her house located at the end of the long road. Jay looked over at Carla. She held a hand up and smiled. Jay returned the gesture and followed after Benu.

◆

Benu's house sat at the end of the lengthy road that stretched on from Carla's house another three or so miles. It was the newest road paved in Cadillac—although, the abundant weeds that shot out of the potholes would suggest otherwise. It was zoned for wealthy houses. If Jay had to guess, every decrepit, massive home they passed by would've had an interior that matched Carla's at some point in the past. But now, broken windows and busted down doors revealed pillaged and ruined rooms—with smiling faces peering out every so often.

However, Benu's house was much like Carla's as they approached. The windows were intact, and the walls were worn, but not in total disrepair. The green paint was cracked and rolling off the vinyl siding. Bits of rock crumbled off the stone porch that was raised three steps. In the driveway sat a rusting Ford F150—the latest model. Even with the metal bent, browned, and decayed, Jay could tell it was the top of the line Ford had offered. Traces of ice still clung to the hood along with splats of white bird droppings.

Benu rushed for the house. She jumped the curb, hopped off her bike, and threw it into the sea of knee-high grass, causing waves of muted green to flutter as the tall blades flung up between the spaces of the bike frame. Jay stood up on his bike and hurried to catch up. He came up onto the sidewalk and parked his bike on the concrete properly. Jogging up the walkway behind Benu, he shouted: "Hey! Wait up! Remember the last time you rushed it?"

"Oh, come now!" she yelled over her shoulder as she ascended the stairs, gliding her hand around a crumbling stone column. "It is safe here. Especially with you around!"

"Well, I can't protect ya if I can't keep up with ya!"

Benu's face was gleaming as if Jay's concern was nothing but a joke. She came up to the outer glass door, pulled it open, and rapped against the massive mahogany door; intricate, stained-glass windows embedded into the wood in two long columns that reached to the floor.

"Mama! *Behan!*" she called. No answer. She rattled the locked doorknob. She stepped over to a large, dirtied window adjacent to the entrance and tried to stare inside, but the caked dust blurred her vision. She knocked on the thick window. "Mama! *Behan!*"

Jay had come up onto the porch. He leaned over to a window on the opposite end from Benu and peeked in. Benu tapped him on the shoulder and said: "We can try the back. Alexis always forgets to lock the backdoor. Otherwise… we can try one of the upstairs windows."

"Why don't we just kick down the door?" Jay asked.

"First off, do you have any idea how hard that *actually* is?" She knocked on the door, emphasizing its rigidity. "And second, mama would not appreciate me breaking the stained-glass on her very, *very* expensive door... I already did that once when Alexis and I were practicing lacrosse inside when she was not home..."

Jay opened his mouth to speak, but Benu took off down the steps and headed for the backyard. Jay sighed and followed her. They rounded the house and stepped onto the driveway where a large, black iron fence stood between them and the backyard. Slats of sun-bleached wood occupied the space between the metal bars, blocking their view. Jay boosted Benu over the fence. She undid the latch and pulled the gate open. The metal creak of the massive, rusty hinges caused Jay to cringe.

As Jay stepped through the gate, he could see a large, two-door, detached garage. He could only imagine what the car collection of a doctor-nurse couple could possibly look like: Mercedes, Porsche, BMW, Cadillac... maybe even a Lambo. As Jay daydreamed, he walked across the vast backyard of the estate. It was completely covered in pavers that surrounded a swimming pool filled with green muck. The cracked walls curved down into a pool of standing water— melted snow that had failed to drain. Azure tiles lined the edge of the pool, broken on one end by a short diving board and, on the other end, a ladder speckled with rust. Broken lawn chairs littered the backyard—one had found its way down into the pool. An umbrella was pegged into the ground between two lounge chairs; drapes of its torn canvas made a flapping noise as it twisted and fluttered in the breeze.

He followed Benu onto a wooden deck that led to the back door. The wooden handrails were damp from yesterday's snow. As Jay grasped the railing, the rotted wood crumbled in his hands. The planks beneath him felt soft and unstable. Benu was rapping at the door, calling out for her family. No answer. She tugged on the doorknob to no avail. Jay's worry grew, but Benu's mind was racing with explanations and excuses as to why her mother and sister hadn't embraced her yet. She had pushed all concerns out of her mind with blind hope.

She backed away from the door and snapped her fingers rapidly. She swiveled on her heels and scanned her eyes across the wooden deck, reading invisible clues in the grain. Finally, she shot her head level with Jay's eyes and pointed towards the sky, dancing her index fingers back and forth.

"Ah! Mama always kept a spare key under the deck. Hold on," she said. She hurried down the steps before Jay could utter any concerns. All he could manage was an exasperated '*um*' as Benu dropped to her stomach and shimmied her way under the deck. Jay called through the slits of the wooden floor: "Just be careful, 'kay?"

"Yes, yes," Benu replied. She had enough room to crouch now. As she rose, her crossbow collided with the joists above, causing her to recoil a bit. She had been so eager that the weight of her crossbow, bag, food, water, map, bolts, med kit, bike supplies, and other bits-and-bobs had felt part of her own body. But the hollow clack of her crossbow against the rotting wood suddenly reminded her of the burdens she carried.

"Careful!" yelled Jay.

She looked up but didn't reply. Drips of water pearled off the edges of the wooden construction. Old, dead cobwebs were balled up in nearly every corner like thin fabric. Benu traced a few spiders scurrying about with her eyes. Some were small. Others were large. And *others* looked like no spider Benu had ever seen—crawling about on hundreds of spindly legs. Their bodies were segmented into two, bulbous masses with a gray exterior and a jumbled mess of eyes on each bulb. Benu kept her head lower than before so as not to disturb the spiders, lest she risk another night bedridden from mutant poison.

Making her way to the far corner, she spotted a familiar, smooth stone, indented in the damp soil. She turned it over and found a silver key. Picking it up, she wiped the caked mud off with her thumb. Carefully, she snaked her way out from under the deck and reconvened with Jay. Holding up the key by her face, she smiled and turned to the door.

Jay snatched her arm and murmured: "Benu, wait."

"Yes, *dost?* What is it?" she replied, turning around.

Jay opened his mouth to speak, but could see the gleam in Benu's eyes. Those eyes were those of someone who knew deep down that a horrible truth was about to rear its ugly head. The eyes of someone who wanted so desperately to believe that her suspicions were just that—suspicions. But Jay could see, behind Benu's shining lenses, that she had already accepted that ugly truth. She just had to see it for herself—for her stubbornness wouldn't permit any alternative proof or reasoning. Jay let her go and replied: "Nothing. Just… take it slow, alright?"

She rolled her eyes and jammed the key into the deadbolt. As she turned it, the slide of the bolt was gritty and sticky, but the *clack* of the heavy lock came. She wriggled the doorknob, found that it was unlocked, and burst through the door. The vinyl blinds swung and smacked the door as Benu made her grand entrance, "Mama! *Behan!* I am home!"

Jay followed as Benu jogged through the massive kitchen. She had already disappeared into the bowels of her expansive home before Jay could finish shutting the door. The house was dim. Diffused rays of morning light fought through embroidered curtains. The dining room table had a thin layer of grime over it. Jay ran his finger across the surface and rubbed the fine powder between his fingertips. A dusty envelope in the middle of the table caught his eye. He reached over and picked it up, swiping off plumes of gray clouds. Red wax was pressed over the fold sealing it with a signet. Flipping the envelope around, he only saw one word written across it in knotty, elegant cursive:

Binaka

"Binaka," Jay whispered to himself. "Hmph, pretty."

He strolled through the house, gazing at the vast array of decorations and expensive objects the Udathas owned. The house was a labyrinth. Each room was dedicated to something. There seemed to be a room for everything! Working out, playing billiards, another—larger—dining room, a reading area in a den styled similarly to Carla's; the house felt like it would go on forever. No signs of break-in or struggle was apparent anywhere. Only a thin sheet of dust covered things throughout. He could hear Benu yelling for her mother and sister as she moved through the maze. As Jay entered an entertainment room at the end of the house, he found Benu standing in front of a marble fireplace.

"Benu!" he called.

She whipped around, startled, and said: "Don't scare me like that, *dost!*"

"Sorry, didn't mean to." He walked up and stood by her side. She was staring at a photo that sat on the mantel. Three women were pictured standing in front of backdrop of greenery and blue sky; their waists cut off by the bottom of the frame. In the middle stood the tallest in a royal blue cap and gown. A bright yellow stole with matching royal blue "M's" embroidered at the ends draped over her shoulders and onto her chest. Jay recognized the young, smiling face as Benu's—a little thicker and a whole lot cleaner. She had her arms around the others.

To her right was an older woman with a tight-lipped smile. Her raven hair was done up in a bun. A red bindi sat between her eyes. Her hands were woven together over her stomach. A glare of sunlight caught the golden trim of her emerald saree stitched with intricate patterns of flowers. To her left, Benu's arm wrestled around the neck of a figure only an inch shorter than her. Her younger sister's face was comical with rolled-back eyes and a tongue hanging from her open-mouthed smile. She grasped at Benu's forearm as if she were doing pull-ups. Long, scraggly raven hair draped over Benu's choking arm.

Alexis wore a matching saree to her mother's, but red like the mark between her mother's eyes.

She pointed them out to Jay and told him their names. She held her eyes on Alexis and said: "Hmph, mama forced her to wear that dress. It was the one Indian thing she imposed on her. Alexis wanted to show up in jeans and a t-shirt."

"You find them yet?" Jay asked.

Benu sighed, "No, but I have not checked upstairs yet. It is strange." She scanned the room. "It is like no one has been home for a week, but it does not look like someone, or *something,* has broken in."

"Yeah…" he twiddled with the envelope he found earlier. "Oh, hey, I found—"

"I am going to head upstairs and check. Could you take a look in the basement? The stairs are over there." Benu pointed past Jay's shoulder at an archway that led into a descending staircase.

"Uh, sure."

"Awesome. Shout if you find anything!" Benu was already heading out where Jay had entered earlier. She left him standing there in a cluttered room of dusty opulence. He spun the letter in his hand and nodded to himself. He headed down the stairs to the basement, lit a flame in his palm, and held it high like a torch. As Jay came down the stairs into the vast darkness, he felt the plush of soft carpet. He held his flame in front and wafted it across his view. The basement was finished with white-painted drywall, carpet, and a drop-ceiling. Moving through the room, he could see that it had been transformed into a home theater. Two rows of three leather recliners faced a back wall where a projector screen hung. In the far corner, he found a utility closet. Inside was the furnace, water heater, washing machine, dryer, and a large backup generator seemingly jerry-rigged into the house's main line. He flipped the switch. The machine clunked a lifeless thud.

Seems Carla hasn't been here for a while.

Jay exited the utility room, searched the basement, and found nothing. Then, he started to head back up to the den. He was halfway up the staircase when he heard a succinct yelp echo through the halls.

"Benu!" he shouted as he rushed up the stairs and across the house, searching for the stairs leading to the second floor. He yelled Benu's name again as he rounded a wall into the foyer and spotted a landing overlooking the entrance to the right, leading into a hallway where he could hear a 'thump' of something hitting the ground above.

"Benu! Hold on! I'm comin'!"

Jay stomped up the carpeted stairs. The dust sprayed off the handrail like rolling waves of smoke as he guided his hand across it. He sprinted down the long hallway, looking left and right into open rooms as he went.

An office.

A guestroom.

A bedroom.

A bathroom.

A laundry nook.

A bedroom.

A linen closet.

When finally, he came upon the master bedroom where he heard soft braying.

He turned into it and stopped in the doorway.

"Ben—" he had called her name before he could fully comprehend what he had seen.

Benu was on her knees, hunched over in front of three corpses that sat under a large, open, casement window. The thin, translucent, purple curtains fluttered from the breeze that rolled into the room. The smell was pungent, and it stung Jay's nostrils. He tucked his mouth and nose into the crook of his elbow and crept towards Benu. Her things were placed upon the bed to Jay's left. As he passed by it, he set the letter addressed to her next to her crossbow.

"Benu?" he whispered, but the only response he received was continued, weak braying.

He took another step, now standing just over her. He could see
the corpses clearly now. Their faces decomposed to the point of being
unrecognizable. The dark skin they all shared had become tinged with
a sickly green as their innards began to rot. Their clothes were stained
and soaked with splotches of black and red. The smallest one on the
left had her mouth open; only a few teeth remained, with the others
resting in her lap. A few pills had spilled from a small white bottle
onto the lap of the rightmost corpse. The middle corpse had her
parents' arms intertwined with hers as she rested her hands in her lap.
Jay dropped his elbow; the smell could no longer overpower the
despair that had taken over. He scanned the Udathas from left to right.

Deepti, Alexis, Ajith.

And then there was Benu, weeping at the sight of her dead family.

"He came home, Jay…" Benu whimpered. "Papa came home…
after all this… just for this…"

Jay knelt at her side and placed a hand on her shoulder. He filled
his voice with as much tenderness as he could muster: "Benu…"

As he came over to her, he saw the glint of the knife in her lap; the
blade pointed towards her stomach. Her white-knuckled grip caused
her hand to tremble. With a bloodcurdling scream, she raised the
knife in front of her, determined to plunge it into her chest.

Jay sprung at her wrists and wrestled her to the floor. Benu kicked
and scrambled, but Jay ripped the knife from her hand and stood up.
Benu was left defeated; she stayed on the ground, propping her upper
body on her elbows. Her eyes stared into the deep plush of the carpet.
Now, she was weeping heavily. Jay could see a steady stream of tears
wetting the beige carpet beneath her face—each drop creating a dark
spot. She began beating a fist into the ground.

"No! You do not get to take that choice away from me!" she
screamed, her voice cracking.

"No! Don't ever go there!" Jay protested.

Benu straightened up and sat on her knees. She looked up. "I have
lost everything, *dost…* everything… my mama… papa… *Behan…* Oh
god! God! I want to die!"

"Get a hold of yourself, Benu!"

"They are gone! Gone! My world… my everything… I was meant to protect them. To keep them safe! But I failed! Failed! I need them… They needed me… Who will need me now? What purpose do I have if not to my mama and *behan*—and even papa! Give me my knife! Give it!" She delivered the last demand with frightening hysteria as she shot forth an open palm.

Jay raised his voice to a bellow, one that seemed to shake the floorboards. "I need you!" he shouted. "I need you, Benu! You talked about being that person that changes someone else for the better, and so, here *I* am!" He stretched out his arms to the side, presenting himself. "I am only here because of you. And I couldn't imagine being here tomorrow without you. You claimed to be that shinin' influence, and you have proven yourself! Here *I* am! The hardships we've faced, and the time we've spent together… the pain you've eased me from… You've taught me I am no island… that for all the power I possess, my greatest obstacles can't be burned away. I am your proof. Here *I* am."

Benu balled her open hand into a fist and retracted it, sniffling.

He tossed the knife on the bed and caught his breath. "I can't go on without you, *dost*," Jay whispered. "I *need* my traveling buddy."

Benu's weeping had simmered down to soft sniffles. She wiped a tear from eye. The golden rays coming through the open window shimmered off her moist cheek. She sniffled again and pulled out her blindfold. After blowing a glob of snot into it, she spoke: "What if they were alive? What if I could not go on with you?"

He offered her a helping hand. "Then, I would've gotten on my knees and begged. Wept as you just did because it would be like parting with a piece of myself."

Benu blushed and couldn't help but smile at Jay's corny tone. She couldn't deny the gullible Detroiter she had shot by accident nearly a week ago had influenced her in a way she had hoped she had done for him. Tearing herself from him now would be just as painful as losing a part of her soul. She took his arm, grabbing it around the forearm just below the elbow. He grasped her just the same and pulled her to her feet. They let go and embraced in a crisscross hug, Jay's chin perched on Benu's right shoulder. Benu buried her mouth and nose into Jay's right shoulder and mumbled: "Thank you, *dost*… Thank you."

{Chapter 24}

2:9:9:43

Puffs of brown dust rolled out from under Jay's shovel as he patted the mound of the shallow grave he had dug. He had done a preliminary sweep of the area; he only found two nopperubo and fended them off. Both times, he saw Her face and, both times, he knew it wasn't Her. He stood up and lanced the earth by his feet with the blade of his shovel. Wiping the sweat from his brow, he looked to his left at the other two mounds he had finished filling before. Jay and Benu's bags were with their bikes, parked on the sidewalk, save for Benu's crossbow which Jay kept on the ground near him. Jay had Benu's knife strapped around his leg lest her dark thoughts return. As he caught his breath, he looked up at the front face of Benu's house. There was an eerie silence in the air, as if the spirits of Deepti, Alexis, and Ajith still clung to their home, slowly finding their way to the afterlife.

Jay's reverie was broken by the metal creak of the gate to his right. Out came Benu, carrying three wooden crosses she had fashioned in the garage.

"Finished?" she asked as she came up beside Jay, the shovel between them.

"Yeah…" he replied. "I wish I coulda dug deeper, but…"

"It is ok. We are short on time."

She pulled the shovel from the dirt and began staking the largest cross at the head of her father's grave. She grunted as she hammered the wood with the bottom of the shovel's blade. Next, she moved to the middle and staked the smallest for Alexis—a candied bracelet looped around the vertical plank, draping over the one that ran parallel with the ground. Finally, the leftmost grave received the middle-sized cross, decorated with her mother's saree—the one she wore at Benu's graduation. Jay watched silently, trying to read Benu's emotions; the knife straps on his leg felt tight. As Benu finished, she returned to Jay's side and dropped the shovel into the earth. The damp dirt accepted the blade with ease, causing the shovel to stand erect.

Benu crossed her arms and silently wept, wiping tears away before they could reach the corners of her mouth. Jay felt a numbness in his chest and a vice grip around his heart. He let out a long-drawn breath to ease himself of grief. A grave was a hard thing for him to see. His memory had been stricken of Hers long ago; he dared not remember it. But it lay dormant in his mind—deep… deep in his subconscious. The faint, blurry image of Her funeral still lingered between thoughts. He put his hand in his pocket and fiddled with his ring.

As moisture began to build in his eyes, Benu spoke: "As you know, I am not really religious… but the crosses were all I could think of for a headstone."

"You did good, Benu." He put his arm over her shoulders and rubbed her arm as he held back his tears.

As he let her go, Benu said: "That bracelet… I made that for her when she was seven… maybe eight. I was visiting during summer break when I did it. She was wearing it… in the end…"

"She never stopped thinkin' about ya. None of them did."

"And I them. Ahh, I wish I could have found something for papa. But… he took everything when he left."

"I'm sure he was proud of ya. They all were."

"Yes…" she wiped another fresh tear from her cheek.

They stood in silence for a while. The air was still and moderate. Birds chirped amongst the trees as the sun neared its zenith. The bright light of day shone over the somber funeral. Somewhere, Jay heard the soft rustling of leaves. He scanned the area and saw nothing; it seemed the creatures had lost interest for now. A soft breeze rolled in, scattering dead leaves across the graves and onto the wilted grass. One wrapped itself around Ajith's cross before tumbling onto the dirt mound.

"Oh," Jay said to himself as he reached into his back pocket, "I almost forgot to give this to ya." He produced the letter and handed it to Benu. "Found it on the dining room table."

Benu flipped it over and read her name.

"Binaka… Bit of a silly name, huh?" Jay muttered as he nudged Benu with his elbow.

"Hmph," Benu allowed herself a meek smile at Jay's successful attempt to cheer her up. "It is the name of the god Ganesha. You may know him: the one with four arms and an elephant head. I never like the idea of being named after a god… I much prefer 'Benu.'"

"Benu, it is and Benu it'll remain, then. Take your time. I'll do a final check on our things—grab whatever food and water I can find inside."

Benu responded with a silent nod.

Jay began walking to the front door—crossbow strapped on his back—as Benu broke the wax seal of the eggshell envelope in her hands. *Wax? Really, mama?* She thought to herself. A small chortle escaped her mouth as she slipped out two letters. Unfolding the bundle, she could see short strokes of twisting loops and hooks, connected by straight, horizontal lines that separated each phrase and word. She recognized her mother's immaculate Hindi and began to read it to herself.

Binaka,

> *You know I like to keep things short, so this will be no different. Your papa came home. We had a fight, but soon we got to the root of the matter. It was you, Benu. He told me, he could not face the end of the world knowing he hurt you or Alexis, so he came home and made amends. You have made us so proud, especially your papa. Every day since he returned, he talked about you. Asked how you were… what he missed. Please forgive him, Benu. He truly has changed.*

So has Mrs. Marlow. Every week Carla checks on us to see how we are doing. She asks about you every week. She has obtained some sort of electric power. We guess it was The Anomaly. What else? At the end of her visit, she offers to end anyone's suffering if they so choose. She can apparently deliver an electric shock that will do it painlessly. Last week she offered it to us.

Do not hate her for it, please. She means well, even if she has problems showing it. I know you heard her that night. I could see it in your face the next morning. Please, do try and forgive her. We had been considering it for a while, but today we have decided to follow through. But it does not feel right, Benu. To lay that burden and guilt on someone else's hands. We have decided to do it ourselves. Papa has some leftover, heavy drugs he took from work that should make it quick.

The days have become mundane torture. Every day we live in fear, simply waiting for the end. I try to tell myself things will change… that Total Convergence simply will not happen, but I know in my heart it is coming. There are creatures in this town. Ones that steal faces. Every day they kill one of us. Every week Carla tells us that fewer people answer their doors. You may think us cowards, Benu, but I know I will see your face if one of those things gets me. I know we all will… I cannot allow one of those things to walk this earth with the face of my Benu.

Please, if you are somehow reading this, see your life to the end. When we meet again, you will stand above us for this. I know it.

We love you, Benu,
Mama

Benu shuffled her mother's letter behind the other piece of paper, teardrops staining the pages. She recognized her sister's handwriting immediately. The scrawled English letters looked childish, but Benu knew Alexis had tried her best; her handwriting had always been a mess. Benu smiled and expelled a quick laugh as she sniffled and wiped away some snot. She began to read.

Hey Ben-Ben,

First off, I don't know what you'll find first, this or us, but either way.......
STOP YOUR CRYING!
*I know it's going to be hard for you, but you're the strongest person I've ever known! People need you, Ben-Ben... not just us. You're a doctor for Christ's sake! And I know you can do stitches and fix broken legs and stuff, but I know just being **you** is going to fix someone who's suffering from something that cuts deeper than any knife. (That was probably the best sentence I've ever written by the way!)*

You know I'm not great with words, so I don't know how much I can express how much I respect and love you. Papa's the same way. He tried to write a letter too... but couldn't bring himself to do it. He said he'll just tell you face-to-face when we see each other after the end.

*We've been scared, but not today. Today, we decided to see for ourselves sooner rather than later. I'll be honest... I don't know if you're going to meet **us** in two weeks or if we're going to meet*

Benu clutched the letters close to her stomach. They began to crumple around her fingertips as she wept. Tears rolled off her chin and darkened the pages, forming wet spots. She let her sister's words penetrate her heart. Soon, she calmed her breathing and stood for a moment, contemplating the words she held in her hands. Her tears trickled down her expressionless face of acceptance. She balled the hem of her sleeve, wiped her tears, sniffled, and nodded to herself. Jay stepped out onto the porch as Benu folded up her letters into the envelop and tucked them into her back pocket.

She met Jay at the foot of the stairs. He handed her an apple and a slice of bread from the bundle of supplies he cradled in his arms.

"Found these in the fridge. Not sure when the power went out, but these look fresh enough. I'm sure they got the bread from Carla. Not sure about the apple," Jay said.

"The Glowackis, the neighbors a couple houses over, have an apple tree in their backyard. I am sure they got it from there," Benu replied as she sniffled, wiped the fruit against her poncho, and took a bite. Her teeth crunched into the apple as she caught a spittle of juice with the heel of her palm. Still chewing, she said: "Yup… definitely fresh."

"Ah, nice."

Jay could see Benu's eyes were bloodshot from crying. He motioned over to the bikes, and they began walking towards the sidewalk as Benu finished her apple and bread. As they packed up their things, Benu looked back at the shovel staked into the ground.

"Should we take that—for you?" Benu asked.

"No way to carry it. I was plannin' on scavenging one in Escanaba, to be honest," Jay replied.

"Hmph, good point… Ah! I have an idea. Wait here."

Benu rushed through the gate and returned a few minutes later with a gardening trowel. It was an ordinary tool bought from a big box store. Clumps of dried mud were caked on the edges of the blade, which was fit into a green, plastic handle, inlaid with black rubber grips. An ordinary, mass-market tool bought by millions of people, so it was no wonder that Jay's wife had owned the same trowel she'd use to tend her garden for years.

"Here, *dost*," Benu said as she flipped the handle towards Jay. He took it and picked off some of the dry mud, studying the tiny shovel. A smile stretched across his face as he remembered the days his wife spent tending her little garden. The days he would sit outside and chat with Her as she watered her black-eyed Susans. The night he gained his abilities and the aloe vera that soothed his scalding hand. Of course, the creeping memory of Her days in bed were there too. The fatigue Jay felt in his shoulders as he toiled over clumps of weeds and mulch. But he would wear the same smile for Her as he did now. Although he took on the burden of two people at times, Her loving warmth soothed his tired soul.

Jay placed the trowel in his bag and thanked Benu. As they mounted their bikes, Benu harrumphed and said: "Jay, my crossbow and knife, please."

"You're gonna be ok?"

"No, but… I am no longer in that dark place. The letters… mama and *behan* knew exactly what to say… you can trust me. I will not try that again, and if I do, you have permission to save me again and take them away for good."

Jay curled his lip. He was hesitant to hand over Benu her means of self-harm, but she would need them to survive… and he would need her in case of trouble. As he unbuckled the knife off his thigh, he peered into her hazel eyes, strong emotions of compassion emanated from his gaze. Benu gripped the sheath as the knife formed a bridge between them.

"Promise?" he murmured, hoping his caring aura would engulf her and soothe her mind.

Benu smiled with a soft expression of appreciation and whispered: "I promise."

Jay let go and returned Benu's control of her life. She strapped the knife to her left thigh and held out her hand for the crossbow. Jay slipped the crossbow off his back and held it to Benu just the same as the knife. This time, they simply nodded to each other as Jay let go and Benu slung her weapon over her back. As Benu resituated herself, Jay asked for her map and began checking the route.

"It's gonna get even rougher from this point. We've mainly been takin' highways, but we're gonna have to go down some country roads and through more forest. No more large towns. I can only *hope* the roads aren't completely chewed up," Jay said.

"Yes," Benu leaned over to look at the map, "and it will be a fairly lengthy ride. Six hours to the shore? And…" She flipped her watch to face her. "We have about two days, eight hours 'till Total Convergence."

Jay pursed his lips and turned his head to The Anomaly. Even in the brilliant daylight, the red aura cut a diamond-shaped hole in the blue sky. Jay could see it now, the thing he had dreaded before—the collapse of reality. As he stared, he realized he had seen it all along. The twisting and twirling of the air around it, warping in waves of iridescent colors. A hum rumbled in his ears as he noted the size of the black diamond.

It's growing.

He ripped himself from the hypnosis of The Anomaly and folded up the map, handing it to Benu. He bit the first knuckle of his index finger and bounced his right foot anxiously on the ground.

We'll make it. We have to.

He pulled his knuckle from his mouth and asked, "How are ya feelin'? Physically, I mean."

"Good. I was a little tired from making the crosses… and crying, but I am good."

"Same. I'm a little sore from diggin' and carrying… them, but I can push it a bit today."

"Agreed, I can too. But remember to keep your wits about you, or you will end up like me on Carla's couch."

Jay chuckled as he pulled out two bottles of water and handed one to Benu. They both drank a bit and packed up.

"You go on ahead of me," Jay said. "That way, if one of those things gets ya I can kill it."

"Sounds good," Benu replied as she took one last look at her home and the fresh graves that lay before it. She nodded to herself, then to her family, and pedaled off.

Jay and Benu were now four hours out from Cadillac. They had passed through the small towns of Mesick, Copemish, and Thompsonville; all were nothing but rubble. The rural roads they traveled were rough, cracked, and pitted—filled with overgrowth. Forest canopies shielded them from the afternoon sunlight, only allowing shafts to waver amongst the pavement. As they traveled more North, the air became cold and dry. Lake Michigan was close now, causing chilled breezes to roll through the woods off the freezing waters. Jay had lowered his sleeves and Benu had donned the hood of her poncho. The hairline cracks of the earth had widened, forming dips and gaps in the terrain. At times, they had to bike around craggy spires and drop-offs that had formed from the earth's splitting. Violet light shone more brightly now. Jay could see the stain of lilac across his hands and Benu's body as he followed her.

They passed through former farmlands. The swaying stalks of amber wheat now smothered by overbearing weeds and tall grasses. Occasionally, they would come across fields of farm animal carcasses. The cows, pigs, and chickens were all free to roam now. Unfortunately, they made the perfect prey for predators, both new and old. At some point, Jay spotted a group of disfigured coyotes feasting on a dead cow on the side of the road. Flies were swarming around the decaying meat as the coyotes, with bloodied teeth and fur, snarled at Benu and Jay. They rode down twisting dirt paths and trudged through thick bramble when the road proved too perilous. Benu caught a flat, and Jay repaired it. In a large, open field, just before the town of Honor, they rode alongside a herd of slackjaws. Their mighty gallops rocked the earth as they leapt into the forest ahead of them, causing the treetops and branches to sway and rustle. Jay and Benu decided to stop just before this forest to take a break. The woods ahead of them were not of the black curse from Detroit or Clare, and they had seen no sign of it thus far.

They led their bikes off the road and down a small, shallow slope just before the field. Laying their bikes over, they took off their things and set them aside. Jay was the first to sit down on the incline while Benu did some stretches. He leaned forward and rested his forearms on his knees. His hands and face were warm from the exercise. As he took off his beanie, a brush of cool air rolled across the top of his head. It provided a short stint of reprieve before quickly turning into needles of frigid ice. Jay pulled his beanie back over his head and could feel cold numbness build in his hands. He reached into his bag, grabbed an apple and water, and began eating.

Benu finally sat down and huffed a swath of hot breath into her hands, rubbing them together. She reached into her bag and pulled out a bottle of water and can of chicken noodle soup. Holding the two items in one hand, she rummaged through her bag. After a while, she came up empty, turned to Jay, and asked: "Hey, do you have the can opener?"

"Yeah, think so," Jay set his water down and searched his bag. "Yup, here it is." He pulled out a can opener and handed it to Benu.

"Ah, thank you." She cradled her three items in one hand and searched her bag again, coming up empty. "Um, what about a spoon?"

"Uh, yeah. I think I forgot to give you one when we were packin' up. Hold on."

Jay looked through his bag, found a silver spoon, and gave it to Benu.

"Ah, awesome! Thanks."

The crunch of thin steel and tin accompanied Jay's chewing as Benu rode the can opener along the lip of the soup can. A small '*pop*' sounded as the tool finished rounding the lid. Benu put down the can opener and peeled off the lid. One end of the lid fell into the soup and dribbled off some broth as she lifted it out of the can and threw it into the field like a frisbee. She nearly plunged her spoon into her meal when she stopped and nudged Jay. "Hey."

"Yeah, what's up?" he replied.

"Could you... *cook* this for me?"

Jay chuckled and held out his hand, "Sure." Benu placed the can in Jay's open palm as he heated his hand. "What am I? Chef Mic?"

Benu chortled and poked phantom buttons on Jay's arm as she made '*beeps*' and '*boops*'. Jay nudged her off as they shared a snicker.

"Ya feelin' better?" he asked.

"Yes, I am," she replied. "I had a lot of time to think during our bike ride." She patted the right side of her hip. "Mama's and *behan's* letters really helped me. Their deaths are... still fresh in my mind, but I want to see this to the end. It is what they would want."

"Good. I'm glad."

"What about you? How are you doing?"

Jay swallowed a pit in his throat. "Nervous. Scared. Tired. I feel like The Anomaly is playin' games with us, y'know?"

"Hmph, I know what you mean. One moment, it feels like it's tearing us apart—imprisoning us in some world of pain. And, at times, it throws us some reprieve—like Lorenzo or Carla. And, other times… it is like it is not even there."

"But it's always there… watchin' us. It's drivin' me insane—eatin' away at my brain."

"Does not seem like it."

"Whaddaya mean?"

"You hide your emotions very well, *dost*. Only rarely have I seen you falter at your feelings. Never have I seen you break down… like I did."

"Well… I've always been like this, I suppose. Just don't want others to worry, is all… but, admittedly, talkin' about… *Her*… has really helped."

"Have you… ever talked to anyone about this before?"

The soup in his hands had begun to bubble. Jay set it down in the grass between him and Benu and warned her to let it cool a bit. He replied to her question: "I've tried. But… it's hard, y'know? Every time, the words just… wouldn't come out. I was advised to go to therapy after her funeral, but… I was too afraid to talk… to feel those feelings again. No one ever followed up on it, either. So, I just kept it inside and dealt with it."

"Keeping it inside is *not* 'dealing with it'. *This* is."

Jay felt his heart drop as a wave of heavy emotion shot into his throat and choked him. He swallowed and sniffled—his nose red from the chill air. Wiping some snot off his upper lip, he took a drink of water and said: "Yeah, you're right, you're right… I think you can eat your soup now. Probably cool enough now."

Benu reached out a hand and rubbed Jay's shoulder—then picked up her hot soup, thanked him, and ate. As they ate, they continued to chat. As they chatted, time stood still. Jay felt strong comfort in Benu's company. She had heightened the goodness in him and quelled the despair in his heart and anguish of his mind.

"Hey," Benu said. "Could you teach me some sign?"

"What for?" Jay asked.

"Just for fun."

"Um, sure. Sure. What do ya wanna know?"

"Hmph, how about… 'My name is Benu?'"

"Mmm, that would require you to know the alphabet which would be kinda hard."

"Then… what about the first thing you learned?"

"Well, that would be the first thing my wife taught me: 'You are my friend.'"

"Oh! Perfect, *dost*."

Jay pointed a finger to Benu and said, "You." Then, he made a hook out of both his index fingers and connected them together, right over left. Then, left over right. "Friend. That's it!"

"Wow! Easy!"

They continued passing time as Jay taught Benu a few sentences in sign language. Their chat on the roadside felt as if The Anomaly had disappeared from the sky momentarily. As they finished their break and stood, the black diamond made its presence known once again.

The earth began to quake beneath Jay and Benu's feet. They held out their hands to balance themselves as Jay looked out across the field. In the distance, he could see chunks of earth lift high into the air as trees on the surface swayed violently. The sound of rocks splitting, like cracks of giant bones, sent birds sailing out of the forests. Benu looked out towards a group of trees that were shaking more fiercely than their neighbors. Deer, slackjaws, and other woodland creatures rushed out of the area as a crevasse began to form around the quaking woods. A piece of land—measuring about five miles in radius—began to lift in the air from the horizon. Waterfalls of dirt and rock began to fall from the edges of the lifted earth. Lagging animals tumbled off the sides and crashed into the ground—some limping away, others lying dead in the grand shadow. Deep roots dangled from out the bottom of the rising land. Jay followed the large, floating island as it levitated high into the sky towards The Anomaly, blotting out the sun. The treetops seemed to scrape the blue sky before slowly disintegrating into specks of black nothingness. The rest of the island began to follow as shadows of crumbling earth were cast over Jay and Benu. Soon, the island was gone without ever leaving the atmosphere—ground into dust by the black diamond.

The two stood speechless for a moment. It was as if The Anomaly felt their joy and thought it necessary to remind them of its power. Jay looked out at the enormous scar The Anomaly had left in the ground. He scanned the horizon around him to see distant slabs of earth rising into oblivion, just like the one he'd witnessed.

{Chapter 25}

2:1:58:49

Jay and Benu were now an hour from the shores of Sleeping Bear Dunes. The forest road they cruised through was rocky with very little pavement. Night had come early, blanketing the sky in blackness amongst a new moon. The only color in the sky was that of the red outline of The Anomaly and the pinpoints of bright, white stars. Benu led the two with her flashlight clipped to the collar of her poncho. As they coasted down craggy hills and bumpy terrain, her light was tossed around in the darkness like a frantic searchlight hunting down an escaped prisoner. The purple hue of the cracked earth helped light the area enough to keep them from crashing but offered no real semblance of aiding their direction. All they had was the broken path they had chosen and their wits. At one point, Benu had checked her compass only to find it spinning rapidly.

After another hour of biking, the forest began to change. Jay felt dread in the air as the red hue began to pour more brilliantly through the canopies. He looked up and around to see a few trees had completely lost their leaves—their branches like spiny, white bones against the black sky. As they continued further, Jay could see fewer Fall trees. For a while, every other tree was dead. After a longer while, most of the trees were dead. Then, the entire forest was nothing but ashy towers of spindly limbs. The purple light that lingered along the ground was now dissipated amongst a rolling mist that chilled Jay below the waist. He could feel his toes numbing as he and Benu pedaled through a tunnel of dead trees.

Jay called out to Benu to stop. She obliged and they pulled over to the side. As they stepped off their bikes, gray leaves crumbled into ash and the particles of black and gray were carried off into the mist by a breeze. He turned to Benu.

"I think we're lost," he said plainly.

"Yeah, me too," Benu replied, scanning the wasteland. "We have not strayed from the road, however."

"Maybe we're on the wrong road?"

"No, I do not think so… I am positive I did not stray from the road. Besides, there are not many roads to turn onto by accident out here anyways."

"True… maybe The Anomaly changed something? Like when a piece of the earth was taken, it changed the landscape?"

"Possibly… Wait… Do you hear that?"

Jay listened intently. The place was dead. Devoid of any rustling from woodland creatures or tumbling of leaves. Even the breeze he felt across his face made nary a sound. The only sound he could hear was the thumping of his heart and the blood moving in his ears.

"No, I don't–"

Benu shushed him and put her ear to the ground. Closing her eyes, she heard the distant movement of water, crashing and churning somewhere far off but closer than before. She continued to listen. The splash of two waves colliding. Water lapping sandy shores. And… something else. A whistling… a hollow howling… a whooshing of large swaths of air. First, just an accent amongst the waves. Then, slightly louder until it fully drowned out the sounds of the lake. She shot up and grabbed Jay's arm, pulling him further off the road.

"Hey!" he yelled.

She looked back at him and shushed him sternly. Jay clamped his mouth shut and nodded. Benu let go of his arm as they sprinted deeper into the dead forest. They leapt and bound over purple-emanating crevasses until they came up a ditch on the other side of a fallen tree. Benu scampered onto the log—still propped up on one end by its stump—hopped into the ditch and sat down against the dirt wall. Jay parted the mist that lingered just above the ditch and took a seat next to her. As they huffed, Jay asked between his heavy breaths: "Benu… What's goin' on?"

"Something is coming… Keep quiet… Keep still…" she replied, her voice wavering as if years had been taken off her life. She flicked off her light.

Jay could hear it now. In the distance behind them, something howled a constant deep, growl accompanied by the whistle of a tea kettle. As it grew closer, Jay felt nothing. The ashes around them were undisturbed and the branches above were rigid, unmoving. The growl became clearer, like a malformed train horn, building as the creature that was surely making it, barreled towards them. It was only a few feet away now. Jay and Benu had recuperated and, as if something primal in them kicked in, they held their breath to hide themselves from the predator that loomed over them.

They were covered in a long, undulating shadow that stretched out past the width of the twenty-foot ditch. A gust of wind rushed past Jay and Benu, coating their cheeks with ash and dust. The beast stopped above them and hovered just over the fallen log. A wave of crumbling leaves poured into the ditch; all around the forest floor, the ground refuse was shot forward as if a giant broom had swept them into the mist before Jay and Benu. The spiderweb of branches above were rocked with a tremendous wave of force. The monster's terrifying siren and whistle had stopped in an instant, now replaced with nothing but the sound of creaking wood and low, whirling winds as it craned its figure side to side. Jay and Benu continued to hold their breath as the black shadow swayed along the ground before them, passing over Jay… then over Benu… then back to Jay… and so on. Then, the pulsing shadow stretch out between them, splitting them down the middle on each edge. The scarlet glow of The Anomaly covered half their bodies in crimson.

It hovered there for a moment. Jay's vision began to blur. Benu's face began to turn purple.

It creaked once. Jay's body began to convulse. Benu clamped her eyes shut.

Then, like a bullet, the creature whipped around and shot off into the forest, smattering Jay and Benu with forest-floor debris. When the wailing of sirens and whistles had vanished from Jay's ears, he slumped down the dirt wall and gasped for air. Benu began gasping as well and turned over onto her left, bracing her hand against the dirt wall. She smushed her ear against the dirt wall and heard nothing. Before she could say it was safe, Jay spoke: "What the fuck was that thing?"

Under any other circumstances, that question would have made Benu cackle sarcastically and taunt Jay with a quip regarding to absolute state of The Anomaly's world and power, but in this instance… she was just as flabbergasted and shellshocked as he was. She simply looked at him, still gasping, and shook her head.

"It felt like death, Benu… I could feel it above me… If it had touched me… Oh God…"

"I know, *dost*… I felt it too." Her voice was heavy with fear.

"What do we do?"

"The lake is close. I could hear it back at the road. It is maybe… less than five miles away. It is your call… we can turn back."

Turn back. The two words echoed in his head.

Turn back. It would be easier.

Turn back. He'd be dead in a couple of days anyway.

Turn back. He could always apologize to Her when they met again.

As Jay sat up to give in to Benu's suggestion, he felt the urn pressed between his back and the dirt wall. He would always be forgiven by Her, but could he forgive himself? He had to see this to the end… even if it meant turning to ash. He had to push on—not only for Her, but for himself.

"No, we keep goin'," he replied. "We head towards the sound of the lake. I trust ya, Benu. You got good ears. We're in no danger if ya can hear it comin'."

"Hmph, all right." The compliment seemed to restore Benu's confidence.

Jay felt it too and felt the urn against his back as he stood along with Benu. They helped each other out of the ditch and examined the open woods. Benu switched on her flashlight. Jay fiddled with his ring in his pocket as the pair walked back to the road. When they arrived, they found that their bikes had been broken and rusted beyond repair. As Benu touched the handlebars of her bike, it crumbled to dust.

The two had crept through the dead woods for nearly two hours since their encounter with the monster. They followed the road, but it seemed to lead nowhere. The crash of waves and shifting of moving waters could be heard nearby, but the forest continued to repeat itself. They were traveling in circles. In the twilight of the stars, the forest of ash and mist felt like a desert. A few times, they had heard the howling sound of the shadow beast from before, but it had not approached them since. Benu dared not light her flashlight. The oppressive trepidation of the ashen forest made it feel as if her light had no place in this land of decay.

Jay's frustration started to overtake his fear. He jogged up to Benu and grabbed her shoulder, stopping her.

"Benu, we're lost. What's your compass say?" he muttered.

She pulled out her compass and watched as it spun rapidly. This was the third, maybe fourth, time Jay had asked; Benu couldn't remember. Clutching it in her hand, she grimaced with her eyes shut. The spin of the needle broke something in her common sense as she tossed the compass off into the woods out of blind frustration. The howling came again, somewhere down the road this time. The two rushed into the woods and found a high outcropping. Clumps of ash and dead roots fell below them as they scurried up the wall. When they made it to the top, they hid behind a boulder embedded into the ground.

They were high above their previous position. Through the purple mist, they saw the beast gliding through the air, only a couple of feet off the ground. It appeared as a formless cylinder, twisting and twirling in a mass of black smoke that left a wispy trail behind it. The center was a solid, entangled mass of black, undulating worms that parted and came together as it went around tree trunks and dead shrubbery. It bobbed up and over crevasses, rocks, and humps. Some tendrils separated off from the colony and swirled up and around tree trunks without touching them, flowing up about halfway before traveling down and off branches, rejoining with the main hive. As the shadow mass moved around the forest, the afflicted area would wither further. Leaves and overgrowth would flutter out of its way as it carried a strong gust with it. The whistle and train horn traveled with the creature.

As they watched the swirling mass draw closer to their outcropping, Benu heard a small commotion to her right. She motioned Jay to follow her as they crept over to the ledge. They peered over, laying on their stomachs, and saw a group of soft, teal lights moving around some bushes and trees about fifty feet away. The sounds were similar to children holding conversations on a playground. Benu carefully unslung her crossbow and peered through her scope. The azure glow belonged to a group of twenty or so small, pudgy creatures. Benu could see the light emanating as bioluminescence from the red tops of their heads which resembled spotted mushroom caps. The large, brimmed caps sat atop petite, chubby bodies of ridged, fungal membrane. Their arms and legs were stubby as they waddled around, making squeaks and calls at each other. The mushroom creatures were picking through bushes and trees, gathering anything edible and tossing them over their shoulders and into wicker baskets they wore on their backs. Benu caught a glimpse of one of their faces. Two plain features were all that occupied the completely flat skin: two black, beady eyes and a puffy muzzle like that of a cat or dog—but smooth and hairless. Their bodies were pill-like with no visible evidence of a neck or waist. Their hands were like mittens with no discernable digits aside from their thumbs, and they had stubby legs that lacked feet—only leaving round imprints as they waddled through the ash. They varied in heights of three to four feet; some had prominent bellies while others were slender. The larger ones carried wooden spears and had no baskets.

Benu tore herself from her aim as she heard the shadow creature round the outcropping beneath them. Jay nudged her and pointed out to the left. The roaring mass barreled towards the living mushrooms as they screamed and scattered, dropping traces of berries and small fruit. As the whirling dark mass passed through the crowd, it left behind dried and dead husks. The spear-wielding members rallied the remaining mushrooms to form a circle that encased the gatherers. They held their spears at the ready as the black mass spun furiously around them like a hurricane. One of the warrior mushrooms let out a fierce, child-like battle cry as his cap shone brightly, warding off the beast. The rest of the perimeter followed suit as the protected members huddled and whimpered in fear. Black tendrils lashed out at the warriors as they lanced their makeshift spears at the shadow monster. Some of the shadow creature's attacks had contacted the mushrooms' spears and skin, turning them to ash.

"They cannot hold out much longer," Benu whispered to Jay.

"Yeah, but maybe once it's done, it'll leave," he replied.

Benu turned to him in disgust. "We have to help them!"

"Do you see that fuckin' thing?" Jay snapped through clenched teeth. "It'll turn us to dust before we even step within a foot of it."

"We *have* to try!"

"Why? Both those things are creatures of The Anomaly. I say let it sort itself out."

Benu rolled on her side, lifted an open palm, and struck Jay across the cheek. He quickly grabbed it, warming his hand out of instinct.

"Maybe I was right when I met you… maybe you are not human."

Jay pointed with a quivering finger at the fight. "*Those* are not human."

"It is our ability to tell right from wrong—good from evil—that makes us human… not how we look or where we came from. Look! *Look* down at those helpless things and tell me if letting them die is the 'human' thing to do!"

Jay sighed heavily.

"Look!" Benu was yelling now.

Jay obeyed. He saw the circle of mushroom creatures close as, one by one, the warriors fell. The cries and screams of the group started to sound distinctly human in his ears. These were not the creatures of The Anomaly that were birthed to destroy; they were made for another purpose. He remembered Nerf, the magical cat, and the slackjaws. He felt a fire grow in his hand as he crushed a handful of leaves and dirt into ash. In his mind, he saw Carla smoking on her deck, telling her story of how she came upon her powers. He nodded a few times and turned to Benu. "All right… All right! I'll head down there and get its attention. You wait till it's clear and get those mushroom guys away from here."

Benu nodded curtly as Jay slipped off his backpack, shot up to his feet, and found his way down the outcropping. The mushrooms' defenses were tight now; only eight remained—two warriors and six gatherers. Jay sprinted towards the whirling spiral of formless clouds and worms. He stopped a few paces from the shadow monster, skidding his feet and kicking up dust. The cyclone towered over Jay about fifteen feet. Without a word, Jay took in a huge breath, rolled up his sleeves, and splayed out both his hands. Unleashing two streams of superheated flames, Jay struck the broad side of the creature. An ear-piercing whistle erupted from the beast as pieces of fluttering flames sprayed outward. The train horn blasted in agonizing pain as the cyclone swirled above and came back together into a barreling piston headed straight for Jay.

He held his ground, delivering flurries of fire until the shadow was a couple of arm-lengths away. Jay cut his flame and dropped to the ground. The mass started to pass over him like a burning freight train, its horn-like cry wailing. Jay watched the ground and waited for the shadow of the creature to pass completely. When he could see the gleam of the purple earth brighten, he rushed to his feet and ran ahead without looking back. He could hear the shadow changing direction to his left.

Curling into the air.

Back down.

Skimming the ground.

And swirling back into pursuit.

Jay ran deeper into the forest, crossing the road he and Benu had been on and luring the beast far from the mushrooms. As he ran, he fired back projectiles that collided into the creature and burst like artillery fire. He leapt and scurried over fallen trees and rough terrain as the booming horn of the shadow grew near. When he saw the shadow of the beast meet his feet, he turned on his heels and let loose a volley of fireballs. Each fired from Jay's blackened and crackling hands with booms of veracious fury. The explosions of each impact were like landmines detonating in an open field. Branches shook and broke into chunks of ash as Jay was deafened. He could only hear his muffled cries as he continued his attack—the train horn but a constant background. The shadow pressed onward, trailing behind plumes of smoke from the streams of flames that burned off its body like ribbons. As it endured blow after blow, it began to relent.

Jay held his ground and manifested a wall of fire that steered the beast around him. The beast, now an infernal tower of hellfire and billowing, black smoke, twirled in the red glow of The Anomaly. Its movements had become lazy and lurching; it seemed to have trouble keeping itself from plummeting into the ground. It faced Jay and readied a final attack.

Benu climbed down the outcropping when she saw Jay initially lure the beast away from the mushrooms. The frightened creatures were still in position, ready to strike any additional threats. Benu crouched towards them with her hands out to show them she meant no harm. One of the warriors let out a small yelp as he was startled by her presence. The spear shook in his little, mitten-like paws. The other warrior stepped forward, braver than the shaking one, and held his spear out. Benu was an arms-length from the tip of the little one's spear. She stopped in her tracks, her hands still out.

The brave warrior furrowed his brow and asked a series of questions in a strange language Benu didn't understand. Its words were a rapid-fire of slurred babbling and garbled sounds; it reminded Benu of a baby's first attempts at speaking. It spoke with a hurried tone and with each supposed 'question mark,' the warrior jutted its spear forward. When it was done speaking, there was only the whimpering of the gatherers behind the warriors.

Benu pointed a finger into her chest, "Umm, me. Friend. *Fa-ren-de.*"

The warriors looked at each other, exchanged some words, and looked back at Benu with even fiercer vigor. The brave one poked his spear forward and caused Benu to flinch back. In the distance, Benu could hear the wail of the shadow creature. The gatherers turned in the direction of the sound and held each other tightly. Benu began to feel a tinge of anxiety in her chest until she remembered the chat she had with Jay.

She looked into the brave warrior's beady, black eyes and pointed to the creature. Then she signed the word "friend." The creature tilted his head; the bioluminescence from his cap flickered a bit. Then Benu drew a circle out in front of her, returning her finger back to her chest. She held out a fist—her knuckles lined up vertically—and placed the open palm of her other hand on top of it. She had asked the creatures to hide with her.

The warriors were unsure. Benu's intentions felt noble to them, but they had no idea what she was trying to convey. Benu made a few more gestures to beg the creatures to come with her, none of which were of Jay's teachings. She had made praying hands to beg and waved open palms towards her, saying: "Come on!"

The mushrooms still didn't budge. Benu then heard echoing explosions and a horrendous howl. Benu felt it in her gut: either Jay would return soon… or the shadow creature. She made one final attempt. She stuck out her hand and slipped off her backpack. The warriors held their spears at the ready. Opening her bag, she pulled out an apple and tossed it to the brave warrior's feet. Benu then slipped her backpack back on, held both her hands out, and lowered her head beneath the warrior's height. The brave one held its spear in one mitt as it knelt and picked up the apple. It held it to his muzzle and sniffed the fruit. It took a cautious nibble and tasted the sweet juices. Then, it took a huge bite, closed its eyes, and made a delighted noise. It nodded its head and tossed the apple to the other warrior who took a bite as well. The apple was passed around to the gathers who all took bites until the apple was nothing but core.

The brave warrior lowered his spear and approached Benu. She stood, towering over the creature—the mushroom's cap just beneath her breasts. The warrior reached for Benu's hand and grasped it. He nodded to her, looked over his shoulder, and waved the rest over to follow. Benu sighed out of relief and led the mushrooms onto the outcropping where they hid behind the boulders.

Jay stared at the shadow creature and wondered if it was staring back. It hovered before him like a king cobra waiting to strike. Jay could imagine the piercing eyes of a serpent amongst the moving black clouds and writhing tendrils leering deep into his mind. He could feel its presence strongly now. It was the same foreboding aura of The Anomaly. This was a remnant of the black diamond. He was sure! Jay convinced himself of this and, as he did, his vision tunneled around the creature.

The monstrosity was smoldering. Bits of black tendrils dropped from the mass and sizzled into the ash below—dead. It studied its prey, rotating slowly along its length. The formless black cloud was silent, puffing out waves of smoke.

Jay dug his feet into the ash. The gray powder shifted beneath his soles.

He ignited his hands and stilled his breathing.

The shadow wasted no more time; it went for the kill!

A screeching whistle burst from the beast as its train horn bellowed louder than ever before. It swooped down across the forest floor and drilled towards Jay.

Jay let loose a torrent of wildfire. As the creature collided with the flame, the two forces splayed out in a grand starburst. Jay's inferno was now a shield of dancing streams of fire that shot off in all directions. He could see the same was happening to the shadow. Charred, burning tendrils were flung into the sky before drifting into the ash below. However, Jay was running out of steam, and the beast continued to fight back out of desperate survival.

Jay could feel his flamethrower being shoved back.

He could feel his feet being pushed from under him.

I have to get out of the way. I have to move!

He dropped his attack and ducked to the right, his left arm lagging.

The black shadow zoomed through and caught Jay's left arm just above the elbow. It barreled past Jay in a smoking, black blur—a tidal wave of dust and ash with it. It howled in anguish as it retreated somewhere deep into the woods, skipping off the ash-laden ground, severely wounded. Jay's ears were ringing, but he could no longer hear the monster's tremendous horn. He lay in a pool of ash, his face dusted in light gray. Jay turned over and coughed up trails of saliva onto the ground. He spat once more for good measure. His teeth ground against each other, traces of ash still between them.

He sat up and wiped his face of the dust. As he stood, he felt a heavy weight drop from his left arm. There on the ground, where he had rested his left arm, was a pile of ash shaped like his forearm down to his hand. He traced the ground over to his leg, up his side, and past his shoulder to see his jacket had been torn just above the elbow with nothing else below it.

With a quaking hand, he rolled up his sleeve to see his bicep had ended in a stump just below the elbow. There was no blood—no pain, even. The exposed meat at the end was just a light gray—the same as the ash. The same color ringed around the end of the stump and up the skin about an inch. Jay held his stump up a bit and waved his remaining hand through the ghost of his left and felt nothing. He dropped to his knees, his stump hovering above his right hand. Quivering gasps left his mouth as he gripped the stump and squeezed it to ensure himself that he had truly lost his left arm.

He felt the squeeze.

He reached down it again and squeezed the air where his forearm had been.

He felt nothing.

He tried to wiggle his left-hand fingers.

He felt them wiggle but did not see them wiggle.

There was nothing there.

As Benu comforted the mushrooms, she heard a bloodcurdling scream somewhere in the distance.

{Chapter 26}

1:20:6:44

Benu peered through her scope over the large boulder she and the mushrooms were hiding behind, scanning the dense forest of ash for any signs of Jay. She had heard the screeching train horn of the shadow creature fade off deep into the forest. The scream that followed indicated that Jay was victorious… or met his death in battle. Benu wanted to believe the former, so she allotted herself some time to wait for his return. Otherwise, she would have to accept the unfortunate truth of Jay's demise and move on. All she could hear now were the whispers of the mushroom creatures behind her as they consoled each other. Then, she spotted a figure clutching his left arm and plodding towards her. As the mist cleared a bit, she recognized Jay's gray beanie and black jacket. She dropped her aim, swung the crossbow over her shoulder, and scampered down the outcropping. The mushrooms followed, lagging a bit to help each other down the side of the dirt wall.

"Jay!" Benu yelled as she snatched up Jay's bag and ran towards the hobbling figure. He raised his head and smiled a coy smile to show that he was 'all right.' As she met up with him, she stopped just a few paces before him and clasped her hands over her mouth; she saw the emptiness below his left elbow. He took a few steps up to her and stood up straight. Benu was still in shock as the mushrooms gathered behind her.

She guided her hands towards him carefully as if he were made of glass and said: "Oh my God… Jay… are you ok? Your arm…"

He reached out his only hand, grabbed both of hers, and replied: "Don't worry; I'm fine. It… doesn't hurt. I didn't even feel it when that thing took it."

Benu rushed in for a hug, held back tears, and said: "I am so sorry… I did not mean for you to…"

He patted her on the back with his right hand and reached up with his stump to do the same with his left; his phantom hand felt nothing. "It's all right. It wasn't your fault."

"Yes, it was! Maybe… maybe we should have…"

"No… you made the right choice. We did the right thing." He pushed her off, gently. "Besides, I wasn't plannin' on doin' much with that arm anyways."

"Hmph," Benu chuckled and pulled out her medical kit. "Let me at least take a look at you."

Benu led Jay and the mushrooms out of the open. They sat crisscross applesauce on the ground as Benu set Jay's bag down. Jay presented his stump as Benu examined it. He asked: "So, how many made it?"

Benu looked over her shoulders as she worked and replied, "Eight. Two seem to be warriors. The others are harmless… To be fair, they all seem to be harmless, but they are brave."

"Are they… friendly?"

"Hmph, as far as I can tell."

The group of mushrooms walked around Benu and up to Jay. The warriors stood over Jay and raised their spears over their caps, gripped them with both hands, and let out a deep *"oooohhhhh!"*. Then, the gatherers raised their mitts up and did the same.

Benu stopped examining Jay to look around and smile. Jay raised an eyebrow and began heating his hand. But, as soon as the thought of defending himself crossed his mind, the chanting stopped, and Jay was gently touched on his right shoulder by the smaller warrior. The sensation that passed from the creature felt soothing and blissful. The dread of the forest melted around him as he cooled his hand and sighed. Another hand touched his right shoulder—this time the brave warrior. He spoke words of gratitude and praise. At least, that's what Benu and Jay could gather from its tone and inflections. Jay replied: "Uhhh, you're welcome."

"They understand sign language," Benu quipped. "Kind of…"

Jay shot her an exaggerated look that read 'Really?' across his face. He shrugged with the creatures' mitts still on him and looked at the brave warrior. He held his right, open palm level with his eyes facing the ground and scooped a swath of air into his belly, upturning his palm to face the sky. The warrior tilted its cap left to right and rolled its pudgy shoulder in a form of a shrug. The mushroom retracted its hand and called the gatherers over. They each took a moment to lay their hands on Jay, muttering words of apparent wonder and extolment.

"See?" Benu said.

Jay just rolled his eyes as Benu applied some antibiotic ointment to his stump. She had wiped away some dead skin and ash with a small towelette soaked in alcohol. Jay could only feel the cool liquid, without any semblance of stinging pain.

"It really does not hurt at all?" Benu asked.

"No. It really doesn't," Jay replied.

"The amputation was not very clean, the adherent scar tissue formed over very roughly but… there is no way it would have formed in that short amount of time. It is odd, to say the least."

"I'm not sure we should even try to make heads or tails of how The Anomaly's monstrosities work. I mean… you've been with me for a while now… can you explain how I shoot fire outta my hands?"

"Hmph, I suppose not." She had finished wrapping Jay's severed arm in gauze as the mushrooms took their hands off Jay and gathered a dusting of glowing spores in their palms. Jay looked around as the creatures caked Jay's jacket in the glowing dust. As they finished, they walked over to Benu and did the same to her poncho. Benu giggled a bit at the soft, spongelike mitts of the mushrooms pressing onto her.

"What're they doin'?" asked Jay.

"I am not sure. Feels like some sort of thank you? Maybe a sacred ritual?" she replied.

"Is it poison?"

"Oh, calm yourself, *dost!* They are harmless."

Jay grumbled as all eight stood to his left. The two warriors bowed, and the gatherers did the same. As the mushrooms rose, the brave one held out its free hand, as if presenting something, and spoke some garbled words. Jay shrugged in return and tilted his head, mimicking the mushroom's earlier movement of confusion. The brave warrior rubbed its flat chin and smacked its inset lips. It then nodded and patted its chest a few times. Then, it grabbed the mitt of a gatherer behind it and marched in place, leading the gatherer down an imaginary path. It then stopped, stepped over, and patted Jay and Benu on the shoulder.

"I think… it is offering us a favor—or maybe offering to lead us somewhere," Benu muttered.

"Hmmm…" Jay pondered. "Can you lead us to the lake?" As he asked this he pointed to the mushroom and towards the sound of the lake he had heard before. *"L-ay-kuh,"* he enunciated as he held the first three fingers of his only hand up to his chin perpendicularly and mimicked waves towards the warriors with his arms. He could feel his left creating the motion, but only his stump moved up and down. As he performed this sign for 'ocean,' he made splashing noises like two waves coming together.

The brave warrior nodded, turned to the smaller warrior, and said some words. Then, the group of mushrooms huddled and held a private conversation. Jay and Benu glanced at each other. Benu shrugged as they both turned their attention back to the mushroom mass. The soft creatures turned back to Jay and Benu as the brave warrior stepped forward. It splayed out his stumpy arms—one holding his spear erect, the other with its mitt open—and said a reaffirming sentence. Jay couldn't help but smile at the petite, five-foot-or-so arm span of the mushroom; Benu covered her mouth as she giggled. The brave warrior lowered his arms and curled his muzzle in a smile as Jay and Benu rose to their feet with their things. Jay looked down into the mushroom's tiny, black eyes as the mushroom craned its neck up to meet Jay's.

"All right, lead the way," Jay said.

The brave warrior took Jay's hand and tugged. The squishy mitt felt like a giant marshmallow. The other warrior had grabbed Benu's as the entourage began to walk.

◆

The mushrooms led Jay and Benu through bending, twisting trees. The deeper the group traveled, the thicker the mist became, turning into a dense fog. Starlight and the red hue of the black diamond dimly lit the blanket of fog. Here and there, Jay could spot areas of greenery. He walked hand-in-hand with the brave warrior at the front while Benu and the other warrior took up the rear. Jay could only see a few feet ahead of him and took each step with caution, but the brave warrior marched with confidence. The air was still and, although the path seemed to bend and wind in several directions, Jay could hear the crashing waves growing closer. He looked over his shoulder—down the line of glowing blue caps—and checked on Benu. She was looking around aimlessly, probably wondering how the lake was growing closer despite the nonsensical path. Just as Jay began to grow skeptical of the mushrooms' competence, they crested over a grassy hill and broke through the fog.

Rolling dunes spread out before them as the waves of Lake Michigan lapped the lakeshore about a mile from where they stood. A brilliant display of gleaming colors lit the orange sands as the aurora borealis danced in the night sky like massive ribbons twirled by giants. They stopped for a moment to take a breather and absorb the view as Benu came up beside him along with the rest of the group. The warriors stamped the blunt end of their spears on the ground as the gatherers clapped and celebrated. Jay looked behind him and could see the ashen forest covered in fog. In front of his face was a gray wall of vapor. He reached out and could pass his hand through it with no issue but, when he pulled his arm back, the fog refused to pass some invisible line.

As he turned back, the brave warrior tugged at his jacket sleeve and pointed his spear in the direction of the lakeshore. Jay peered at the shoreline, blocking the bright lights above with his hand. He spotted figures in the distance moving around what looked like a pier with a small structure attached.

"Hey, Benu," Jay called over, pointing at what he saw. "Can you see through your scope? What's over there?"

Benu unslung her crossbow and took aim, "There are more mushrooms. Maybe… thirty? They are carrying things… Looks like they are organizing or something… and there is a boathouse some are moving in and out of. It looks… 'Makeshift' is the nicest way to put it. There is also a small village of some sort on the beach."

The brave warrior tugged at Jay's sleeve again and beckoned with its spear. They descended the hill and stepped into the sand. The loose earth accepted Jay and Benu's feet gladly. With each step came a plume of sand that trickled off the sides of their shoes. Jay had it worse in his Chucks; their loose, canvas construction allowed for heaps of sand to build up in his shoes.

Benu felt *she* had it worse as her boots were far heavier and required far more effort to lift out of the shifting sands. The mushrooms, however, were far too light to be affected by this trek, leaving tiny, round footprints as they moved ahead of the struggling pair.

At one point, they came upon an exceptionally large dune that forced Jay and Benu to crawl upward. Jay found it difficult to crawl with one arm, but he adapted quickly and soon, he stopped reaching with his phantom hand and, instead, used his stump to balance himself. He looked up to the peak to see their two warrior escorts, looking down at them and waiting patiently. He felt like Blondie in *The Good, The Bad, and The Ugly,* pulling himself along the desert floor—a pair of Tucos waiting for him above. He was exhausted and battered—so tired he could almost hear the *'wah wah waaaahhh'* of the movie's theme in his head. He licked his lips and could feel they were badly chapped from the dry air; he thought again of Blondie's sun-bleached face on that desert floor.

Benu reached the top first. She placed her hands on her hips and caught her breath. Jay came over the top and plopped onto his belly in front of the brave warrior. Sand clung to his cheek and beanie. He wanted to lay there indefinitely as his eyelids grew heavy. The sand had been as cool and inviting as he imagined, sinking in like a plush mattress. The brave warrior reached down and nudged Jay's back in a manner that conveyed: *'C'mon, time to get up.'*

"Thanks, lil' guy," he muttered as he rose to his feet—his knees quivering like stilts. He swiped the sand from his torso and face. As he stood up straight, he could see they had reached the shoreline. Just down the dune, the six gatherers rushed to the colony by the boathouse and greeted each other. Some larger ones were hugging smaller ones and others chatted in their strange language.

"Thank God," Benu said wearily.

"Yeah, no kiddin'," replied Jay. "Say… what time is it?"

Benu flipped her watch towards her. She wiped grains of sand off the watch face as she pressed the backlight button on the side. The watch beeped a small electronic chime. The fluorescent glow painted Benu's face green in the night. "Damn, it is late. 2:36 in the morning."

"Doesn't make any sense… How were we so far from the shore?"

"I do not know, but I am too tired to question it right now."

"Agreed."

Jay looked down at the brave warrior who waited patiently for the conversation to finish. It then nodded and led Jay and Benu into its small colony. As they walked towards the boathouse, they passed by stacks of crates, raised vegetable beds with nothing but dirt, tiny structures too hard to make out in the dark, and small burrows where a few mushrooms had nestled themselves into the ground and slept— only visible from the neck up. It was like walking through a miniature village built for garden gnomes.

The mushrooms gathered around their new visitors as the warriors, presumably, explained what happened. The crowd made the same sounds of bewilderment and astonishment as the gatherers before as they reached out and touched Jay and Benu. Other warriors stepped in, warded off the crowd, and made way for the brave warrior and the pair to pass.

The brave one led Jay and Benu onto the pier of the boathouse. Its cobbled construction of logs, 2x4s, and pallet wood creaked and groaned under their feet as black waves splashed underneath. They came up to the door of the boathouse. A structure of various woods, sheet metals, differently sized windows, road signs, and bricks stood before them. The brave warrior reached up and turned the doorknob. It pushed the door open and held it for Jay and Benu to enter. As Jay stepped in, he found it odd that the door was sized for humans.

{Chapter 27}

1:17:48:28

The brave warrior shut the rickety, South-facing door behind Jay and Benu as the two stepped into a small dining room and kitchen combo. Jay wiped the sand from his jeans and jacket. The small boathouse was a hoard. Piles of knickknacks and junk were stacked everywhere in cardboard boxes, pushed against the walls. The small room housed a dining room table with six chairs sitting on a large oval rug; a row of four or so hanging cabinets; a counter and sink beneath that spanned the length of the wall; and a fireplace with a cauldron placed on a pile of logs. Along the walls were random decorations of street signs, taxidermy deer heads, landscape photos, and other cheap wall decorations that felt more at home in a thrift store. Everything was jerry-rigged—a mash of mismatched woods, shoddy mortar work, and rough placements. If Jay had to guess, the mushrooms weren't exactly masters of home renovation or construction.

There were no lights hanging above, only the blue glow of the caps of the brave warrior and another mushroom that was working at the corner of the kitchen counter. To Jay and Benu's right was an open doorway which led to another room. The brave warrior motioned the two to sit at the dining room table as it walked into the other room, where it could be heard talking its quick language. There was another, muffled, deeper voice; this one sounded human. Jay and Benu took a seat facing the doorway.

Benu leaned over to peek inside the adjoining room. She could only spot a dirtied rug on the ground and a small, ragged dresser.

Jay ran his finger along the grain of the mahogany table—*heavy and sturdy*. He was watching the kitchen worker. The mushroom stood on a child-sized wooden stool as it moved and organized glass jars of varying sizes. Jay could see colors of red, green, and yellow in some of the jars. *Preserves,* he thought.

After the worker finished, it patted its hands on a little white apron it wore and stepped down from the stool. It turned around and jumped a bit when it faced Jay and Benu. It had heard them come in but was too busy with its task to notice who had stepped through the door.

This was a smaller mushroom, maybe three feet tall, and Jay could only see above its muzzle from across the table. He raised his hand and waved. "Hello."

The worker placed its hand on its chest and exhaled, then raised a hand and went: "Ah!" Then, it turned to Benu. "Ah!"

Benu returned the gesture with a wave and smile. As the worker left, it hung its apron on a nail that protruded low on the doorway leading to the other room. As it crossed to exit, the brave warrior came into the dining area and took a step to the side of the doorway. Jay and Benu could hear the rustling of bedsheets and the metal squeak of old bedsprings just beyond the kitchen wall. Between the wooden slats, Jay could see a shadow move across the adjacent room. As it rounded the doorway, a tall, slender man ducked through. The man looked tremendously old—with dirtied, fair skin and patches of bark-like scabs that creaked as he moved. All he wore was a pair of striped boxers and a yellow bucket hat with no evidence of any protruding hair coming from beneath it. His "beard" and "mustache" consisted of a bundle of green leaves and branches that stretched down to his bent knees. He scratched his cheek with one of his jagged, yellowed fingernails and yawned. As he did, it sounded as if his vocal cords were like cello strings being plucked.

His cheeks creaked as he smiled. "Oh, hello thar!" he said, his voice jovial and pleasant with a warm wave of hospitality. Jay could immediately tell from the slight Finnish inflection that he was dealing with a genuine Yooper—a U.P. native. His accent was strong and slightly higher-pitched than average. As Jay's mother-in-law would have described it: *It's the Michigan accent with a hint of genius! E'yup!*

Jay and Benu both greeted him mildly, taken aback by his odd appearance. The man lumbered over and took a seat. "Can I get ya two ehnythin' ta drink or eat?" He hooked a thumb over his shoulder. "Gilnup 'ere tells me ya guys had a run in with da Narlath… Oh, terrible thing that thing is!"

"You can… understand them?" Benu asked looking over at Gilnup—the brave warrior.

"Oh! The mushies? Oh yah! I can understand dem plenty. It took me some time, but dontcha know? It's not too different from English!"

Jay placed his right elbow on the table and his stump as well. He was drifting in and out of sleep, exhausted from the night's events. Resting his cheek in his hand, he yawned greatly.

The old man spotted Jay's bandaged stump and asked: "Ahhh, the Narlath got yer arm, eh?"

"Yeah," Jay replied wearily. Benu covered her mouth to yawn herself.

Jay had several questions racing through his mind: *What is this place? What are the mushies? What is the Narlath? Is there a boat to get across the lake? What time is it? Is it safe here?* But Jay could only muster one question. "Hey," he muttered, "are you Captain Quigby?"

The old man raised a creaky eyebrow and chuckled, "Captain Quigby? What kinda name is that? Sounds like ya made it up!"

Jay nodded sluggishly.

The old man's chuckle grew into an animated laugh as his chest jumped up and down. He smiled big and stood, saying: "I think ya two need some sleep. Ya can sleep 'ere. I'll move da furniture for ya sleepin' behgs."

The two stood out of the way without saying a word. They each took their chairs and placed them against the South wall. As they went to grab more, the old man had already placed the other four chairs on the table. He squatted and grasped the edge of the table, lifting it without so much as a grunt. His knees groaned like a settling house as he carried the hefty furniture a few feet in front of him and placed it against the West wall, clearing the floor. Then he scooted some boxes of junk out of the way, placed his palms on the edge of the table, and pushed it forward. The table bumped the wall with a force that caused the hanging decorations to shake.

Jay and Benu were too tired to convey any sort of awe. With heavy eyes, they plodded over and spread out their sleeping bags. The old man walked past them, towards his room. He stopped in the doorway, looked over his shoulder, and said: "Oh! Where're my manners? What would ya like ta call me?"

"What do you mean?" Benu asked.

"Well, I haven't seen another human bein' in so long… and I lost my name when I died. The mushies gave me a name… but… ya wouldn't be able to pronounce it, I'd think! So, what'll be?"

Jay was on the absolute verge of passing out—too tired to even ponder what the old man meant by 'when I died'. He mustered one last reply: "What about Captain Quigby?"

"Nah, nah. I dun like that name… little too *weird* for me! Hmmm…" He looked to the ceiling and stroked his leafy beard. "We'll keep it simple, then. Cap'n Q! There! Has da same connotation, eh?"

When he looked down, Jay had already passed out before hearing the old man's new name. Benu was also snuggled into her sleeping bag, but replied: "Good to meet you, I am Benu. This is Jay." Then, she drifted off to sleep.

Cap'n Q grinned, "Sleep well, you two."

Jay awoke to the sound of soft-padded feet moving around him. As he slid open his eyes, he could see petite, smooth legs moving in and out of view in front of him. It took him a moment to remember the events of last night and to recognize that these were mushie legs moving hastily about. He rolled onto his left side and slipped when he tried to push himself up with his phantom limb.

Oh, that's right, he thought. He rolled onto his back and sat up. His skin stretched as he cupped his hand just below his eyes and pulled down, yanking the grogginess from his face. He reached behind him and slipped on his beanie which had fallen off his head in his tossing and turning. One of his jacket sleeves had rolled up; he pushed it back down and rubbed his hands together vigorously for warmth. The mushies paid him no mind as they moved about the open kitchen and worked. Some were cleaning while others were pulling junk out of boxes and taking them outside. A small group was gathered around the cauldron over a fire, cooking something that smelled earthy. They were handing out the daily meals to any mushies that approached. They would line up on the left side of the cauldron, take a bowl of soup, then follow the kitchen counter out of the boathouse.

"You sure do like to sleep, *dost*," Benu said as Jay turned to his left and saw Benu sitting on her sleeping bag finishing some of the bread they packed from Cadillac.

"Hey, gimme a break... had a rough night. What time is it?"

"About a quarter past noon."

"How much time do we have?"

Benu rolled her eyes to the ceiling. "Mmmm, about a day and a half."

"Shit..."

"Oh!" Cap'n Q's voice came from the doorway. "Yer awake! Good mornin'!"

"Good morning, Cap'n Q," Benu replied.

Cap'n Q? Jay thought. *Oh right...*

"Good mornin'," Jay added aloud.

As the two rolled up their sleeping bags, Cap'n Q lumbered over to the kitchen cabinets, pulled out three bowls, and set them on the counter. He wore the same yellow bucket hat from before but had gotten dressed in a white shirt and blue overalls. His bare feet were completely covered in bark-y skin. "Didja sleep well?" he asked.

"Um, yeah, just fine," Jay replied.

"Das good, das good. See if ya can get da table back in place and we'll have some breakfast—Oh, sorry... Excuse me, excuse me." Cap'n Q was weaving his way through the crowd of mushies, towards the cauldron, as Jay and Benu began taking the chairs off the table. They placed their hands on the table opposite of each other.

"You got this?" Benu asked Jay.

Jay adjusted his one hand on the table's underside, pursed his lips, and nodded curtly. They counted to three and lifted the table. Grunts expelled from the two as they remained slightly crouched. Jay could see veins strained across Benu's forehead and could feel his own facial muscles tighten. Jay found the weight unexpectedly heavy with just one arm, but he and Benu were able to shimmy the table clumsily into place. The mushies parted to make way for the two. The table hovered just an inch above the floor as the pair dropped it, creating a thud that shook the boathouse. Jay and Benu set the chairs as they both huffed. Cap'n Q set three bowls of unknown soup on the table. "Please, sit," he gestured. Jay and Benu obliged.

Cap'n Q turned around, retrieved three soup spoons of differing lengths and designs from a drawer, and sat down. He handed each person a spoon and took a slurp of soup himself. Hot dribbles trickled through his bushy beard and traveled down the creases of a few leaves, dripping into the branches. He closed his eyes and shook his head. "Mmmm, mmm! Those lil' guys sure know how ta cook! Go on. Dig in!"

Jay picked up his spoon and pulled his bowl closer. He inspected the soup. The broth was clear with chunks and strands of various vegetables. Haphazardly cut broccoli, carrots, and green onions all floated around in the soup. Jay scooped up a spoonful and took a sip. The flavor was clean and fresh, almost as if it had no taste at all. It was clear the little chefs hadn't used any seasonings. The meal was bland, and frankly, Jay didn't feel like eating it. He looked to his left to see Benu slurping away greedily. As her messy, bedhead hair jostled about, he could see a dark scar had formed on her neck where the nopperubo had pierced her. Resting his spoon in the soup, he asked Cap'n Q: "So how long ya been 'ere?"

That's not what he really wanted to ask. What he *really* wanted to ask was 'can we stop eating?' and 'can you take us across the lake?' but even with the end of the world looming over the horizon, he respected his ma's teachings to 'mind his Ps and Qs'.

"Oh…" Cap'n Q replied between slurps, "das a tough question to answer… All's I know is I *was* a man once and, at some point, I was 'ere on dis beach. I just remember wakin' up with da mushies surroundin' me with their lil' hands on my chest, glowin' with their blue glow. There was shipwreck scattered across da beach. As far as I'm concerned, I died… and the lil guys brought me back. After a while, my beard turned into dis 'ere bush and my skin started to get all bark-y, ha!"

"Well… how long has it been since then?"

"Oh, another tough question. I dun have any sorta clock or ehnythin' to tell me da date. When I woke up, I tried ta walk back ta town, but da Narlath stopped me."

"That shadow monster?" Benu chimed.

"Yah… Whatever it touches, turns ta ruin. Da mushies warned me, although I din' understand dem at da time. But luckily, a group of dem had tailed me and led me back 'ere."

"You were lost?"

"Oh yah, dat ash forest is cursed to us humans, I think. Or… the mushies just have it figured out. Eider way, I'm grateful for da lil' guys, and they're all I got now."

"They were out gatherin' food, it looked like," Jay said.

"Yah, yah. They go out nearly ev'ry night scavenging for food. Some things still live in dat forest, it seems. Sometimes, they bring me random things they find. They seem to go out real far ev'ry once in a while. Even scavenge da things dat helped build dis house!"

"We lost a few… when the shadow attacked."

"Oh, I know. Gilnup filled me in on ev'rythin'. Real shame." Cap'n Q wiped a tear from his eye. "They're like children, yah know? So innocent… like kid drawings come ta life. And yet… they got da spunk! They really look after their own!"

"And others, it seems," said Benu.

"Oh yah, leave it ta sweet innocence to assume ev'ryone is good, eh?" Cap'n Q sighed. "I guess, at one point, they thought the Narlath ta be good as well…"

"The Narlath… What is it?"

"Death… destruction… some by-product of evil. Dunno. No idea other than ta stay away from it! I know whenever I look up at dat diamond in the sky, it reminds me of it."

No memory from before he 'died,' Jay thought.

"Cap'n," Jay said, "ya don't remember anything from before you woke up on the beach?"

"Eh'nope! Nada! There's some residual stuff, I'd say. Like, I remember dat this 'ere is Lake Michigan! And that da Earth is round, and two plus two is four… and how ta eat n' sleep! And, thankfully, I remember how ta shit and piss!"

"But you said you hadn't seen another human being in a long time… When was the last time?"

"Oh, yah know, I think dat was just part of my residual stuff I mentioned. All I've known are da mushies, da dunes, and da forest. But I *know* I had to have seen another human, eh?"

"Do you remember anything about Total Convergence?"

"Mmmm… sounds familiar, but das about it."

Benu harrumphed, calling Jay's attention. He turned his head to Benu as she shook her head slowly. He shouldn't tell the old man, should he? Jay also secretly longed to live in blissful ignorance. To be free of The Anomaly's existence and hold. In a way, knowing the exact time and date of his death had been a curse for the past five years— when the eggheads calculated Total Convergence at the time of the black diamond's arrival. But to ignore the loose bolt or leaky fuel line located deep in the machine, doesn't prevent it from falling apart eventually.

Jay turned to Cap'n Q and said plainly: "That black diamond in the sky is called The Anomaly. It's been tearin' the world apart and, in about a day… it's gonna finish the job."

"Ah, yah know… I think I knew dat at some point. Dis is really helpin' my memory!"

"You… do not seem worried about this news," Benu said.

"I suppose I'm a bit… ambivalent 'bout it. Time hasn't had much meanin' ta me since I awoke. I dun even remember when all dis bark and leaves grew on me. Ev'ryday seems ta just move on with no real sense of consistency. Some nights I dun sleep… Others, I sleep for what feels like several nights! Maybe it's dis place… maybe dis is how da mushies perceive time…"

Benu checked her watch—1:02 PM. Time had moved normally.

Jay had decided it was time to get down to business. He asked: "Cap'n, is there a way to cross the lake?"

"Oh yah! The mushies ride Leviathan all around all da time! Sometimes, I go with dem when I'm bored."

"And the Leviathan can take us to Escanaba?"

"Oh, yer gonna haveta show me where dat is."

Jay asked Benu to pull out her map. She obliged and laid it out across the table. Jay placed his index finger on the town of Escanaba, about eighty miles across the lake.

"Hmmm, it's not a journey I think da mushies have ever made before… Typically, they just take Leviathan a couple o' miles out. I'm sure Leviathan can make it but… furthest da mushies been is just past da islands, maybe…" Cap'n Q pointed to two islands about ten miles North on the map.

"Do ya think they'd be willing to *try*?" Jay asked, lowering his head and looking from beneath his brow.

Cap'n Q leaned back and shifted in his chair. He crossed his arms and pursed his lips. As he twisted his lips side-to-side, small creaks and squeaks eked out. He pulled on his beard. The leaves fluttered as the branches crunched from his grip. He pulled on it again; this time, a leaf had become detached and seesawed onto the table. Cap'n Q brushed it off onto the floor and asked: "Can I ask what for?"

Jay sighed and told Cap'n Q his story. At some point, a group of mushies gathered around to listen. Nothing held Jay back now. The words of his promise to Her flowed like a tranquil stream. He paraphrased his and Benu's journey. His heart felt calm and still and, by the end… a final weight fell from his being. This would be the last time he'd have to explain his purpose.

"Ah!" Cap'n Q exclaimed as he wiped tears from his eyes and sniffled. "Ah! We'll get ya there! We will!" The mushies went to comfort Cap'n Q as a few talked amongst themselves.

"That's great!" Jay exclaimed as he stood. "When can we leave?"

"Oh, we can leave now, if ya like. Let me just gather a few mushies to handle Leviathan and we can go!"

"Hmph, excellent," Benu said as she stood and gathered her things. "Um, Cap'n Q… I did not see a boat when we arrived last night. Maybe it was too dark… is the Leviathan docked somewhere else?"

Cap'n Q tilted his head for a moment in silence, widened his eyes with stark realization, then laughed hardily.

"Oh! Leviathan ain't no boat!"

{Chapter 28}

1:6:30:27

Cap'n Q stepped out of the door and onto the pier, patting his stuffed belly. Puffs of dust expelled from his dirtied overalls. He walked a few paces to his right, down the pier, as Jay came out the boathouse with his things.

Jay looked down the pier. At the end were two mushies sitting on the edge, swinging their stubby legs in the afternoon sun. Jay looked across the vast expanse of Lake Michigan. If he had fallen out of the sky from some alien world, he might have thought he was staring at an endless ocean. The waves were moving steadily across the waters, splashing onto the pier like buckets of paint being thrown across a canvas. It was as restless as Jay had remembered the news reporting a couple years back when the waters around Michigan began to grow violent. The color he had seen last night was not just the lack of a fresh moonlight or a discoloration of the aurora borealis that flowed with its brilliance. Lake Michigan had truly turned black.

The water was a sea of ink, crashing about with whitewater edges. As the tides receded, Jay could see the sand stain for a moment like a spill of coffee on a pair of beige khakis. It would seep into the shore, leaving behind fading, gray shadows, before lapping back again to darken and reshape the stains. Jay could feel the mist of splashing water brush his face. At one point, a large wave hit the pier and threw some droplets against his cheek. He wiped it off with two fingers and inspected it. The liquid had the consistency of water and, when thin, was transparent. But as Jay rubbed the wetness between his fingertips, he could feel a strange, moving texture like microscopic slugs flopping and rolling around.

"Da water's cursed," said Cap'n Q, who had watched Jay wipe the water from his lips. "Ya can't drink it. Not a lot of it at least. I tried a gulp once… just once. Just because I was thirsty."

"What happened?" Jay asked.

"It causes ya extreme pain. The kind ya can't really sleep off."

Jay wasn't sure what Cap'n Q meant by this. He wanted to prod further, but he could feel the creeping hands of The Anomaly grip his shoulders. Looking up, he could see it had grown again. He felt his stomach crawl. Jay asked, "Was the water used in the soup last night from the lake?"

"It's ok once ya boil it. Kill all da lil' creepy crawlies."

Creepy crawlies, Jay thought as a wave of nausea lapped against his stomach. "So, how long till we set off?"

"Oh, just gimme a few minutes to round up da mushies, then we'll bring Leviathan to da pier. In da meantime, have a look around. Da mushies are quite da lil' architects!"

Cap'n Q crossed the entrance behind Jay, towards the steps that led to the mushie community. Jay watched Cap'n Q as he lumbered to the rear of the village, calling some mushies over to him. Jay was growing impatient as he tapped his foot. He fiddled with his ring as Benu stepped out of boathouse.

She did the same scan of the lake and turned to Jay. "The lake… why is it…"

"Black? Dunno… Cap'n says not to drink it. Says it hurts like hell," Jay replied.

"Hmph, do not have to tell me twice." She pulled out a cigarette and lit it.

"All set?"

"Yup, just wanted to double-check my equipment. Everything is good to go." She flicked the cap of her lighter closed and threw it back into her bag.

Jay started walking towards the beach. "Cap'n says he needs some time to get the crew together. Might as well look around."

Benu followed. As they stepped off the pier, they found themselves strolling through a tiny village that had become clear in the daylight. Shoulder-high houses of the same materials as the boathouse were built up along the shore in a haphazard arrangement.

Some were shaped like shacks while others were like the average Midwestern home with a chimney and steep, inclined roofs. Between them, were twigs and branches—speared into the sand and tied together with twine—that formed fences to separate the houses. The fences formed variously shaped yards in the front and back of the houses. As Jay and Benu passed by, some mushies were out, sweeping their plots of land with tiny makeshift brooms of twigs and straw. Clouds of dirt rolled from underneath the brooms as the mushies swept. In some areas, others were tending to the vegetable plots, crates, and burrows the pair had seen the night before. At the back of the village were three larger structures. One was shaped like a warehouse, where Jay spotted a mushie warrior enter with a spear and leave without it. Adjacent to it was another warehouse which Jay had assumed was for storage of materials and community supplies. The third structure was across from the warehouses. It was about the size of the two warehouses combined and more ornate with various decorations lining the sides and a wooden awning with supporting columns. On the other side of this structure, Cap'n Q was discussing something with a couple of warriors and a mushie who wore a tattered 7-11 hat.

"It feels like a movie set, huh?" asked Benu as the two strolled towards the rear of the village.

"Yeah… like one of those cities they'd build for Godzilla to smash up," Jay replied.

"Hmph, I could never imagine smashing up these little guys. They are adorable! Oh, look at that one!"

Benu pointed at a mushie out on its front yard, watering a tiny sapling in a terracotta pot that was about half its size. Benu giggled to herself.

"C'mon they're not zoo animals," Jay teased with a nudge.

"I know… more like children, but smarter… They obviously are self-sufficient to a point, but their behavior is… peculiar."

"Like they're blissfully unaware of The Anomaly."

"Yes. As if this has been their world the entire time… and as if it will be here tomorrow. Their only concern seems to be taking care of each other."

Like children, Jay thought. This little village and its little residents reminded him of his childhood, playing make-believe with his friends at the playground. He thought of a first-grade class project he had to participate in. The class was to construct a little town out of milk cartons, carboard boxes, tape, glue, etc. Each student was given a role to study and build their corresponding building. Jay was the mayor. He built his little town hall not too dissimilar to the large, ornate structure that stood before them. If Jay had been more superstitious, he'd say the mushie town hall was a mirror image of the twig and Mod Podge structure he had slapped together as a seven-year-old. He thought back to the couple in Flint, whose names had escaped him long ago—and their infant worrying about nothing other than the wondrous, unknown sights and sounds around it. To it, The Anomaly was just another one of those objects, something to *ooo* and *ahhh* at. In many ways, Jay envied that child and the mushies; maybe it was better to spend his final days as a child.

Blissful ignorance.

Jay looked at Benu's profile as she continued to observe the little residents. Her sunken eyes were darker than usual. Jay could see veiled grief under her mask—the same he had worn for a long time. He frowned slightly and asked: "How're ya holdin' up?"

"I am hanging in there…" She shot him a tight-lipped smile of false reassurance.

They stopped for a moment to let a mushie cross in front of them. The little creature was carrying a bundle of sticks up to the door of one of the houses. Jay and Benu watched as it knocked on the door and was greeted by another. The two mushies exchanged a few rapid words and traded goods for profit. The homeowner handed the stick-monger two quarter-sized stones shined to a high-gloss finish as they said their goodbyes. Jay could recognize the distinct patterned surface of a Petoskey stone any day. The rocks were fossils comprised of ancient coral colonies that formed fingernail-sized, warped hexagons of jagged, edged silhouettes across the surface; each butted up right up against each other—with a dark circle at the center of each shape.

Plip… plip… plop!

"Wow, that sucked," Stacy teased.

Jay's wife waggled the universal sign of "fuck you" to Stacy as she told Jay it was his turn.

Plip… plip… plip… plip… plip… plop!

Jay raised his arm, balled a fist, reeled it back in victory, and smiled at Her. She rolled her eyes and motioned to Stacy to go.

Plip… plip… plip… plip… plip… plip… plip…

The little stone had plipped across the lake so far, no one could hear it plop. All they could see across the gleaming orange lake was a little droplet jumping out of the water in the distance—the setting sun nearly blinding them as they peered. Stacy raised her hands up and danced around Jay and his wife, gloating about how she was "the best" and how the two losers could "suck it." Jay's wife shook her head as Jay mumbled, "Man, what the fuck…"

"Y'know I *live* on this lake right?" Stacy said sarcastically. "I've got plenty of practice."

"Yeah, yeah," Jay said as he picked out another stone from left hand and held it by his waist to skip it. Just then, he felt Her grab his wrist to stop him. He stumbled a bit and looked to Her. "Hey? What's up?"

She gently pulled Jay's wrist out in front of Her and plucked the rock out of his hand. She inspected it and grinned. She told him it was a Petoskey stone.

Jay took it from Her and inspected it. "Oh yeah," he said to himself.

"Sweet!" Stacey said from over Her shoulder.

Jay's wife smiled as She took it back and held it up in the setting sun, turning it as She looked at the little fossils. Then, it fell into the sand. Waves lapped against it, pulling it slightly towards the lake.

She started coughing and placed Her hands on Her chest.

Stacey rushed to Her side, opposite of Jay, as he quickly wrapped an arm around Her, "Hey, hey. You ok?"

Jay's wife patted her chest, swallowed, and nodded. She told him she was fine and that it was just some sand in her throat.

◉

Jay and Benu passed by the two warehouses and rounded the larger, decorated building. Cap'n Q was still discussing a few things with the 7-11 mushie. He spoke their language—the same garbled, baby-talk at lightning speed. Even though the language was totally alien to Jay, he could tell Cap'n Q still stumbled on a few words here and there. He could also tell Cap'n Q changed the inflection of his U.P. accent to more closely match those of the mushies, but it was clear his Finnish flair was still present. As Jay and Benu approached, the 7-11 mushie looked past Cap'n Q's legs, cutting off itself mid-sentence.

Cap'n Q turned around. "Oh, hey there!"

"Hey, Cap'n," Jay replied. "How's everything lookin'? We good to go?"

Jay looked past Cap'n Q as the 7-11 mushie and two warriors leaned to look at Jay and Benu. The 7-11 mushie stepped in front of Cap'n Q as the two warriors flanked it and stood at attention. Jay recognized one of the warriors. Although its face was identical to nearly every mushie Jay had seen before, he was sure this was the brave warrior Gilnup.

The 7-11 mushie raised a mitt and greeted Jay and Benu: "Ah!" Jay and Benu returned the greeting and, after lowering its hands, the 7-11 mushie explained something to the two in its unintelligible language as it talked with its hands. When it was done, Jay looked at Cap'n Q and shrugged.

"Ah! Right," Cap'n Q said. "First off, this is da mayor, Pillup. Mayor Pillup directs ev'ryone 'ere… except me, o'course. They typically hold meetings at da city hall on big decisions like dis." Cap'n Q pointed to the larger structure across from the two warehouses. "I

333

explained to da mayor da hurry you were in and, at first… they said 'no' but then, Gilnup 'ere vouched for ya. Gilnup told da mayor what happened in da forest, and da mushies always pay back their life-debts. So, Mayor Pillup's makin' an exception for Gilnup ta take ya!"

Gilnup raised his spear and stamped the broad end into the ground.

"What about the others?" asked Benu as she finished her cigarette and pitched it into the sand. "Will the other seven we saved be joining us?"

"Ah, Mayor Pillup has decided dat da journey across da lake would be great enough ta cover those seven life-debts, if Gilnup were ta carry dat responsibility."

"So, there'll be four of us?" Jay asked.

"Nah, Gilnup also has another dat owes them a life-debt. Nuup is their name and they happen ta be pretty good at navigatin' Leviathan."

Jay turned to Mayor Pillup and Gilnup. "Thank you," he said, bowing his head. The two mushies looked to Cap'n Q who translated Jay's thanks. Jay turned to Cap'n Q. "Can we set off now?"

"Oh yah! Let's go call Leviathan!"

Jay, Benu, Cap'n Q, and Gilnup stood on the end of the pier. The lake was restless with high waves that crashed against each other, sending splashes of water into the air. The tide rolled into the pier and splashed onto their shoes. Jay could feel the microscopic movement of whatever was in the water seep into the canvas of his Chucks and slowly dissipate. Cap'n Q had put on a pair of wellies he had sitting by the entrance of the boathouse.

The sound of soft-padded feet rushing down the pier came from behind them. Jay turned to see a four-foot tall mushie, carrying two child backpacks, running towards them. The mushie stopped just before them, dropped the backpacks, placed its mitts on its hips, and panted. After a moment, it raised a hand and said: "Ah…"

Gilnup stepped over and slung one of the backpacks over its back. It then rubbed the tired mushie's back to soothe it. Jay examined the cap of the new mushie. Its spotted, red exterior was noticeably faded compared to Gilnup's and was laden with scars from scratches. It glowed the same blue luminescence as Gilnup's but was dimmer and had a grayer tone. As it raised its head, Jay could see aged wrinkles around its eyes, down its cheeks, and on its muzzle.

"Ah, Nuup!" exclaimed Cap'n Q. "Always late to da party, eh?"

Nuup huffed and made a dismissive, but friendly, sound.

"Nuup 'ere is a sailor—one of da older ones, from what Gilnup has told me. He's also taught me a thing or two!"

Jay and Benu greeted Nuup who straightened up and stepped to the edge of the pier.

"Ok," Jay said, "we're all here. So, where's Leviathan?"

Cap'n Q's cheeks creaked as he smiled at Jay. He turned to Nuup and asked something in the mushie language.

Nuup looked up at Cap'n Q and nodded. Nuup signaled for everyone to stand back. Gulnip obliged, stepping back about ten paces. Jay and Benu stood where they were and turned to Cap'n Q for an explanation.

"Ya might wanna listen to Nuup! Trust me!" he shouted as the sound of crashing waves grew and his leafy beard was rustled by a fierce gust. He placed a hand on his head to hold down his hat.

"I think we should do as he says," Benu said, her eyes wide with bewilderment.

Jay nodded as they joined Gilnup.

At the rear end of the pier, about forty feet back, the mushies had gathered along the shore to watch. They jittered restlessly as some tried stretching upwards to look over taller ones. Some had taken a break from whatever task they were doing, still carrying vegetables or bits of junk. A couple of warriors stood guard at the pier entrance to make sure no onlookers could interrupt what was about to unfold. The crowd conversated amongst themselves as Nuup raised his tiny mitts to the horizon.

Nuup bellowed a chant of several rapid, alien words, but Jay could catch repeated patterns here and there. He could also hear the imperative tone in Nuup's voice, as if the mushie was calling out to a god for divine intervention while singing praises on top. Then Nuup howled and turned his arm over to Cap'n Q.

The half-tree-half-man raised his hands above his head in a 'V' shape. A pair of waves collided in front of him and rained down black water atop his and Nuup's heads. Trickles of ink dripped off his bucket hat as well as Nuup's cap.

Cap'n Q shouted: "And I speak for da humans! Oh, great Leviathan! We seek yer compassion and trust! Allow us a but a taste of yer awesome power so dat we may bask in yer glory! We—mushie, human, Leviathan—shall travel as one! Please, take us to da other side! Let us bear witness to yer strength! Come, Leviathan! Come!"

Nuup and Cap'n Q stood there with their hands stiff in the air. The gust began to swirl and buffet the boathouse violently. Jay could barely hear rattling sheet metal and decorations against the wooden walls above the howling winds that vortexed around them. Jay and Benu shielded their faces from the wind as gray clouds swirled above the lake. As the clouds moved, the rays of sun shimmered through open spaces and glistened off the inky lake. Below the cloud vortex, a massive whirlpool had formed. Jay couldn't estimate the exact size; it seemed to threaten to swallow up the entire pier and boathouse. As he watched the maelstrom, he heard the low, drawn-out grumble of something deep beneath the water's surface. It shook the ground beneath them as Jay lost his balance and nearly fell over. Benu had caught him, and they were now supporting each other.

"What is going on?" Benu shouted.

"I dunno!" Jay replied, trying to match Benu's volume. "Cap'n Q! Cap'n Q!"

But Cap'n Q was a rock—his hands still held high in the air. At some point, when Jay went to shield his face, Cap'n Q's yellow bucket hat had fallen off his head and dangled by its pull-string around his neck, revealing a tiny bonsai tree that had grown atop his head. It's little bundle of leaves and branches jostled heavily in the wind. Jay looked down at Gilnup, who had no trouble holding his ground. He looked down at the brave warrior's feet and could see tiny roots had protruded from Gilnup's feet and embedded the mushie into the pier's wood. Jay looked back and could see the crowd was faring a little worse. Their roots were having trouble finding hold in the loose sand, but they still held fast. Jay and Benu, on the other hand, were now falling to their knees as they held each other in the torrential storm that had formed over the lake. The cyclone of clouds began to drop towards the lake as the waters below started to rise, meeting the clouds and forming a thick waterspout.

Then, as if some great director in the sky yelled 'CUT!', a clap of thunder exploded from the waterspout, and all was quiet. The cyclone slowly receded into the sky as walls of water fell back into the lake. The whirlpool unfurled and evened out as the waves of the lake returned to normal. The clouds parted and sunlight returned to the pier. No rattles came from the still boathouse, and the wood of the pier let out soft creaks and groans as it settled.

Jay and Benu stood up—their knees shaky. Gilnup was already waddling towards the end of the pier. Cap'n Q and Nuup had lowered their arms. Cap'n Q turned around and waved Jay and Benu over. The two obliged as they stumbled to the end. As they stood next to Cap'n Q, they felt a growing rumble beneath their feet, coming from where the whirlpool had been. Jay took a step back and planned to continue doing so, but Cap'n Q placed a hand on Jay's back and turned to him. "Dun be scared. Have a bit o' sisu, eh? Yer gonna need it for dis ride, dontcha know!"

Jay had heard the Yooper term before, from his mother-in-law. Many times, she'd say it to Her: *'I like Jay, he's got alotta sisu for visiting us in the winter! E'yup!'* Jay remembered hearing it a few times before he finally asked Her what it meant.

Sisu, Jay thought. *Gumption. Perseverance. Balls.*

The rumble grew and grew until Jay could start to see the water's surface start to ripple and rush away from the area. Suddenly, a massive mass of brilliant azure burst from the lake, sending blankets of black water onto the entourage. Jay and Benu instinctively shielded their faces as they were soaked by a tremendous splash. The serpent hump rose high in the air, forcing Cap'n Q to crane his neck upward to watch it. Then, it settled into the water and flattened out as its azure scales moved in the sunlight and shifted into a reflective emerald. Jay lowered his arm and studied mighty Leviathan.

The width of the hump was just over the width of the pier which could already fit the five of them comfortably shoulder-to-shoulder. Down the center, there was a beige ridge that looked like a miniature mountain range. It emerged from one end of the beast, crested over its curved apex, and plunged back into the depths. The scales moved and fluttered in ripples down Leviathan's back, flicking off flecks of black water. Cap'n Q stepped out onto the hump and resituated his hat onto his head. As he did, the sparkling plates formed a stairway that allowed him to ascend the shallow angle to the peak, which was about fifteen feet above the pier's surface and twice that length away. Cap'n Q's wellies squeaked and squelched as he climbed. Nuup and Gilnup followed Cap'n Q to the top. As the scales curled out to form the steps, Jay watched the beauty of the color-changing armor glisten in the sun. They reminded him of iridescent car paint that would change colors depending on the angle or light source.

Jay didn't have time to continue staring in awe. He had already accepted that this enormous serpent, whose head was presumably somewhere deep underwater, was the only way he'd be getting to Escanaba. He jolted a bit to give himself some sisu and stepped off the pier towards Leviathan. As his foot hovered over the space between Leviathan and the pier, one of the scales pivoted from the sea-serpent's body and formed a large scaly step that was nearly twice the size as Jay's foot. Jay stepped onto the platform that appeared as smooth as glass to find it tacky and grippy like sandpaper. This took him by surprise which caused him to misstep when he brought his left foot onto the beast. But the plates changed shape and jutted out, forming a wall to prevent him from tumbling off as Jay fell onto his side.

"Careful!" Benu taunted.

The fall had blurred his vision for a moment and, when Benu's taunt recovered him, he saw that she had already ascended a few steps ahead of him on the other side of the ridge. Jay pushed himself from Leviathan's body and stood. As he lifted his foot, he found that the step's tackiness had subsided and easily let him go. He was last to the top on which he could stand steadily. Behind him, a wall of scales curved up forming a small, chest-high wall that then surrounded the group and came together in a U-shape at the front. Cap'n Q was crouched with Nuup, pulling out some rope and meat hooks from the mushie's bag. Cap'n Q and Nuup each tied a rope to a hook. Then, they went to opposite corners at the front of the wall and lifted a scale, plunging the meat hooks into the soft flesh of Leviathan. Small spurts of blood sprayed from the punctures. Leviathan grumbled and shivered a bit but seemed mostly unbothered by the hooks. To the sea-serpent, they might as well have been mosquito bites.

"What're those for?" Jay called to the front.

"Oh! Dis is for controllin' Leviathan. He never pokes his head up from underwater. I dun know if he actually has a head! So we have ta guide him and make sure he dun pull us under!" Cap'n Q replied as he handed his end of the rope to Nuup.

The mushie then straddled the spine of the beast. The scales then rose the mushie just over Cap'n Q's height. Jay could see the flesh of the sea-serpent now. Towers of white, fishy meat supported the mythical platforms. As the wind rolled over the beast, Jay could smell the exposed flesh—a combination of dead walleye and stale tuna. He and Benu grimaced at the strong, deep-sea stench. They stepped to the side where the wind wouldn't blow the stink directly at them.

Nuup tugged at the ropes to check if they were secure and nodded at Cap'n Q. Nuup looked over at Gilnup and exchanged nods. Gilnup sat against the West wall and laid its spear across its lap. Then, Nuup looked to Jay and Benu and signaled them to take a seat.

Jay and Benu obliged and sat against the East wall.

They were ready to set off.

Nuup looked to the Northwest, towards Escanaba, and whipped the ropes against Leviathan like a musher. Another hump emerged from the lake in front, but this one's spinal ridge had what looked like five enormous porcupine spines stacked along its length; alternating stripes of white and black wrapped around each one. Nuup whipped the ropes again. The spines unfurled into the air, forming a webbed fin that caught the wind like fabric. Jay peered up at the fleshy dorsal fin. Gargantuan red veins spiderwebbed throughout the translucent, pink webbings.

Finally, Nuup whipped the ropes with great force and a loud *"Hup!"*

The sea-serpent groaned a hefty roar as Jay and Benu fell onto their sides from the force of Leviathan's launch. The things in their backpacks clattered as the waves parted behind them, crashing down onto the lake's surface. Benu sat herself up, reaching a hand behind her to support her crossbow. As Jay worked his way onto his knees, he looked over the South wall to see the boathouse shrinking rapidly as the mushies on the shore waved goodbye.

{Chapter 29}

1:3:45:35

Jay opened his bag and took out the last of his food and water. He held a half-jar of applesauce and a slice of bread in one hand and a plastic bottle he had filled at Benu's house between his legs. In hindsight, he regretted not eating his bland, morning soup or asking Cap'n Q for a jar of his preserves. He could do with the taste of something other than apples, but he wouldn't need to worry about what he ate for much longer. The soft red hue of The Anomaly dimly lit Leviathan's reflective scales. Jay looked up at it; it was even bigger now. He set his water aside and stood up, bracing himself with his stump on the scale wall to look over the lake. The waves were vicious and reaching high, peaking like temporary mountains. Some splashes crossed between him and the black diamond. The smattering of ink would leap into the air and smack onto the water's surface, as if The Anomaly itself was dumping fresh liquid into Lake Michigan.

The water rushed against the scaly body of the sea-serpent. White waters eddied away as Leviathan cut through the massive waves with its fleshy fin. They were about thirty-five miles into their journey and by this point, Jay had gotten used to being constantly damp from the splashes of water. Just a few miles ago, there was nothing but the cloudy sky and blackness all around, but now Jay could make out the protrusion of the upcoming line of islands that floated about twenty-five miles out from the shore of the U.P.. They were faint, but tiny silhouettes of trees shot up from the lake like distant spires.

Leviathan swam steadily. The chilled, lakefront wind that buffeted Jay's face reminded him of an evening cruise in his Miata down Woodward Ave. Home felt so far away now. Just a couple weeks ago, Jay was simply sitting on his couch watching reruns of whatever Detroit's local archive decided to put up that week. He couldn't remember the show or the channel, but he remembered his mood.

Apathetic.

Unmotivated.

Suddenly stricken with a nagging feeling of anxiety as Total Convergence crept near. He remembered that it was then that he had decided to make his journey. There had been no come-to-Jesus moment or sudden burst of emotion. It was just like any other day that his subconscious decided to kick him in the ass and get him moving. Now, he had been kicked in the ass across the entire length of Michigan and beyond, surrounded by cursed waters on top of a sea-god being piloted by living mushrooms.

Jay smirked at the thought of it and sat back down. He placed the bread in his lap and held the jar in his left armpit. Then, with his right hand, he unscrewed the applesauce lid and dabbed some of it onto his bread. He closed the lid, placed the jar back in his bag, and had his meal. He looked over at Benu to his left who held her crushed packet of cigarettes near her mouth; the butt of one was sticking out. She stared at it while flicking the lid of her lighter open and closed... open and closed.

"What's up?" Jay called—bread stuffed in one cheek. His voice was heightened, trying to outdo the sound of rushing water.

"This is my last cigarette. I am contemplating if I want it now or later," she yelled back.

"Might as well, right? Now or never!"

"Yes, but I feel like the water or wind will ruin it. I think I will save it."

Benu closed her lighter and tapped the cigarette back into the pack with her index finger. She placed both items into her bag and scooted over to Jay.

"Can I take a look at your arm? I know you have been managing well, but I should still check it."

"Sure," Jay replied as he presented Benu with his stump.

She unwrapped the bandages. They were tacky from the ointment she had put on but otherwise were completely clean. She pursed her lips and tilted her head with a nod. Then, she threw the bandages overboard.

"The state is gonna fine you for that," Jay quipped.

"Hmph," Benu replied and sat back against the scale wall. She craned her neck to the sky. The clouds were growing thicker and grayer—not overcast, but it would begin to drizzle soon. Benu sighed, "I wish *behan* was here. She was always the more adventurous between us."

"Alexis? *She* was the adventurous one?"

"Yes. When I was out surviving in Royal Oak, I thought of her to give me strength—not in a holy way, but in a 'how is it that my *little* sister is braver than me?' kind of way."

"Coulda fooled me," Jay replied with a short laugh.

"Whatever you say, *dost.*"

"Say, you never told me why you didn't evacuate with the rest of us to Detroit."

"I think I just did," Benu replied with a wink and smile. "Ah, I am not sure, to be honest. Part of me wanted to prove myself *to* myself, but another part of me just did not feel it was right. I did not want to be coddled—did not want to rely on someone else or be relied on."

Jay was puzzled. He asked, "So then why did ya save me? Why did ya ask me to join ya?"

Benu looked away and said nothing. At first, Jay thought he wouldn't get an answer at all. Then, when Benu opened her mouth, he thought he'd get the same answer he got way back in that decrepit house in Royal Oak. Instead, Benu answered: "Because I realized I am not an island, and neither are you."

They shared a smile as Jay patted Benu on the shoulder.

It began to drizzle as Cap'n Q walked over to Jay and Benu. They had just passed the line of islands. The overcast thickened. The diffused light of the sun melded with the red glow of the growing black diamond and filled the air.

Cap'n Q crouched next to Jay—his knees creaking like old wood. "We're about an hour and a half out now!" he said. He hooked a thumb over his shoulder. "Nuup is gettin' tired so I'm gonna take over. Holler if ya need ehnythin'!"

Jay and Benu nodded as Cap'n Q stood with that same aging creak. As he walked away, the drizzle turned into a steady rainfall. Cap'n Q took the reigns from Nuup as Leviathan lowered the mushie. Cap'n Q was plenty tall enough to see over the wall, but he still required good footing. He dug his wellies into the tacky scales as they formed around his feet, holding him in place. As he pulled the reigns taut, his joints groaned like old floorboards. Nuup waddled over to Gilnup and sat down. Gilnup rubbed Nuup's cap, soothing the elderly mushie as he panted. In the darkened air, their caps glowed bright blue—Nuup's dimmer than Gilnup's.

Soon, the rainfall turned into a torrent as the clouds overhead darkened further. Leviathan leaned and swayed with unrest as the waves of Lake Michigan grew massive. Jay and Benu grunted and groaned as they were tossed from side to side on the floor. They clumsily slipped on their bags and tightened the straps. Jay, afraid he might lose his ring, pulled it from his pocket and stuffed it in his bag. He felt his beanie slipping off, stuffed that into his bag as well, and zipped the bag up—checking the zipper twice to make sure it was secure. Benu had one hand clutched on her quiver to hold her bolts in place. The great, dorsal fin of Leviathan rapped and fluttered violently as it split twelve-foot waves in half, splashing the crew with blankets of black water. They were absolutely soaked, and Jay and Benu did their best to keep as much liquid out of their mouths by spitting up globs of it. However, Jay could feel the residue of the black water crawling along his teeth, working its way up the inside walls of his cheeks and somewhere through his gums. He could feel something wriggling its way under his eyes… through his brow… and into his skull.

A hum.

A whisper.

A voice.

Jay shook his head violently. He could hear his own voice transforming from grunts to yells as he fought against the storm. Benu's screams were there too. She dug her hands underneath a pair of scales as they cut into her fingers. The tacky plates clung to her knees and boots as water crashed against the floor and sailed overhead. Jay faired a bit better in his balance. He clung to the scale wall and looked back at Benu, yelling: "Hold on! Just hold on!" He turned his head to Cap'n Q. "Cap'n! Cap'n!"

But his words were lost in the vicious winds and crashing wakes. Cap'n Q was preoccupied pulling hard on the reigns. His bucket hat had torn at the strings and flew off some time ago into the storm; the little bonsai tree shuddered in the wind. He had wrapped both ropes around his wrists and gripped them with all his might. The thick, coarse hemp tore at his hands, coating the soaked fibers in fresh blood. His joints were creaking heavily now. His body teetered and tottered, jostled by the storm. Across from Jay and Benu, Gilnup and Nuup dug their roots deep into Leviathan. Gilnup held Nuup close as the elderly mushie's roots struggled to find a solid hold. As the waves cracked open, Jay could see the shore of the U.P. approaching along with something else, rushing towards them just beneath the waves. He recognized the approaching hump of water as that of another sea-serpent.

"Cap'n!" Jay screamed desperately; his voice hoarse like gravel.

But Cap'n Q heard nothing but whistling gusts and crashing waves.

Jay started trudging towards him.

Cap'n Q howled, "Rage! Rage, mighty Leviathan! Rage against da storm of annihilation! Cut through da walls of destruction! C'mon ya sea-beast! Fight, damn you!" He yanked on the ropes hard as blood spurted from the meat hooks. The rumbling groan of Leviathan complemented the thunderous boom from above as the sea-serpent lurched its fin upwards and broke through another wave. Jay could see that the rolling hump approaching them had moved to the left and began to surface with a flash of ruby. He stumbled up to Cap'n Q and caught himself on the tree-man's right bicep. Jay shook the soaked, barky arm violently as Cap'n Q turned his attention to him. Jay pointed over Cap'n Q's arm towards the ruby hump.

"Cap'n! There! Look!" he yelled.

Cap'n Q whipped his head to where Jay pointed—leaves of his bushy beard fluttering and breaking off in the wind. The hump had rose higher, and another appeared in front of it. The same webbed fin as Leviathan's rose from the leading hump. Then, it turned to Leviathan and filled the depths with a monstrous roar like that of a collapsing, steel hull.

The shore was only ten or so miles away now. Cap'n Q bit his lower lip and yanked the reigns to the right. Leviathan howled a reluctant cry as it shifted its course to starboard. Jay fell onto his side, the shoreline blurring past him like a dark streak. Benu crawled her way up to him as they helped each other up. He pointed to the ruby hump that was now one more wave-split away from direct impact.

Cap'n Q looked to his left and yelled: "Brace yerselves!" as he curled his torso to the left and pulled Leviathan around in a curve.

The enemy serpent bashed into Leviathan with a mighty strike.

Jay and Benu were thrown off their feet for a moment. They crashed onto the floor as the ruby sea-serpent collided with Leviathan and scraped across its portside. Benu's hand was lifted from her quiver as a few bolts were thrown overboard. She quickly scooped up what bolts she could. Twinkling, jagged scales of shifting colors rained from the collision like confetti as the fin of the ruby beast dove underneath Leviathan and appeared on its starboard side. Its trailing hump also dove underwater and lifted from below.

The muffled sound of crashing bodies underwater shook Leviathan's hump. The scales gripped Cap'n Q's feet tightly as he pulled the reigns to the right for a counterattack. The enemy sea-serpent was now swimming alongside Leviathan's starboard side. Its dorsal fin leaned toward the crew as Cap'n Q hollered a war cry and pulled violently on the reigns towards the ruby beast. Blood sprayed from the meat hooks as splashes of black water washed it away.

Leviathan matched Cap'n Q's cry as it crashed into the enemy creature. Scales rained down as before, exposing bits of soft flesh from both beasts. Benu looked over the scale wall and saw an opportunity. She began unslinging her crossbow.

The two monsters battled it out as they twisted and turned just five miles from the shore. Jay tried to ready his arm for a shot but found himself rushing back to grip the scale wall for support.

Damn this missing arm! he screamed in his head.

Benu held her crossbow in one hand; she supported herself with the other on the scale wall. She tried several times to let go and load a bolt but found herself going back for the scale wall every time. Desperate, she cried out, "Leviathan! Let us help! Please, hold our feet like you are doing for the captain!"

A groan sounded off as scales wrapped themselves around Jay and Benu's feet. Jay straightened up and took aim at the opposing fin as Benu loaded a bolt. From behind them, Glinup and Nuup trudged across Leviathan, their roots receding and extending as they walked over the spinal ridge. As they joined Jay and Benu, Jay heated his hand and held out his stump to his side as best as he could for balance. The fin whipped and swayed in the turbulence.

Jay watched the pattern of the swaying fin and aimed where it would be next. The spray of black water against his eyes stung like needles. He squinted as his hand crackled and blackened—tiny embers trailing off as a baseball-sized fireball formed in his palm. He watched the movement of the ruby serpent's fin and waited for the moment when the sways of the fleshy fabric would stay still. When the opportunity presented itself, he attacked.

Jay unleashed a volley of fireballs along the serpent's fin as it stood erect. Explosions railed the fleshy flaps like cannon fire as it tore holes through the giant's thin membrane. Ribbons of burning skin hung from the tattered fin as the wind ripped strands of flaming flesh from the beast. The ruby sea-serpent cried pain as it rolled onto its starboard side a few feet, exposing the lining of a soft belly. Benu took aim and fired. Her bolted pinged off the scales just above it.

She loaded another bolt and fired.

Another miss.

She loaded another bolt and aimed for a patch of pulsing, white flesh that had been ripped free of its protective scales. She ran her hand over her face, brushed tufts of wet hair over her head, and peered through her scope.

This time her aim was true, and the bolt lodged itself deep into thumping veins. Sanguine burst from the beast like an erupting geyser and misted the crew with fresh blood. The beast groaned in agony. Benu reached for another bolt and grabbed air. "Shit!" she yelled as the ruby beast howled an aggressive threat.

Cap'n Q reeled Leviathan back for another counterattack; they were quickly coming up to the shore and he needed to slow down lest they crash. Cap'n Q maneuvered Leviathan Eastward along the shore as he collided with the ruby beast again. He looked to the flaming dorsal fins, wondering if he had somehow missed a lightning strike that struck the beast while he was preoccupied steering. They rode along the shore. The ruby serpent, in a state of heavy agitation, smacked its body against Leviathan.

Cap'n Q hollered, "Holy wah! Off with ya! Off! The great Leviathan knows no equal ya 'ear? Go on back into da murky depths of da black waters and wallow in yer pain!"

Jay looked to the shore. He squinted through the spray of misty blackness and could see the buildings of Escanaba coming up. He looked over starboard, past the ruby serpent and across the lake, to see several blue and red humps clashing in the waters. He followed the trail of protruding fins and iridescent scales along the waters and watched as the shifting colors of azure, emerald, and ruby corkscrewed around each other.

"Benu! It's comin' this way! This big bastard is gonna pull us under!" he cried.

"I know! But I am out of bolts!" she cried back.

Then from Benu's right, Gilnup—brave and bold—climbed to the top of the scale wall and stood tall. Spear in hand. Roots planted firmly. It puffed out its chest and looked down at the bleeding wound where Benu's bolt had previously struck the enemy serpent. Behind him Nuup climb up as well next to Gilnup with its shaky, elderly roots. Gilnup looked over to Jay and yelled something triumphant in its language. Jay didn't understand the words but he understood the meaning: Gilnup was ready to pay his life-debt.

"H-hey! Whoa! W-wait a minute!" Jay yelled, but Gilnup held his spear at the ready as Leviathan shook Jay and Benu from their scaly hold. Leviathan moaned. It was growing tired. The walls began to recede as Cap'n Q began to lose his footing—his wellies slipping and squeaking along the surface. The ruby serpent's hump rose in the air, high above Leviathan. It was getting ready to wrap itself around the crew. As it drew near, Gilnup readied its spear.

Its muzzle flared as its eyes sharpened. It readied itself to leap in a final hoorah of glory to lance the beast and drive it back into the deep.

Brilliant ruby filled Gilnup's vision; the sky had become a repeating pattern of glistening wet scales with a patch of writhing, blood-stained flesh. Gilnup bent its knees when it felt its spear yanked from its hands as Nuup pushed Gilnup to the floor into Benu's arms, knocking her crossbow out of her hand. Her weapon slid along the glassy surface and was swept away by the gushing waters. Nuup burst forward into the air, its spear held forward as it lanced the weapon deep into the exposed meat. The ruby monster cried bloody murder as its hump crashed straight down onto the starboard side of Leviathan, sending Jay, Benu, and Gilnup tumbling into the inky depths.

The final sight Jay caught before going under was Nuup's little body flying over the red hump. He bobbed back up as black water rushed down his throat and into his gut. He saw the meat hook of one of the ropes had broken loose from Leviathan. It sailed through the air and into the water as Cap'n Q screamed in terror and plunged into the lake—the bonsai tree on his head ripping asunder.

Jay kicked and flailed his arm and stump wildly. The adaptation of his phantom arm was suddenly gone as he struggled to wade water with his absent left hand. He was tossed and turned in the waves, bobbing up and down to the site of the sandy shore just before him. Slowly, the shore showed up less and less. Jay wanted to cry for Benu, but his mouth was filled with black poison as he gasped and spat. The pain was unreal now. There was a constant stream of agony piercing up his face and into his brain. His vision was black. The sunlight above could not penetrate the inky surface. He was now submerged and at the mercy of the waves. Soon, his limbs stopped moving, and he simply floated in a world of darkness. The pain had left but there was now something else.

He could hear it clearly now: the voice of The Anomaly.

{Chapter 30}

1:1:15:8

I am human.
I am human.
I am human.
I am human.
I am human.

Oh? And is one who is so sure in need of constant affirmation?

I am human.

No, my friend. My very close friend. You are rot. A self-serving mass devoid of empathy. You parade yourself with veiled compassion but, in the end, you are destruction.

Shut your mouth! Shut your goddamn mouth!

Feed on these words. These neglected words you have buried deep in your soul. The thing you claim so heartily to be is a disposable creature to you. You've stopped caring.

That's not true! Shut it!

They are gone now. I speak to them too.

Stop it… you're not real! You're some trick. Some monster birthed by The Anomaly… in the black water.

And does The Anomaly not float itself in the sky? Perpetuating its very real influence on your world? Soon, it will pull you into its Total Convergence just as it does the earth beneath your feet. It is very real. Accept it. This is the end. Your ambitions were but dying light, ready to be snuffed out.

No... I refuse! I promised Her... I promised Her... No-no-no-no...

Ah, Her. That is what it all comes to. The reason you ran from me. But, deep in your mind, you held onto me. You claim I am but an illusion, but I have merely been incubated in your warm and nurturing obstinance. Here, let me remind you of my inception. The time of your little death that marked my birth.

{Chapter 31}

2557:17:6:19

The bright red banner lit the night as Jay passed under it. The sliding hospital doors parted as he walked into the vestibule. A call had come in that jolted him from his slumber. He had been awaken this way a few times before in the months prior. Every time he saw ROYAL OAK HOSPITAL spelled out across the screen of his phone, he felt as if the ringing was a piercing drill burrowing deep into his ears. He agonized over the fear that when he answered the phone, a somber voice on the other end would deliver the grievous news of Her passing as the piercing drill would strike his brain and kill him. However, this call was just as the one's before – Jay's wife had been resuscitated from a sudden attack of sharp chest pains and coughing.

The doors behind him slid closed, sending eddies of snow into the vestibule. The harsh white lights above Jay made him squint and blinded him for a moment, then his eyes adjusted from the chilled darkness of night. Purple rings cupped his eyes, and his clothes were disheveled from being hastily thrown on. Ahead of Jay were a pair of inner sliding doors. In his drowsiness, he nearly smacked his head against the doors when they didn't open. Taped on the RFID reader to the right was a note that read: DOOR BROKEN. PLEASE SEE SECURITY.

He looked to his right at the security office. He yawned and huffed as he waved at the friendly security guard that sat behind a glass window. On the lapel of the guard's black security uniform, a nametag read "DARNELL."

Darnell knew Jay well. The guard had worked at the hospital for many years and, when Jay started as the local biomedical technician, Darnell was the one to assign him a security badge that would get him through the doors. When Darnell had worked the day shift, he had seen Jay frequently pass through with his tool bag in hand. Some days, Darnell would see Jay jog out of the entrance and return later with Her, hand-in-hand. For the first few instances, the guard simply greeted the couple as they briskly walked through the vestibule. Then after a few more visits, Jay walked with her arms clung tightly around his elbow as she hobbled along. Eventually, Jay was pushing Her through in a wheelchair.

One afternoon, Darnell stood wide-eyed as an EMT team rushed Her in on a stretcher with Jay close behind. Then, later that evening as the guard was packing up to end his shift, he watched as Jay left by himself. That was two months ago.

Eventually, Darnell began working the graveyard shift. Ever since, Jay would stay hours after work to spend his time with Her. He would then leave around 11 P.M. to get some shut-eye at home, greeting Darnell as he clocked in to start his late shift. On occasion, Darnell would find himself greeting Jay again just a few hours later. Tonight was one of those nights.

Darnell leaned forward towards the silver, round intercom imbedded into the glass and pressed a button on a little, gray box.

"How's it goin' Jay?" he asked in a crackly voice.

Jay wiped one eye with his knuckles and nodded. "I'm doin' alright."

The buzzing white lights above shone on Jay's weary, sleepless face. Darnell had seen that face before. The face of a person stricken with an indescribable mixture of worry, anxiety, and pure exhaustion underneath. Drained of energy and sagging heavily as if it carried ten extra years. However, those eyes always held a glint of anticipation. Darnell had seen many Jays and had known all of them to be of unrelenting loyalty. He had seen them come and go… come and go— visiting their loved ones in hospice. But… eventually, Darnell would see these weathered, yet hopeful, faces enter one day and leave hours later as shrunken husks of grief—never to return.

"The door's been havin' some issues. I'll open it for ya." Darnell said.

"Thanks," Jay replied.

Darnell reached to his right and pushed some unseen button on his desk. A short, shrill beep sounded from the RFID reader as the door slid open. Jay waved to Darnell and walked through.

The emergency room lobby was an expansive, open space. A large, analog clock hung from a girthy, oaken joist above—3:25 A.M. To Jay's left was a waiting area, lined with rows of chairs with blue cushions and curved wooden armrests. Between every three or so were small round tables. Three of the chairs were extended horizontally to fit larger patients comfortably.

In one of the mid-row chairs, a young man dressed in baggy clothes bounced his knee vigorously as he chewed on his nails. Against the far wall, a teenage girl sat with her arms wrapped around the shoulders of an elderly man hunched over on his cane. He let out a raspy cough as the young girl patted his back and said something to him in Spanish.

Ahead of Jay, a young, female employee dressed in blue scrubs approached him, wheeling a stark white podium with a laptop resting on it.

"Hello," she said in a friendly tone as she began entering information into her laptop. "What brings you into the emergency room today?"

"Ah-h, I'm not here for me… I got a call concernin' my wife, who's been stayin' here for a while. I'm just here to visit," Jay replied.

"Oh," the employee said as she stopped typing and rested her hands on the gray handles attached to the side of the podium. "Do you know where she's staying?"

"Yeah, I know the way."

"Alrighty then. Have a good evening. Hope she feels better."

"Thank you," Jay said as he began trotting towards the large hallway.

He passed by reception, a round office enclosed by glass windows and a chest-high wooden counter. There was a man at the counter, discussing something with one of the workers through a group of holes cut out of the glass. The other workers were too busy shuffling papers and pecking away at their keyboards to notice Jay. Down the hall was the main hospital, bathed in darkness and closed for the night. Only the expansive hall that led to a pair of elevators at the end was lit. Jay could see the glow of a row of red EXIT signs trailing off into the void along with various, random, dim lights scattered throughout.

All Jay could hear as he moved down the hallway were the sounds of his shoes squeaking along the freshly mopped tiles of white and beige. At the corners of each were small, black diamonds connecting the tiles together in a pattern. He passed by a painted mural of doctors and patients of various ethnicities, genders, and ages. On the left was a large painting of a female doctor from the waist up in a stark, white coat. She looked middle-aged with poofy, curly hair and thin-brimmed glasses. Opposite from her was an older doctor with gray hair—bald with a thin-lipped smile. Between them were scenes of nurses, other doctors, and patients doing various things: a child patient was being pushed in a wheelchair through a lush park, an older woman sat in a bed with her doctor's hand in hers, and an elderly couple were depicted leaving the hospital in good health. Every one of their faces were smiling with expressions of hope. Across the top read the words "CARE, COMPASSSION, COURAGE" in deep blue text.

The dim, fluorescent rays passed over Jay as he walked under the wooden joists and arrived at the elevators. He pressed the up-arrow button. A faint orange ring lit up around it as a frosted, arrow-shaped light pointing upwards above the elevator doors illuminated with the same orange shade. Between the up-arrow and down-arrow lights was an LED display with the current floor shining in sharp blue. It had started from seven and continued counting down. Jay waited with his arms crossed, bobbing his heel on the ball of his right foot. His mind was a blur, racing with thoughts of Her.

Is she ok? God, I hope it wasn't serious. This is the third time this week. Why isn't the medicine working? They said it would work this time. I wonder if she's hungry. I bet she hasn't eaten yet. Why is this damn elevator taking so long? I wish I could do more. She's probably feeling horrible right now. Damn it, I should've brought some food for her. Or some clothes. I'm sure she's tired of the hospital gown. Holy shit, hurry up... Maybe, they'll let me take her out for a bit even though its late. She really likes the little garden they got here...

"Jesus Christ, what's takin' so long..." Jay said to himself, under his breath.

Finally, after what felt like an eternity, the elevator's display read "1" and dinged. As the elevator doors slid open with a mechanical clunk, Jay dropped his arms to his side and walked towards it. He nearly collided with a female, dark-skinned doctor exiting the elevator. As she recoiled, her thick, raven hair jostled back and revealed a face with a slender nose and sunken eyes surrounded by dark rings.

"Oh, excuse me," she said wearily in a rapid, Hindi accent.

"Sorry about that," Jay said as he shimmied past her.

He turned to face the row of floor buttons and pressed the one marked "5." His heel continued to bob as the brushed steel of the elevator doors accordioned closed and dinged. As the elevator ascended, the same LED display chimed with each floor passed. Jay paced around the elevator with lips pursed and arms crossed. All he could hear were the mechanical workings of the elevator; the hospital automatically shut off the generic, smooth jazz that normally played during the day. His jacket felt damp from the melted snow under his hands, and he had only started to notice the small tinge of discomfort on the tip of his nose that came from cold flesh being warmed up.

The elevator began to slow as Jay stepped up just inches from the exit. A round swath of condensation appeared and shrunk on the mirror-like elevator door as Jay breathed onto it. He hadn't been doing anything physical that would warrant his racing heart. Still, he found himself panting and stressed.

Jay squeezed himself out before the elevator doors could fully open. He turned left past the empty, dark reception and towards the hall of patient rooms. The tiles were the same white and beige with black diamonds, but the walls were now a salmon pink with framed pictures of random, outdoor scenes. Along the bottom was a stripe of fake wood paneling with thick, textured handrails of gray lining the entirety of each wall. The halls were dimly lit to help patients sleep. The only noise was the sound of buzzing fluorescent tubes and Jay's echoing footsteps as he trudged down a row of metal, teal doors and took a right down another hallway.

Room 342, he thought. *Just around that left corner.*

As he approached the T-intersection, he heard the clunking of rolling wheels ahead of him. He recognized the familiar sound and looked up at the quarter-sphere, convex mirror mounted just above the intersection that allowed him to see down either hall. Just as he suspected, a nurse was wheeling a patient in a gurney from down the left turn. His heart sank for a moment as the nurse turned down towards Jay. He half expected Her to be laying in that gurney as he stepped to the side and let the nurse and patient through. As they rolled by, Jay looked down to see a drowsy man curl his lip in pain as the nurse reassured him that they were *'almost there'*. Jay turned down the left hall and passed by a mounted, bronze sign that read:

←330 – 350

350 – 370→

A pair of bright, vending machine lights to his right caught Jay's attention. He paused and thought to himself: *I should get Her something.* He peered through the streaked glass that had been recently wiped down by the custodian. Scanning the snacks, he thought: *Sour things. She loves sour things.* He pulled out his wallet and bought himself a bag of Doritos and, for Her, a bag of Sour Patch Kids. He stuffed his snacks into his jacket pocket and power-walked past several rooms. As the room numbers on little, brown plaques blurred past, he read them in his mind: *337… 338… 339… 340… 341…*

He was now standing outside room 342. Looking through the cross-hatched slim window, he could see that the lights were on. He turned the handle, heard a chunky 'click' as his wedding ring clinked against the metal, and opened the hefty hospital door. As he stepped into the room, he heard the laugh track from a TV just behind a pair of ceiling-to-floor, beige curtains that hung from large metal rings along a curved rail. They were closed to give Her some privacy. He crept forward and slowly parted the curtain with the back of his hands.

He saw Her sitting up in Her hospital bed with a blanket pulled over Her legs, staring up at the flat screen TV in the upper corner of the room. She had Her hands in her lap as She continued to watch. Jay glanced at the TV to see racing captions overlayed on a sitcom he didn't recognize. He slowly crept into her periphery as She ripped her attention from the TV and waved excitedly with a smile. Jay raised a hand and smiled timidly. Underneath the TV was a large chair for visitors. Jay had spent many weekend nights sleeping in this chair and found it ironic how incredibly uncomfortable the cushions were, despite their plush appearance. He pulled it up to Her bedside and sat down.

She forced a smile as he fought to smile back, but all he could do was frown for a moment. Her complexion had grown so pale and thin. She looked ragged and worn. The color in Her once-brilliant eyes was now fading like a dying star. The strands of Her disheveled hair were but a shadow of their former, luscious beauty. He took one of Her hands in his and rubbed the top of Her fingers gently with his thumb. They felt boney and cold. Jay saw beauty in the woman he had dedicated his life to. He saw the part of him he had given to Her in those dim eyes. Anytime he was in Her presence, his heart felt warm.

"How're ya doing?" he asked calmly.

She told him she was doing fine—Her delicate hands signing weakly.

"They said you had a pretty serious coughin' fit."

She nodded and started to tear up. Jay leaned over and held Her as She cried into his shoulder. A commercial sounded off behind him as he caressed Her back. His eyes felt moist as he heard the lingering beep of the heart monitor to the left of the bed.

He buried his cheek into to the top of her shoulder as he looked around. Several cables and tubes were leading into Her. He could see the leads of the heart monitor reaching under Her shirt and onto several parts of Her torso. In the crook of Her right elbow, an IV drip had been inserted—the bag of which hung from a silver pole attached to the head of Her bed. And finally, another tube was snaked under her gown's collar and into an implant under Her collarbone. The bag that fed this tube was filled with the medicine the doctors said would keep Her heart pressure low.

Jay loved Her.

He loved Her with every fiber of his being.

If he had his way, he'd rip out every damn cable and tube and plunge them into himself if it meant She could be healthy again. He'd suffer through hellfire and fury even if it meant Her health would show a microscopic hint of improvement. When She started to sniffle, he pulled away and looked through glassy eyes at the face of his wife. The tears rolled down sunken, pale cheeks as She wiped them away with the heels of Her palms. Jay saw Her as gorgeous as the day they married under the sunlit conservatory but couldn't deny She was withering away like a wilting flower.

He stilled his heart, sighed, and reached into his jacket pocket.

"Here," he said softly and handed Her the pack of Sour Patch Kids. "I figured you might be hungry, and I know how much you like those."

She tilted her head, smiled, and thanked him. Jay unfolded the tray on the side of Her hospital bed. He heard a meek grunt as he looked at Her struggling face. She was twisting the bag desperately to try and tear it, but Her weak grip proved inadequate. Jay set his bag of chips on the tray and tapped Her on the wrist. She handed him the bag. He easily opened it and handed it back. She thanked him as she pulled out a powdery, red gummy and popped it into Her mouth. She puckered Her lips and squinted as She made small smacking sounds with her lips. She chewed a bit and swallowed. Jay thought he saw a bit of color return to Her cheeks as She smiled at him. A laugh track sounded off behind him.

"You mind if I shut off the TV?" he asked.

She asked if he could just mute it since She still wanted to watch. He rolled his eyes and pecked Her on the cheek. He reached over to the tethered remote on the side of Her bed and muted the TV. Now, only the slow beeping of the heart monitor and the crinkling of junk food bags filled the room. As they ate, She asked him how work was going.

"Y'know how work was," he teased. "You asked me how it was before I left last night."

She told him She knew but wanted to hear anyway.

"Hmm, well that CT on the second floor went down. Looks like it's gonna need a new x-ray tube."

She asked him when that would get replaced.

"Not sure. They're shipping it out tonight, actually. Should be here tomorrow, but with all the snow… who knows, right?"

She shrugged as She placed her half-eaten bag of candy on the tray.

"All done?"

She nodded and picked at Her fingernails in her lap. Jay crumbled up his finished bag of chips and tossed it in the trash. He then took Her candy and brought it over to a desk by the head of Her bed. He placed it down next to a thick hardcover with a green, ribbon bookmark hanging out the bottom. Raising an eyebrow, he picked up the book and turned to the bookmarked page.

"Hey," Jay said as he sat down with the opened book, "you weren't supposed to read ahead." He flipped back through several pages. "Damn, you read like five chapters ahead."

She blushed as She curled her lips.

"Was my reading really that bad… I thought my Frodo voice was pretty good…"

She held out a horizontal, splayed palm and pivoted it a few times—"*so-so.*"

"Hey, be *nice*," Jay said as he gave Her a little pinch on Her hip. She recoiled slightly and giggled. Jay chuckled with Her. He stopped and tilted his head with a loving smile as they simply looked at each other. The feeling was beginning to overwhelm him before he decided to save himself the crying and leaned in for a kiss. She craned Her neck as their lips met. Her lips were like ice. He closed the book and set it in his lap. The heart monitor continued to beep.

Jay leaned back in his uncomfortable chair, rubbed one of his eyes, and yawned. He glanced at the clock but didn't catch the exact time. It was twenty minutes—give or take a few—past four in the morning. He looked over his shoulder at the large windows that lined the wall. Through it was a cloudy night sky and the twinkling of random city lights. Across from their hospital tower was another one with a few rectangular lights shining through windows. On a raised platform off the ground, a helicopter pad sat—surrounded by red lights that slowly faded in and out in sequence. Blankets of pure white covered the rooftops of buildings as snow trickled down steadily. Jay's wife tapped his wrist to get his attention.

She asked him if he was tired. It didn't matter what time it was, or how he felt when he spent it, as long as it was with Her.

Jay smirked and chortled. "No, I'm ok."

She apologized.

"No-no-no. You have nothin' to be sorry for. I was thinkin' about takin' some time off so I can spend a week with ya. We can go down to the park, and I'll bring some board games for us to play. Maybe they'll even let me bring a DVD player, and we can watch some movies!"

She let him prattle on as She bit her lips and nodded along. Then, She started crying again.

"And we can— Hey? What's up, honey?" Jay asked as he thumbed tears off Her cheek.

She took a deep breath.

She knew it was time. Deep in Her subconscious, a fluttering sense of conclusive anxiety traveled down Her throat and throughout Her chest. She sniffled and cleared Her throat. She looked at Jay with a stern expression.

She asked him to listen.

He listened.

She told him to save his time off, that he wouldn't need to take it. He opened his mouth to ask "why?" but she held up a hand to stop him. She thanked him for their time together. Their wonderful memories they shared from the day they met in high school. She recounted that memory to him. How he tried so hard to win over the affection of 'the weird shy girl who never talked'. And how She had wanted nothing to do with him until the day he asked Her to be his Valentine in broken sign language. She told Jay She couldn't imagine Her life without him and that the joy he brought Her was something She wished she could repay him for. Taking a hand in one of Hers, She told him that once they met again, She would smother him with the culminated love and affection he would be missing out on while She was gone. And that, in that afterlife, She would become the woman he married again.

"Sweetheart, stop," Jay said. Tears streamed down his cheeks and met as drops under his chin. "You're not goin' anywhere and besides… you've always been the woman I married… and always will be. Never has a day passed that you weren't who I've always loved."

She squeezed his hand and shook Her head, breaking Her stern expression into a sullen look. Jay's head sunk as well; Her hand was so cold… so very cold. His tears dripped onto the back of her hand— beading up, rolling off the side, and absorbing into Her bed sheet. He felt Her other hand pull his chin up. She held that same serious expression as She caressed Jay's cheek. She pulled Her hand back to sign.

She asked him something he hadn't wanted to see or hear or think about.

No, he thought to himself as he looked down at their hands again. *I can't* move on, *honey.*

She pulled his face up again—forced him to face reality. She urged him to be brave just as he had taught Her to be.

"I-I can't, honey," Jay babbled. "I-I can't do this without you. You're the only r-reason I *can* do this."

She assured him, gripped his hand tightly, and pursed Her lips. She let go of his hand and jammed a finger in Her chest. Next, she crossed her arms over Her chest in an "X" with balled up fists. Then, She jammed the same finger into Jay's chest.

"I love you too, sweetheart," he replied.

She repeated the sign.

"I-I love you too… God, I love you so much. Don't do this… please…"

She coughed.

She begged him to promise Her that he would move on.

"No… No I can't. I could never!"

She rubbed Her chest in a circle: *"Please."* She coughed again.

Jay bit his lips. He sniffled and wiped his cheeks. "No…"

She held his face in her hands, leaned forward, and touched Her forehead to his. She rubbed his cheek with Her thumb gently. *So cold,* Jay thought.

She pulled back and coughed again. Letting go of Jay's face, She asked him for a favor since he wouldn't let Her go.

"Of course. Anything… anything…"

She told him if he couldn't let Her go, then he could hold onto Her. Hold onto Her as long as it took—until he was ready. And, when he was ready, to take Her across Michigan one last time—like they used to when they were young. She wanted to be with Her mother… She wanted to be with him. She thumbed the blue diamonds along his wedding ring on his left hand.

She coughed twice.

"Honey… I…"

She curled Her left ring and pinky finger into her palm and clamped the fingertips of her middle and index finger to her thumb: *"No."*

She did it again with more force: *"NO!"*

Extending Her left index finger from a closed hand, She held it against her chin and pointed towards Her nostrils. Then, She brought it down—opening it into a chop onto the palm of Her other hand.

"Promise."

Jay bit his lips and said nothing.

Coughing, She did it again.

"PROMISE!"

"Ok! Ok… I promise, honey. I promise," he said while signing the word back to Her. She continued to cough. "Let me get you some water. You're–"

She leaned forward as She hacked and gasped violently into her palms. Jay shot to his feet as he looked down and saw that Her hands were coated with blood. The heart monitor began to beep quickly. Jay threw the book in his lap onto the desk, reached over the head of the bed, and spammed the red nurse call button. He jogged to the door and swung it open.

"Nurse! Nurse!" he yelled down the hall as a nurse in blue scrubs jogged towards him.

"Coming! Coming!" the nurse yelled back.

Jay stepped out of the way as the nurse rushed past him and put a hand on Jay's wife. She asked Her a few questions and only received coughing for answers. The nurse saw the blood on the sheets and immediately turned to a black phone on the wall, picked up the receiver, punched in some numbers, and hung it up.

Jay rushed to his wife's side and tried his best to comfort Her as he babbled. She tried to raise a hand to sign, but quickly found it returning to her mouth to catch more blood.

Soon, a doctor and two more nurses burst through the door as the heart monitor continued to race. The doctor crouched by Jay's wife and signed Her some words; She responded with only nods and shakes. One of the nurses was busy tapping away at graphs and charts on the heart monitor. Another nurse pulled Jay's chair to the corner under the TV as the third nurse led Jay to it while saying: "Please, let us handle this."

Jay crashed into the chair, staked his elbows into his knees, and buried his face into his hands. He rocked back and forth as he squeezed his eyes shut. In the darkness, he could hear the nurses shouting medical terms he didn't understand at each other. More like, he chose *not* to understand. And whether or not he chose to understand the phrases he had heard countless times in Her hospital visits before, the panic in the hospital worker's voices now told him all he needed to know. In the cacophony, the heart monitor continued screeching. Jay's mind was a typhoon.

No-no-no-no-no-no-no-no-no.

The beeping cut through louder. Jay heard Her gasp heavily.

Please! Stop! STOP!

He could hear feet shuffling as more people rushed in.

No more! Oh god! No-no-no… please…

Then, his heart shattered. He felt a significant portion of himself die inside; he felt incomplete—inhuman. The room fell silent for only a split second as the heart monitor held a constant high-pitched note.

The typhoon became nothing in an instant. Her coughing stopped as Jay heard someone yell "She's going into cardiac arrest!" He felt a sharp pain behind his eyes as he opened them to a slits of light that shone between his fingers. His world had gone silent, save for his heavy breathing and the flatline of the heart monitor.

He didn't want to open his palms.

He didn't want to accept the sight that awaited behind them.

He didn't want to leave his safe, little cave and enter a world without Her.

I'm sorry, honey… Your promise… I can't let go… No… No-no-no…

Two years later, astronomers would discover a new space anomaly orbiting the earth.

{Chapter 32}

0:20:40:57

Seagulls, Jay thought in the darkness. *I hear seagulls.*

The squawks and calls sounded as if they were behind a thick wall. Jay's eyes stung and his skin was cold and damp. He could feel water lapping against his heels; the fabric of his shoes were soaked. He attempted to lift his left hand to his face and felt clumps of sand drop from his stump. *Oh right…* he thought. He tried to roll over onto his left side, but a small force on his right arm held him down. The starlight burned his eyes as he opened them. He felt as if his eyes were smeared with Vaseline. Above him, the white pinpoints twinkled like starburst gems in the clear sky. Cosmic clouds of purple, green, and brown streaked across the sky as Jay followed them to the red hue that blotted out all starlight around it. The Anomaly continued to grow. To the left of the black diamond, Jay could barely make out the waning crescent of the moon through the red film.

Jay's head pounded as his vision started to glaze over with a blue glow. His headache receded for a moment as he lurched forward and expelled mouthfuls of black water onto his lap. He collapsed back onto the soft sand as a small force pushed his chest down.

Jay's mind was clear now. He was no longer delirious, but his vision was still blurred. Now, he could plainly see the small force was Gilnup's two mitts pressing into his right bicep as the brave warrior sat on its knees. There was a soothing warmth emanating from it and moving into his body. This warmth was different from Jay's destructive power. This was one of healing and amiability; Jay could feel his fire returning. One side of the coin mending the other.

His hearing returned to normal as a low hum faded into the still night. At first, Jay nearly went into a panic. The memory of Second Convergence flashed across his mind. However, the comforting touch of Gilnup's hands calmed Jay's heart and soul. He traced Gilnup's mitts to the mushie's face and could see the creature's beady eyes closed tight as its muzzle vibrated with the low hum. Gilnup's fungal membrane was severely shriveled, like a prune, across the entirety of its body. A few times the humming stopped as the brave warrior huffed to catch its breath. Jay looked to Gilnup's cap—bruised and gashed badly. Jay rolled his face to the sky and closed his eyes.

Another surge of energy rippled through Jay, forcing his eyes open.

The world around him became clearer now. He gripped a handful of sand in his right hand, turned it over, and lifted it a few inches off the beach. As he opened his hand, streams of sand trickled between his fingers. The feeling of rolling granules perpetuated across his palm as he began to feel his backpack—soaked and tattered—pressing against his back. He felt a wave of relief pass over him as he came to realize a distinct, hard, round object pressed against the small of his back. Jay tilted his head towards Gilnup and could see, behind the brave warrior, Benu's hands resting on a green lap. Jay looked up to her face. She was sitting on her knees behind Gilnup, smiling wearily. A thick circle of black surrounded her eyes as she blinked rapidly. She swayed to the left, ready to pass out as if she was stuck in a three-hour lecture covering the history, intricacies, and medical significance of the first gallbladder transplant. Then, she jolted and caught herself on the sand with her left hand. Her eyes widened with the look of *'I'm awake! I swear! I'm listening!'*.

Jay eked out a smile and even a small chuckle. The blue glow illuminated brighter as Jay's chuckle turned into laughter. Benu tilted her head and began to laugh as well. Gilnup's hands pulled away from Jay as the brave warrior stood up and plopped its butt onto the sand, causing small mounds to form around Gilnup. Jay sat up as his laughter morphed into sorrow. He frowned as he looked out into the raging black waters. Gilnup had saved him from death. He bit his lower lip as he began to sob. Trash littered the beach. Little islands of plastic bags, cardboard, and pop cans drifted amongst the waves. To

Jay's left, a ship had run aground—scattering splintered wood, ripped fiberglass, and twisted metal across the sand.

"Jay..." Benu murmured from behind him.

He turned around to see Gilnup—its eyes closed and cap dimly glowing—limp in Benu's arms. Its shriveled membrane looked gray and dry. The once vibrant, spotted cap atop Gilnup's head had desaturated to a pastel pink. Its little chest moved slowly up and down as it breathed. Jay crawled over to Gilnup's side, sat on his knees, and joined Benu in holding the petite creature.

"Gilnup used up all its strength to revive us..." Benu whispered.

"I don't understand," Jay said. "Cap'n Q didn't mention this when he was revived on his beach."

"But he was *surrounded* by mushies when they revived him... Reviving us must have been too much for Gilnup alone."

"Cap'n Q... is he?"

Benu shook her head, "I have not seen any sign of him."

Jay looked to the brave warrior. In the little creature's final moments, it looked at-peace and pleased.

Bravery and a sense of closure filled Gilnup's heart as it felt Jay's hand on its chest—its life-debt repaid. Gilnup let out a soft moan as it passed—its muzzle fluttered as it exhaled. The blue glow faded out as the air filled with the red hue of the black diamond. Through the grains of sand, the purple gleam illuminated Gilnup's cheeks.

Jay laid eyes on the face of a hero.

Benu wept as Jay said: "Thank you, lil' guy."

Benu pulled her palms away and onto her eyes as she continued to sob. Jay remained silent. A dormant eruption of emotion brewed inside him, but he gulped hard and swallowed it—his Adam's apple bobbing noticeably. He sat on his knees in silence for a bit as he held his savior in his lap. He set Gilnup's body back on the sand.

Finally, Jay said: "We should bury the lil' guy."

Benu lowered her hands and agreed. Jay searched his waterlogged backpack and found the contents were wet, but not soaked. He pulled out his beanie, wrung it out, patted it against his arm, and put it on.

Next, he tossed aside his now-useless bike pump and repair kit. The homeowner's toolkit was next to follow. He found the trowel completely unharmed and staked it into the sand. He had reached the bottom of his bag. Smatterings of sand coated the walls and floor of the backpack. Sitting at the bottom were Jay's ring and the urn. He retrieved his ring and shoved it into his right pocket, feeling grits of sand under his fingernails. Knowing that the urn was safe, he zipped up his bag and threw it on.

Taking the trowel in his hand, he looked over to Benu to find her tossing something into the lake. He heard the 'plop' of the small item as she zipped up her bag. She had also organized her things, and Jay wasn't sure what she had kept and what she had tossed into the inky blackness. For now, he didn't care.

"Can you carry Gilnup?" he asked Benu.

"Yeah... Where should we..."

Jay pointed towards the rear of the beach with his trowel where the sand turned to grassland. The land was severely split, forming small crags. Purple shone through the cracks.

"There, in the sand. We should bury Gilnup in the same sorta land it called home."

Benu scooped up Gilnup and stood; the body was as light as a feather but dry as a bone. They walked to where Jay pointed—the lake to their backs. Benu set Gilnup down as Jay began to dig.

He sat on his knees, reached out far with the trowel in his hand, and lanced the blade into the soft sand. Then, he sat up, pulling the trowel through the sand. He continued to do this as a mound built up between his knees. He longed for his left arm. Benu had joined in, using her hands to dig like a child gathering material for a sandcastle. They dug for nearly an hour until they were sure the hole was deep enough to cover Gilnup in its entirety.

They lowered the brave warrior into the grave and covered the body. Standing over the grave, Benu said, "Gilnup deserves a tombstone... Even a crude one at least."

Jay went to stake his trowel at the head of the grave when Benu held out her hand to stop him.

"No," she said. "You need that to bury your wife." She then reached for her knife on her thigh. The buckle had held firm in the torrent and kept the knife from being swept away. She unclasped her knife from the sheath and knelt by the head of Gilnup's grave. She drove the knife deep into the sand until only the military green hilt could be seen.

"Lil' guy would've like that," Jay said. "Gilnup was a fighter, after all."

Benu nodded as she stood. They shared a moment of silence for Gilnup, the brave and fearless. Jay felt a strange thought cross his mind. He asked himself *"Why bury anything or anyone when, in less than twenty-four hours, it would be as if this grave never existed? Soon, this grave will be nothing but space dust—just as the rest of the countless graves across the globe, old and new. A grave is a memorial. Who will be left to remember this one?"*

He had no answer; it just felt like the right thing to do. Jay's mind was silent as he thought of Her. No memory of a specific event they shared together—just Her. He felt that dormant emotion well up again, but this time had no way to quell it. A lump traveled from his chest and up into his throat, choking him as he fought to hold it back. His head felt tight as he grimaced and sobbed. As he gritted his teeth, he could feel Benu's eyes on him. Throwing the trowel into the ground, Jay let out a harrowing bellow as he whipped around and shot a volley of fireballs at The Anomaly. The jacket sleeve around his forearm burned away as he watched his projectiles shrink into nothingness against the pitch-black backdrop as if the black diamond snuffed them out consciously.

"WHAT THE FUCK DO YOU WANT FROM ME?!" Jay screeched out into the silence. "You've ruined my entire life… my entire world—clawin' and rippin' my mind to pieces! You've taken everything from me—EVERYTHING—my home, my life, my very being… And yet, that is not enough… You torment me! You torment me with your endless hunger! You eat away at me like a rabid animal!"

"Jay!" Benu cried out.

Jay turned to Benu, pointing at The Anomaly. "Do you know what it showed me? In the black water… I heard its voice and it took me back… It made me relive Her death! The fuckin' monster revels in it—feeds on my anguish! It must know… It *must*…"

"Know what, *dost*?"

"It must know I've relived that fuckin' day, *every* day, since it happened. That damn heart monitor won't shut the fuck up! And it knows… So, it eats away at my mind like a disease—takin' away what makes me human!"

"Jay, stop!"

"What time is it?"

"Wha—"

He continuously snapped his fingers as he pressed. "The time! The time! How much time is left?"

Benu scrambled to check her watch. The digital display was dead. She spammed the buttons and smacked it few times, but the little screen remained a solid gray without numbers. Looking at the moon, she replied: "I do not know exactly but… it has to be less than eighteen—maybe sixteen—hours?"

Jay turned away and threw up his right hand and phantom left hand and yelled, "This is Hell on Earth! The hellscape of my mind has fully come to fruition! If I can't do this… If I can't keep my promise…" He let out an aggravated grunt. "Why can't anyone understand what I'm goin' through?"

Benu's face grew hot with anger and felt a surge of latent energy. She furrowed her brow and promptly stepped over to Jay. She spun him around by the shoulder and stared daggers into his eyes. Jay huffed and said nothing. Then, Benu backhanded him across his right cheek. The blow forced him to look to the ground. He brought his head up to meet Benu's tight-lipped grimace. Then, she slapped him across the left cheek, forcing him to look the other way. He felt assaulted and, by instinct, began to heat up his right hand which sizzled. Benu gripped the lapels of his jacket with both her hands and yanked Jay in. She took up his entire vision as he felt her hot breath against his face.

"Go ahead," Benu murmured. "Burn me. Burn me, because it could not hurt me more than what you have just said. You think you are the only one suffering from that thing? You think it did not show *me* something as well in those waters? I was back in that room, Jay... staring at three. Rotting. Corpses. You say no one understands. Well, *I* do! Have you ever spared a moment to think there are others like you? And you think that pain is not fresh in my mind? You think I have not felt The Anomaly's grip tighten ever since? I know that I am not alone in my pain. And I have told you before... neither are you." She loosened her grip and backed off a bit as Jay's hand cooled. "Why? Why do you not just *talk* about these things?"

Jay clenched his fist and replied, "I'm conflicted. I want to be strong for Her. Strong enough to carry her promise to the end. But I'm finally at my breaking point and I don't know what to do. I... I don't wanna be a burden or be seen as weak. How can I carry Her if people feel the need to carry me?"

"*Dost...* Nobody is above needing help. You are human, just like anyone else." Benu felt for the letter in her back pocket. Miraculously, it hadn't been swept away by the cursed waters. "It is ok to be weak... You just cannot embrace those weaknesses." She stepped forward and embraced Jay in a hug. "Please... be strong enough to ask for help."

Jay's hand quivered. His eyes danced between random grains of sand, then to The Anomaly. The hesitation in his mind was like a creeping fog, snuffing out the light. The desire to bundle up his emotions and tuck them deep within his being beckoned to his consciousness. He began to step away from Benu, when he felt the urn against his back.

In the blackness of The Anomaly, he saw Her face, gleaming with compassion and strength that cast away the fog. He steeled his resolve, wrapped his arm around Benu, and buried his face into her shoulder.

"Thank you, Benu."

{Chapter 33}

0:7:13:18

Jay and Benu had collapsed on the beach shortly after Jay's breakdown. The soothing, shifting sands wrapped them in cooling comfort. And although the Fall air was chilly, there was a warmth emanating from the earth that night. The sounds of tides moving in and out of the shore was like a caressing hand on their backs, lulling them to sleep. Their exhaustion, both physical and mental, had caused them to sleep a few minutes past noon. A few times, Jay had woken up in the middle of the night in a panic to rush to the cemetery as he felt the grip of inevitability squeeze tightly, but the thrashing he had done in the water and the digging he had done for Gilnup made his whole body feel like Jell-O. And soon, he would pass out.

When they awoke to the sound of seagulls, Benu pulled out the last of her food: half a jar of Skippy, waterlogged fruit, and water. They ate and went on their way.

For the past hour, Jay and Benu had walked the empty streets of Escanaba. The sun shone brightly, but the sky was no longer blue. The Anomaly was nearing its finale—Total Convergence. It had grown so large, Jay swore that, if he were to stretch out his right arm, he'd dip his fingertips in the black diamond's inky blackness. Its red aura filled the sky and painted the earth a muted sanguine. Purple gleams from the splintered earth shimmered between the wide crevasses that zigzagged in all directions. The rough terrain had caused much delay in their trek towards the northern cemetery where Her mother had been buried.

They passed by the ruins of collapsed buildings and disheveled sidewalks. The overgrowth of large trees loomed throughout with thick bramble occupying the spaces between structures. Through large, broken, storefront windows, Jay could see various wildlife scurrying about, eating at grasses and weeds that had invaded the floors and walls. What would normally have been a two-hour walk looked more like three, or even four, by Jay's judgment.

After another half hour, the pair arrived at the center of town where a wide ditch had eaten up about a mile of road. Jay looked for a way around, but the ditch had spanned far into the horizon on either side and was surrounded by crags of upturned streets and buildings. The two stood on the edge as Benu leaned over and peered into the ditch. She could see rubble of concrete, rebar—and the mangled, rusted corpses of old cars. Just below her, about ten feet down, a large sewage pipe jutted from the ditch wall. She straightened up and looked to Jay, "We can cross this. I can lower you down to that pipe, then you help me down. After that, we move into the ditch. Looks about another ten feet."

"Yeah, sounds good," Jay replied.

Just as he finished, the familiar rumbling of land being ripped away caught their attention. They looked West, towards the lake, over the crags, and could see several plates of land being pulled towards the sky—enormous waterfalls pouring off the edges. Then, they heard the rumbling again that shook the ground beneath them. They held out their arms for balance and turned their attention to the East where more chunks lifted into the sky and dissolved. The crash of waters and groaning trees filled the red-stained air with devastation. For a moment, Jay thought the land under them would begin to lift as well; but the rumbling came to an end, and the two were still standing over the ditch.

"C'mon," Jay said, catching his breath. "Let's move."

Benu nodded as Jay stepped in front of her and turned his back to the ditch. He dangled his left leg off the ledge, checking over his shoulder a few times to make sure he was above the pipe. As his right leg bent to meet his chest, he braced himself on the ground with his right hand. He pursed his lips with effort and motioned for Benu to grab his hand. Jay slipped a little at the momentary loss of balance as Benu knelt and locked her hand with his. Her faced strained as she lowered Jay towards the pipe. She rested on her stomach as Jay's toes met the pipe.

"I'm good!" Jay called up.

Benu let go as the hollow thud of Jay's Chucks landed on the large iron pipe. Benu licked her lips and tasted the salt of fresh sweat. She thought back to a week ago when she dragged Jay's limp body down the street of the Royal Oak neighborhood she met him in. And, although she figured she was in better health back then, Jay's body was heavier for some reason, despite being a limb short. Benu was nearing her limit. The world would end in a matter of hours, and she knew it. At this point, the only thing driving her was a bullheaded sense of loyalty, duty, and compassion for her friend.

She rose to her feet, turned her back to the ditch, and began to work her way over the edge. As she got both feet over the edge, she dug them into the ditch wall and hung by her hands. Jay raised up his right hand and stump as if to catch Benu if she fell.

"Be careful! I've never caught anyone one-handed before!" Jay called.

Benu shook her head and chuckled. "Only a few hours till the end of the world, and you are still cracking jokes?"

Jay shrugged. "I dunno. Guess I got it all out last night. C'mon, I got ya."

Benu lowered herself enough so that Jay could place his hand on her waist. When she felt it, she let go and dropped onto the pipe; Jay's hand and stump had slid up and caught her weight under her armpits. The pipe creaked as it began to buckle.

Jay and Benu held onto each other for balance as the metal creaked under their feet. The pair grunted as the pipe dropped sharply down a couple inches but remained in the wall. When the two felt it was sturdy and safe, they helped each other into the ditch and began trudging through the debris.

"Besides," Jay continued as if the event with the failing pipe never happened, "I wanna be in good spirits when I bury Her." He looked to his feet. "At least… the best spirit I *can* be in."

Benu smiled and patted Jay on the back. They moved through piles of brick and stone. Rusty, green light posts poked out from the rubble like twisty, metal plants. Chain link fences were chaotically tangled and wrapped around debris like thistle. The sound of flowing water dripped into the ditch from broken pipes and the air was filled with the stench of sewage. Above them, only the crumbling pavement of broken streets and the tops of faltering buildings could be seen.

Jay looked to his right as he heard a group of rocks break free from a nearby, collapsed building and tumble into the ditch. The useless, rusted metal of cars groaned and creaked as the pair hopped along the vehicles' hoods, roofs, and trunks. They helped each other cross uneven ground and supported each other over jagged hurdles.

Soon, they arrived at the other side of the ditch where a landslide of dirt and rock had formed a shallow incline. Jay and Benu trudged up the slope, out of the ditch, and back onto the street. Jay stood up straight, put his right hand on his hip, and caught his breath. Benu hunched over and rested her hands on her knees.

"Hey," Jay said, "thanks for last night."

"Hmph, no problem," Benu replied, straightening up. "It is what friends are for."

"That's what they say, *dost*," Jay smirked. They began to walk with Jay leading—Benu just over his right shoulder. They were now less than an hour away from the Northern cemetery.

Benu smiled and tilted her head curiously. "You are in *awfully* good spirits. Are you sure everything is ok?"

"Do I really have the luxury of being ok or not? The answer *is* no, but… I haveta admit, I feel different. I don't feel as empty anymore. I feel in control, y'know? It's like… I realize even though I can't control the world ending, I can choose how I want to end it… how I want to approach it. I think I'll be at peace when all is said and done. Especially after I bury Her. Then, I think I'll be complete, truly."

Benu placed her hand on his right shoulder.

Jay turned to face her as they passed the rear of the bus.

"Oh, *dost*. That is what I—"

A 'bang' cracked through the dry air as Benu's falling body tugged on Jay's shoulder, pulling him back. Jay instinctively caught her with his right arm and stumbled back, bracing their weight with his right foot planted in the ground. He whipped his attention down the road and scanned his eyes between a collapsed, four-story hotel on the left and a gas station on the right. The air crack again as a small, lightning-fast projectile pinged off the roof of a car behind them. Jay ducked out of instinct and shouldered Benu to the side of the school bus. He put their backs to the fading yellow wall and slid down it together. Benu was grunting and gripping her left ribs as Jay sat her up against the rear, deflated tire.

As Jay pulled his arm from under her, a streak of crimson ran from the crook of his elbow, down his bare forearm, and onto his palm. He looked up at the bus wall to see its yellow paint brushed with red where Benu had slid. He followed it down to Benu's grimace as she coughed a splatter of blood onto her shoulder.

"No-no-no-no," Jay said in a frenzy as he gripped Benu's shoulders and scanned his eyes frantically around her body, unsure of what he was looking for. "Benu! Benu! Tell me what I gotta do!"

Benu gasped and lifted her right hand off her wound. She gripped the hem of her shirt with her blood-stained hand and touched her chin to her chest to look down. The white of her poncho around the entry point of her wound was now stained a deep crimson. The blood continued to expand the red stain outward from the frayed hole that the projectile had created. It continued to soak through as it reached a portion of the vines and roses embroidered along the hem. She slowly started to lift her poncho and shirt together before Jay quickly went to her aid and lifted both. Jay rolled them up just below her left breast.

Jay had only ever seen gunshot wounds in movies and TV shows, but the real thing was far more sinister in its subtlety. The entry wound was a clean hole where the skin and flesh had caved in and collapsed just beneath the surface. Steady wells of blood leaked from the wound with each pulse of Benu's heart.

Jay pulled Benu's bag carefully off her. Its bit of plastic, paper, and fabric spilled across the ground through a tear that had been made by the bullet. Jay recognized the transparent plastic of Benu's medical case. He pulled Benu away from the bus slightly, lifted her poncho over her head, and felt her bare back. Although he couldn't see it—or dared not see it—he could feel the exit wound was far closer to the Hollywood dramatizations. Between his three first fingers, he could feel strands of meat and skin hanging off Benu's back like torn curtains. The exposed meat under his fingers felt mangled and destroyed. It was then that he realized his hand was absolutely soaked from a steady stream of warm blood and his nose stung with the smell of dirty iron.

"Benu," Jay said curtly. "I haveta try to cauterize this, ok?"

Benu's eyes widened as she shook her head, grabbed the back of Jay's neck, and mouthed *'no-no-no-no'*.

Jay bared his teeth and heated his hand, pressing his fingers into her wound. Benu yelped and screeched in horrific agony as she dug her nails into Jay's neck. Blood trickled from the back of Jay's neck as his blood intermingled with Benu's under her fingernails. Jay continued as Benu bit into her sweater's thick sleeve to brace for the pain. She lifted and stomped her heavy heels on the pavement. The smell of cooking flesh caused Jay to wince. When Jay could no longer feel blood, he removed his hand and moved to the clean wound under her breast. He allowed her to catch her breath. Benu's eyes glazed over for a moment as she craned her neck back and rested her head against the bus. Then, she rolled her head over towards Jay and nodded.

"This one should be quick," Jay assured her and penetrated his index finger up to the mid knuckle and cauterized Benu's wound. She squirmed and grimaced but was too fatigued to kick or scream this time. As Jay removed his finger, he asked, "Ok, that should be good for now… is there anything else I can do?"

Benu exhaled a hurried breath. Her face had quickly grown pale and was drenched in sweat. She licked her lips and said breathlessly while shaking her head: "My… medical supplies were ruined… in the water… Nothing else you can do."

"No-no-no, don't say that! There's got to be something! Anything!"

Benu closed her eyes and sighed heavily. "You can… wrap it… needs pressure."

"Ok-ok," Jay said as he threw off his jacket and pulled off his shirt—his beanie falling off his head and onto the ground. He tucked one end of his shirt in his teeth and placed it against Benu's frontal wound. Then, he fed the shirt under her and back around, laying it across itself. He held the overlayed fabric down with his stump and clumsily tied a knot, cinching it tight against her entry wound with his right hand and teeth. She grunted and cringed.

"How's that?" he asked.

Benu simply replied with a closed-eyed nod.

"Don't move."

Jay crept to the end of the bus. He looked to the gas station that was in full view across the street. *No, the shot must've come from the hotel,* he thought. He peeked around the taillight of the school bus with his right eye. Just down the road, about a block away, was a four-story hotel whose Western half had collapsed completely. Hefty cracks crawled up what remained as Jay scanned the windows from top to bottom—but his view was obstructed from his position. As he moved out to get a better look, he caught the glint of something from a broken window from the fourth floor on the Eastern edge. Jay quickly ducked back as another 'bang' echoed through the air and a bullet skipped off the payment by his feet, breaking up the ruined asphalt and kicking up small black rocks.

He slunk back to Benu. Her breathing had calmed but her normally rich complexion was growing paler. Jay's thoughts were a flurry of what-to-do-next's and flashbacks of Her, laying in that hospital bed. He shook the thoughts away and wiped away some sweat from Benu's forehead.

As he pulled his hand away, she murmured: "Hey… two things… please…"

"Yeah? Yeah, what's up?" Jay replied.

"My letter… in my back pocket."

Jay nodded and reached under her bottom as she struggled to lean to her side. He slipped out the water-damaged letter and handed it to her.

"And…" Benu continued, "I want that last cigarette." She motioned with her chin over to her bag.

"You can smoke that at the cemetery. I don't think—"

"Hey," she demanded with a raspy voice just above a whisper. "Do not deny someone their last cigarette, *dost.*" She then curled her lip in a meek smile and coughed a heap of blood onto her chest.

Jay looked to the ground and nodded a few times to himself before crawling over to her bag. He unzipped the front pocket and retrieved her crumpled box of Marlboro Reds. The carton papers tore and disintegrated as he spread open the pack. He plucked out the last, bent cigarette.

Benu let out a weak moan as she scooted up the school bus tire a bit—her letter in her left hand. She slipped the papers out of the envelope, staining them with blood. The waters had made the ink run, but the words were still legible.

Jay knelt by Benu's side and offered her the cigarette. She puckered out her lips slightly as Jay fed her the butt of the cigarette. Working it to the side of her mouth, she said: "I… need a light."

With the tip of his finger, Jay held a small, crackling flame to Benu's cigarette. The red glow of The Anomaly made it seem Jay's little flame wasn't lighting up anything at all, until he saw the glimmer of his fire in Benu's dim eyes. She drew and puffed with no success, coughing as she did. Jay opened his mouth to say something, but Benu drew one last time as the end of the cigarette glowed with hot embers. She puffed out a plume of smoke and leaned her head back. Pulling the cigarette from her mouth, she harrumphed as droplets of blood dribbled on her lips. Jay could see her yellowed teeth stained with swaths of sanguine.

"Thank you, Jay. I… should be good now," Benu whispered. "I just need to… take a break, I think." She started reading her letter as she brought the cigarette back to her mouth.

Jay bit his lower lip and nodded. "I'll be right back. Don't go anywhere," he said as he set his backpack next to her, threw on his beanie and jacket, and moved towards the rear of the bus.

{Chapter 34}

0:5:25:48

Jay crouched halfway up the bus with his chest to its rust-spotted, yellow side and his right hand curled around the edge. He looked behind at Benu, who sat against the deflated, rear tire just a few feet away. A thin wisp of smoke was trailing from the cigarette between her lips. Jay watched closely to see the embers glow from another draw. He turned his attention back towards the shooter. Pulling himself to the edge, he peeked his right eye around the corner again. The glint Jay had spotted before was in the same spot: fourth floor, East corner.

The sniper's nest was less than a block away.

Between it and Jay were two broken-down cars parked against the curb. The first car, an SUV, was about a bus-length away from him. The second car, a newer Camaro from what Jay could tell through the thick layers of rust, sat about twenty feet from the SUV. From there, Jay would need to cross over the curb and into the parking lot where two cars had seemingly T-boned yards from the entrance. Only a handful of cars remained across the rest of the parking lot, none of which would provide Jay with ample cover on approach.

The glint flickered and swayed in the red-tinted sunlight. Jay could feel his heart racing as he peered at it from around the bus. It was at the East corner of the building, facing out a fourth floor, South window. He wondered what sort of firearm-wielding creature The Anomaly had produced. He also doubted the reality of the gun itself. The world had been without the crack of gunfire for so long, Jay thought that maybe the black diamond had spawned a monster with a tail or arm that could shoot bullets like a gun. But, as Jay squinted, he could clearly see the black barrel of a hunting rifle leading back onto a wooden forestock which rested on the ledge of the hotel room window.

The sniper held their aim on Jay's position with stalwart discipline.

Jay could feel the sniper's crosshairs on him, swaying around his barely exposed head. Jay looked down where the second shot had taken a chunk of pavement out of the street. The sound of the whizzing bullet past his ear echoed in his memory. Jay couldn't risk making a dash for it; he'd have to find a way to cause a distraction.

He reeled back slightly and took a step away from the bus, being sure to stay crouched beneath the bus windows. From this angle, Jay could see a small leak underneath the Camaro had formed a slick, large puddle with an iridescent sheen. The smell of gasoline wafted through the air.

He glanced over towards the sniper's position, making sure his body wasn't exposed. As Jay took aim, his hand blackened and crackled with dancing embers. He held this position as he took one last peek at Benu over his shoulder. Her eyes were shut, with her blood-stained letter resting in her lap, but her chest was shakily moving in and out. Jay breathed in through his nose and out of his mouth. He turned his attention back to the Camaro's underside, steeled his focus, and fired.

The fireball zoomed through the air with an echoing *'fwoom.'*

As it clashed with the shimmering puddle, it burst into flames that skipped past the rear of the sports car. The inferno engulfed the car as the puddle of fuel ignited into a fluttering wall of fire.

Jay didn't spare a second.

As soon as the fireball ignited the puddle, he burst forth, past the bus's rear, and dove behind the SUV.

Just as his feet cleared the front bumper, a gunshot cracked through the sound of the explosion and echoed through the air. Jay slammed into the craggy asphalt hard as his bare chest bounced off the ground and his elbows and knees skidded across the pavement. He could feel the sting of freshly scraped skin on his dry knees.

He lay on the ground for a moment—his face tucked into the crook of his right elbow. He cringed as he readied himself for the surge of pain that would surely come from a gunshot wound to his foot or leg or waist or torso, but the pain never came.

He was safe for now.

Jay let out a held breath as he scrambled to a crouching position.

Just as he did, another gunshot rang out and the window just above his head shattered and sprayed glass across his back. The bullet ricocheted off the asphalt and into the gas station behind Jay. "Shit!" he screamed as he instinctively ducked with his right hand over his head and his stump mimicking a left hand doing the same.

He did his best to calm himself as he stared at the raging inferno before him. The Camaro had now been completely engulfed. Jay was panting as options raced through his mind. He'd need another distraction, one that could buy him more time. The old adage of *'Fool me once, shame on you. Fool me twice, shame on me'* flashed across his mind. Then, the addendum his uncle had made to it came next: *'Fool me thrice... Well then, you're a dead man.'*.

Fuck, man, Jay thought. *This is so fucked!*

Just as Jay was ready to curse out loud, the earth rumbled. He readied himself for the ensuing quake to follow. This would be his only chance. He knew he'd have to forgo taking cover behind the Camaro. His next move would be to sprint between the cars and take cover once again behind the crashed cars in the parking lot. Then... he'd test his uncle's proverb.

Jay peeked his left eye over the windowsill of the broken window. The sniper's glint was still flickering like a bright star. Then, the quake came.

It was a violent one, nearly shaking Jay off his feet. He caught himself as he saw the bright, fourth-floor star reel back and disappear.

Go!

Jay sprinted between the cars. The ripping of the gas station from the earth behind him did nothing to stop his stride. He could feel the boulders of falling rocks at his back, but he remained fixated on the T-boned crash a few yards in front of him. He had passed over the grassy field between the parking lot and sidewalk and stumbled over a crumbling parking block as the land shook under him. As he caught his balance, he swore a bullet had passed between his legs, but the deafening holler of the ravaged earth behind him masked the sound of the gunshot.

Jay ran for the crashed car—his vision warped by beads of sweat that dripped off his brow and eyelashes. As the scene of the parked cars bounced before him, he noticed shimmering wires between the crumbled cars. The thin wires connected something from the front seat of the bottom of the T crash, through the windshield, and into the passenger seat of the other car. As Jay came within ten feet of the crash, he noticed more wires were strung between the undercarriages of the cars. A large jerrycan was squeezed in between where the cars had collided.

Fool me thrice…

Jay swiveled his foot and turned tail to the right without breaking his stride.

The earthquake began to subside as Jay passed the booby trap.

He was about twenty feet away from the rigged cars when the earth settled, and another gunshot fired.

The crack of the sniper's shot startled Jay as the 'bang' came directly above him, but the explosion that followed sent his ears into a deafening ring and blurred his vision. In his mind, he saw Her heart monitor.

Jay wasn't sure how he ended up under the hotel's portico entrance. Either he continued sprinting and collapsed from the explosion or he was sent flying by the shockwave and ended up where he lay. He also wasn't sure how he was still breathing. Either he was at a steep enough angle that the Sniper couldn't see him or Gilnup's miraculous revival had somehow protected him. Either way, he was still alive and, other than being shell-shocked into a thumping headache, mostly unharmed. As he recovered from his shell shock, he looked up at the cracked, stone portico and analyzed his situation.

He was at the East entrance, protected from the Sniper's gaze that faced out a South window. As Jay stumbled to his feet, he realized his clothes had been scorched and were smoldering. He patted off some parts of his pants and jacket whose frayed ends were still glowing with embers. As he faced forward, he could see that a dinner-plate-sized piece of rusted debris had flown over him and lodged itself in the glass of the sliding entrance door. Over his shoulder, he saw the crashed cars raging with soaring fire. The smell of burning fuel permeated the afternoon air.

Jay winced at the soreness in his joints and muscles. He felt a wetness traveling down his right forearm. As he brought it up, he saw drips of blood falling off his pinky finger from along the length of his palm. Streams of blood ran from his scraped elbow and down his forearm. Seeing this, he realized: the sniper couldn't be sure if Jay was alive or dead. As far as whatever took pot-shots at him knew, Jay was a cremated corpse underneath this portico. Jay could feel other streams of blood running down his knees as he looked down to see his jeans had been torn. He cauterized whatever scrapes and cuts he could feel and moved into the hotel through a broken, full-length window adjacent to the sliding door entrance.

The lobby of the hotel was in ruin, bisected at the far end by a crevasse that had caused half of the building to collapse into it. Mountains of concrete slabs, rebar, and hotel furnishings were piled in the ditch between the remains of the lobby and the West end. Looking out at the remains of the structure across the ditch, Jay could see four stories of exposed hallways and rooms like an open dollhouse. Rocks and waterfalls of debris tumbled from the edges—no doubt, shaken loose from the earthquake.

Jay stood in the center of the lobby. The carpet was blackened by mold and squelched as Jay walked across it. The stuffings of the green leather seats were emerging out of ripped stitches, forming poofy, static clouds that clung to the furniture. All around, Jay could hear the moan of buckling steel supports. Red rays of The Anomaly's light gleamed over the edges of steel beams and concrete platforms that jutted out over the crevasse. Wind whistled through the open structure, causing scattered papers and trash to swirl and skip across the ground.

Jay searched the area for the stairwell and found the doorway to the service stairs at the Southern wall, near the crevasse. The large, metal door had fallen off its hinges and had lain flat against the first few steps leading upwards. Across the top of the door, faded black letters read "EMPLOYEES ONLY". Jay entered the dark, dank stairwell and lit a fire, no brighter than a match, in his hand. Holding it forward, he hovered it around the fallen door and up the wall to his right. He moved it along the handrail, searching for any signs of more traps. He began to ascend.

Step by step, he scanned with his flame.

He moved meticulously and kept an eye out for the shimmering silver of taut fishing wires. Streaks of white moved from side to side along the steps. Jay looked over the edge of the railing and could see more jerrycans and other home-rigged explosives hanging off the sides. The wires he sidestepped and weaved around were tied to some sort of ignition device wrapped around the caps of the containers. Jay didn't care to analyze them in detail, but his handyman brain went to work.

He imagined the tripwires were attached to some sort of plastic or thick paper sheet that was being squeezed by a clothespin or hair clip. The sheet formed a barrier between two metal plates. One was hooked to the positive terminal of a small battery—a 9-volt would do the trick—and the other was attached to a piece of wire that connected to a fuse leading into gallons of fuel. Another cable would need to be attached from the negative terminal of the battery and to the ignition wire. When the tripwire was activated and the plastic sheet was yanked from the clamp, the two metal sheets would meet, completing the circuit. Then, the ignition wire would heat up, light the fuse, and the entire stairwell would go up like some freak fireworks accident on the

4th of July. Yes, that's how Jay would set it. And while he didn't fear the flames, he did anticipate the stairwell was rigged to collapse and crush its intruder, judging by the jerrycans placements and the key supporting points of the stairwell landings; the inferno would just be a bonus. Jay also thought, if he were the sniper, he'd also lay tripwires at chest, or even face, height. Just as he thought this, a flash of white shot across his vision. He held his flame near the wire before his face just to confirm it wasn't his imagination running wild. Ducking under the wire, he continued to carefully slink his way up the stairwell.

As he reached the third-floor landing, he heard the low hum of The Anomaly. He stopped and braced himself for another quake. Only a minor tremor shook the building; small pebbles trickled from the cracks in the concrete walls. Jay's heart skipped a beat as he was reminded of the time he was wasting by being so careful. He picked up the pace—his footsteps echoing through the stairwell—and reached the fourth-floor landing.

The beige metal door that led to the fourth-floor hallway was dented and battered. Jay peered through the crosshatched window. The feeling reminded him of Her hospital room all those years ago. But he couldn't dwell on that now; he buried the memory. Through the window, he could see down the dimly lit hallway. Shafts of red light illuminated the corridor through open hotel doors. By Jay's logic, he figured he was at the opposite end of the building from the sniper. Somewhere at the end of this hallway, the creature that shot Benu waited for its next prey. Jay extinguished his flame and reached to open the door. The broken handle turned clumsily and with some resistance.

As Jay slunk through the door, he felt the snap of a wire near the top of the door.

Then, he heard the sizzle of a short fuse to his left.

Before he knew it, his left ear was assaulted by the violent popping of firecrackers.

Jay jolted to his right and hollered "Fuck! Fuck!" as he attempted to cover his left ear with his phantom hand—to no avail. He clenched his teeth and grimaced as he slammed into the wall to his right. As he opened his eyes, he caught the glimpse of the sniper at the far end of the hall, aiming at him.

Instinctually, Jay fired off a shot and dove into an open room to his left before the sniper fired theirs. The fireball went wide and punched a hole in a wall somewhere to the right. The sniper's shot went off-target as well as they recoiled back into their room to dodge Jay's attack.

Jay stood in the doorway of his room as the firecrackers continued to pop away. He caught his breath and wiped the sweat from his brow. The sniper's shot had glanced Jay's face. A fresh cut across his cheek bled generously onto his chin.

Jay ran his finger across the deep cut and winced at the stinging pain. He quickly cauterized it and shook his head. Jay had never been in a firefight. He had seen plenty in movies and TV shows and played plenty of paintball, but the intensity of having real, life-threatening bullets whizzing by him shook his entire being. His hand was numb, shaking violently with some unknown mixture of fear and adrenaline. He could even feel his phantom hand grow clammy. His knees shook like stilts as his heart beat so hard against his chest, he swore it was ready to fracture his sternum.

He wiped another streak of sweat from his brow and blinked hard.

His nostrils flared as he contemplated his next move. As the firecrackers began to peter out, he heard the distinct rattling of metal and wood down the hall; the sniper had taken aim.

Damn it… I'm stuck, Jay thought.

He was right.

The sniper was a crack shot. It was only by sheer luck and his element of surprise that Jay had survived this long. Now, the sniper was aware of Jay's abilities; they wouldn't be caught off guard again. Jay looked around the ruined hotel room. He was in a single suite with a living area, kitchen, and separate bedroom. He spotted a broken lamp on a table by a tattered, cushion-less sofa and ripped it from its socket. Holding it by his side, he bent his knees and readied himself to run to a room further down the hall if what he had planned worked. He tossed the lamp into the hallway and flinched.

No shot was fired. The sniper wasn't stupid.

Jay might as well have poked out his beanie on a stick to complete his embarrassment of a tactic. He paced around the room a bit with his hand on his head.

"Fuck-fuck-fuck-fuck," he murmured to himself. He was properly trapped. As far as he was concerned, he had two options: move out into the hallway and die or jump out the window and die. Frustration and anxiety began to build in his mind as he faced the mangled sofa. He huffed and yelled "Goddammit, man!" as he kicked the sofa with the flat of his foot.

The sofa was sent clean through the wall and into the bedroom behind it. Jay recoiled back as the wall caved slightly—drywall dust puffing thin clouds into the air. Jay flinched, unaware of what he had done. Bewildered, he began to remember the stark imagery of lanky, old Cap'n Q lifting the heavy walnut table back at the boathouse. Cap'n Q did not possess the strength of a normal man. He was once human until a group of mushies revived him. Now, Jay had shared Cap'n Q's fate in a fractional manner. Once he realized this, Jay sprang into action.

I hope to see you soon, Gilnup. I owe you big time, he thought as he moved into the kitchen. Pulling the back side of the fridge, he found it easy to yank it away from the wall. The fridge screeched across the tile as Jay pushed and pulled it out of the kitchen and into the doorway. He let out a deep breath. He could hear the sniper readying themselves at the sight of something they couldn't quite make out in the doorway down the hall from them. Jay grimaced and pushed the fridge into the hallway.

He quickly slinked between the doorway and fridge as the Sniper took a shot that pinged off the steel of the fridge and punched a hole in the ceiling. Jay pressed his palm to the back of the fridge and buried his left shoulder into the mechanics. He grunted as he began pushing the fridge down the hallway.

The sniper began firing shot after shot.

The hallway echoed and reverberated with the piercing bangs of the hunting rifle's bullets. The sharp metal-on-metal dings felt like stabbing knives in Jay's ears. He began screaming a deep war cry as he marched. The hallway was filled with the loud scrap of the fridge's feet as its doors creaked from each shot that deformed its surface.

As he moved, the fish-patterned wallpaper of the walls scrolled by his vision, breaking up every six or seven feet by a hotel door. He saw the room numbers flash by and counted them in his mind.

409…407…405… 403…

The Sniper's shots began to speed up. Now, they were firing frantically, desperate to stop Jay from advancing. With each shot came the robotic and quick sound of rifle's bolt being pulled back, expelling the shell, and feeding another one into the chamber. Gun metal sliding against gun metal. Brass casings pinging off the walls and floor.

In the hellfire of bullets, Jay could hear the deep scream of terror from the creature on the other side of the fridge. Jay's push was cut short when a bullet finally penetrated the steel construction and pierced his left thigh.

Jay's war cry and the scrap of the fridge were silenced.

He bit his lower lip hard and immediately cauterized the entirety of his gunshot wound. The wound wasn't severe, as the bullet's velocity was hampered by Jay's thick, steel shield. The bullet could still be lodged inside, but he didn't have time to think about that or tend to it anyways. Then, the cacophony ceased.

For a moment, Jay's ears rang. As his senses began to clear up, he could hear the distinct, rhythmic sound of something from the sniper's room, just on the other side of the fridge:

'Click… chk-chk… click… chk-chk…'

He's reloading! Jay screamed in his mind.

He shoved the fridge past the sniper's door and turned into the doorway with his hand splayed out. He caught the sniper at the other side of the room as they turned around.

Jay's hand ignited with an intensity like none before. He could feel the skin across his hand cracking and splitting wide as they glowed intensely. Embers poured from the tiny valleys as his hand blackened and crackled.

This was the creature that shot Benu.

This was the final obstacle between Jay and Her.

Jay's hoarse and tired throat screamed with thunder as the corner of his eyes expelled small ribbons of flames.

Jay aimed for the kill and fired.

The sniper did the same.

The pain from the gunshot wound in Jay's leg was only matched by the explosive agony he was now feeling in his left shoulder. Through willpower, bullheadedness, and a surge of adrenaline, Jay was able to dodge the bullet meant for his chest. He began to cauterize the wound, but the range at which the sniper had shot him had blown out Jay's shoulder blade. Blood and bone fragments had sprayed behind him and onto the fridge in the hallway. Sanguine poured steadily down Jay's missing arm and onto the floor but, eventually, he was able to fully cauterize his wound. The shot left Jay stunned, but he was still standing.

The sniper, on the other hand, was dead.

Jay limped over to the corpse and stood over it.

The sniper's head was completely obliterated by Jay's attack. All that was left was the lower jaw and neck with a mangled tongue attached. The window they lay beneath was splattered with a sunburst of blood and brain matter. In the Sniper's right hand was their rifle; their finger was still on the trigger. A line of bullets stood on end upon a round, wooden table next to the window. A couple more were scattered on the ground by the sniper's chest. Their torso was plaid—

red and black—which came down to a pair of jeans around their legs, ending in brown boots.

To Jay's right between two beds, a woman clutching a little girl screamed.

It was only then that Jay realized the sniper was a man.

The sniper was human.

Jay's head was killing him now. He covered his mouth and looked to the woman. His lower lip quivered as the woman screamed at him in a language he didn't understand. She was hysterical, wrought with anguish and anger. She flailed her arms at the dead man's corpse and Jay. He held his hand towards her as she recoiled and held her child close. She hyperventilated in fear.

"I-I-I'm sorry," Jay stuttered. "I'm… sorry… sorry."

He backed away and said no more. As he limped down the hallway, he could hear the echoing the cries of the woman and her child. He shut his eyes and kept moving.

{Chapter 35}

0:2:52:20

Jay's shadow flickered in front of him as the fire of the T-bone crash raged on behind him. He had worked his way out of the hotel the same way he entered, clutching the gunshot wound on his left shoulder. The pain set in fast and hurt like hell. His leg was fairing better due to his accelerated healing, but it still caused him to limp. However, he couldn't focus on himself right now. Just past the burning Camaro and SUV was the bus where Benu had been left.

Jay walked down the sidewalk towards the bus—his left foot dragging against the battered pavement. His face was smattered with black smudges of dirt and soot. Beads of sweat rolled from the V of his neck down his bare chest, creating streaks through his dirtied body. He breathed through his mouth steadily. The cool air felt good against his cracked lips. As he passed by the burning Camaro, he coughed as he breathed in a swath of searing fumes. He tucked his face into his elbow where his jacket sleeve had unrolled itself at some point. His jacket smelled awful, like a year of B.O. and ash had been compacted into the black fibers.

The earth continued to rumble and shake as Total Convergence loomed just over the horizon. The Anomaly was enormous now, blocking out the evening sun. The bottom point of the black diamond sat just above the Northwestern horizon while the opposite point nearly touched the apex of the sky. Jay lowered his arm and glanced over his shoulder at the black diamond. The darkness of its body swirled in eddies of shifting waves as if it was comprised of corkscrewing serpents moving through ink. Jay turned away as he passed through the tall grass between the sidewalk and the street in front of the SUV. The dead grass kissed his hand as he stepped off the curb and headed to the rear of the bus. The orange light from the fires danced in the reflection of the bus's rear window and exposed chrome between flaking yellow paint.

As Jay rounded the corner of the bus, he called: "Benu! Hey!"

She lay there in the same position Jay had left her—her back against the deflated rear tire with her legs stretched out. Jay limped along the side of the bus, gliding his hand against the rusted metal.

"Hey, sorry I took so long," he said, but Benu didn't answer. Jay stood over her and saw her chest wasn't moving. Her right hand was motionless in her lap, loosely clutching her bloodstained letter. A smoldering cigarette sat between her hip and left hand on the ground; a wisp of smoke trailed off from a dying ember. Jay knew in his heart that Benu wouldn't answer his call. In a way, he knew the words she had said to him before he left were going to be her last, and yet he shakily knelt and murmured again: "Hey… Benu… C'mon let's go."

He placed a hand on her shoulder and contemplated shaking it but knew it would mean nothing. He moved his hand to her eyes and pulled her eyelids shut. He brushed her hair back as his fingers ran across her ice-cold cheeks. He saw the silhouette of her delicate face against the darkness—the orange fire from behind accentuating her slender nose and sunken eyes. Jay ran this thumb across her lips and wiped the blood from them. Despite the stains across her cheeks and chin, she looked tranquil, as if she were dreaming of something peaceful. He scanned his eyes down her torso and could see her wound had bled through the shirt he tied around her and stained her own with a great splotch that encompassed her side.

Jay reached back and slipped on his backpack, wincing as he worked his immobilized stump through the strap. His strength was failing, but he didn't want to leave her in the street. He placed her left hand in her lap along with her letter and reached over and draped her poncho over his right shoulder. Bearing his pain, Jay weaved his stump under her knees and wrapped his right arm under her shoulders. He pulled her away from the bus and awkwardly lifted her, teetering as his left leg buckled. As he limped past the bus's rear, he looked down at Benu cradled in his arms. The torment of The

Anomaly was but a fleeting memory in her eternal sleep, never to be suffered from again. Her face was of soft and peaceful beauty.

Jay plodded over the curb and into a small field adjacent to the hotel parking lot. He collapsed to the ground, making sure not to drop his dear friend. The grass parted as he laid Benu down. Jay gently set her head down as he slipped his right hand from under it. He took her hands, placed them in her lap, and laid them over each other on top of her letter. The envelope sat on top of the two letters; fragments of Benu's true name, Binaka, could be seen between her fingers.

Then, he covered her body with her poncho up to her neck. Hunching over, he met his lips to her forehead and kissed it gently. As he pulled back, he rolled his chin to his chest and touched his forehead to Benu's.

The ringing in his ears returned as a cord that connected his heart to his mind snapped. Palpable anguish gripped his throat as he felt the need to weep, but his cognition simply wouldn't allow it. His dear friend lay dead beneath him and yet, he could not cry.

He whispered: "Thank you, Benu… I'll see ya in a couple hours."

He pulled the poncho over Benu's face. Reaching into his backpack, he retrieved his trowel and staked it into the dirt above her head. He stayed there for a moment and exhaled. As he stumbled to his feet, he zipped up his bag and threw his right arm through the strap. He let the bag hang from his shoulder as he shoved his hand into his pocket and fiddled with his ring.

Now, the last good thing in this world had left him; there was nothing left here to anchor him to reality. His thoughts separated from his feelings. In his heart, he felt a part of him die. But the promise he made Her wouldn't let his mind rest.

He had reached the end of his journey just as he started it.

Alone.

{Chapter 36}

0:1:9:44

The cemetery that sat just thirty minutes North of the hotel was a broken mess of hills and deep crevasses. Shattered chunks of marbled tombstone were scattered throughout the overgrowth of grass, bushes, and dying Fall trees. The wildflowers had grown rampant, and vines had fully encapsulated crumbling mausoleums and disintegrating statues. The air was clear with a sea of stars strewn across a cloudless sky. The dancing ribbons of the aurora borealis flicked rays of colorful lights upon the land, mixing with the overbearing red hue of The Anomaly that made the greenery shimmer with curtains of bright emerald and cobalt.

Jay's bum leg had made the trek difficult. He hobbled and pulled himself over and across lifted outcroppings as he grunted with each climb. The wounds in his shoulder and leg screamed with piercing pain, but his mind remained fixated on one thing: Her mother's grave. His face was like stone, expressionless as if he walked through a waking dream. And although his mind begged him to rest, his heart pushed him forward.

Jay knew the cemetery well. He and his wife had visited Her mother's grave once year on the anniversary of her passing. The tombstone he searched for was located at the Northwest end. He plodded along a winding stone path as The Anomaly hummed above.

In the red-stained night, he could see blue wisps drifting about. As they flowed through the trees, ghostly apparitions of dead faces faded in and out of existence. They hovered along the ground and wrapped around the twisted iron fences and broken statues. Their expressions were those of peace, with their eyes closed as if they were sleeping. As they flew around, they whistled through the air as the wind parted around them. All around, Jay could hear soft whispers.

Jay couldn't recognize the faces, but he felt their anguish. Their woes. Their history and regrets. This land was mystical, brought to life by something otherworldly. Either by divine intervention or The Anomaly malformation. Jay paid the spirits no mind. He trudged through the cemetery with the blinders of single-mindedness flanking his dull and empty eyes. As he moved, his mind only allowed thoughts of the present; he thought of neither the past nor future.

The ground beneath his feet quaked as he fell to his knees and caught himself against the cobblestone path. Sweat dripped onto the smooth stone and blotched it with dark marks. The urn in his backpack bounced off his spine and settled against his back. He could hear pieces of the earth's crust scraping against each other as they lurched about. Behind him, the cemetery entrance—with its large, ornate iron gate—was lifted into the air along with a hefty chunk of land. Jay stood and continued walking.

After about fifteen minutes of limping, climbing, and crawling, Jay arrived at the Northwestern corner of the cemetery. Before him was a small hill that had formed from the earth's destruction. At the top was an uprooted tree that leaned to the left—its roots jutting from the land like wild hair. He recognized the tombstones that had been moved and upturned along the hill's surface; Her mother's grave was near the top. He began to climb the hill.

The wispy spirits twirled around him as he passed unearthed coffins of splintered wood and exposed corpses. Jay trudged onwards. As the ground quaked beneath him, rocks and pebbles tumbled down the hill past his feet. He faced upwards and spotted the gravestone just under the shadow of the teetering tree.

He stood over the ruined headstone. And, although it had been reduced to rubble, he knew in his heart that this was the correct one. Miraculously, his mother-in-law's coffin remained completely buried. Jay knelt in front of the gravestone ruins, kissed his first two fingers, and touched them to the cool earth beneath him. Then, he scooted to the left and unslung his backpack. As he unzipped it, he felt a cool breeze brush his neck as a wisp passed through him. The sensation sent chills down his spine as he pulled the urn out of his bag. He set the urn down over his mother-in-law's grave, threw his bag aside, and began to claw at the earth with his bare hand.

As he ripped and tore handfuls of dead grass and dirt, his mind went into deep thought as his hand worked autonomously. The world faded into the background as Jay lost himself in his thoughts.

I stand here on the precipice of self-immolation. The culmination of rot that ate up my mind long ago has built up to this inevitable climax. The beauty of this world, a veil for the ever-driving force of self-collapse.

A husk remains. Alone and silent.

Somewhere in France, a man digs as I do in the hills of the Ardennes. In New York, a man slits his throat in a rusted cab. Thailand, a mother holds her children close. In Flint, that lovely couple hopes for an afterlife with their baby. I see their faces amongst these graves. The faces of those who have suffered the same affliction as I.

I am a child of The Anomaly just as they are. A product of its destructive rampage. I see my own face here, amongst the others. Beneath the flickering colors is a man who left his home with a purpose. The only control he has is the ability to destroy himself. Now, he is on his knees digging… digging… digging.

I dig because I must. But I am changed. Oh, Benu… How could I ever repay you for teaching me how to face my demons? Physically, I am alone, yes. But, in this world of decay and desolation, I have those who care for me and those I care about. I will bury the part of you in my heart here as well.

Ah, that should be deep enough.

The urn is heavier in just one hand, but it nestles itself comfortably in my palm just as Her hand once did. I turn it slowly and feel the raised carnations. Its petals and leaves brush my callused skin. I place it down deep into the hole.

I reach into my pocket.

My ring. Warped and malformed. It reminds me of myself at the time of Her passing. I run my fingers down the sides. Smooth and without imperfections. On the surface, twisted and unnatural. But in my hands, exactly how it should be. I place it on the urn. I move the earth over it without a sound. Like a drone.

It is done.

My heart is empty now. Its contents buried here. All that is left are my body's autonomous functions and an urge to lay down.

I lay down and place my hand under my head.

I stare at the wavering ribbons of light.

To either side of me, the land splits as I rise towards the sky.

Sounds fill my ears, but I don't care to hear them.

I close my eyes.

I can see my veins against the red glow and bright lights.

I wish you had been with me, but I will see you soon.

He could feel it.

Her head pressed against his right collarbone, nestled under his chin. A petite, tender hand rubbed across his chest, passed under his right pec, and came to a rest over his heart.

She spoke in the voice she always wished she had.

Jay recognized that voice as if she always had it.

"I was always with you. Here."

Kathryn… Oh, Kathryn… my trauma was never mine to bear alone.

Acknowledgements

This book is a culmination of a flood of emotions I could have never expressed without the unwavering support of those who are dear to me. Without your support throughout my life, I don't think I would have ever gotten to where I am now. I would have never had the courage to continue my work on this book if it wasn't for you guys always being there.

I'd like to thank, first and foremost, my loving wife, Kristyn Clary. You are my everything, and I will fight to hold you up just as you've done for me. You're the strongest person I know, and your courage inspires me every day. You know I will always need you, and as I wrote this book I thought of you every page of the way. I know reading this book may have hurt, but now we can grow closer together as we do every day. I love you.

I'd like to thank my mother for always supporting me in all my ventures that have positively affected me. And I'd also like to thank her for *not* supporting me in any ventures that seemed like dumb ideas. You've saved me from a lot of trouble! I love you ma.

If it weren't for Uncle Bob's persistent push to "feed your head" then I don't think I would have ever picked up a book in my life. You will always be a shining pillar of intelligence and eloquence to me, and this book is proof I read the dictionary just as you always encouraged!

Darian and Chris. Hopefully you've read this far (or skipped to the end…) Either way, I know I'm horrible at expressing my feelings to my two best buds, but I can only hope through this book you two can understand much of the pain I feel every day. And how you two are always there to alleviate it. Thank you for always being there for me. You've saved me from many nights of crying, even if you guys don't know it.

Landon. I still stand by my claim that your compassion is beyond human comprehension. It just comes to you so naturally, and the fact you don't even know it kind of proves my point. Thank you for all the times you've cheered me up and kept me from sinking into despair. Your support has kept me sane and loved, and I try every day to hold onto that because of your friendship. Chocolate shakes have always tasted sweeter since that day in college. どうもありがとう、ビッグボーイ！

I'd also like to thank all my beta readers for telling me what sucked and what didn't. I always appreciate constructive criticism and even harsh criticism is something to grow by. David Kovacek, in particular, pulled no punches. Your suggestion to kill two chapters was the best piece of editing advice I think I got through this whole process. Thank you for working overtime to read my book. You'll receive a complementary gift basket by mail in 2-3 business days.

Finally, I'd like to thank Alisha Harvey for professionally editing my first book. Your services were invaluable to sculpting my story and vision. Thank you for all the hard work (as I've said several times through our email exchanges) and if I were an octopus, I'd give your editorial services a solid eight thumbs up.

Thank you all again.

Also thanks to my three cats (Nerf, Casper, and Mochi) for trying to lay on my keyboard as I typed.

About the Author

Jesse Clary grew up in El Paso, TX and moved to the Detroit area in 2015 after graduating from college. He makes his living as a service engineer. In his free time, he enjoys making music as a drummer with the band Quadrovek. He can also be found tinkering with his Miata or playing the latest video game. This is his first novel.